The HOUSE *of* SMOKE

Also by Sam Christer

The Stonehenge Legacy
The Turin Shroud Secret
The Camelot Code

The HOUSE of SMOKE

SAM CHRISTER

sphere

SPHERE

First published in Great Britain in 2016 by Sphere

1 3 5 7 9 10 8 6 4 2

A CIP catalogue record for this book
is available from the British Library.

ISBN 978-0-7515-5092-4

Typeset in Bembo by M Rules
Printed and bound in Great Britain by
Clays Ltd, St Ives plc

Papers used by Sphere are from well-managed forests
and other responsible sources.

MIX
Paper from
responsible sources
FSC® C104740

Sphere
An imprint of
Little, Brown Book Group
Carmelite House
50 Victoria Embankment
London EC4Y 0DZ

An Hachette UK Company
www.hachette.co.uk

www.littlebrown.co.uk

To Myla

May your unfolding life be more joyous than any story ever written.

PART ONE

I sought my death, and found it in my womb,
I looked for life, and saw it was a shade,
I trod the earth and knew it was my tomb

'Elegy', Chidiock Tichborne

New Year's Eve. A momentous night.

One I spent alone, in the most inauspicious of dwellings. Certainly not where I had envisaged passing the final hours of the nineteenth century, in the thirty-sixth year of my existence.

On the hard bunk in my fetid prison cell, I closed my eyes to escape the horror of what awaited me. But even in the private darkness of my mind I found no respite. *They* were always there. The ones I had killed.

The young. The old. The men. The women. Their faces formed and faded like the snowflakes falling beyond my barred window. Death by knife. Death by garrotte. Death by my bare hands.

Midnight bells rang out across London. I pictured people of all ages kissing and making their New Year wishes. Hoping for brighter tomorrows. Resolving to do better and change their ways.

Such fools. The ways of mankind cannot be altered. Lord knows, I have tried. At best, our habits and instincts may be managed – even controlled for a short period – and our lapses into old ways can be hidden or disguised. But ultimately our true self surfaces. We are exposed for what we really are.

And I am a murderer. The taking of life defines me. Indeed, it is the very thing that drives me to escape this dreadful hovel. For peace of mind, I *must* wreak absolute vengeance on the man who has hurt those closest to me and ruined my life.

You shall be hanged by the neck until dead.

The decree of the Old Bailey judge rang in my ears louder than those midnight bells. Without a flicker of emotion the old bastard set the date and place of my execution. It raised cheers in the public gallery, a smile on the face of the famed detective Sherlock Holmes and a wince of annoyance from his nemesis, James Moriarty.

On the break of dawn on the eighteenth of January in the nineteen hundredth year of our Lord, you shall be taken to the gallows at Newgate Gaol and hanged by the neck until dead.

A little over seventeen days from now. Four hundred

4

and eight hours. Barely long enough for me to find a way beyond these walls and shed so much blood I swear it will drip from both the sun and moon.

Please forgive the brutality of my language, my ugly outburst. It is not how I wish you to think of me. Not a side of my personality I care to show the world.

My name is Simeon Lynch and when I was arrested the police recorded my height at five feet and eleven inches. I weighed twelve stones, nine pounds and three ounces and was said to have 'a muscular build, dark hair and brown eyes'.

Those who knew me as a child would describe me as 'rough and working class'. In my twenties, circumstances shaped me into a more educated and professional being. My ways and manner of speech became refined and allowed me to present myself as a kindly, courteous and reliable fellow.

But I will tell you who I truly am.

Despite my best efforts, I am a creature of the dark. I am the menacing silhouette that falls across your path. The unexpected hand on your shoulder. The shiver that turns your blood cold.

I am the manservant of Death.

17 Days to Execution

Night slipped silently away. Dragged with it the tatters of the old year. Left me to view the virgin dawn of the twentieth century from the squalor of my prison cell.

Newgate Gaol is as duplicitous a building as the offenders it harbours. On first appearance, like me, it seems pleasantly respectable. Demurely dressed in grey granites and adorned with sombre sculptures, it stands a stone's throw from the sacred dome of St Paul's Cathedral, much as a murderer might in his best suit join the devoted at Sunday Mass.

But inside, all pretence is dropped. It sheds its mask of culture and shows its true face. One that witnessed executioners boiling severed skulls in kettles of camphor. One that still watches over condemned men as they rot in the Devil's parlours.

Such has been the demand of late for the hangman's services that an old part of the prison, one even more decayed and stinking than the rest, has been opened in my honour.

I paced the musty, cramped space and ran my fingers over dampened walls. The span of the arched ceiling had been curtailed, suggesting the cell had once been larger. There was little else. A pot to piss in. A small, single window, barred and high off the ground. A heavily locked door.

My examination concluded that, as decrepit as it was,

6

the gaol had all the features of a modern fortress. Its architects had intended no easy escape. But I was not deterred. My life had seldom been easy and I had overcome tougher opposition than stacks of bricks and mortar guarded by fat and lazy men.

I sat on the floor among the dirt and cockroaches so I might glimpse clouds shifting in the grey morning sky. Light and Dark had always been my accomplices in murder, and I hoped would be again. Fewer guards at night meant fewer men to kill. Daylight brought with it fast means of escape – automobiles, trains and ships that could speed you halfway round the world within a week. It was all a far cry from the first time I had spilled blood and been forced to flee London.

MANCHESTER, AUTUMN 1884

I had not quite reached my twentieth birthday when I crossed that line – the blood-red division between decent souls and those who have taken another's life. But I was already feral.

The murder I committed had been unplanned. Blood spilt in a split second that stained my soul for eternity. There will be a time to explain it all in detail, to give perspective to my life, but this is not it. For the moment, let us just say that as a result of that terrible act I scurried from the capital, scavenged my way through the Midlands and up to the north-west of England where I stayed out of the grasp of the Metropolitan police.

The journey was a long one. By the time I reached the outskirts of Manchester, England's trees had yielded their green and were cloaked in copper, gold and pewter. The first winds of autumn blew chill. Winter was coming. Living rough would soon be unbearable.

The big farm that I came upon did not need workers. Nor did the nearby colliery. Nor the factory that made bearings and wheels. Nor the carpenter or blacksmith, or even the undertaker who had a card in his window testifying that he did.

They all had good reason to turn me away. I had seen myself reflected in windows of carriages, houses and shops and I looked uncivilised: tattered, filthy and riddled with lice. If I was to find honest labour then I needed to cut my hair and cleanse both myself and the stinking clothes that made people wince whenever I came near them.

The secluded slopes of a river, fringed with oak and maple, gave me an opportunity to wash. I stripped and lowered myself into the cold water, dipped beneath the bracing surface and rubbed my face and hair. A crop of floating lilies made flannels for my body and I managed to banish some stench from my skin. I climbed out onto the bank and shivered while I rubbed myself dry with grass and leaves.

I was still only half-dressed when a man's voice turned my head.

'That's a right dangerous place to swim.' He spoke in

a thin, nasal northern accent. 'Looks calm round 'ere but there are undercurrents that will suck you all the way down to the weir.'

The fellow was short and stocky. Five or more years older than me. Bearded, with big brown eyes that belonged more to a bear or dog than a man. He had long, black, curly hair. His hands were clustered with rings and held the leashes of two slobbering black bulldogs.

'What's it to you, where I swim, mister?' I picked up my shirt and put it on.

'Nowt.' He allowed the dogs to move nearer to me. 'Except I'd rather this place wasn't infested with coppers pulling your body out of the water.' He walked close enough to allow a dog to sniff at me. 'My name is Sebastian.'

'Good for you.' I pushed his mutt away.

'People call me Sebastian *the Jew*.'

'Good for them.'

'My name means *nothing* to you?'

'I suppose it means you're Jewish.' I fastened the rest of my shirt. 'Is that your Jew gang, mister?' I nodded to a group of young men forming behind him.

He glanced over his shoulder. 'Yes and no. They are my acquaintances, but they are not Jewish.'

'*Acquaintances*,' I repeated sarcastically. 'And do you intend to have your *acquaintances* beat upon me?' I rolled up my sleeves and clenched my fists so the knuckles cracked like snapped twigs. 'Or are they charged with picking up what remains after your dogs are finished?'

'These?' He laughed as they pulled their leashes. 'The worst *licking* Dee and Dum will give you is with their tongues.'

'Strange names for dogs.'

'That's because they are strange dogs. Brothers they are, like the twins Tweedledee and Tweedledum. Dogs look the same but are very different. One's lazy and one never rests. Only thing they have in common is they can't manage a dangerous bark between them, let alone a bite.' His eyes assessed me in the manner a farmer might choose cattle at a market. 'That's an intriguing scar on your face.'

'You must live a very boring life to find a scratch like that in any way interesting.'

'On its own you might be right. But it's not on its own. Your skin is browner than a berry, meaning you've not been labouring in any local factory but living rough. Your boots are fair knackered, a sure sign you've walked your legs short. Those clothes of yours stink worse than my mutts' arses and your accent is not local. Not local at all. So you see, there's a handful of reasons why your scar is interesting to me.'

I picked up my footwear and regarded him with suspicion. He was no toff, nor was he a working-class ruffian without brain or charisma. Behind him, more of his gang ominously gathered. There were now eight, maybe ten of them, I could not be sure because they were not still enough to count. 'You're right; I've been travelling a long while. Looking for work and food, that's all.'

'I can give you work. And shelter.' He knelt and rubbed one of the dogs' ears. His eyes met mine. 'A roof, hot food and even clean clothes.'

'And *why* would you want to do that?'

'Because a man on the run from something that put a scar on his face might be useful to me.' He smiled and added, 'In return, I'd want hard graft, no cheek or any drunkenness.'

'I am sober, disciplined and can do an honest day's toil.'

'*Honest?* That's the last thing I want.' He looked to his men. 'He wants *honest* work, lads.'

There was laughter but no one spoke. They knew their place. Don't interrupt the boss. Just stand close and wait to be called upon.

I picked out a man second from the left and another, farthest right. These were the hard boys. The ones not crossing their arms and puffing out their chests to look tough. The ones who had nothing to prove.

Sebastian held out his palm. 'Shake my hand and join us. Or else be off. And if you refuse my hospitality, then make bloody sure you stay well away. This is Scuttler turf and you'll find we don't take kindly to strangers around here.'

I grasped his hand. It was soft. Had never done anything more strenuous than hold a dog leash. 'Terry,' I said, mentioning the first name that entered my head. 'Terry Perch. What, may I ask, are Scuttlers?'

'*Scuttlers?*' He smiled easily, 'Without a doubt, they are the best group of men in *all* of England.'

He jerked the two sniffing dogs into a slow amble along

11

the river's edge and I followed, thinking all the time about the men behind us and whether something worse than a beating could befall me.

We halted at the rear of a large mill built of red bricks. There were endless rows of long windows and through the lower ones I saw the scaffolds of loom beams, spidery webs of multi-coloured wool, chimney spindles of wound cotton and armies of busy women.

In the cool shadows of the building, Sebastian introduced me to his men. Most were no older than me and had names I instantly forgot, save those of the two who stayed closest to their leader. Danny was my height and weight but with blond hair and blue-green eyes. He sported a wispy, waxed beard that he seemed to derive great calmness from regularly stroking. The other was a small, fidgety man they called Fingers. I guessed this was because he constantly fluttered a ha'penny back and forth across his knuckles. The coin would always tumble from the smallest to the index finger; he'd roll his hands together and repeat the dextrous manoeuvre across the knuckles of his other hand.

'We have rooms below the steps,' said Sebastian. He let the dogs off their leashes and they bounded and skidded down a steep grass bank. He motioned to a black iron staircase. 'This way's safer, I think.'

The 'rooms' transpired to be nothing more than a large, open and unused part of the lower floor of the mill. Rows of bunks had been erected in a far corner. In the centre stood rough wooden tables and benches where men gathered to eat, play cards and swap stories. The rear wall contained a polished oak door guarded by a muscular young man.

'That's *my* place,' said Sebastian, following my eyes. 'You and the boys have the run of all this, but nowhere else.' He jabbed a thumb over his shoulder. 'Back there, and what's *kept* back there, belong to me. You don't go inside. Not unless I invite you. That's another rule.'

'Lots of rules,' I said, my gaze rolling over the high cold walls and long floors.

'Only one,' he answered. 'Do as I tell you. If you obey that, then you'll be fine.'

'And if I don't?'

His eyes grew large with excitement. 'Then, my new-found friend, you'll be lucky to escape with your life.'

17 Days to Execution

NEWGATE, 1 JANUARY 1900

Fifteen years after that warning from Sebastian the Jew, I reflected on it in the solitude of my cell.

I have known little good luck in my life. And Sebastian certainly brought me none. Indeed, had I known his true character when I met him, I swear I would have walked away from the riverbank and never darkened his turf again.

And had I done so, then my first visitor of this New

13

Year might have been a beautiful maiden rather than a middle-aged gaoler, ruddy skinned with a thick black beard that crept high up a thin face and almost crawled into the pits of his soulless dark eyes. He let the squeaking door bang on its rusted hinges as he strode in, proud of the noise and drama of his entrance.

At the end of my bunk he stopped, kicked my feet and shouted, 'Stand up, Lynch! Turn around and put your *bloody* convict hands against that wall!'

I was on my feet instantly. Not out of obedience, but because I sensed a chance to overpower him. He clearly was a gaoler of authority and might have sufficient keys to afford me the opportunity of escape.

I was mistaken. He was far from alone. A gang of loury men trailed after him and as I placed my palms on the cold bricks, a prison baton cracked the back of my legs.

I fell to my knees and through gritted teeth managed a verbal response: 'I sense you boys have not come first footing then? No ale or gifts to welcome in the New Year?'

'Shut your insolent mouth!' shouted my uninvited guest. Heavy hands pushed my face into the brickwork. 'I am Mr Tobias Johncock, the assistant keeper – or deputy governor, as *modernisers* like to say.' He pronounced *modernisers* with contempt. 'Turn 'im around, men. Let's get this over with.'

They kept me on my knees but dragged me around to face him.

Johncock stepped closer and smirked wickedly. 'I have been tasked with the pleasure of organising your *execution*.'

He spread his arms wide to his colleagues. 'I am the man to lynch Mr Lynch.'

They gave him the laughter he craved.

I've 'anged more scoundrels than any other screw in London,' he boasted. 'And I can name all the toppers, right back to Thomas de Warblynton in the thirteen 'undreds and clumsy Jack Ketch, that blessed bungler who shamed the Duke of Monmouth with a blunt axe. Messy, messy, messy. I don't like messy, Lynch. Don't like it at all.'

I lowered my head. The cell's cockroaches had gathered in one corner as though frightened of Johncock. The sight of them made me smile. Given a chance, I could kill this cocksure cove quicker than I could exterminate them.

'Look at me!' he shouted.

His men tugged my hair so I had no choice but to raise my eyes to his.

'There's fierce competition on the 'Angman's List for the 'onour of stretching a double murderer like you.' He reached into his tunic pocket and produced a handsome pipe. 'The clever money is on James Billington. Though I'd top myself rather than let a northerner do it.' He raised an eyebrow and smiled. 'I was 'ere when Billington did that bitch Amelia Dyer. The "Angel Maker" they called 'er. She swung for the murder of only one infant but I 'ave friends in the constabulary and they say she killed 'undreds, bloody 'undreds of poor babes in arms.'

Johncock pulled tobacco from a pouch and pushed it into the pipe's bowl. 'Then there was the "Ripper" 'anging. A doctor he was. Went by the name of Thomas Cream. Stood right on the traps where you'll be quivering.' He stretched out his arm to demonstrate the next movement in his tale. 'Billington was pulling the lever when Cream shouted "I am Jack the—". *Boom!* The traps rattled open and 'e swung. Never got a chance to complete what 'e wanted to say. If 'e 'ad, it might've been the confession of the century.'

Johncock struck a match. The acrid smell brought relief from the putrid stink of the cell. He took several quick, short draws to raise a red crackle in the pipe bowl, exhaled and announced, 'I 'ear you're an 'andful, Lynch. Got a bit of a temper on you. Now that's *not* desirable in a prisoner. No, no, no. Not desirable at all.' He checked the tobacco was lit, then added, 'I thought it of mutual benefit to pay you a visit and explain my ground rules. They are very simple. You give me no trouble and I give you no beatings. Because I promise you my beatings will cause you twice the pain of any trouble you inflict upon me.'

He nodded to the others and walked away. A cloud of tobacco smoke rose as he neared the doorway. His men had landed the first of their blows before he reached the corridor outside. A knee hit the side of my skull. A kick followed to the ribs. A stick set fire to my spine.

I could not manage to stand, so I grabbed a leg and upended one of my attackers. Others rained blows on me. I, in turn, inflicted maximum distress on the fellow I had brought down. His shrieks of agony alerted Johncock, who whistled down the gallery for more men.

16

They came piling into the cell, flailing sticks. I knew I had little time before they overwhelmed me and absolutely no hope of overcoming them all.

I got up on my toes but they beat me into a wall. A hand snagged my wrist. Someone pulled at an ankle. Boots piled into my stomach and genitals. My right arm was twisted up my back. A big skull butted my face.

'Come away! Leave 'im now,' said Johncock. 'Much as I'd like to kill the bugger we 'ave to save that joy for the 'angman.'

Voices shouted around me. Feet slapped stone. Keys jangled.

I slipped into blackness. Drifted in time. Back to my youth, to when I was free. When I first met Sebastian the Jew and he warned me about life and luck.

MANCHESTER, 1884

I settled easily with the Scuttlers and quickly found them to be a gang unlike any other I had encountered.

They stole for a living. Nothing unusual about that. They were capable of extreme and cold-blooded violence. Again, commonplace. What made them different was Sebastian. He was organised. Controlled. Calm. From my experience, gang leaders tended to be the toughest and loudest, the biggest and most brutal, the braggarts and the bullies.

Sebastian was none of these.

I doubt he had ever thrown a punch in his life. He led through intelligence and cunning. Was quietly spoken yet always had everyone's attention.

An insight into the small man's power came soon after I arrived. He had departed early in the morning, without his animals or any of his men. When he returned in the middle of the day he was smiling broader than a loom beam. He was well dressed, in green check tweed and polished brown boots. Tucked beneath his arm and balanced in his hand was a long, rolled-up, beige document tied with ribbons.

Heading directly to his private rooms, he motioned to Fingers and Danny to follow him, which they duly did. The rest of the afternoon was spent behind closed doors with them and other men who, one at a time, were also summoned into his sanctuary.

By early evening, the only people left in the big room were me and a dim-witted scrag of a boy called Zack.

'What's going on back there?' I asked.

'Dunno,' he shrugged. 'They never tell me nuthin'.'

Zack got told plenty, just not anything he wanted to hear. His role was to clean and empty things. Sort out the piss pots. Unblock the shit pits. Sweep the floor. Wash plates and cutlery.

'But what do you *think* they're doing?' I pressed. 'They're up to something, aren't they?'

'Work,' he offered. 'They're *up to* work.'

Work, I took to be thievery and the exact details most

probably lay on that big roll of paper Sebastian had carted in.

After a time, Danny appeared in the doorway. 'Terry, you're wanted.'

I rose quickly and covered the twenty yards to Sebastian's quarters at a pace indecently close to running.

His quarters were handsomely decorated but dark except for splashes of light thrown upwards by the gas lamps. Instead of the bare bricks present in the rest of the mill, the walls were panelled in cheap oak, punctuated with oils depicting hunting scenes. There was a small, open fireplace, stacked with fresh coal, and a long and heavy trestle table flanked by pew benches that looked as though they'd been stolen from a church.

'Time to earn your keep,' said Sebastian. 'Come and join us.'

I took a seat in the midst of a pool of smoky yellow light.

'Let the dog see the bone,' he urged his men. One by one, they moved hands, pipes and arms so I could view the plans spread across the table.

'Goddard Grange,' Sebastian explained. 'Stuffed to its old woodwormed rafters with Persian carpets, Dutch oils, Roman silverware and Indian jewels.'

'Very nice,' I said.

'Very *beautiful*. The lord of the manor, a Mr Wilberforce Singleton, is an antiques trader. In a few hours' time he will be meeting a ship in Southampton and taking delivery of prized Etruscan artefacts. We, meanwhile, will be taking possession of everything of value in his lavishly furnished country home, the place detailed on the plans in front of you.'

We all scanned the large document, already marked with crosses, showing where the family silver, jewellery, oils and sculptures were located.

'What do you want of me?' I asked.

'Tonight, you will be a carrier,' replied Sebastian. 'Joel, tell our young friend what his duties are.'

A thickset fellow with receding brown hair coughed to clear his throat and shifted his feet nervously as he spoke. 'You waits outside, by the windows, then when the *stuffers* brings you their sacks you carries them to the carts.' He coughed twice more then added further instructions, with the emphasis of someone who had clearly been told the procedure many times. 'You does it *quickly* but *carefully*. No *running* or *stumbling*. No *dropping* or *throwing* sacks down – not unless coppers come and you have to leg it!'

His last remark brought laughter from the entire group. Once it had died down, Sebastian looked at me with an intensity I had not seen since our first meeting on the riverbank. 'Can you do that, Terry? Does it fall within your abilities and your definition of *honest* labour?'

'I can do it. And more if needs be.'

'Needs will be. But not tonight. Tonight you start at the bottom.'

*

Night fell.

In an instant of near-military coordination we all moved. More than a dozen covered carts rumbled out from our riverside abode and took us miles through the deepening blackness of the countryside. I was at the back of the convoy and noticed each driver kept a good two minutes' distance from the one in front, presumably so as not to attract undue attention. Down long unlit roads, rutted country lanes and winding hillside tracks we travelled for hours.

We halted with the same precision that had moved us. For twenty minutes or more we idled in a tired silence. Coughs were stifled with cupped hands. Patience of the highest kind was called for.

Finally the pointsmen came. Called us from the carts in whispers. We clambered out. Dropped noiselessly onto soil and grass. There was no need for prompting. Every man knew his job. We moved quickly, and calmly.

Bent low and backlit by the moon, we trod carefully across the carpet of turf that rolled up to the big house.

As instructed, I watched for the swing of a lantern outside the east wing. When it came, I dashed over with my arms full. I was laden with large hessian sacks, specially made for the oil paintings. Deep bags packed with balled newspapers to swallow silver goblets, urns and plates. Soft cloth pouches for delicate personal jewellery such as bracelets, rings and necklaces.

We descended like locusts.

Within the hour we had stripped the house bare.

By the time the last of the carts had been loaded, my lungs were on fire and my legs had turned to jelly. Thick sweat greased my face as I walked the mile to the crossroads where I had been told we would be picked up.

Joel was already waiting with a large four-wheeler drawn by big black horses. He handed us ale then sat up top with the coachman as four of us climbed inside and exchanged excited chatter about 'the job'.

There was more drink when we got back to the mill. Enough to float a ship. The tables in our lodgings creaked from the weight of the food piled upon them. Huge slabs of beef and pork. Great rounds of cheeses. Baskets of fruit and bread.

There were women, too. Blondes. Brunettes. Redheads. Young. Old. Tall and small. I felt too awkward to go with any of them. Their light dresses and heavy sexuality repulsed rather than attracted me.

Celebrations grew noisier by the hour and by the glass. Once singing began there was no stopping the Scuttlers. They mangled many music hall numbers, belted out bawdy shanties. And more than once, they roared at the top of their voices a song I'd heard during my days in London:

Up and down the City Road
In and out the Eagle
That's the way the money goes
Pop goes the weasel!

Tankards rose and clanked together on the final line. Ale had to be downed in one and was followed by riotous cheering. The only voice missing was that of Sebastian.

Nor was it heard the following morning, when even the sound of bird song was too loud for our delicate heads.

Not until late afternoon, when the last of the drunks were sober again, did he return. On seeing him, the older men roused themselves from their seats and headed over like moths to a flame. He in turn welcomed them to the warmth of his guarded quarters.

I counted the time that passed, mere minutes, before one by one they returned to the main room. All were smiling. The younger ones were then called through. They returned in similarly happy spirits. None flaunted the money they had been given, but from their excitement it was apparent they had been paid well for their labours.

I was not. Not a penny. My name was never called.

The moneyed men spent the night discussing what they would do with their newly acquired clink. There were clothes and women to be bought. Debts needed settling. Dreams to be chased.

I went to bed and dwelled on the events of the day but not the fact that I had been excluded from the payout. This, I assumed, was simply part of my initiation. I had to earn my way in.

So be it.

No, my mind was on other things.

I was focused on the easy success of the burglary and the many questions it raised.

The whole caper had been aided by architectural plans of the house and precise information about when it would be deserted, save for a dithery old butler, sleepy cook and young housemaid who most sensibly did not put up any resistance. I thought it quite strange that the owner had left no beefy brutes to guard his goods and concluded that Sebastian had either paid them off or had his men tackle them before we arrived.

None of the coachmen who carried away our haul had been known to any of us in the mill, except to Sebastian and possibly Danny. Yet they were allowed to drive away with the haul in the dead of night. To where? Some industrial warehouses, dockside sheds or farm outbuildings? I had no idea. Did Sebastian have even more Scuttlers working for him? Men other than those I slept and ate with every day? Or was *he* in fact working for someone else? I felt certain the latter was the case, although it occurred to me there was another distinct possibility.

Perhaps *nothing* had been stolen. Things might simply have been *moved* to another location. Sebastian could have been hired by the owner to empty the house while he was away, so he could fraudulently claim money from some big London insurance company.

The real reason never materialised. Not that I cared. In the months that followed, I was given a fair share of coin as I graduated from carrier to stuffer, then from stuffer to lifter, and from lifter to breaker. Finally I made it to pointsman, the role that under Danny's tutelage involved coordinating all ground operations, transport, men and timings. It made a welcome change to use my brain rather than my fists. Nevertheless, I was wary of going soft, of losing my physical strength and the protection it afforded me.

Every morning I would train hard. As soon as light broke through the big mill windows I would rise and begin a two-hour regime. At first, it involved nothing more sophisticated than a long run then sessions of lifting and squatting with heavy rocks.

I had boxed, during my childhood in a London workhouse, so I always finished with furious bouts with my silhouette. Initially, some of the other men came and laughed at me. Then they wanted to join in. Sebastian got us gloves and we began to spar. There were even calls to stage matches between ourselves and take bets, but for reasons that will soon become apparent, this was something that I refused to take part in.

Often I would swim in the river at the back of the mill. I had taught myself to do it after escaping from London, venturing deeper and deeper into streams, rivers and canals and then panicking my way back to dry land via a mixture of sinking and swimming.

One day, I was emerging from a post-run dip when I saw Sebastian approaching with his dogs. It was unusual for him to be out so early in the day.

'Good morning!' I shouted, still dripping water while I grabbed a towel.

Normally he had a smile for me, but on this occasion

only a hardened stare. 'Get yourself dressed, then come to my quarters.' He turned and tugged the dogs around to follow him. Dee and Dum yelped objections at having an anticipated walk curtailed so abruptly.

I towelled dry, dressed and made my way into his sitting room. It was, as always, in virtual darkness bar a crack of light through the curtains. Sebastian was in his wing-backed chair, looking through the gap into the daylight. 'You need to pack your belongings and leave, Terry. And you need to do it now.'

'Why?'

'Because I told you to.'

'What have I done wrong?'

A voice that wasn't his replied, 'Nothing.' It came from the darkness at the back of the room.

'What's going on?' I moved towards Sebastian but he shook his head to warn me not to.

'What is *going on*,' continued the man's voice, 'is that you are leaving here to work for me.' He spoke without class or accent, English but with an almost foreign drawl that was beyond my ability to place it.

'*I* choose who I work for,' I protested.

The speaker appeared inchoately in the shadows. 'Not any more.'

I didn't answer. The man finally stepped into the light.

He was only slightly smaller than me. I put him around forty but he could have been older. Brown hair, eyes the colour of roasted chestnuts, a dark beard speckled with grey but well-groomed enough to reveal gentle cheekbones and a powerful neck. A richly tailored woollen suit of chequered browns fell from broad shoulders and tapered at a waist that had probably once been as firm as his shoulders but was lost now to little exercise and lots of food.

Cradled in his hand was a stout unlit pipe, trimmed in silver with some form of crest embossed on it. He thumbed tobacco into the bowl and smiled. 'I think I'll call you Simeon. *Simeon Lynch*. That, after all, is your real name, isn't it?'

I turned and ran.

The door I had come through was now locked. The handle twisted hopelessly in my fingers and would not open. I spun towards the window – if necessary, I'd hurl myself through the glass.

Sebastian stood and with one tug of his hand, those soft, quiet dogs now growled menacingly and strained on their leashes. The stranger calmly lit his pipe. White spirals rose and swirled. Behind him appeared two more men. All hope of escape had been crushed.

Those chestnut eyes followed me through a cloud of newly exhaled smoke. 'Please do not inconvenience us by running around any more, Simeon. It is both fruitless and childish.'

'My name is Terry,' I insisted. 'Terry Perch. You've got the wrong person, mister. That *Simeon* – he's not me.'

'Tut. Tut. Tut.' He shook his head and walked nearer. 'I know exactly who you are, young man. Know it better

27

than *you* do.' His hand gripped my bicep. Seized me like an iron clamp. 'You were born in a cankerous hovel in London and your mother, a local harlot, died while bringing your wretched body into this world.'

I tried to hide my fear but there was something about him that chilled my bones and silenced my tongue.

'Don't you want me to say more, Simeon? More about her? About you? About what you have done and why you ran away from London?'

'No!' I snapped. He had made enough revelations to set my heart racing. It was beyond me how he knew these things and the very fact that he did made me feel all the more vulnerable.

'A wise choice,' he said, unhanding me. 'There are indeed parts of your life best not spoken about.'

'Who *is* he?' I asked Sebastian.

'He's not police,' he said reassuringly. 'Not the Old Bill.'

'Most certainly not,' confirmed the stranger. 'My name is Moriarty. Professor Brogan Moriarty.'

16 DAYS TO EXECUTION

NEWGATE, 2 JANUARY 1900

When I regained consciousness, I felt the full pain of the beating Johncock's men had meted out.

I also realised I had been moved to a different cell. Dressings had been fixed to my head, arms and legs. Poorly applied, I might add. One had sagged and obscured the vision of my left eye, causing me to blink repeatedly as it rubbed against my lid and lashes. My arms felt inordinately heavy, so it came as little surprise to discover my wrists and ankles clasped in chains. They were fixed, I imagined, to sturdy rings set in the floor, though I had no more than a meagre view of the ceiling and a far wall. I was spread-eagled on a hard bunk, and my throat felt as though hot tar and broken glass had been poured into it.

For the rest of the day, I drifted in and out of consciousness and must have been in that amorphous antechamber between worlds when I heard keys rattling and the door creaking open.

I braced myself for another ordeal. Perhaps new guards arriving to administer a fresh beating. I had even heard tell of doctors using experimental drugs on prison patients to control them. But the footsteps were from soft shoes, not prison boots. The voice was richer and more cultured than that of a turnkey.

'I believe you are not an unintelligent man. That beyond your savagery is a cultured brain. One capable of reason.'

I forced open my eyes. The silhouette of a head slid briefly into my limited view. Unexpectedly, the manacle around my right wrist grew tight, then slackened. Seconds later, the same happened on my left side.

'You can sit up,' the shadow added. 'I have loosened your

restraints to grant you some movement. Do it slowly, or you are most certain to pass out.'

I lifted my arms. Chains slithered away like heavy, cold snakes. I struggled upright. The pain in my chest was agonising. Blood rushed my head. I felt woozy. But one thing was clear: I now recognised my visitor.

Sherlock Holmes.

'*Simeon Lynch*,' he proclaimed. 'Caught, convicted of two murders and now condemned to death.'

'Go to hell, Holmes.' I peered at him and remembered how close I had once come to killing the legendary detective. Moriarty owned an entire building opposite the investigator's modest chambers in Baker Street and for three weeks had tasked me with occupying a room there, overlooking 221b. I had chronicled Holmes's every movement and also those of his sycophantic biographer and doting housekeeper.

As wise and nocturnal as an owl, the man had allowed me little sleep during those days. In the end, I traced both his main cocaine supplier and a lady of the night with whom he took comfort in a less-than-salubrious brothel in West Street. I chronicled his vulnerabilities, his weak spots, and given the word would have done my duty. 'I could have killed you several times,' I told him.

'That is a *preposterous* assertion,' he answered with such levity it was as though I had told him a tale of great amusement. 'I know you followed me and spied upon me. Hid in shadows and peered from windows as I sought recreation and work. But dear fellow, you could never have been anything more than my voyeur.'

'What do you want, Holmes?' I sounded disinterested, but my mind was racing to fathom out why he had come and what advantage his presence might afford me.

'Well,' he began in a thoughtful tone as he walked towards the end of the bunk where my feet remained securely chained to the floor, 'you have asked two questions of me and they require different but of course not unconnected answers. Like most decent people, *what I want* – is to see you hang. Unfortunately, I have been charged with offering you a way to avoid the noose.'

He paused to gauge my reaction, but I gave him none. I stared at the medieval iron cuffs fixed on me. These were certainly too strong to break without a chisel and a heavy hammer. I had no chance of endangering him, taking him hostage or in any way using him to fashion an escape.

'You have committed a great many crimes,' Holmes continued. 'Of that I am certain. But I suspect you did so entirely at Moriarty's behest. And yet, here you are, alone in this cell, while that *demon* enjoys all the trappings of a wealthy and free man.'

'Come to the point, or preferably just leave. Time, I have learned, is not something I have an abundance of.'

'Turn Queen's Evidence. Give the police details of that scoundrel's criminal activities and the home secretary will hold a clemency hearing. Your death sentence will be commuted to life imprisonment, and then if a successful prosecution of James Moriarty follows, I believe you may be pardoned.'

I laughed at him for not knowing the real power lay with Brogan. 'You want me to testify against *James* Moriarty?'

'I do. I most sincerely do.'

'Save your breath.'

'I can afford to squander a little, as I, unlike you, have many more years to replenish the supply to my lungs.'

'My, aren't you the wit.' I laid back and stared at the ceiling. A spider had spun a fine, taut web in the far corner. A still-fluttering fly was already caught. Its struggle to escape was pointless, but struggle it did. The predator moved slowly towards it. Death would soon be dispensed. I knew the ritual all too well.

'I am offering you the chance to save your life, wipe the slate clean and begin again.'

'Deportation, you mean?'

'Not necessarily. There are options on English soil. But wouldn't even that be preferable to death?'

I looked at Holmes and wondered who was the spider and who the fly. He thought me about to get caught in his web, but I saw things differently. I was needed. The law needed me. I could, for the moment, safely reject this offer for I was certain Holmes would come back to press his case and in doing so he would perhaps afford me a chance to escape without me having to make any traitorous testimony. My mind was made up.

'Please go away, Mr Holmes. And take your desperation with you.'

He scowled at me, then walked to the door and rapped on it to summon the gaolers. Before it opened he added, 'I must tell you one last thing: I have had a wager with my colleague, Dr Watson. He's a military man as you might know, and he says people like you behave in a military manner.'

'Go away!'

'It is his belief that you will take your intimate knowledge of Moriarty, his crimes and his cohorts to your grave. My bet is to the contrary. You are a killer, Lynch. You deal in death and therefore know the value of your own life, which is of course greater to you than any loyalties you may have. So I have wagered twenty pounds that after some vacillation and pretence to the contrary, you will eventually seize my offer with all the eagerness of a young thief left alone in a cloakroom.'

The door opened and a gaoler asked, 'Are you ready, Mr Holmes?'

'I am,' he answered, 'I am, indeed.' He threw a final comment to me. 'No sooner will this door close than you will begin to consider my proposal and its attractiveness. Use your brain, Lynch, instead of your fists, it might just save your neck.'

The door banged shut. Keys clicked in the lock and once more I was fastened in.

The great Sherlock Holmes had visited and propositioned me. Now wasn't that a thing?

Above me, the spider devoured the fly. The scene made me smile. Perhaps when I escaped I would visit Holmes with a proposition of my own. Death by knife? Or by my bare hands?

MANCHESTER, 1885

Brogan Moriarty.

The name had meant nothing to me when the steely-eyed stranger introduced himself in the shadows of Sebastian's rooms. Had it done, then I would have fought to the death to escape. But I was young, ignorant and arrogant. Mistakenly confident that I could bide my time and give him and his men the slip, as and when the fancy took me.

In the light outside the Mancunian mill, the first of Moriarty's companions appeared to be a well-built, handsome man in his mid-twenties. He was a professional type, a senior clerk perhaps, with shoulder-length black hair, grey eyes and a blue twill suit as perfectly tailored as his smile. With him was a smaller, thinner fellow, drearily clad in an ill-fitting, baggy grey jacket, tattered brown vest and frayed pants, topped by a flat cap far too big for his ragamuffin head. I supposed him to be an errand boy, kept close at hand to run hither or thither as his master wished.

The four of us climbed into the grandest carriage I had ever seen. Painted glossy black, it boasted a golden crest on the doors and gleaming brass lamps to the front. An immaculately uniformed coachman, sat soldier-straight above the elegant steeds, controlled a team of white horses.

I settled into a rear-facing seat, opposite Moriarty and the thin scrap of an errand boy, while the well-dressed one installed himself next to me. I already had the measure of things. As soon as the carriage stopped for any reason I would open the door, dart out and disappear.

The professor caught my eye. 'While I have quite taken to steam travel and appreciate its speed and convenience, I find old carriages like this afford me invaluable privacy.' He ran a hand proudly over the door panel at his side. 'It is a former mail coach, so it is roomy enough. Though I had the springs adjusted by a French mechanic, as the French understand the necessity of a less tumultuous ride.'

'Where are you from, mister? You talk like a toff but have an accent unlike any I've heard.'

His companions laughed and a thin smile moved his lips. 'I'm as English as you are, but I spend a lot of time in America on business. It's like a second home to me and I have only recently returned. The accent sticks for some time because I spent a lot of my childhood there.'

I had grown bored with his tale and my impatient eyes had spied a set of cut glasses and decanters fixed on pads of velvet, tethered by straps of leather and stowed in a door well. I couldn't help but think that I knew plenty of flash houses where fancy goods like that would fetch a pretty penny.

'We'll refresh ourselves in a moment,' he said, in a voice that chastised my gaze. 'But first, some introductions. This is Miss Surrey Breed.' He placed his right hand on the urchin's left knee and smiled. 'Quite an extraordinary young lady.'

'*Lady?*' I blurted.

'Aye, a *lady*,' she stressed in a thick Scottish accent, 'so doon' yoo go playin' the daft laddie an' forgit it.' She took off the large cap, withdrew a hairpin and a waterfall of black locks tumbled over her narrow shoulders. Now she looked undeniably feminine and not a lot older than me. She tilted her head in a coquettish manner and her whole countenance, voice and status instantly changed. 'Honestly, don't you find that first appearances can be *dangerously* deceiving, Mr Lynch?' She had assumed the most refined of English accents. 'It is such an aberration of sound judgement to make sweeping presumptions of class, status or even gender, based solely upon how a stranger appears.'

The professor laughed. 'Miss Breed is a cultural chameleon, an invaluable creature given the pomposity of the age we live in.' He nodded to the man next to me. 'And this is Mr Sirius Gunn. Do not be deceived by his occasional good manners and his constantly prim appearance. Beneath that fine facade lurks a devil that puts Satan to shame.'

Gunn lifted his hat indifferently but spoke not a word. His eyes conveyed in one fleeting look that he did not care for me. In return, mine told him that given the chance I would beat him black and blue and rob him blind.

I turned my attention to the carriage window. Trees and fields flew past as the magnificent horses picked up speed. Soon we would be miles from Manchester. I looked to the professor. 'Where are we going, sir?'

'We will come to that in a moment. First, it is time, I think, for those refreshments.' He leaned to his left and plucked three shimmering glasses from their holders and handed them round. Next, he grasped the cut-glass decanter and added, 'A little *aqua vitae*, to stiffen our resolve for the journey.' He removed the stopper from the decanter and poured a generous amount of pale amber liquid into my glass.

'Try it,' he nodded at me in encouragement. 'I am intrigued to know what you think.' He dispensed similar measures for the others and then took a fourth glass for himself.

I lifted the liquid to my nose and smelled it. In the work-house I had learned that meals and drinks with a bad odour were best avoided if you didn't want to spend the rest of the week in the privy. The best I could discern was that it contained some sort of alcohol. 'What spirit is this?'

'Whisky,' answered Miss Breed, back in Scottish guise. 'Now dunny be a stookie, git it doon ya neck.'

I sank most of it like a dose of medicine.

'*Aqua vitae*,' added the professor, contentedly sniffing his own drink, 'Latin for "water of life". It's also a term applied to distilled alcohol, one Gaelic distillers use for whisky. Mixed with water, or other substances, it can have trans-formative effects on the body's physiology.'

I wasn't quite sure what he meant, but I was thirsty enough to drain the glass.

'For example,' he continued, 'your brain is now telling you that you have almost quenched your thirst. That's a good feeling, isn't it?'

I nodded. He was right about that. It had been some time since I had drunk anything and my morning exercises had left me parched.

He looked pleased. 'A little more?'

I held out my glass. This time he was less generous in his measure. He resealed the decanter and returned it to its holder as I drank. 'You are currently relaxing in the assured knowledge that you are rehydrating. That is because water comprises an enormous amount of the human body – more than half, possibly as much as three quarters.'

I couldn't see how that could be, but I emptied the glass again.

'Better?'

'Yes, I suppose I am almost, what's the word, *rehydrated*?'

'Very good.' He smiled, then leaned forwards and studied my face. 'Your pupils have already dilated. I suspect you are feeling light-headed and a little weak?'

I had not noticed the sensation until he mentioned it, but again, he was correct.

Moriarty reached out and took the glass from me. 'I'll take this from you. It's expensive and I'd hate you to break it. You see, I have given you a sedative and you are now in the process of losing consciousness.'

'What?'

'The drink contained a sweet toxic honey called rhododendron nectar. It lowers your blood pressure to the point that you become dizzy and pass out. It's a crude form of anaesthetic.'

I made a clumsy move for the door.

Gunn slapped an arm across my chest. I tried to lift my hands to fight him, but my limbs felt numb. I stumbled off my seat.

'Don't fight it,' said Moriarty. 'You'll sleep now. When you awake, we will be at our destination.'

The sedative sewed my eyes together. In the blackness, our carriage rose from the ground. Horses galloped into clouds. The air became thin and cold. We were high in the night sky and beneath us everything was turning black. Gradually, images floated up at me.

A tavern. Bawdy men clinking ale tankards, playing cards, arguing over winnings. Coarse women laughing and flaunting themselves. The noise was deafening.

Then suddenly silence; people moved apart. A woman collapsed. Screamed in pain, her face twisted by the agony. Men were laughing at her. Some of the women pulled at her clothes. There was blood. Blood everywhere.

It was my blood. My birth blood.

In that sedated nightmare I heard my mother's screams. Saw her eyes become fixed and dead. Watched her corpse carried from the tavern to a wagon. Heard it rumble over the cobbles, off to the pauper's pit where rotting strangers were piled high upon each other then all were mounded in earth. I heard my own infantile screams.

And a voice from the present not the past: 'Wake up! Wake up! C'mon now.'

The raggedy errand-boy-come-woman slapped my face. My eyes blinked open.

A lantern swung.

'He's coming round,' she said to someone.

'Get him out of the carriage.' Moriarty sounded far, far away.

'Watch his head,' the girl warned.

Strong hands slid me out of the vehicle and into the crisp air. My heels banged the footboards of the carriage. I heard my drug-numbed feet being dragged through gravel.

'Bring him inside,' Moriarty commanded. 'Downstairs. Let him sleep it off.'

More hands now. Scooping up my feet. Lifting me. Floating me again. Down, down, down. Flickering lamps. Feet clapping stone steps. The air stale. My body rising and falling. Different smells. A match. Candle wax. The creak of a door.

'In here. Put him in here until morning.'

Stillness. Flatness. Groans and sighs of men, relieved to be free of carrying me. Their hands disappeared. Light faded. Cool sheets comforted my face. Darkness took me again.

15 Days to Execution

Darkness.

I knew his tricks and powers all too well. Darkness was a conjurer. A demon. He would throw blankets over lovers and soil over the dead. Here, in prison, he was busily employed as the most terrible of torturers.

By keeping out light, he helped the turnkeys crush our spirits and made it all the more difficult to devise ways to escape.

Even in the new cell, where I recovered from my beating, Darkness stood guard from the end of the turnkeys' night rounds until slivers of morning light were smuggled through my window bars.

Asleep, I either dreamed of escape or became a child again. I was reacquainted with Mario the Italian organ grinder, who worked a street corner near where I was born and would play every day except Sundays. Once more, I held out my hands for sweets wrapped in cut-up newspaper and played with wooden toys that other boys had grown out of. I looked into the faces of the mother and father I had never known. I grew up with them. Grew old with them. Placed grandchildren in their loving arms.

In the cold, black, early hours of the third day of the new century, I woke in the midst of a dream so vivid that I still imagined myself surrounded by the people in it.

They seemed to have fallen noisily from the realms of my imagination and now, as my eyes opened, they stumbled, disorientated, around the darkness of my cell.

Feet crept across the stone floor. I smelled sweat and tobacco.

This was no dream.

My mind checked off what I knew. No keys had been heard turning in the lock. No screw had broken my sleep with his booming voice. No doctor had demanded a light to inspect his patient.

I did not sit up or cry out. Did not let whoever lurked in the pool of shadows beyond my bed know that I was awake and aware of them. The fingers of my right hand slowly stretched out for the chain that tethered my wrists.

I heard a whisper.

One whisper equalled two people, or else a dangerous imbecile talking to himself in the darkness.

Cloth brushed my knuckles. The unseen intruder was beside me.

I sat bolt upright.

Desperately, I cast the loop of the wrist chain in the direction of the whisper. Metal clanked bone and a man cried out.

I pulled quickly. A gasp came from the darkness.

Flesh pressed against my fists. The chain was around a throat. Choking noises from the mouth of my haul.

Metal clattered nearby and someone else cried out. The second man had fallen over my slop bucket.

I held tight on the chains between my hands. The fellow caught in them grunted. I dragged him up the bunk until he lay across my chest, facing the ceiling. Desperate hands clutched at me. His body weight shifted, his back arched.

He jerked. The fight went out of him.

His body turned limp.

The cell door opened and yellow light from the landing flooded the room.

I slackened my hands and saw the top of the man's head as he slid off me and flopped onto the floor.

I lay back, exhausted.

Evidently, I still hadn't recovered my strength from the thrashing Johncock's men had dispensed. Seconds passed. Then what seemed a minute, or even more.

Why had no gaolers come? Surely the fall of light into my cell had been caused by a screw opening the door?

I was wrong. I pulled myself upright. The dead man lay partly in shadow, his face obscured, but I could see that it was not *I* who had killed him. A metal shank had pierced his chest and blood was emptying from him like an uncapped mountain spring. A shank that undoubtedly would have pierced my heart, had I not by chance hauled the intruder across my body as I snared him with the chain.

'Door open!' shouted a screw in a panic. 'Cell five is open!'

Whistles blew. I braced myself.

All hell was about to break loose.

The surroundings I opened my eyes to, that first morning in the house of Brogan Moriarty, were by far the grandest I had ever seen. Foolishly, I did not realise that it was but a well-furnished prison and I no more than a pampered inmate.

'Good morning,' said a male voice from somewhere beyond my view.

I lifted my head from the pillows, and as I did so it ached like I had been punched. My fingers fell on crisp white linen. Across the room, I saw a fine wooden dresser topped with a free-standing mirror, a painted washing bowl and a large willow-patterned water jug.

'Are you feeling sick, or dizzy?' asked an elderly man as he walked into view. Slightly hunchbacked and bespectacled he had white hair and a well-trimmed, wispy white beard. Kind eyes in a wrinkled face. He was dressed in a brown and red chequered waistcoat with brown trousers, the sleeves of his white shirt rolled up over his bony elbows.

He sat on the bed and, while introducing himself, stared curiously into my eyes. 'I am Dr Reuss. I need to look you over.' He took my wrist and flipped out a gold pocket watch. 'Relax. Let me and my ticker here see how your ticker is faring.'

For a good minute, I watched him watch me and his watch.

'You are fine,' he concluded and returned the timepiece

to his waistcoat. Without further comment, he stood and left.

I listened to his footsteps in the corridor. They were joined by lighter ones. Voices mingled and hushed. Confidential tones became mere murmurs. I strained but could not hear what was being said.

Dizzily, I made my way to the bowl and jug. Poured water. Checked it didn't smell strange, then lowered my face and splashed it, cupping cool handfuls to assuage my stinging eyes and aching brow, finally drinking what was left in the jug.

Very briefly, the foggy pain disappeared from inside my head. I took a white towel from a brass rail and looked out of the large window as I dried myself.

Grass. Endless grass. There were gardens within gardens. Trim hedges, like mazes, separated roses and fruit trees, gravelled pathways, fountains and ponds, summerhouses, vegetable plots and lawns. Lawns that stretched further than my eyes could see. Out on the horizon were all manner of large, small, flat and jagged hilltops. But no houses, factories or chimneys billowing smoke.

This was not the worst place to be in. Not at all. Once I had my bearings, and perhaps a sack full of stolen property to sell, then I would leave much richer for the experience.

My thoughts were still forming when Sirius Gunn appeared in the doorway. 'So, you are awake,' he declared with a grin on his clean-shaven face. 'Our little Briar Rose has finally surfaced from sweet slumber.'

'Briar Rose?'

'It is the tale of an innocent princess woken after a sleep of a hundred years.'

'I am not a princess and not one for stories. Where am I?'

'You are in the county of Derbyshire. More specifically, a place of great natural beauty known as the Peak District. Now gather your ignorance and follow me.' He headed out of the door.

I wished I had the strength to catch him and break his perfect nose. But I hadn't. I was weaker than a newborn deer. My legs wouldn't lock or move without immense effort. Muscles had mutinied and my feet dragged lamely.

By the time I had navigated the corridor and climbed a steep stone staircase, my face glistened with sweat. Around the corner, Gunn leaned on a wall, a smirk pinned to his face. 'Do you want me to carry you, old boy?'

'Die and go to hell.' I slapped a steadying hand on the wall.

'*Hell?*' He laughed sarcastically. 'You and I are already *in* hell.' He stepped towards me. 'Do you not have any idea *why* you are here, Lynch? Who the professor is? Why you were chosen?'

'I am *here* . . .' I struggled to catch my breath, 'because you and that American bastard drugged me and I had no choice.'

'He's not American, you idiot. His mother was American and he is infatuated with the damned country, but he's British. Now get a move on, you ignoramus.'

He walked away and I shouted after him, 'Call me that in a few days' time, you foppish ponce, and I promise you won't look so handsome then.'

He stopped and walked back. 'You are about to be educated, Simeon Lynch. Those rough edges *will* be knocked off you and your coarse ways smoothed into something resembling pleasantness. Now come along! They're waiting for us. And try to speak politely, or I'll have your filthy mouth washed out with carbolic.'

It took him less than twenty steps to reach a room, open a dark oak door and disappear inside. I was pained to follow.

Gunn was already in conversation with Surrey Breed and several others by the time I dragged myself through the doorway. It was an airy room with a chessboard floor of black and white marble. Most astonishingly, the rest of it seemed to be made entirely from glass. Aside from a small wall no more than two feet high, there appeared to be no bricks, only glass and metal frames that held interlocking panes. And there were plants and fruit trees. So many that it looked like an entire garden had been dragged inside the house.

I spotted Moriarty. He was smartly dressed in a dark suit with a white, wing-collared shirt and red bow tie. One hand was occupied with a glass of water while the other stroked his well-trimmed beard. He was holding sway near a long table covered in white cloth and stacked with food and drink. Large glass jugs of milk, water and fruit juices. Baskets of bread. Plates of meat, cheese and fish.

Standing incongruously beside him was a large, bald, broad-shouldered man in his mid-forties who wore nothing more elegant than an old grey shirt, baggy trousers and unpolished boots. I supposed that at one point he might have been an athlete of sorts, but not now. Bouldered biceps had sagged. A strong torso turned into a barrel for beer. His form did not warrant further attention because opposite him stood the prettiest woman in all of Christendom.

She was tall and in her early thirties. Blue eyed with strawberry-blonde hair tied back beneath a wide-brimmed off-white hat pinned with flowers. A blue day dress emphasised her narrow waist and generous bosom, then flowed to the floor in a flurry of frills and pleats.

Looking at her made my heart feel like it had been trampled on by stampeding horses. Never had I felt like this. Such emotional churnings and excitement were alien to me.

'Chan!' shouted Moriarty to the bald man. 'That bloody interferer will be the death of me!' His voice boomed with anger and frustration. 'He is a godforsaken reptile! He and that odious offspring of his are getting above themselves.'

Before the fellow could reply, the woman leaned close to Moriarty, whispered and looked in my direction. He glanced at me then beckoned with his free hand, 'Simeon, come in. Don't hang back there. You need to be introduced.'

I walked further into the room and did my best to conceal the apprehension growing inside me.

'Good to see you up and about!' Moriarty grabbed my shoulder and deftly angled me towards the whispering lady.

'Elizabeth, my dear, this is Simeon Lynch, the new fellow I told you about. And Simeon, this *heavenly* creature is Lady Elizabeth Audsley. She will be in charge of your *cultural* education.'

This was clearly not the moment to question what was going on, to argue that I did not want 'education'; I simply wished to rob him blind and be on my way.

'Simeon!' he snapped.

I had never met a lady before. She had offered her hand and I had not responded. Once Moriarty shouted, I gripped it firmly and shook so vigorously that she was caused to yelp like a kicked puppy.

'Not so hard, sir, I pray.' She pulled away from me and nursed her fingers.

My face reddened.

'He has much to learn,' said Moriarty in mitigation for my behaviour. He grabbed my shoulder again and turned me to face the inappropriately dressed man at his side. 'This, Simeon, is your *physical* tutor, Mr Michael Brannigan. You may do to *his* hand as you wish, for Michael was once a champion wrestler and remains stronger than all of us put together.'

The bald man stepped forward and challengingly presented his palm.

Everyone smiled.

I took it, knowing he would endeavour to balance my indiscretion by deliberately crushing my bones until I begged for respite.

I was not disappointed. Brannigan closed his fingers like the jaws of a metal vice tightening on soft wood.

Only, I was not soft.

Our eyes locked. My hand returned his pressure in more than equal force. Veins in his arms bloated with blood. His face flushed red as he squeezed to his maximum.

Brannigan turned his head to the watching crowd. 'The youth has the strength of a man,' he grinned at them. 'Wonder whether he has the courage as well.' With his free hand, he feigned a punch to my chin.

To my shame, I did not see it for the playful ruse he intended. Instead, I smashed his hand away with my forearm and endeavoured to headbutt him in the face.

The old fighter stepped swiftly aside and expertly avoided the blow. His eyes widened. 'My, he is indeed a wild one, Professor.'

'Take care when handling him,' answered Moriarty, coolly. 'He has killed already, Michael, and I believe is quite able to do so again.'

My eyes caught Lady Elizabeth's. To my surprise, I saw no shock there. No judgement or repulsion. And in that second, I knew that her opinion of me was the only one that mattered.

Brannigan pushed a finger into my chest. 'Tomorrow morning, nice and early, we'll do some *training* and discover how tough you really are.'

I looked the old wrestler over again. Despite his age and weight, there was something disturbing about him. A quality not discernible in his shape or voice. It was a secret. One very dark and dangerous.

The professor broke my gaze. 'There is a *final* person I wish to introduce you to.' He stepped to one side and revealed a man in a chair. Crutches flanked both his arms and I could see he had only one leg. He was every bit as young and handsome as Sirius but the loss of his left limb, just below the knee, masked his face in what I imagined was permanent misery.

'This is my very good friend Alex,' said Moriarty warmly. 'Mr Alexander Rathbone, from Boston in Massachusetts.'

Lady Elizabeth gently nudged me.

I remembered my manners, stepped forward and offered my hand. 'Simeon Lynch, mister.'

Alexander shook it. His hazel eyes held mine only as long as necessary, then returned to introspective examination of the floor.

Moriarty led me back to the table groaning with food. 'I know you have questions, and I promise in time they'll be answered. But eat now. Get your strength back.'

I snatched a small loaf of bread and ripped off a chunk. The freshly baked smell set my stomach grumbling. I was about to bite off a mouthful when he grabbed my wrist. 'Do you not see either the servants or the plates?'

I glanced to the end of the table, where two young, black-suited men stood with napkins over forearms. One stepped forward, lifted a large white plate and asked, 'What might I get for you, sir?'

I put my bread down on the plate. 'That, and more of it. And some meat. As much as you can fit on there.'

He nodded and set about the task.

'Let us sit.' Moriarty motioned to a table laid with cutlery. 'We always breakfast in the orangery,' he explained as we took our seats. 'I consider it quite the most important room in this house. Can you guess why?'

'Because it has food and servants in it?'

'No, no,' he laughed. 'It is because things *grow* in here. When they come in, they are tiny and ugly. Little seeds and roots. We nurture them with our knowledge and skill. Raise them to their full potential.'

The waiter placed a heaped plate in front of me. My hand went again for the bread. Moriarty allowed me several mouthfuls before he added, 'I have a good friend, a Bostonian, who says fish, meat and drink to us are like sunlight, water and good soil to plants. Basic nourishment.' He leaned across the table. 'You are unique, Simeon. A highly prized specimen of youth. You are what my American friends describe as "the real deal". Rest assured, I will grow you to your fullest potential.'

His words sparked defiance in me and amid a splutter of food I told him, 'I'm not a bleeding plant, mister.'

His eyes turned to granite and he slapped my face.

Noise in the room behind us evaporated.

Moriarty stared challengingly at me.

Instinctively, I stood in anger, my chair making an abominable raking sound on the marble tiles before it fell over with a clatter.

'Sit back down,' he demanded.

My hands balled into fists. Violence boiled inside me.

'You look foolish, Simeon. Pick up your chair and be seated, before someone mistakes you for a serious threat and shoots you.'

My eyes darted across the room. 'I see no weapons.'

'That doesn't mean there are none. Now *sit* and finish your food!'

Reluctantly, I picked up the fallen chair and returned to the table.

'Carry on!' Moriarty shouted to the room.

His guests resumed their chatter and I resumed my assault on the laden plate.

'We will pretend that little incident never happened.' His eyes bored into mine and asked more questions than any words could.

He toyed with his beard while he watched me devour the food and I wondered what thoughts came and went behind his cold, unnerving eyes.

I ate greedily with my fingers not the dainty knife and fork, for fear that any moment the food might be withdrawn. By the time my plate was empty I had so much in my mouth it took me an eternity to chew and swallow it.

Moriarty watched, with what appeared to be a mixture of amazement and disgust.

'You are fed, so let us leave things there, for today,' he announced. 'Go to your room. Rest. Think of what has been said. Contemplate the new you that has the opportunity to rise from within your old life.'

I rose, still chewing strings of meat caught between my teeth, and nodded politely.

Judgemental heads turned as I walked out of the orangery. This was no place for me. That Elizabeth woman was achingly beautiful but I vowed once I had my strength back, I would flee this dreadful place faster than a fox spotting a farmer with a gun.

Back in the room where I had regained consciousness, the bed had been remade in my absence, and the chamber pot, bowl, jug and soap all renewed.

A book had been left on a table. I supposed it to be some American nonsense that Moriarty wished me to ingest. A plain card on the top of the volume bore a handwritten note, which thanks to some basic schooling I was able to read.

Simeon,

  Read what you can, when you can. A day without reading is a day of decay. Yours

                                                            Elizabeth

I turned the card, desperate for more words from her, but there were none, only the title of the book: *Queen Mab: A Philosophical Poem*, by Percy Bysshe Shelley.

One look inside filled me with despair. I was used to rhymes and simple stories. Bible passages and prayers.

Nothing like this. Clumps of long, intense words knotted my brain. Words and phrases I had never heard of hit me like intellectual slaps – *tainted sepulchre* – *roseate morning* – *celestial coursers*.

I threw the book on the bed.

Maybe I would get round to trying it again. Maybe I wouldn't. If I did, then it would be solely to please Elizabeth and have her think kindly of me.

15 DAYS TO EXECUTION

NEWGATE, 3 JANUARY 1900

'Open door, cell five!'

The alarming cry from the guard set off a stampede of heavy-footed gaolers down the corridors of the condemned wing. Whistles blew. Gates to the rest of the prison clanked shut and were locked down.

At first, they thought I had escaped then when a young screw poked his head into my cell he saw only the crumpled body of my attacker on the floor and shouted, 'He's dead! Lynch is dead. Someone's offed him!'

The poor fool almost died of shock when I spoke from the depths of the shadows that covered my bunk. 'Actually, I am very much alive. That corpse is someone else.'

The gaoler fled in terror. I should have guessed the next

wrong assumption would be that the death had occurred as the result of some bold escape plan I had hatched and bungled. Older and meatier screws rushed in, brandishing sticks and fists but little intelligence.

'I am chained!' I shouted, raising my hands so they could see the manacles.

The action spared me a beating but still they bundled me face down onto the floor and pinned me with knees while they checked my restraints were secure and satisfied themselves that I was no danger to them. For once it was a relief to hear Johncock's voice.

'Boardman, Baker, get off 'im! Sit the bastard prisoner up so 'e can explain 'imself.'

Weight shifted off my shoulders and legs. Boardman, a screw in his late thirties, face ablaze with untrimmed red whiskers, turned me over and sat me up. He had hands as hairy as a chimp and I remembered him as one of the men who had previously beaten me. I also recognised the younger screw, Baker. He was a leathery strap of a lad, with the eyes of a rat and the smell of a skunk. He pulled at my chains and told Johncock, 'The manacles are intact, sir. They've not been unlocked.'

Johncock raised his boot and inspected the sole. 'Messy,' he declared, pulling a sour face. 'Messy, messy, messy.' He rubbed his boot on the floor and then on my blanket. 'Show me the dead man's face, Baker.'

The younger turnkey angled the corpse's head for the assistant keeper, but I could not see it, nor did I hear

56

Johncock mention a name. All I could discern was that he wore no wrist or ankle restraints, meaning he was a trustee, a class of prisoner used by the gaolers for cleaning work, slopping out and any other chores they were too lazy to do themselves.

Finally, Johncock turned to me. 'Why was this fellow in your room, Lynch? What 'appened 'ere?'

'I don't know. I woke and he and another man were near my bunk.' I nodded to the corpse. 'That one attacked me. I held onto him to protect myself and I surmise his runaway friend stabbed him by accident.'

'Oh, you *surmise* do you?' He laughed at me. 'Proper gentleman you think you are with your *surmising*.' He stepped over the blood and kicked my leg. 'Well, I *surmise* there was no other man. There was only you. You, this dead fellow and some ill-conceived notion to escape that went fatally wrong.' He put his boot up on my bruised ribs and pressed. 'Now, speak with 'onesty, Lynch, or so 'elp me God, I will kick the words out of you a syllable at a time.'

'Do you really think I would still be in this stinking hole if another convict had been able to open the door for me?' I winced through a sharp pang of pain and added, 'Had I been in possession of that shank and been fit and able to spring to my feet, then I promise you it would be sunk in one of your men's chests, not that dead imbecile's, and I would be free by now.'

Johncock glowered at me. He knew I was telling the truth. If I had been stronger and that passing turnkey had come five minutes later, there would have been a lot more blood on the cell floor than the spatter he had walked in.

'Get 'im out of here.' The assistant keeper banged his knee into my face as he walked past. He stopped in the doorway and told his men. 'Put Lynch back in his original cell; we're done mollycoddling 'im. Then lock this door. Don't move the stiff until I've got to the bottom of what 'appened 'ere.'

DERBYSHIRE, SEPTEMBER 1885

Moriarty's grizzly companion, the fat, old wrestler Michael Brannigan, came for me just after dawn. As I guessed he would. Men like him know the rewards that the element of surprise can bring.

But I had been ready for such an eventuality. I had risen a good hour earlier, washed and changed into the clean clothes that had been left in my room for me, and I was sitting on my bed, full of smiles.

He held the door open and smirked. 'So, you can dress yourself. That at least is something. Now are you ready to do some work?'

'Are you?'

'You would be well-advised to show me some respect.'

'Is that right? Even the young and ignorant, like me, know respect is *earned*, not freely given.'

He headed out of my room and I followed, feeling much

stronger than yesterday. Last night, I had eaten well. Stayed clear of ale and wine. And aside from a fevered dream about Lady Elizabeth had managed a refreshing seven hours of sleep.

Brannigan took me past storerooms and larders, out of a tradesmen's door and beyond the entrances to coal bunkers and an ice house that was in the process of being filled with fresh produce. We walked briskly around the side of what I saw for the first time was a splendid three-storey Jacobean mansion. The walls were made from a fine blue-grey stone, matched with golden brown lintels and steps. Carefully trimmed ivy aspired to grow higher than the bedroom windows where it had been halted by diligent gardeners. Above tall windows perched grim gargoyles, their ever-open eyes keeping vigil over the vast grounds beneath them.

Presently, we came across a warped and weathered barn with a broken roof through which the sky could be frequently spied. Skipping ropes lay coiled like sleeping snakes on a straw-covered stone floor. Behind a stack of hay bales stood a slackly roped-off ring.

Brannigan caught my stare, looked across to the arena and laughed. 'That's not for you. Not unless you want to die before breakfast.'

I walked towards it. 'I am a young and fit boxer and you are a fat and old wrestler. I know washerwomen who could beat you as easily as their clothes.'

He had been in the process of heading away from the ring but turned now and approached me. 'They haven't told you about me, have they?'

'What is there to tell that your fat stomach and wasted arms haven't already said? Age has caught up with you and made you half the man you were. Am I right?'

'You're as cheeky as fuck. That's what you are.' He looked me up and down. 'Boxer are you? Self-taught?'

'I was trained by one of the best.'

'Where would a toerag get such tutorage?'

'In the workhouse, by a great fighter of African descent.'

'*African*? Now you're havin' a bleedin' joke.' Brannigan spat on the ground. 'I am a *Romany*.' He punched his heart with pride. 'That makes me tougher than any bloody African, or for that matter a mouthy piece of London shite like you.'

'Then let's see.' I pointed to the ropes. 'Or have we got up this early just to swap insults?'

'We got up to train you, and we should get on with it.' He flapped a hand dismissively at me. 'You're not ready to fight me. Happen you never will be.'

I turned and walked to the ropes. 'I'm getting in the ring. Follow me and fight, or else be off and feed that fat gut of yours somewhere I can't see you.'

There was no answer.

His bluff had been called. I was young and fit and he clearly didn't fancy a beating this early in the morning.

I was toying with the ring rope when Brannigan kicked my legs from under me and hurled his big old body down on my chest like a carriage filled with clinkers. Air whooshed from my lungs.

60

He hauled me upright. Grabbed me by the throat and testicles and lifted me above his head like I was a sack of flour. The pain was excruciating, but nowhere near as agonising as when he threw me into the post of the ring.

I feared he'd broken my back and was still working out how injured I was when he reached down for my wrist.

I snatched it away and rolled into the ring.

Brannigan ducked the rope.

I got to my knees.

He kicked a boot at my head.

I caught it and twisted hard.

He spun and fell.

I was on my feet before he was. But only just.

He rose in a crouch and ran at me with his head down.

I hit him with an uppercut that would have felled an elephant.

It didn't even rock him. He ploughed into me, barged me across the ring.

When we hit the ropes on the other side he stamped his foot, shifted his weight and slammed my entire body into the ground.

I made an involuntary noise that fell pitifully short of the agony I felt.

Brannigan dragged me upright, locked his arms behind my back and squeezed. That's all he did. But he squeezed so powerfully that I was unable to breathe. He hoisted me further up. Got a better grip. Increased the pressure and pain.

I pulled my elbows free and smashed them on the top of his skull.

He dropped me.

I doubled up. Sucked in air, while I could. The blow to the skull should have knocked him out, but it hadn't.

Brannigan came running.

I dodged this time. Focused.

He turned, sighted me.

I stepped forward and snapped a punch into his face.

His jaw was like granite; he rubbed his chin and grinned.

I bounced to the right, smashed a left into his temple.

Pain barely registered on his face.

My right whipped out two more jabs, then came a rock-breaker of a left. His lips bust like a dropped tomato, but still he didn't go down.

Brannigan spread his arms wide. Spat blood through busted teeth.

I bounced on my feet, kept moving.

He lunged.

I circled him.

He grabbed at me, missed.

I drove a fist into his face.

A second punch hit his temple. A third, the bloody mass of lips and teeth.

The old wrestler closed the space between us.

I spun away, dodging a grabbing hand, and smashed my left into his cheek.

He grabbed and held me. Butted my nose. Giant hands locked again behind my back.

My arms were trapped. My eyes streamed. Blood snotted from my nostrils.

The hurt that followed was unbearable. The best I could do was hold my breath and hope he quickly ran out of strength.

He didn't.

Pain tingled through my arms and chest. I blew precious air from my mouth and he shut off the last space in my lungs.

'Should I choke you to death?' he whispered into my ear. 'Or bite through your neck and have you bleed out like a slaughtered chicken?'

I struggled. Kicked.

'Choke, I think. Choking is always more certain.'

My lungs were on fire. Flames scorched my throat. The back of my eyelids blackened and I lost consciousness.

My limp body hit the ground and I was aware of nothing until a bucket of cold water brought me spluttering back to life. I raised my head and saw it had been thrown by Mr Gunn. Another followed from Miss Breed.

I gasped. Covered my face. Spluttered some more.

When I removed my hands, Brannigan was standing by my feet, urinating over my legs. 'You owe me your life, you little bastard. Your life and your respect.'

I made no attempt to pull away. He was right. I deserved to be pissed on. The fat, old man emptying his bladder had soaked up the best of my blows. He had swallowed pain like it was naught more than sugar and could have killed me without breaking sweat.

'You have it,' I managed, my voice raw with hurt. And then I added the word he had wanted to hear. 'Sir.'

He shook the last drops of his steaming urine on me, fastened up and stepped back. 'Get out of my sight and clean yourself up. You're a disgrace.'

Getting up was easier said than done. My ribs felt as though they had been ground into dust and I struggled to rise further than my knees.

'Nothing is broken,' mocked Brannigan. 'I was instructed not to hurt you too badly. The professor has a soft spot for you. Ain't that so, Sirius?'

'As soft as your heart, Mr Brannigan.' He looked at me. 'Either that or he simply doesn't want the trouble of having to dispose of his ugly, useless carcass.'

'Ignore him,' said Miss Breed, helping me to my feet. 'He's either all charm or all hate. There's no in between with Mr Gunn.'

He tipped his hat at us and walked off towards Brannigan, who had also turned his back and was now a good five yards away.

'Let me help you inside.' She draped my arm over her shoulder and allowed me to lean on her for support.

To my embarrassment, Miss Breed guided me all the way to my room and even to my bed. I made a pained noise as I sat on the mattress and slowly leaned back. She lifted my feet, unhooked my boots and then tugged at the bottom of my urine-stained trousers.

'No!' I shouted. 'I am quite capable of doing that.'

'I don't think you are.' She grinned, then yanked them all the way off.

I grabbed a sheet to cover my embarrassment.

It seemed to amuse her. 'If it makes you feel better, Mr Brannigan pissed all over Sirius during their early days together.'

'It doesn't.'

'It will. *Eventually.*' She threw the trousers down near the window. 'If you like, I can make you a poultice.'

'Poultice?'

'It is a medicament of bread and herbs . . .'

'I'm not hungry.'

She laughed. 'It's not to eat, you idiot. It's for your chest. You put it against your ribs and it draws the bruising out and takes the pain away.'

'I don't want the pain to go away.'

'That doesn't make sense.'

'I *need* the pain. Need it to remind me how much harder I have to try tomorrow, when I take that old beast down.'

'You don't fight him again.' She moved closer to me. 'No one fights Michael Brannigan twice.'

'I will.'

'Then you are even more stupid than I thought.' She started to walk away then turned. 'Do you know who he is? Why you, me and Mr Gunn are here?'

'No. I don't know. We are all criminals, I suppose. Rounded up by an even greater rogue.'

She shook her head in dismay. 'You need to do some thinking. Grasp what we have all done and what unites us. Then you will know why you must never challenge Michael again.'

'Why don't you save me all that trouble and just tell me?'

'Because that's not my place.'

'Excuse me, miss,' said a woman's voice from the doorway. 'The professor has sent me for *him*.'

'He is all yours,' answered Miss Breed, stepping aside. 'I am quite done with him.'

A young maid in a black and white uniform with a frilled apron and cap entered the room. Over her arm lay a long flannel robe in a dark chocolate colour, trimmed with gold piping.

'I am sorry to disturb you, sir. I am Jane, one of the Between Maids.' She had a voice as soft as the dimple on her chin. She laid the robe on the bed. 'The master says you are to wear this while I fetch your soiled clothes to the bathhouse and leave them there to be laundered.' She nodded politely. 'I will wait outside, sir, while you dress.'

Jane left and I struggled to my feet. The beating was already stiffening my joints and putting on the robe, which was a good few inches too large, was an agony. I tied the belt then gathered the soiled garments and joined her.

The route she took was long and led to the end of the west wing, where she relieved me of my soiled clothes and opened a door. 'This is the bathhouse, sir. I will leave you here.'

I thanked her and walked into a room filled with steam. Through the mist I discerned the outline of various tubs. Plungers. Roll tops. Slippers. All on a raised wooden platform.

Out of the fog came a voice and a small moustachioed man. 'Please be careful, sir.' He took my arm. 'I am Bailey, head of Heating, Bathing and Laundry. Watch your step there. That's it. Take it slowly. We have four sunken baths, two cold and two hot, and you almost took a very chilly dip.' There was a hint of glee in his voice as he guided me along the platform. 'The professor told me you were to be soaked in hot seaweed for twenty to thirty minutes to help you recover from your altercation. After that, you must use the plunge pool to cleanse and close the pores. Here, let me help you in.'

He stopped beside a cast-iron tub that brimmed with foul-smelling green-black water. 'You won't be needing that robe, sir.'

I took it off and handed it over.

'Thank you.' He extended an arm for me to steady myself as I raised a leg and stepped in.

'Lower yourself slowly now, sir. Enable your flesh to become accustomed to the temperature.'

The water was surprisingly hot. I inched down until my back rested on the rear of the tub and I managed to stretch.

Bailey bent low so his head was level with mine. 'There

are two doors, which I don't believe you can see from your perspective, but they are in the far corner. One leads into the Turkish bath, quite the professor's favourite. The other is to the laundry, where Jane has taken your clothes.' His chest filled with pride. 'I have to say, we have made quite an astonishingly economic use of the heat provided to the bathhouse, for the hot water pipes go into the room next to the mangles and they provide a wonderful way to dry the wet washing. Within the next month or two, we will be fitting cast-iron heating appliances imported from America and then we will be able to heat every room in this fine dwelling.'

I am unsure whether I fell asleep during that declaration or whether Mr Bailey sensed my lack of interest and simply wandered quietly away. But sleep I did. Not for a long time, but sufficiently for the sludgy bathwater to have cooled and for the prescribed time to have expired.

When I awoke, the great domestic orator ushered me to the plunge pool and after the briefest of teeth-chattering dips, he provided me with thick white towels to dry myself. 'You will find clean clothes in your room, sir, and Lady Elizabeth awaits you in the drawing room.'

'Lady Elizabeth?' I used the edge of the towel to wipe water from my face.

'Yes, sir.' He smiled. 'It seems you have more than one lesson to learn today.'

15 Days to Execution

Baker and Boardman took great delight in roughly bundling me back to my old cell. In truth, old red-beard and his chum all but dragged me there, as I still had problems with my right knee following the last assault.

Only when I was settled again did I remember how badly the old part of the gaol stank. My resting place must have been close to a service opening of Newgate's sewers, and like some incontinent old drunk it was forever leaking the foulest of odours.

Peculiarly, I felt some satisfaction at being back in my original cell. A little familiarity apparently afforded considerable comfort. The blanket on the bunk had remained ruffled, exactly as I had left it, and I discerned the unique smells of my body as I settled beneath it and hoped to sleep away my pains.

It seemed that no sooner had sleep come than bright light and the noise of keys in the cell lock woke me. Crisp winter sunshine cast shadows of window bars across the floor, slim soldiers of Dark and Light standing side by side for inspection.

Boardman was still on duty and yawned out the reason for his appearance. 'You have a visitor, Lynch. Move your sorry bones.'

My attention drifted past him to the man a pace behind,

a fellow holding a handkerchief to his face to mask the smells.

Sherlock Holmes.

'Mr Holmes here has come to interrogate you,' continued Boardman. 'Ain't that so, Mr Holmes?'

The detective stepped forward. 'The keeper has requested that I ascertain the facts behind this morning's death and I believe you are integral to that process.' He faced the gaoler. 'Is Lynch wearing the same attire and restraints as he was in the refractory cell?'

'He is, sir.'

'Very good.' He turned to me. 'Could you please stand up and extend your arms?'

'I need water and food. Before I do anything for anyone, I need to drink and eat.'

Holmes regarded me for a moment and then nodded. 'He does indeed require refreshment. Dry skin. Crusted lips. Words ill-formed because of a sticky mouth. This man is dehydrated and needs sustenance, gaoler. Replenish him and I will return.' Holmes spun on his heels and left.

Boardman gave me a hateful look and followed, slamming the door in protest.

An old orderly duly appeared and delivered a bowl of gruel, mug of weak tea and chunks of stale bread. He stayed until I had wolfed it all and then cleared everything.

A few moments later, Holmes returned. He was alone and had evidently instructed Boardman to wait outside.

'Are you now able to comply with my former request?'

I stood and stretched out my arms as previously instructed.

He ran his hands around the manacle cuffs, inspected the chain then the lock and made several tutting noises. He stood back and studied my tunic, plucked at the cloth around my waist, knelt and examined my trousers.

As he did all this, I wondered whether the famed detective was more valuable to me alive than dead, for at this moment he afforded me a clear opportunity to kill him. Moriarty had once tasked me with this very chore but other events had taken priority. Now all I had to do was loop that chain around his neck and strangle him to death.

Holmes pulled at my ankle chains and then stood up. He extended his left hand and showed me a spring knife that had been concealed there. 'You made a wise decision. I would *easily* have killed you had you tried to overwhelm me.' He flicked the blade back into its steel body casing. 'Sit down, please.'

I lowered myself onto the edge of the bunk and grimaced a little. 'Before you ask, I was half asleep when I was attacked. I never even saw the face of the dead man, or the fellow with him.'

'I realise all that.'

'You do?'

'Obviously,' he said with a hint of irritation. 'The large bruise on the deceased's skull, distinctive injuries under his chin, abrasion on the front of his neck and patterned indentations on his skin all validate your claim.'

'In what way?'

He looked perplexed. 'I just explained the *way*. It would appear that like a hopeful fisherman on a darkened day, you cast your manacle chain blindly and got lucky with your catch. The bruises on his forehead show where you snagged him.' He raised his fists and mimed the actions as he continued. 'Once you had him, you yanked hard on the chain and reeled him in. Where, from the look of the skin around his neck, you set about choking him.' His eyes lit up. 'Somewhat ingeniously I imagine, for you must have been seated or even lying on your back. To escape strangulation, the fellow tried to grab at your face and injure you.' He pointed down my left cheek. 'You have fingernail scratches consistent with this on your face.'

'I didn't kill him . . . '

'Also blatantly true. But you *would* have done, had his accomplice not mistakenly driven a makeshift knife into his heart instead of yours.'

'Then I thank him for his mistake and you for your exoneration. Who was he and why did he try to kill me?'

'Dear, oh dear.' The detective frowned at me disappointedly. 'Those are *entirely* the wrong questions to ask. The name of the dead man is of no consequence to you. None whatsoever. Of far more value is the identity of his accomplice, the man who killed him and then vanished into the gaol.'

I began to see his point. 'How was it possible that two prisoners could come and go from their cells as they wished?'

'It wasn't,' declared Holmes, 'unless they were assisted by a turnkey, or indeed, if one of them was a turnkey. Either of those options proffers a credible explanation. But of even greater interest is the identification of the person who commissioned them to carry out such an act.'

'I have a long list of enemies, Mr Holmes.'

'Of that I have no doubt.' He grew thoughtful then added, 'Tell me, Lynch, if you were to assemble said list in order of those who despise or fear you the most, whose name would be top of it?'

'I have no idea.'

'Think, man! Who is so impatient to have you buried that he cannot wait but a fortnight for the hangman to do the job for him?'

My mind spun with possibilities. Relatives or business associates of people I had killed. Perhaps police officers who had hunted me over the years. Rival gangs and criminals. Maybe even Johncock.

'I see you are overwhelmed with candidates, so I will tell you.'

'Please do.'

'Moriarty.'

I huffed out a laugh.

'Mark my words. This is the work of the master schemer. James Moriarty wants you dead. I saw it in his eyes in the Old Bailey courtroom when you were convicted. That man would hang you himself if he could.'

'And why would he do that, Mr Holmes?'

'You may spill family secrets. Might endanger him and his cohorts.'

'You are a fantasist, sir.'

'To the contrary. I am a realist. Moriarty's agents will have told him I have been here. He will suspect an offer has been made to you and he knows that turning Queen's Evidence would save your neck and endanger his own. The betrayal of a wicked master by a desperate servant is a common enough occurrence to prompt his hand and his darkest acts.'

'You are deluded, Mr Holmes. As brilliant as you are, you are a blind fool when it comes to James Moriarty. He is not my master and I am not his servant. You really should stay clear of those opium dens or at least reduce your cocaine consumption; your judgement is impaired.'

'I suspect you are more proficient at dispensing violence than insults.' He rapped on the door so he might be released, then added, 'Madness is coming for you, Lynch. Be certain of that. Make your deal now, before the stink and solitude of this place takes your sanity, before time runs out and, most importantly, before those playing chess with your life become bored and resort to other means of dispelling their worries.'

Mr Bailey, the effusive head of Heating, Bathing and Laundry, had been correct. Hanging in my room was a selection of shirts, both with and without collars, some ties and neckcloths, formal and informal trousers, waistcoats, a suit, several hats and caps, a pair of black shoes and sturdy boots. It was more clothing than I had ever owned.

I chose a pair of brown striped trousers, a red silk waistcoat and white flannel shirt. Dressing was an ordeal. Not because the items didn't fit. They did. Perfectly. Someone had either guessed my size to the exact proportions or measured me in my sleep. No, the ordeal came because of the pain in my ribs. It seemed to me that the seaweed bath had done precious little to ease the suffering.

Having struggled into the garments, I stood before a wall mirror and considered myself quite a dandy. But why had I been given these clothes? Why was I here? Why had I been plucked from the spartan rooms of a northern mill and brought to this luxurious country estate?

What did the professor want of me?

I was still searching for answers when a well-dressed man appeared in my open doorway and gave a genteel cough to catch my attention. He was tall and gaunt, in his late forties, with greying hair and heavy, curly eyebrows.

'I am Cornwell, sir, the butler. I am here to show you to the drawing room.'

I smoothed down my new clothes and nervously glanced again in the mirror.

The reflection of Cornwell appeared over my shoulder, 'Might I recommend the *brown* waistcoat instead of the red, sir?'

'You might, but I like this one.'

'It is not a *good* choice; but as you wish, sir. Are you ready to attend Lady Elizabeth?'

I took one last look at myself, pulled at the waistcoat for a final time. 'Yes. I most certainly am.'

Cornwell's lips twitched with the suggestion he might once more try to talk me into the brown garment then he turned and walked out.

I followed his well-polished heels along the now-familiar route into the main body of the house, across polished parquet floors and richly woven carpets and rugs. He opened a door, stepped aside and announced, 'Master Simeon, my lady.'

Elizabeth broke from looking out of the window on the far side of a large room and thanked him. She was dressed in a delicate white blouse and simple black skirt. To her left stood a round wooden table, covered in lace and laid for tea. Adjacent was a small piano and a little further away a sloping-topped writing desk.

Cornwell closed the door and Elizabeth's smile lit up the room like a thousand gasoliers as she approached me and asked, 'How are you, Simeon? I heard you endured something of a bruising encounter with Mr Brannigan.'

'You could say that, my lady.'

She looked amused and motioned for me to take a seat at the table. 'When we are alone, you should be informal and call me Elizabeth and I shall call you Simeon. I presume you are already on such first-name terms with Sirius and Surrey?'

I tried not to show my awkwardness as I sat. 'Not yet.'

'Then from now on, you will be. You must set the pace or next thing you know they'll have you doffing your cap to them.'

'I understand. Thank you.'

'You are very welcome.' She smiled as she settled. 'This room is, ironically, called a drawing room.'

'Why?

'Why do you think?'

'Because people draw in it?'

Her eyes laughed at me. 'No, but I see why you might hazard such a guess.'

For a moment, my mind was not on her words, her explanations or whatever lessons she had in mind for me. It was on the locks of her hair that glistened like spun gold. It was on the soft creases near her eyes and mouth that underlined how beautiful she was. It was on her voice, how sensual it sounded. 'Are you listening to me?'

The question pulled me up and made me redden.

'I was saying,' she continued, 'the name is derived from its original title, the *withdrawing room*. It was a place where people of great wealth could withdraw from company in the house and be alone, be less social. And as my task is *not* to make you more withdrawn, but to enable you to be more social, it is ironic.'

'And is withdrawn such a bad thing to be?'

'Not by choice. But you must also have the skills to be outgoing, in order to mix with all and sundry.'

'Why?'

She laughed. 'Is *why* your favourite word? The short answer to your question is, because this is what the professor wants. And we all do what the professor wants.'

'Do we?'

'We do,' she said, sternly. 'And if you learn nothing else today, learn that we do *whatever* the professor wants, *whenever* he wants it done.' Point made, she relaxed again, 'Now, tell me about yourself. About your family and upbringing.'

'I would rather not.'

'I heard you were orphaned,' she persisted, 'which means you were probably brought up in a workhouse, where education is seldom a priority. Can you read or write?'

'I was taught some reading and writing. Enough to create a hunger for it. And I was around good people who encouraged me to think for myself and talk proper.'

'Talk properly. Not proper.'

I reddened again and wished the damned lesson were already over.

'So tell me then, what books do you have knowledge of?'

'Many,' I lied, then checked myself, 'but none to speak

to you about.' I looked down at my feet to avoid her questioning eyes.

'The professor is very interested in Russian writings on nihilism and American developments in ontology. Do you have any particular views on these kinds of subjects?'

I shook my head. 'I don't even know what those things are.'

'Ontology is the philosophical study of the nature and relations of being. Nihilism is a belief that all values are baseless.'

I am sure that by this time my face must have been the colour of a beetroot, for Lady Elizabeth put one of her cool and gentle hands over mine. 'Don't be ashamed, my dear. I am not trying to humiliate you. We are finding our starting point, a mark from which we can measure your progress.'

I believe I struck such a sight that she took pity, for she stood, straightened her dress and walked closer to me. 'Just look at you! You are unbearably tense and crumpled. Your head is bent and those big fists of yours are clenched so tightly your knuckles are white.' She pushed me gently upright and slid my arms down by my side. 'Relax a little. Allow your mind to open up to new challenges and to grow.' She used her cool, slender fingers to unclasp my right fist. 'You can't fight yourself out of every eventuality in life, Simeon. Sometimes you will have to think your way to victory. Battles are more often won with the mind than the body.' She worked free the fingers of my left hand and I fought an urge to hold hers, to raise it and kiss it, to place it against my heart so she might feel how insanely it beat for her.

Contrary to all my previous desires for the lesson to end, I now wished it would never cease, for I was sure I wanted to spend eternity with this beautiful, beguiling woman.

Two Weeks to Execution

NEWGATE, 4 JANUARY 1900

Some force other than the Crown wished me dead. One not limited by the letter of the law or the bureaucracy of having to make an appointment to take my life. This force was powerful enough to bypass the turnkeys of Newgate, unlock my cell and attempt to cheat the hangman of his coin.

I had three suspects in mind as perpetrators of the attack on my life: Tobias Johncock, James Moriarty and Sherlock Holmes.

Holmes was the cleverest but the least likely. He certainly had the ability to disguise himself, pick locks and then fade into the shadows.

Johncock was more probable. The assistant keeper's hatred of me and the savagery of the beating he orchestrated made me believe he bore me a personal grudge. Perhaps I had wronged someone close to him. Or he was in the pay of a rival gang to the Moriarties and would only be financially rewarded if I were killed in prison.

Then there was James Moriarty. He and his family had the most to lose, should my tongue and hand choose to give testimony against them. I had not lied to Holmes. I was no servant of James nor was he my master. And I was not wrong in stating that the detective's impeccable powers of deduction were blinkered as far as he was concerned, for it was the reclusive Brogan, not the extrovert James who was the driving power of the family. Brogan, who from the obscurity of Derbyshire and his connections in New York and Boston had shaped a criminal empire that stretched across the world. His brother, brilliant as he was, had merely been foolish enough to draw Holmes's attention in London and to have personally baited and toyed with him.

In all honesty, it was difficult to rule James out as the architect of the attack on me. While we had never previously crossed swords, it was well within his character to have me killed, rather than risk me betraying the family. Brogan, on the other hand, would never dream of such a thing.

I could also not discount the possibility that my would-be assassin had in fact been a gaoler and not a convict. If that were the case, then it was possible he murdered the convict deliberately so his part in the attempt on my life could never be told.

Cell five! Door open!

The declaration came back to me, and the more I

thought about it, the more I believed the second man in my room might well have been the turnkey who raised the alarm. What could have been easier than to have simply stepped outside the cell and shouted for help? The best of illusionists know the centre of attention is the perfect place to hide.

I was sitting on the pot in the corner of the cell when my thoughts and privacy were rudely interrupted by the opening of the door. I expected Johncock and his cronies but instead there was Boardman and with him a fresh-faced turnkey I had never seen before.

The vicious gaoler closed the door and the stranger strode towards me. He was tall but thin, had thick sandy hair and long sideburns. His uniform was spotless and smartly pressed, his boots freshly shined.

'My name is Huntley,' he announced. '*Harrison* Huntley.'

'And what do you want, *Mr Harrison Huntley*? As you can see, I'm somewhat busy forcing shit out of my backside.'

'Mind your fucking manners!' shouted Boardman. 'Or I'll kick that shit out of you.'

'You will do no such thing,' said Huntley. 'And if I hear you make another threat like that, I'll have your job. Now stand back and be silent.'

To my amazement the whiskered old thug straightened his shoulders and slunk obediently against the wall.

Huntley stared ominously at him and then turned to me. 'In light of the attack on you, I have been brought in from another prison to ensure you are protected and kept in good health until the eighteenth of this month.'

I laughed. 'Until my execution! That is ironic.'

'It is. You are quite correct. But it is my job. Mr Johncock is to remain in charge of your lawful despatch but not your daily welfare. From this moment onwards, that is my specific duty.'

'Forgive me if I don't express how grateful I am.'

'There is one other thing.' Huntley stepped nearer. He eyed the irons around my hands and the rolled-down trousers snagged above my ankle chains. 'I am here also to inform you that we have been notified you have new legal counsel. A man called Theodore Levine.'

Now this was a name that I did recognise and my spirits lifted. Levine was Brogan Moriarty's external legal counsel, though very few people knew of such an arrangement. He was the lawyer I had asked for when I was arrested. Unfortunately, he had been out of the country and I ended up with a dimwit junior. 'Do you know when he plans to visit me?'

'I do not. The fact that the keeper asked me to inform you indicates it is probably imminent.'

'Imminent? *Overdue* is the word I would use.'

'I understand your impatience. If I were you, I too would hope my counsel moved quicker than the money leeches and desk snails that populate his profession.' He sounded surprisingly sympathetic.

Huntley was well spoken but beneath the veneer was a familiar accent.

'Where are you from?' I asked.

'Birmingham. Why do you ask?'

'No particular reason,' I lied. 'Just the way you said *you* and *me*, more like *yow* and *moy*.'

'I try to cover it up,' he said with a smile.

'*Yow* need to try harder, Mr Huntley,' I joked.

He smiled and turned away. Banged on the mighty slab of door and with a nod of his head left me with my thoughts. Memories from sixteen years ago, when I was in the city of Huntley's birth and would rather have been in the bowels of hell.

THE WEST MIDLANDS, MAY 1884

Birmingham was the first place I settled after I fled London. I welcomed its noise and crowds after months of self-imposed exile in lonely forests and meadows where I had been living off the land, stealing and killing whatever I could, like a country fox. Hens. Chickens. Eggs. Rabbits.

I had roamed farms and cottages, becoming an adept scavenger. I snaffled ragged clothes, cuts of useful twine, dregs from bottles to quench my thirst, even discarded newspapers or periodicals to read and keep my mind alive.

The Londoners I had grown up with had all had skin the colour of slate and eyes as dull as ditchwater, while the poor country people I encountered were ruddier of face and seemed fitter, happier and healthier. I presumed this was

84

because they spent so much time out in the fields, where there is no smoke to cover the sun and as a consequence their hands, arms and faces had turned multiple shades of brown. But this was not the case in Birmingham.

This city's skies were blackened by coal smoke and its inhabitants had all the pallor of those in the capital. Its streets boomed with the same urgent clatter of carts, horses, loud-mouthed traders and surly inhabitants. Beneath that coke-smudged canopy of clouds stood endless rows of workers' homes, and factories belching soot through a forest of chimneys.

I knew I cut a strange sight as a sun-browned ragamuffin boy sat by the roadside in this city, reading old papers, but I didn't care. Reading was one of my few joys and talents. As a child I had received little instruction but took to it like a duck to water and this served me well when I found faded, sun-crisped sheets of Birmingham's *Daily Post* blown against walls and railings.

Much print was dedicated to the growth of railways and football. The papers also divulged that there was plenty of basic work to be had. I could take my pick of manual jobs with the railway, council, waterworks or all manner of engineering and metal companies.

In the end, I landed a labourer's post in the grounds of the All Saints Mental Asylum at Winson Green. I supposed it to be a place that not many people would visit. Where the daily inhabitants, some three hundred imbeciles, wouldn't be reliable witnesses if ever called upon to answer questions about me. Perversely, its close proximity to the city's giant gaol, also appealed to my sense of humour.

I was assigned to the chief gardener, a stooping, white-whiskered man by the name of Ralph. He told me that I was his only helper and would be 'doing most of the diggin', plantin', fetchin' and carryin', because he suffered terribly from a bad back. My knowledge of gardening was meagre but this gamut of functions did seem to cover every imaginable task and it made me wonder what, if anything, would be left for him to do.

All was made clear when Ralph confided that he was a former alcoholic and had recently taken up with a washer-woman called Betsy who was 'much demanding' of his attention.

'She's saved me she 'as,' he confided. 'Without Bets, I'd be dead an' buried now. I used to drink ev'ry day, from morn' 'til the moon went out. Now I don't touch a drop. Cross me 'art on that.' And he did, with the nail-less grubby fingers of his right hand. 'Yow can watch moy. Yow won't see a bottle to moy lips.'

The asylum had grounds that stretched for forty acres or more and there was endless soil to be dug, grass to be cut, wood to be chopped and things to be 'fetched'. Ralph's gardening shed was my refuge from both him and the world at large. It was bigger than most houses I'd been in and filled with all manner of tools, pots, plants and country mice.

At the end of my second day, the old man found me bunked down on a mattress made from vegetable and seed sacks. 'Yow can sleep there, providin' yow does no 'arm,' he decided. 'an' *con-dish-nal* yow don't steal owt, or sell owt that belongs to 'ospital or moy. Yow do that an' yow're owt!'

His accent was painfully thick but the message was clear. I needed to be on my best behaviour.

And I was.

You could not have found a harder-working or more polite labourer in the whole of Birmingham. I seldom went into the buildings themselves, but when I did, it was usually to take tons of vegetables or potatoes to the kitchen. The staff kept themselves to themselves and were never keen to exchange more than a few words. On occasions, I saw such dreadful sights that I understood why they were not so talkative. Emaciated wretches in grey gowns wandered barefoot and glassy-eyed down corridors. Some sat rocking in the corners of rooms, deliberately knocking their troubled skulls against the walls.

The work was brutally hard and as the weeks passed I became increasingly tired and ill-tempered.

'Yow need to gow into town an' blow sum steam,' declared Ralph. 'Find yowself a cheap drinkin' hole, an' an even cheaper lady to befriend.'

I ignored his advice until the end of the following week, when things finally got too much for me.

Looking back, I wish I hadn't.

I wish I had found some extra resolve to keep me away from the city centre, the taverns and the terrible trouble that was brewing.

13 Days to Execution

Two turnkeys took me to a small visiting room where my lawyer, the elusive Mr Theodore Levine, apparently 'waited in eagerness to converse with me'.

The venue for this auspicious first meeting was a simple cell devoid of convict's bunk and the basic sanitary facilities that most convicts had at their disposal.

While the screws chained me to iron hoops sunk into the floor beneath a wide bolted-down table, the lawyer paced with hands clasped behind his back. He was lamppost thin, had black hair and a neatly trimmed beard speckled with grey. His suit was a luminous blue, worn over a frilly white shirt and a red four-in-hand knotted tie.

Once I was secured and the gaolers gone, he placed his topper on the table. Before saying a word, he walked to the door and pushed to make certain it was firmly shut. He then paced the entire cell again and tapped various bricks. 'Walls have ears,' he proclaimed. 'It has been known for the police and various institutional governors to have genuine bricks replaced with paper ones, so conversations may be covertly listened to. For that reason, we must be circumspect in what we say.'

Finally, he sat and smiled at me. 'Don't look so worried, Mr Lynch. I have come to save you.'

'Save me?' I couldn't help but laugh. 'And how might you do that, sir?'

'By hook or by crook, Mr Lynch. By hook or by crook. Before we proceed, a personal apology that I could not attend your trial.' He cleared his throat. 'There was a certain matter, one best not discussed within these walls, that needed my urgent attention on foreign soil. And, I must say, the Crown acted with surprising swiftness in their case against you. By the time I had extricated myself from those other duties, I am afraid your fate had been sealed.'

'I accept your apology, but find it of no comfort.'

'But comfort I *will* bring. We have already begun preparations to file appeals on your behalf. The procedure is somewhat archaic, but file we shall.'

'Based on what?'

'Whatever can be found, or if necessary, invented.' He stretched out his hand dramatically, and clenched and unclenched his fingers. 'I am the proverbial clutcher at straws, the great grasper of the most minuscule of opportunities. But you must assist me in my pursuit of something upon which I may build your appeal.' He let his dramatic hand fall and rest upon the table. 'First, I have some direct questions for you.'

'Then I will strive to answer them as best I can.'

'That's the spirit.' He interlocked his fingers and manipulated them until they all cracked. 'A little arthritis,' he explained with a smile. 'Now tell me, the other day you were visited by a Mr Sherlock Holmes. What did this troublesome fellow require of you?'

'For me to testify against certain people.'

'In return for what?'

'Clemency.'

Surprise flashed in his eyes. 'A full pardon?'

'Yes, the promise of a clean slate and a life to begin anew.'

'That was indeed a *most* generous and beguiling offer. How did you view Mr Holmes's proposition?'

'I found it *most* agreeable. And it remains so. I am sure a fine legal mind such as yours understands that it presents a far better alternative to being hanged.'

He smiled. 'It does. It most certainly does. You are quite right. Will you accept it?'

'I do not know.'

His eyebrows arched a little. 'It is my duty to remind you that you swore an oath of allegiance to our mutual employer. One from which you benefitted greatly.'

'I did. You are quite right. And I would not break such a bond, if indeed the breaking of my neck was not a distinct possibility.'

He shifted in his seat. 'You are being very honest with me, so I shall reciprocate in kind. Prisoners often get very badly injured in institutions like this. Even killed. I understand you have had one altercation already and I fear that unless we extricate you from here as a matter of urgency you may suffer another.'

I flew at him. The manacles drew tight and stopped my

hands reaching his throat. Levine looked as startled as a rabbit being charged down by a carriage.

'Were *you* behind those men?' I challenged.

'Good Lord, *no*!'

'If you *were*, then so help me, I will kill you.' I strained against the chains.

'What a terrible question.' He pushed his chair back to ensure his safety. 'Mr Lynch, you unjustly impugn my integrity and that of our mutual employer.'

'Fuck your integrity. A man tried to murder me.' I was so angry I snorted the words out. 'Someone sought to plunge a shank through my heart.'

'I know the particulars of the attack.' He fussed with his tie. 'Who do you think it was who complained to the board of this prison about your ill-treatment and forced the keeper to take steps to have you protected from Johncock and his brutes?'

His words silenced me. I sat, fists clenched, glaring at him.

'Every day we are looking after your welfare, Mr Lynch. You may not see us toiling, but I assure you we are hard at work.'

I looked up at Levine. Was he truly trying to have me freed? Had he and the family really intervened and used political influence to protect me from Johncock? Or was it all a pack of lies?

'I am presuming you have been briefed well, Mr Levine, so you will know that I am a man of my word. Tell those

91

who need to be told that my oath is intact and I have every intention of keeping it that way.'

'I am delighted to convey such news.' He rose swiftly, collected his hat and extended a trembling palm over the table. 'I believe we have a gentlemen's understanding. Am I correct?'

I grasped his hand and held it painfully tight. 'I believe we do.'

Levine winced until I let him go. 'Then I will get to work. There are appeals to be lodged, people to be spoken to, wheels to be set in motion.'

THE WEST MIDLANDS, MAY 1884

It had been a hot, windless day in the grounds of the asylum and I had sawn and moved a forest of logs. Ralph had been in a foul mood all week because of a row between him and his precious Betsy. Whatever work I did wasn't good enough and his bad temper meant that he did even less to help me than usual.

Once we had downed tools on the Friday evening I told him, 'I'm going into town. I need that drink after all.'

'Yow'll find all yow wish for in the Bull Ring,' he advised. 'An' if yow sees a quiet woman there, one what down't want to be gittin' married, then be a mucka an' bring 'er 'ome for me.'

'I shall.'

He shook my hand and we parted on good terms.

As I made my way towards the bright lights, I realised that until that night, I hadn't been off the grounds of the asylum since starting work. It felt like a holiday to be free of trees, grass and most of all the sight of the big brick walls of the hospital and nearby gaol.

As night unfolded, the taverns teemed with happy drunk men and carelessly dressed women. Unwisely, I lost track of both time and the amount of ale and gin I consumed.

The hour must have been very late when I downed my last drink and stumbled into the virtually deserted streets. Sensibly, the masses had made their way home, which was where I was headed once I relieved myself of the excess liquid straining at my bladder.

A few meandering minutes away from the flickering gas lamps brought me to an alleyway and the blessed relief my body craved. Leant against a wall in urinal bliss, I heard a rough voice shout, 'Lissen to that. Sounds like there's a cheeky stallion pissin' on our patch.'

Two, maybe three men laughed. One added. 'A pissing *mare*, more like. A stallion wouldn't hide 'imself in the dark. 'e'd want to show off all 'e'd got.'

More laughter. Different voices. I was sobering up and realised I had underestimated the number of strangers. There were four, maybe five men, not three.

I finished and buttoned myself up. I was growing more alert by the second. Maybe relieving myself had restored my faculties.

Boots moved on cobbles. My eyes adjusted to the light. Street lamps cast shadows into the alley and I saw their outlines. Big men, huddled together, all with caps, and sticks in their hands.

The sight made me smile, not tremble. I knew their business better than they did. One would step forward and show his mettle. The weaker ones, the followers, would stay a safe distance away until they were sure the fight was won, or necessity demanded they all piled in mob-handed.

I opened my hands and raised them to show I had no weapon. 'Lads, if it's clink you are after, then you are out of luck. The last of it was drunk more than an hour ago and just pissed out on my boots.' I swayed a little. Gave the impression I was an easy cove. 'I don't want no trouble; I just want to walk on home.'

''Appen yow do,' said a shadow. 'But from the way yow speak, it sounds like yow're a very long way from home.'

'Too far away for yowr own good,' added another. The laughter that followed was thin. A cold broth of bravado and evil intent.

I focused on the task presenting itself. Moonlight lay to my right. I shifted away from it so less of me would be visible. The big silver crescent smiled coolly in a puddle on the cobbles at my feet. I edged further into the darkness.

A big hand hit the middle of my chest. Pulled me back into the light. 'Now then, where do yow think yow're goin'?'

'Teach 'im a lessin, Billy,' shouted a crony. 'Crack the basta'd, then we'll tip 'im up an' empty 'is pockits.'

Billy was apparently the brave one. Gangly, but not without muscle or nerve. He had a firm grip and spoke calmly. 'Yow can go on 'ome, once yow've paid a toll.'

I looked down at his clenched hand. It was a tough man's hand. Even in the moonlight I could see knuckles chequered with cuts and scars. I felt my heart beat against his other pressed palm. 'Toll?' I asked.

'Yow'z on a *toll road,* moy friend. Meanin' yow'z 'as to pay. *Or* suffer the consequences.'

The shadows around him chuckled and closed in on me.

'Take your hand away,' I whispered to him.

The shadows mumbled.

'*Please,*' I said more forcefully.

'An' if I don't?'

I leaned into his fist so he felt me push back and Billy the Brave did what I expected him to do. The very thing he shouldn't have done. He gave me a good hard shove.

Or, at least he tried to.

I slapped both my palms over his fingers, so he couldn't remove them, then I bent quickly. He had a choice: fall to his knees or have his wrist broken.

Billy made another wrong decision. He stood tall and brave. His bone broke with a sickening crack and he doubled up in pain.

I held on to his busted hand. Stepped over it. Twisted his arm and dislocated his shoulder.

Billy screamed like a trapped animal and I confess my brain fizzed with excitement. I had missed the mental relief of being in a fight. The primordial rush of crushing another predator.

'So who's next then?' I swaggered challengingly into the moonlight. 'Who fancies a little of what Billy just got?'

I took their silence as submission, which was almost as stupid a mistake as the one Billy had made.

Almost in unison, they took off their caps. Respectfully, I thought. As though a priest or someone of great standing had entered their purview.

Then they let out a roar and rushed me. A callow youth swiped with his cap. I raised a forearm and felt the peak slice my jacket.

Now I understood: some form of blade was concealed beneath the stiffened fabric. This changed things. Not only was I outnumbered but these boys were more dangerous than I'd anticipated. I crunched an elbow into the face of a man to my right. Instinctively, my cut-throat razor clicked open in my hand – a fellow had crept noisily behind me and I slashed his leg with it. He squealed loudly.

Someone shouted, ''Enry? Yow all right, 'enry?'

I slipped deeper into the darkness. Heard the others rush to their friend's aid. Their preoccupation provided me with the opportunity to shift, unseen, along the alley wall and disappear into the street beyond.

I ran hard. Put as much distance between the gang and myself as quickly as I could. It wasn't long before I heard police whistles and the clatter of carriages and hooves. They were heading in the opposite direction to me but I still stepped back into the shadows and waited until silence returned.

Once I felt safe, I moved again. A street-corner gas lamp cast a golden sheen across a cobbled junction. I stopped there, panting for breath, and looked myself over. There was blood on my hands, glistening as black as tar. My jacket had been ripped by a blade. My cheek stung from a cut. I put a finger to it and then licked fresh blood from the skin.

The whistles came again. They were closer now. The coppers had probably reached the gang and been redirected. I took deep breaths then set off once more.

Only when I came to a canal basin did I slow to a walk. Barges lined the water's edge but those lingering on them were either asleep or drunk. On the towpaths, I saw only men too inebriated to make it to their crafts, or those who had stopped to spend the last of their pay with dollymops too ugly to work in the light of the taverns.

Off the back of a barge, where no interior light shone and no sound of life could be heard, I lifted a swill bucket from a hook and pumped fresh water into it. There was enough illumination from the moon to clean myself as best I could.

The rest of the journey back to the asylum was reassuringly uneventful. No sooner had I curled up in my pile of sacking inside the shed than I fell into a deep sleep.

The following day was one of silent reflection. I couldn't get the encounter with the razor-capped gang out of my head and I spent the morning lost in thoughts as I chopped wood for old Ralph.

'Yow're very quiet today,' he observed. 'Cat got yow tongue? Or yow feelin' badly from the ale?'

'I was just thinking things over.'

'*Things* to do with that cut on yow face?'

It looked worse than it was. A raw red line that was really no more than a deep scratch had drawn blood and was trying to scab. Still, it ran from the middle of my cheek to the lobe of my left ear and would be visible for some time. 'Had a bit too much to drink and caught myself on a bush last night.'

'And this *bush*,' Ralph said sceptically, 'woz it over-chargin' yow? Or woz it someone else's *bush* an' yow got a good beatin' for messin' with it?'

'I'm not like that.' I downed the axe and glared at him. 'I've never been with a woman like that, and I'd certainly never hurt one. Never.'

'I'm glad to 'ear it.' He could tell I was offended. 'So tell me then, wot's the matter with yow?'

I moved more wood into position to be chopped, then decided I would tell him. 'The first bit was true. I took a drink too much. Then I got cornered by some gang demanding money from me.'

'Lads yow'r own age?'

'About that.'

'Dressed smart, with caps?' he said knowingly.

'Yes.'

98

'Yow needs steer clear of the likes of them. Bad news theys are. Bad news indeed.' He planted a foot on his shovel, and drove it into the soft soil of a small vegetable bed he'd been working all week. 'They're Blinders. Yow're lucky they didn't take yowr eye out.'

I wasn't sure I'd heard him correctly. 'Blinders?'

He removed his own cap and ran a filthy finger around the well-worn peak. 'They gets their name coz they sews sharp metal into 'ere. Then they blinds people like yow by slashin' 'em in the eyes.' He looked more closely at my cut. 'Inch or two different an' yow'd be needin' a stick.' As an afterthought he asked, 'Did they take yow money?'

I didn't answer. Didn't want to give away that they'd come off worse than I had. That the police may well be looking for me.

'I thought so. Explains them sour looks. Anyroadup, don't go askin' me for money. I've none to give.'

'I wasn't going to.'

'I'm relieved to 'ear it.' He studied my cut a little more. 'Did they beat yow bad?'

'Not so much.' I put my hand to the cut. 'Just this and some bruises. Once I turned my pockets out they left me alone.'

He nodded. 'Yow did right. Money can be replaced. An eye can't.' He put his cap back on, then had another thought. 'Yow best make sure yow stay out of trouble.' He nodded towards the prison. 'I'm not gowin' in there on account of yow. I'm not gowin' in there for no one.'

'I understand.'

He turned and looked me over. 'Thinkin' on it, any lad wot comes away from a scrap wit' the Blinders, bearin' only a scratch, 'as to be more 'n' lucky.' He studied me again and didn't like what he saw. 'I'm owld enuff to smell badness a mile away. An' standin' 'ere right now, yow stinks of it.'

I said nothing, just picked up the axe and sank it into the oak.

Old Ralph put his hand on my shoulder and stopped me swinging again. 'I reckons it's time yow moved on, no offence.'

'None taken.' I knew he was right. I needed to put miles between myself and the trouble snapping at my heels. 'Guess I've got some money coming?'

Ralph paid me to the end of the week, we shook hands and I walked away without a word or a backward glance. But even as the miles between Birmingham and me opened up, I sensed I wasn't done with the Blinders. A grudge as strong as steel swords had been forged between us and blood would be shed again. Of that, I was certain.

PART TWO

The charge is prepared, the lawyers are met,
The judges all ranged, a terrible show

The Beggar's Opera, John Gay

I was infatuated with Elizabeth, but being young and immature there was simply nothing I could do, except suffer.

The blessed woman was on my mind from the very second that I woke. She occupied all my final thoughts before sleep and attended my every dream. And in that phantom world, she looped her arm in mine and I was not the fool of the drawing room who used the wrong words and lied about what he knew – I was her protector, her guardian, her lover.

Until Elizabeth, there had been no woman who had turned my head and set my heart racing. Not even a little. While boys and men around me had slept with all manner of girls and women, I harboured no such desires. I was curious about the fairer sex. But every time I looked at an elegant lady in the street or a laughing harlot in a tavern my mind would fill with notions of my birth mother and then a terrible flood of childhood memories would extinguish any sparks of passion.

To distract myself from Elizabeth, I wandered around Moriarty's mansion. Never had I been anywhere as luxurious as this, unless carrying a sack to stuff with silver.

From an upper landing window, I watched deer amble in a distant field. From another, I saw a great owl settle on the slated roof of a private chapel, built I later learned, to stop bodysnatchers stealing any Moriarty corpses and selling them to medical schools. And from a third window, I followed fast-moving water as it broke white on rocks and tumbled around the sharp bend of a river.

What I did not see was any other house or sign of civilisation. Moriarty's home was isolated. Hidden. And judging from the number of men patrolling the distant hedges and fences, it was a fortress.

I descended the grand main staircase and studied a wall filled with oils. They depicted generations of men bearing varying resemblances to Brogan Moriarty. Some were grandfatherly figures, standing behind chairs that bore women and babes in arms. Others were more heroic: men on horseback, in battlefields or hunts. All had the same piercing stare as the one I had first encountered back in Manchester.

I had some time before my lessons so I explored the corridors, more out of boredom than curiosity. Raised voices spilled through a door left slightly ajar at the foot of one landing. Sirius Gunn and Surrey Breed were in heated conversation. I pressed myself to a wall so I could hear but not be seen.

'The Chinese are *not* a threat,' insisted Gunn. 'The old man is obsessed with them. Just because they want more profit from their opium and are interested in gambling, doesn't mean they are becoming our enemies.'

'Raising prices is not a friendly thing to do.'

'Nor is it a sign of war. Moriarty should look more to the tinkers and the English gangs massing in London; they present far greater dangers than the Chinese.'

'Do they? The professor says the Chans are more organised than the English and one day opium, cocaine and even laudanum will be illegal.'

'Illegal? What poppycock! Surrey, you really should confine yourself to concocting poisons and trying to look more feminine. You are not informed enough to comment sensibly on these matters.'

'I'll confine myself to kicking your bollocks,' she retorted. 'If Moriarty sees the Chinese as a threat, then that's good enough for me.'

'Good Lord, woman, do you not know that we get more opium from India than we do from China? We should forge *closer* ties with Chan and his clan and not fear them. There are but a couple of hundred Chinese in London. We can muster as many men in an hour.'

I must have moved my weight a little because a floorboard creaked beneath my right foot.

'What was that?' asked Surrey.

'What was what?'

'There was a sound. Outside.'

I had been rumbled, and had no choice but to walk to the door and open it fully. 'Excuse me,' I said, 'I am lost and looking for Lady Elizabeth.'

They glanced at each other and then at me.

'Have you been listening in?' asked Gunn.

'I have just told you what I have been doing,' I answered curtly. 'Now can you please tell me where I might find Lady Elizabeth?'

'I'll show him,' said Surrey. 'Follow me, Simeon.' She walked past me and into the corridor. For a second or two, Gunn and I glared at each other.

'Don't you have a *lesson* to go to?' he said sarcastically.

'I do. But I would gladly delay it to teach *you* a lesson.'

'*Simeon!*' shouted Surrey.

I left to catch her up. 'One day, I will swing for him,' I said as I drew level with her.

'He's not your enemy. None of us is. You just have to get used to us.' She gave me a friendly look. 'We're not so bad, given a chance.'

'I believe that of you, but not him.'

'Did you really forget where the drawing room was?'

My face owned up to the lie, even before I did. 'I was bored, so walked around a while before my lesson. I wasn't listening in, honestly.'

'*Honestly?*' She laughed. 'Be wary of anyone who says "honestly", Simeon. It is always an attempt to conceal a lie.'

'I'll remember that. Why are you worried about the Chinese?'

'Oh, so you *were* listening!' She seemed pleased to have got it out of me.

'I heard only a few words.'

'Then you will hear the rest soon enough.' We descended the main stairs, turned a corner and she gestured to a door. 'And lo and behold, here we are, the elusive drawing room.'

'Thank you.'

'Entirely my pleasure.' She knocked on a panel for me, smiled again and departed.

'Come in!' shouted Lady Elizabeth.

I felt a rush of excitement as I turned the knob and entered a room ablaze with sunlight. She looked up from the writing desk. An elegant black fountain pen paused above a buff-coloured document. 'Simeon?' She glanced at a gold clock ticking loudly on the mantelpiece. 'You are a full five minutes early.'

'Would you prefer I went away for a while?'

'No, certainly not.' She rose and shook out the ruffles of a gold and red day dress, then glided to the table where we normally sat. 'It is good that you are eager to begin.'

'What do you know about China and the Chinese?' I asked as I held a chair for her.

'The *Chinese*? My goodness. Let me see.' She sat and smoothed the dress over her legs. 'They are one of the most populous nations in the world and are a wonderful race of people. Quite brilliant. They invented gunpowder, paper money, silk, the abacus – all manner of things. Why do you ask?'

'I overheard Surrey and Sirius speaking about them.'

'Ah.' Her tone became subdued.

'Sirius said there were a couple of hundred or so in London but I never saw any when I lived there. Where are they all?'

'There are communities in Pennyfields and Ming Street in Poplar.' She glanced at the clock. 'Time for us to move on to other matters.'

'Who are the Chans?'

'*Please*, Simeon. We need to begin our work.'

'The Chans?' I persisted.

'Very well. They are old business acquaintances of the professor and his family.'

'And there is a dispute, some bad blood between them?'

She reached for a pile of books on the table. 'I have said enough. More than enough on this matter.' She opened a book. 'I want to talk today about art and artists. What kind of art do you like?'

'I like shades,' I answered enthusiastically. 'I like them very much.'

'By *shades* you mean black-and-white portraits, silhouette art?'

'Yes.' I was pleased to have a subject I could talk about without feeling stupid. 'I have some.'

'You have some?' She seemed surprised.

I dug into my pocket and handed over two printed portraits, both small enough to fit in the palm of her hand.

Elizabeth studied them like diamonds. 'They are

exquisite. Simple, but enchanting shades of a mother and child.' She passed them back to me. 'How did you come by them?'

'I didn't steal them, if that's what you mean.' I returned them to a fold of leather I kept in my pocket. 'Someone special gave them to me. Please do not ask me more than that.'

'As you wish. Do you know where the word *silhouette* comes from? How this type of art materialised?'

'No.'

'In France, there used to be a very austere finance minister called Etienne de Silhouette. He was known for making severe cuts to the country's budget during an age of frugality. At the same time, there was a demand for portraiture, which was usually done in oil or by photography. For those who couldn't afford such luxuries, portraits were made by sketching a facial outline on black card, cutting it out and sticking it onto white card. Because this had been done so cheaply, so *meanly*, it became known as a silhouette.'

'I like that story. Like it very much.'

'Yet you sound sad. Have I upset you, somehow?'

'Showing you the shades awoke some old memories, that's all. And mixed with how you make me—' I stopped before I said anything embarrassing.

'Make you what?'

My tongue was stilled.

'Tell me.'

'Feel.'

She laughed. 'And how *exactly* do I make you feel?'

Now I was lost.

My foolishness had led me to a precipice that I was too inexperienced and afraid to cross.

'*Simeon?*' she pressed, saying my name in the softest of tones, 'I asked you how I made you feel.'

I stayed silent. That fragile ground beneath my clumsy feet crumbled a little more.

'Just speak!' she snapped in frustration. 'Don't censor yourself, just speak.'

'I feel like you raise a storm within me. You make me want to be close to you, to protect and care for you—'

'Oh dear.' She cut me off with a small sigh. 'I hope you do not have a crush on me. That would be awfully sweet but exceptionally awkward.'

'I am sorry. I take it all back. I'm stupid. Forget what I—'

'There is no taking back things like that. The professor predicted you might develop some affection for me but I thought him silly. Now I see I am the foolish one.'

'Should I leave?'

She nodded. 'It is best you do.'

I rose and felt a terrible shame. It was as though I had broken some priceless vase that even if repaired would never be the same again.

'Simeon.'

I turned. 'Yes, my lady.'

She smiled gently. 'Thank you.'

I was confused. 'For what?'

'For your courage. Many men go through their entire lives without saying what is in their heart. Many women never hear words as sweet as the ones you said to me today. So thank you.'

Panic filled me. I had no reply. No mature response. I rushed for the door. Rushed outside. Kept on rushing, until I was far across the lawns and deep in the orchard, where I could roar at the clouds and be alone with my bursting joy, my sweet sadness and my intoxicating uncertainty.

TWELVE DAYS TO EXECUTION

NEWGATE, 6 JANUARY 1900

January the eighteenth. That infernal date with death was branded into my thoughts. No notion, no distraction, nor any precious memory could dislodge it; it was forever present and noisy in my troubled mind.

Hanging day.

I did not want to perish like that. Pinioned. Powerless. Impotent. Shitting my pants swinging from a rope. That wasn't me. If I could not escape, then I wanted to go out fighting, grabbing at the throats and tearing at the eyes of my opponents.

Hanged by the neck until dead.

That's what the old owl of a judge had hooted.

But how long would it take?

Ten, twenty seconds. Thirty? More? Was I destined to kick and spin for inglorious minute after minute? Or would my head pop clean off my body, as many wished it to?

And what of the pain? How bad would it be? Worse than the most terrible beating I had ever endured? Than the bullet shot through the bone of my arm in Paris? Than the knife stabbed in my back in Dublin?

I had broken someone's neck once. Done it cleanly, quickly, just the way I had been taught. A perfect combination of speed and technique. 'Twist and pull,' I had been told. 'Only hard and fast. Harder and faster than you've ever done in your life.'

It had been good advice. The man I killed was much bigger than me, and it would have been a bloody battle had I not been so well instructed. But that was a lifetime ago.

I looked at my hands and remembered all the flesh I had touched, both in anger and in passion. Fingers that gouged and choked had also stroked and soothed. Could these limbs have done better things? Could this brain have created rather than destroyed? I wished I had fashioned something of value. Nothing grand – perhaps just wood or bread. Good bread for good people. Fine furniture for fine families. Not for monsters like me, or those who made me this way.

Or had I made myself what I was? Was it I and I alone who had sought out their instruments of evil and used them to shape myself?

I picked up the long chain that was now permanently attached to the leg irons and manacles chafing my wrists. It stretched across the icy floor of the cell. Ran up through an iron ring sunk in the stone wall beneath the window, then back on itself into another ring set in the floor by the door. Its length enabled the turnkeys to pull me like a dog, to drag me back and forth across the cell whenever they wished to enter. It rendered me harmless. Or so they thought. I was confident I could pull it away from them, unless two of them held the chain when it went slack. Certain I could then, within seconds, loop it around one of my captors' heads and strangle him long before any army of screws could stop me.

The musing was empowering. I was a caged lion. Disorientated by the strange and cramped habitat but still lethal. Respected for my explosive and unremitting violence.

Such imaginings – the worst of me – were all I had left to cling to.

A rattle of keys in the cell door turned my head. 'Stand away, Lynch. Get to the back of your cell! Face the wall!' The shouting came from Briggs, my gaoler for the day. He was as round as an ale barrel but weak. Even the strain of opening the door showed on his bloated face.

I stood obediently by the window. Felt the chain pull

tight. He took an age to fasten it at the other end. 'You have a visitor,' he announced.

For a moment, I did not turn. I wanted to savour the expectation. Was it Holmes, returned to question me? Johncock, full of new ways to hurt and belittle me? Or the man I really wanted to see: Moriarty.

'Mr Lynch.'

The voice was not one I could place from memory. I watched his shadow climb the wall I was facing. No hat. Tall. Clad in some long cape.

I turned and saw an old cleric. Wispy white hair fell over the dandruff-sprinkled shoulders of his long black cassock. A face red from either the wind outside or an early belt of rum greeted me. 'I am Father Deagan.' He stretched out his hand. 'Father Francis Deagan.'

I raised my manacled wrists. 'I'd shake your hand, Father, but as you see, that's a little difficult.'

'Slacken his chains, man,' the priest demanded. 'Give the poor creature some dignity.'

Briggs loosened and reset the chain, then banged the door shut in protest as he left.

Deagan immediately took my palm and clasped me tightly. 'May God have mercy on you. The Prison Ordinary told me you were a Catholic and I hoped that I might be of comfort.'

'I was, Father. *Was.* A very long time ago. And only as a child.'

'He said he visited you on remand and found you praying.'

114

'Complaining more than praying, Father. It did me no good.'

He smiled. 'It is not too late to rediscover the path to the Lord.'

'Oh, with the greatest of respect, I think it is. You know why I am here and what I have been convicted of.'

'I do. And I know that it is not so very long ago that these walls and the hangman's noose once punished priests like me for the "offence" of being a Catholic. Criminal acts are *seldom* what they seem.'

'Mine is. And be I Catholic, Protestant or Jew, I am damned for my most dreadful crimes.'

'Not so. God forgives the smallest and the greatest of sins. Not unconditionally, of course. But He forgives.'

'So even the Lord has conditions in his contracts.'

He saw the joke and smiled. 'Only one.'

'And it is?'

'Repentance.'

'Repentance?'

'Yes. It means being contrite. Turning your back on sin. Regretting what you have done and wishing you had not done it.' He studied my face and saw that he had struck a nerve. 'Tell me, my son, *do you* repent? Do you feel contrite and wish you had not lived the life you have?'

I gave him an honest answer. 'I am not sure I do. There are people still alive that I dearly wish dead and people dead whom I very much wish were alive.'

'That is not the answer I was searching for.'

'I know.'

'Only God has the right to *make* or *take* life. You might have the will and strength to kill another man, but you have no right.'

'Father, I understand that. Maybe I *do* regret the life I have led. I wish I could have written poetry and painted, had many children, grown old and been a grandfather. But it was not to be.' I glanced pointedly to the barred window. 'Maybe *this* is what was meant to be. If there is a God, then perhaps his grand plan for me is being played out.'

'Then let me take your confession, heal your soul and prepare you for the moment you meet your maker.'

'I am not ready for that, Father. Not now. Perhaps not ever. But thank you for coming here today and for not judging or berating me. That in itself has lifted my spirits.'

He bent his head respectfully. 'Then I will leave you to contemplate and will seek to try again.'

'Please do not waste your time ...'

He laughed. 'You are a captive audience. Such things are rare and present opportunities that must not be squandered.'

I laughed along with him.

'So, be certain that I will return. Your soul may yet be saved.'

'I have no soul, Father. I sold it to Satan a long time ago.'

'Then we must get it back.'

I watched him leave then listened for the door to close and the locks turn and bolts slide. One at the top. One at the bottom. One in the middle. They missed none. I stared at the recessed hinges. Old and rusted, but firm.

I kept on staring.

There had to be a weakness. Most doors I had come across had a weakness. And if they didn't, then the men behind them certainly did.

DERBYSHIRE, SEPTEMBER 1885

I spent the afternoon skulking in the orchard. Climbing the bigger trees. Biting and throwing sour apples at large black crows come to peck fallen fruit. When I was done with them, I edged up as high as the laddered branches would allow and there in the thinned-out foliage gazed at distant hills and forests.

I thought about the police in London and how vigorously they might be hunting me. About Elizabeth and whether she could ever feel towards me the way I felt towards her. And the Chans. The mysterious Chinese family I had heard Sirius and Surrey talking about. Were they really a threat to Moriarty? He seemed so rich and powerful that it was difficult to imagine him being bettered by anyone.

My reflective state was broken by Brannigan's voice booming from below the boughs of the tree. 'What in sweet Jesus's name are you doing up there?'

He was dressed in his usual filthy vest and baggy training

pants. Pleasingly, his sweaty face now showed bruising from the punches I had landed during our fight. His right eye in particular was a satisfying riot of purples and reds.

'Nothing,' I finally replied. 'Just looking.'

'Then get the fuck out of that tree and do your *looking* down here.'

Reluctantly, I descended. At the bottom, I rubbed my hands on my trousers to clean them of dusty bark and sticky apple juice. 'Is there some law against climbing trees?'

'Yes, my law. Now, what were you up to in those branches?'

'Like I said, I was just looking.'

'At what?'

'Them hills,' I pointed. 'Them big ones over the other side of the fields.'

'That's Dovedale over there. Big one is Thorpe Cloud.' He looked at me suspiciously. 'Shouldn't you be in lessons with Lady Elizabeth?'

'She wasn't feeling well, so we stopped and I came out here. Had nothing else to do.'

'Right then, if you're at a loose end, I'll find you something. Follow me.'

My heart sank.

Brannigan left the orchard at a brisk pace, while I deliberately lagged behind. The longer it took to reach wherever he wanted to go, the less time there would be for me to do whatever he had in mind.

It soon became evident he was suffering from a bad

cough for every hundred yards or so he had cause to stop and bark out disgusting mouthfuls of phlegm.

'If you're not feeling well, Mr Brannigan we don't have to do anything.' I called him *Mr* to soft-soap him a little. 'I can go back to the house if you prefer.'

'I'll tell you what I prefer.' He quickened the pace again. 'I prefer you don't talk too much. I *prefer* that I could spit you away like that horrible cud. But thanks to the professor, I can't. I am stuck with you.'

'I fear we are not going to be friends, then?'

'That mouth of yours is most unfriendly. It will get you killed one day. Not that I care. But I do mind if it endangers others close to me. So learn to shut it. Listen and don't speak. Do you understand?'

I deliberately didn't answer. If silence were to be my new weapon, I intended to use it immediately.

'Do you understand?' He stopped and clenched a massive fist.

I halted and shifted my weight. Balanced myself. Lifted my hands into a boxing stance.

His eyes lost their intensity and instead sparkled with amusement. 'You would, wouldn't you, you little bastard? You *really* would fight me again.'

'In a blink,' I answered defiantly. 'And to my death if necessary.'

He laughed. 'It may well be necessary. But not today.' He winced a little and put his big hand to his chest to quell another bout of wheezing.

119

'What's that?' I pointed at a tattoo on his bicep. 'Some kind of sailor's tat?'

Brannigan flexed his bicep so the inked image grew. 'Do you have no idea what it is?'

'A flabby arm marked with a black triangle that has a red ball inside it.'

He slapped it proudly. 'It is a drop of blood, not a ball, you young fool. And the symbols represent our brotherhood. This a *very* special tattoo.' He looked at me scornfully. 'Mucus like you should never be considered for such a badge of honour.' He added bitterly, 'But apparently the professor thinks you should.'

'Fuck you! Fuck your tattoo and fuck the professor. I don't want—'

His massive hand grabbed my throat. Fingers found flesh faster than I could blink. Shock hit my brain. Air bulged in my throat. Brannigan's reach was so long, the desperate punch I swung fell inches short of his face. I kicked out – my foot failed to reach him.

Hot with anger, he raised his big muscular arm and forced me up onto my toes. 'I told you to *listen* and not speak. Now if you value what life you have left you will obey me.' He lifted me clean off my feet. My toes twitched in the air.

Fortunately, Brannigan began coughing again and it was so severe he had no choice but to drop me.

I stumbled as my feet hit the ground. Gasped for air.

He fell to his knees and vomited. Panted for ten or

twenty seconds then wiped his mouth with the back of his hand.

'Sour ale,' he announced as he rose. 'Get up. We set out to do something, so let's get it done.'

I followed him again, my hands nursing my throat as we walked. When we next halted we were at the far side of the estate, where crops grew and farm animals were penned.

'Pigs, cows and bulls over here.' He pointed them out. 'Over there, chickens, ducks, geese and rabbits.'

'The professor likes his pound of flesh,' I noted.

'Spread out in front of you is all manner, shape and size of life. Young, old, weak, strong, small, big, parents and children, brothers and sisters.'

'What of it?'

'Choose which one you want to kill.'

'*What?*'

'You heard me. Every day, from now on, you will perform this task. So make your choice.'

'Then it's a rabbit or a chicken.' My eyes roamed the pens. 'I've killed both before, but only to stay alive, to eat.'

'This is no different. You are learning to kill, in order to stay alive. Take your pick.'

I knew from experience that cornering a chicken was trickier as they could fly as well as dart around. 'Rabbit.'

'Rabbit it is.' He walked towards the pens.

I followed. 'Do you have a knife?'

'No knife. Just your hands. Your hands are the only

weapons you are guaranteed to have. You must learn to use them to their fullest abilities.'

The wire cages were as tall as me and ran for maybe ten yards. Inside was a line of rough wooden hutches where fat parent rabbits lay with their offspring. Cabbage leaves, straw and excrement were scattered across the stone-flagged floor that prevented them burrowing away.

For a moment Brannigan rested on the fence, then he unpegged the door and let me in. 'Be quick about it.'

More than a dozen rabbits bounded back to hutches or corners. I wondered if they were used to the sight of cooks coming here to gather them for dinner.

I had used rocks in the past. Caught the animal, held it and despatched it quickly. There was no such implement of death inside the wire cell.

'Get on with it!' came the shout from outside.

Rabbits scurried away. I had to run right, left and right again before I cornered one. It wriggled in my hands and kicked to escape. I stroked it. Beneath the soft fur, a heart beat furiously and in young, black eyes I saw a reflection of myself.

'Don't make me have to come in there!' shouted Brannigan.

Anger flashed inside me. I remembered something from a long time ago, from a period I had hoped never to recall. I dangled the animal by its ears and then chopped the back of its neck viciously with a rigid left hand. I dropped it to the floor, where it lay motionless.

Slow, sarcastic slaps of applause came from outside the wire, then Brannigan let himself into the pen.

He walked straight to a corner and grabbed a rabbit. 'Let me show you a better way.' He grabbed a large rabbit. Held it tightly by the back legs. Slid his fingers down and around the neck. Pulled hard and twisted. There was a cracking noise, and the rabbit's head lolled loosely in his hand.

He swung it and threw it to me. 'Dead in under three seconds. No fear. No struggle. You just pull until you hear the bones crack. Now you do it.'

I did.

'Again!'

I had to kill ten more before he shouted, 'Enough! Now gather them up and take them to the kitchen. They'll skin 'em and cook 'em for servants' suppers.'

I looked at the broken bodies strewn around the pen and then at Brannigan. 'Does it please you to kill things?'

'Neither pleases nor displeases me. It is just death. Every kill makes the next one easier. You'll learn that. Learn it fast. Now be off with you; kitchen likes to have those creatures while they're still warm.'

I did as I was told and trudged back to the house.

Mrs Ellis, the cook, was a fat woman in her fifties, dressed in an apron as white as her hair, except for brown and red smears where she had recently wiped her hands. 'Put 'em on the block,' she ordered wearily as I lumbered forward with my arms full of victims.

I dropped them on a large wooden butcher's block and

123

she and one of her maids inspected the haul while I washed in a deep white sink near the window. Outside, I saw Brannigan sitting on a low wall, lighting a pipe, coughing and spitting by his feet.

I left the kitchen and resolved to settle some unfinished business. Not with Brannigan and not of a violent kind. I returned to the drawing room and knocked.

'Enter,' called Elizabeth.

I opened the door quickly for I was afraid my courage would disappear.

She was in a chair reading and looked shocked by my visit.

'Forgive me – I must speak with you before the day passes and with it my bravery.'

She put the book down on a side table and rose cautiously. 'What is it, Simeon?'

'I know you said that I did not need to apologise for my words, but I feel I must. I am clumsy around you and people like the professor.' I approached nervously. 'Especially clumsy around you, and I . . . well I just don't want you to hate me for my awkwardness . . . and—'

She cut me off by putting a hushing finger to her lips. 'Simeon, you are not awkward; you are just a little innocent in emotional respects. Behind every hardened young man lies a childhood without a great deal of love and feminine affection. Am I correct?'

My face confirmed that I did not know how to answer her.

She looked pained for a moment, then continued, 'The professor instructed me to prepare you for *whatever* challenges society can throw at you.' She smiled. 'And that includes issues of the heart.'

'So you are not angry with me?'

Her face softened again. 'Of course not. But if I am to be of assistance, then you need to help me understand you.'

'I should like that.'

'Good, then answer me this: has there been anyone?'

'What do you mean?'

'A woman in your life, one who has given herself to you?'

My embarrassment set my face aflame. 'No. There has been no one.'

'My goodness. But you have been kissed, haven't you?' Hesitatingly, she added, 'And *loved* of a sort?'

I felt such peculiar shame that I could not answer.

'Oh, my dear Simeon.' Her eyes grew soft and she gently embraced me. 'You should have been loved, cared for, taught these things.'

My heart thundered. Boomed its feelings against her clothes, all but pounded them into her skin, her blood and bones. I clung to her out of dizziness and excitement.

Elizabeth's face touched mine. Her hair brushed my skin. A gentle sigh she breathed filled my lungs and yet left me breathless. My eyes were drawn to hers and once there were irrevocably locked. I could not look away. Could only close them and hide in my hopelessness.

Her lips touched mine. So softly, I was unsure it had happened.

Then more firmly.

Then not at all.

I stood there dazed, my eyes shut. Uncertain what to do, how to respond. Then I blinked and looked.

She was gone.

All that remained were traces of her perfume, the sound of the clock ticking and the pounding of my heart.

ELEVEN DAYS TO EXECUTION

NEWGATE, 7 JANUARY 1900

I have over the years become something of a learned man, but I confess I know not of any word, in any language, that adequately describes the mental torment of being condemned to death.

It is more than the sum total of the worst of your worries. It is greater than the accumulation of your darkest fears and most awful days. It is all those things, multiplied by each waking second of your sentence.

Imprisonment turns your thoughts into deadly enemies, mutinying troops that lay siege to your soul and your sanity. They are reinforced by personal regrets and you are powerless to defend yourself.

At first I thought the small window in my cell beyond my reach. Then I learned it was possible to jump from the end of my bunk, grab one of the iron bars and hang for a while. Not that the view amounted to much. But it was a view. A gun-metal sky and a yard below, the place where all condemned men, except me, were allowed exercise. It was called the Press Yard, because stones used to be loaded onto the bodies of remand prisoners who had refused to plead, in order that they could be 'pressed' into confessing their crimes.

Hour after hour dragged by. Time was chained as heavily as me and I in turn was manacled to my past, to my crimes and of course to Moriarty and the life he forced me to live in return for keeping me from the noose.

It was late in the morning when two gaolers entered my cell. Both had mutton-chop whiskers and grey hair. Two peas in a wrinkly old pod. 'We're 'ere to take ya to chapel, Lynch,' said the larger one. 'Git ovva the other side, by that piss pot, an' turn ya back to us.'

'*Chapel?* I don't want to go to chapel.'

'Well you're goin'. Mr Huntley said you should go, so you're goin'.'

'I am a Catholic,' I protested.

The larger man shrugged. 'We don't have no place for Cat-o-licks, so you'll just 'ave to make do with the bleedin' C of E, won't ya?'

I succumbed. Not out of a lack of principle, but because it at least offered an hour away from the stench and bore-dom of my cell.

Once I was secured in walking restraints, they marched me to the chapel.

It was a wretched place. Dank, dour and dirty. Only the strongest of daylight penetrated its high, filthy window. In a tainted shaft of light that broke through the grime, dust motes hovered like souls suspended in purgatory.

My chains clanked on the floor and the eyes of all prisoners and staff turned to me. Everyone knew who I was. What I had done. Even here in the company of thieves, rapists and killers the exact nature of my convictions marked me out as a monster.

I shuffled into a pew reserved solely for those awaiting execution. Close to a dozen men were penned in like cattle. Singled out and separated from the rest of the convicts. Destined for the Newgate abattoir.

Tall wooden railings divided female prisoners from the men. The altar looked nothing more than a long table with a cloth thrown over it. Thankfully, the old habit of putting out a coffin for the condemned men had either been forgotten or dispensed with.

Johncock and the governor, a small and pale man whose name I did not know, sat in a private, roped-off area, and did their best to look holier than the chaplain. Huntley was there, too. But he did not sit with them. He walked around, vigilantly checking his men were doing their duties.

My attention drifted from him to the rest of the turnkeys and to the congregation. Was one of the men who entered my cell and tried to kill me among them? Had it indeed been a turnkey, as I suspected? Or was there a convict here who could come and go from cell to cell because he had some kind of master key? Such a person would be most interesting to find. Find and deprive of such a valuable instrument.

An orderly ambled along the aisles carrying a box, out of which he distributed bibles and hymn books. He was a frail man, bald and bent, bowlegged by rickets and awkward in gait. When he reached the condemned pew, his bloodshot eyes caught mine and he stopped in front of me. He handed me my books but seemed to hang on to the bible as though he thought I wasn't worthy of it. I was forced to tug it from him. His eyes caught mine. But there was not a look of judgement there, just acknowledgement. But of what?

As he moved away, I realised it was the book.

I opened it but saw only holy words. Words that over the years had lost much of their meaning to me. Slowly, I thumbed through the pages. There was nothing unusual. I closed it and began to think I had been mistaken. The spine rested against the palm of my hand and felt strangely uneven. I slid a finger down the outside. There was something concealed behind the binding. I opened the dark cover to release the tension on the fabric.

Now I saw it.

Glued vertically was a thin iron nail about four inches long, gleaming and sharpened at the end. I could think of a thousand uses to put it to. But first, there was the problem of removing it from the book and concealing it about my person.

Prayer followed prayer, but there did not seem to be a moment when the eyes of the turnkeys were not on me.

And then it happened. Five minutes from the end of the service, one of the female prisoners fainted. In the confusion that followed, I freed the nail and slid it through the waistband of my trousers into my drawers.

The orderly collected the volumes and his gaze never met mine. Diligently, he gathered everything and under the supervision of a screw stacked the books at the rear of the chapel.

No one moved until the keeper and Johncock made their exits. The gaolers then descended and our manacles and leg irons were checked before Huntley gave the signal for us to be escorted back to our cells.

Inside the condemned wing, the two screws guarding me stopped outside my door to conduct a body search. 'Spread your arms and legs then lean against the wall, Lynch.'

I had manoeuvred the nail into the fold of my groin but the risk of it being discovered was still high. Hands felt my neck, shoulders, chest and waist. They grabbed my left ankle. Patted their way up my leg.

'Hey!' I kicked out at the screw doing the searching. 'There's no need for you to be touching me there, you sick bastard!'

'Shut up, Lynch!'

His inquisitive fingers jumped from my left thigh to my right ankle and once more inched their way up to my groin. As they neared the hidden nail, I shouted again, 'For God's sake, are you some kind of pixie?'

They spun me round. An angry screw jabbed a fat forefinger into the middle of my forehead. 'We're doin' our jobs, that's all. Now get back in your bleedin' cell.'

As I chain-waddled through the door, I felt a much-anticipated kick in my backside and fell face first to the floor. The pair of them dropped on me, switched my chains, mumbled insults and left me with the big question: who had given me the nail?

Not the orderly; he was just a harmless go-between, relied on to do as he was told and ask no questions. Who had decided to put the nail in that book and told him to ensure it was delivered to me and no one else?

Had it been another prisoner? A man with power and sway within the gaol, someone who had heard about the attack and taken pity on me? Did I have a secret supporter within the community of convicts? Someone who knew who had attacked me and hated them enough to arm me against them? Or was it a gaoler? Huntley perhaps?

The two screws who came to my cell said he had insisted I go to chapel. Had it been him? Had I finally found the perfect ally to escape this hellhole and all its demons?

My next lesson with Elizabeth proved to be an awkward and disappointing affair. Not that this surprised me. I had spent a sleepless night fearing it would be so, while at the same time hoping it wouldn't.

In my wildest dreams I imagined entering that awful drawing room and sweeping her off her feet. She would surrender herself to me in a spontaneous embrace that would see us descend in passion to the Persian rug while grand old men in oils frowned down on us from their jaded golden frames.

The events that unfolded were nothing like that. It seems moments like this, ones preceded by such high anticipation, are destined to disappoint.

I took a calming breath before walking into the room as confidently as I could manage.

The cold blankness on her face warned me that my hopes were about to be crushed. Elizabeth was already seated at a table, my study books spread over it, a chair pulled out in readiness for me. 'Come and sit, Simeon. We have much to learn today.'

I took the chair. 'You seem distant with me. Is that because of yesterday?'

'It is. You are correct.' Her tone was brusque. 'Simeon, I overstepped the professional line that should divide teacher and scholar. I promise you I will not let it happen again.'

'But you were nice to me. You encouraged me to talk of how I felt—'

'I know what I did and it is something I should not have done. Oh Simeon, you are so young and I am charged with developing your character, not confusing you.'

'I am not confused. I love you.'

She looked startled. A moment passed. She shook her head. 'You are too young to know anything of love. Pick up your books, please.'

'What age does a man have to be to be capable of love? Can you teach me that?'

She ignored me and held up her book. 'I left a copy of this, Shelley's Queen Mab, for you to read. Have you?'

'I do not wish to talk of stupid poets!'

'What you wish does not matter! The *professor* wishes for me to teach you lessons of culture and that is *all* I will do with you.' She stood so quickly she knocked over her chair. 'Or shall I leave this very minute and tell him you refuse to be tutored by me?'

I began to rise.

'Stay seated. Tell me your answer. Do we continue as we are meant to, or do I go to the professor?'

I felt so much anger and frustration that I could not speak. I found my fists clenched and my mind urging me to strike out at something, to break the table, to rip apart all her damned books, to smash the whole room into a thousand pieces.

Elizabeth righted her chair and placed her trembling hands on the top of it. 'Do we resume, Simeon, or not?'

'We resume,' I answered. A more sensible part of me reasoned this was a better option than explaining my foolishness to Moriarty.

'Very well.'

She sat. Pulled her chair closer to the table. 'Did you read any of the poetry I left you?'

I could not look up at her. I studied my clenched hands and slowly stretched out my fingers. How could she make me feel like this? One moment my spirit was higher than those tree branches I had climbed in the orchard. The next, I felt lower and more wretched than the tiniest, vilest insect in all of Christendom.

'Did you read it, Simeon?'

I looked up at her. 'I did. I read of death and sleep, and right now I wish I were consumed by either of them. Anything other than this.'

'Did you understand the poem?' she persisted.

'In parts. But most of it made no sense to me. There were too many words that I had never heard of to make a story out of it all.'

'Then let me explain. Shelley has taken a character from Shakespeare, Queen Mab, and he pairs this fairy with the soul of Ianthe, his first child. Mab uses her powers to take him on a journey through time. She shows him how evil flourishes inside institutions that appear good, like religion, business and monarchy.'

'That is not what I thought it was about. Not at all.'

'And what did you think it was about, Simeon?'

'I thought it was about a clever and beautiful woman who awoke wonderful and frightening feelings in a stupid and clumsy young man. About how she was able to see beyond what he was and could understand what he could become, if only she would let him, if only she would help him.'

For a second Elizabeth did not answer. A second during which I saw that my words touched her and melted some of the coldness.

'No,' she answered, unconvincingly, 'that is not what it is about. Not at all.'

ELEVEN DAYS TO EXECUTION

NEWGATE, 7 JANUARY 1900

With the cell door closed and the turnkeys engaged in their Sunday evening duties, I retrieved the nail from my under-clothes and looked at it with a wonder that I imagine few men had ever felt in consideration of such a mundane piece of ironmongery.

I wrapped my fist around it. It was less than half the width of a little finger and was not rusty, implying it had been selected from clean storage, not scavenged from old wood. Rightly or wrongly, this made me inclined to believe it had come from someone able to leave the gaol and return at will.

Outside of the prison walls, the nail would have but one purpose and only a brief moment of use. It would be positioned on some specific part of timber, balanced on its point between thumb and forefinger, then hammered so flat it would become almost invisible. That would be its life.

But inside this wretched place, my humble nail had many lives and more possibilities. It could pierce a man's throat. Gouge out an eye. Rupture a temple. Slide through a rib cage. Perhaps it could even pick a lock. Given patience and dexterity, it might even dislodge a window bar.

As precious as it was, I could not continually carry it on my person. Regular body searching would discover it sooner or later. I needed to hide it.

My eyes roamed the dank walls of the cell until I saw the perfect place. A small gap in the wall, between door frame and brickwork, where years of banging and vibration had taken their toll. A sliver of space, large enough to push the metal into, small enough to escape the eye.

It fitted perfectly.

For once, I wished away the rest of the day. Longed for night to come and for the lazy screws to lock us all down until daybreak and settle into their nocturnal habits of skiving and drinking.

And when the sun did finally set and the iciness of night

crept across my floor, God was good to me. He blessed my little piece of hell on earth with enough moonlight to see what I was doing and I slid the point of that nail into the big lock on the leg irons.

Several hours later, I had undone it.

The chain lay loose at my feet and despite the locked door and barred window, I felt free. I stretched, luxuriating in the freedom of movement. I even smiled.

But I knew my happiness was a delusion. The door was not only locked, it was bolted from outside. I ran my fingers along the nail and cleaned it of dirt. I would have to take a turnkey by surprise to use it as a weapon on him. This would entail sitting on the floor by my bunk in a way that showed the leg irons but concealed that they were unlocked. Then I would pounce. Hold the nail to his throat, force him to undress and give me his uniform and keys. I would bind and gag him, then like the man who tried to kill me, I would calmly leave the cell and walk away.

I was fooling myself.

Gaolers never entered the cell alone. There were always at least two of them. I had nothing with which to tie them up and gag them. I could possibly rip the sheet on my mattress, but unless used immediately its destruction would soon be discovered.

My best chance of escape would be breaking through a wall or window during the cover of night and then surprising and overpowering whoever stood between me and the outside world before an alarm could be raised.

I studied the small moonlit window above my head, jumped and grabbed a bar. One-handed, I hung there, and used the nail to scrape inquisitively at the bricks beneath the iron that held me.

Keeping my balance while applying force to the nail was nigh on impossible. The actions cancelled each other out. I either pressed too hard and fell, or scraped too lightly and made not a jot of difference.

I was annoyed at how quickly I tired. How wasted my muscles had become. Yet I resolved not to be dispirited. The window would not easily yield but there were hundreds of bricks to try.

Alas, not this night.

Exhausted and angry, I returned the nail to its hiding place, snapped the leg irons back around my ankles and collapsed on my bunk.

The moon had shifted. It was the middle of the night. Another day had come and gone. I counted the time I had left.

Ten days.

Two hundred and forty hours before my execution.

DERBYSHIRE, NOVEMBER 1885

Winter was fast approaching. The fat trees that in their summer greenness dappled light, now stood skeletal and black against the moody skies.

With sharp seasonal change came personal transformations. Emotionally, physically and mentally I was becoming a different person. Being well fed and well cared for enhanced my physique, while the lessons prescribed by the professor developed me in ways I had never imagined. I gave little thought to Moriarty's benevolence, save considering it a stroke of good luck that he had been kind to me. Not for years would I realise that his motive was selfish.

Sadly, Elizabeth stuck steadfastly to her promise not to again cross that boundary between pupil and teacher. She took me on a broad cultural journey that encompassed not only her beloved Shelley but also Shakespeare and the etiquette of eating, drinking and speaking in the company of higher society. I learned how to waltz a little and to listen a lot. How to feign interest in the most boring of conversations and if pressed, how to diplomatically voice disapproval. She taught me to use dictionaries, write business letters and showed me how to conduct myself in meetings with professional people.

And I learned about tea.

Yes, tea, of all things. Those precious leaves turned out to be Elizabeth's greatest love. To steal a step closer to her heart, I used my newfound social skills to seem enthralled by her tales of taking tea in the gardens at Vauxhall and Ranelagh, where apparently she liked to stroll of a summer afternoon. And I was nothing short of entranced by her disclosure that the custom of tipping had originated from overworked waiters placing boxes on tables marked T.I.P.S. – To Insure Prompt Service – and how they wouldn't serve anyone until they heard the clank of a coin.

But these moments of closeness were rare. And never a lesson passed without me thinking about that kiss. *The mistake* as she hurtfully labelled it.

In contrast to my cultured sessions with Elizabeth came the brutal tutelage dispensed by Michael Brannigan. Under his guidance, I graduated from the barehanded strangling of rabbits to the deadly despatching of chickens, pigs, cows and even bulls.

I learned that soft and silent art of choking. That sustained pressure across an airway can strangle the most massive of opponents, even if they have four legs and want to gouge you to death.

I even learned to *like* Brannigan. I admired his strength and expertise. He used his hands like a craftsman used a box of precious tools passed from father to son. Grips. Locks. Levers. His fingers were all those things and more. And his fighting brain was faster than any punch I had ever thrown. He fought like a chess player, anticipating his opponent's next two moves. When we grappled in training, he was always several steps ahead of me.

At the end of our sessions, we often walked back to the house and talked of the fishing and shooting he'd done on Moriarty's estate. He didn't like cities, hated London and had visited both Paris and Rome, which he disliked even more 'because of their peculiar ways'. Most of all he hated the Chinese. 'Sneaky bastards. All of them,' he insisted, without giving any justification to his condemnation.

On one such occasion, we were on our way back to the house when the professor came heading our way.

'Michael, please pardon my interruption. I am hoping your lesson with Simeon is at a close because I am in urgent need of his assistance.'

'All done, sir,' answered Brannigan. 'The lad's put in a good day's work but still has energy to do your bidding.'

'Very good.' He looked my way. 'Walk with me to the courtyard, Simeon.'

I fell in step with him and he explained the reason for seeking me out. 'Miss Breed has had to address a problem we have with some Chinese associates and has been delayed. It means she cannot complete a chore I banked on her performing.'

'By Chinese, do you mean the Chans, sir?'

'Who I mean is currently of no consequence to you.'

'But they are your enemies, aren't they, sir?'

'Anyone who is not my closest of friends is, to a greater or lesser degree, my enemy. Now clear your mind and focus on the task.'

Moriarty walked me to where a carriage awaited. Inside was the handsome, one-legged man I had met in the orangery. 'Please get in,' urged the professor. 'Alexander will instruct you en route.'

I stepped up into the carriage and was immediately taken with its smells of polished leather. Moriarty shut the door, tapped the leg of the coachman and the hansom pulled away with a jolt.

Once the horses gathered pace and settled into a rhythm, the young American reached for a cloth bag at his feet. His disability meant he had some difficulty lifting and swinging it towards me. 'You will find everything you need in there.'

I took it and loosened the drawstring. Inside was a pristine revolver with a sleek steel barrel and polished wood stock. Also powder, fresh ammunition balls and a rolled parchment sealed in thick red wax.

'It is a Remington,' explained Alexander. 'The professor and I brought several back from our last trip to New York. Do you know how to use such a firearm?'

I half-cocked it and levelled it at his head. 'This is a normal cap and ball, with powder and metal enough to kill a man, is it not?'

He shrank back. 'It is.'

'Then I know how to use it.'

From behind raised hands he implored me, 'In God's name, be careful with that thing.'

'I'll be more than careful.' I made the gun safe and returned it to the sack. 'You can keep it. I have no intention of taking anyone's life.'

His wall of hands came down. 'You shouldn't need to. It is precautionary, that's all. We are going to an estate in Warwickshire, owned by some of your English gentry.'

'Who?'

'A Lord and Lady Graftbury.'

'And why should we do that?'

'Because, currently visiting them and their hideously rude and highly unlovable daughter Victoria, is a French aristocrat by the name of Thierry de Breton.' He warmed to his story. 'There is belief in the Graftbury household that monsieur may this very day ask for Victoria's hand in marriage. Hence our special visit.'

'And what am I to do – shoot him?'

'Good heavens, no! You are to steal a particularly valuable item of jewellery, while the family is immersed in talk of marriage. It is called the King John tiara and is an exceptionally beautiful and rare headpiece made of countless pearls and finest gold. It is finished with a circle of blood-red rubies and a perfect diamond in the centrepiece. It seems your old King John was something of a master thief himself.'

'Is that so?' I said uninterestedly.

'*Johnny* used to break up sets of jewellery that his soldiers looted and have new pieces made. The most stunning of which were the tiaras he gave to his three most pleasing mistresses. This particular one, the one we're after, is the last in open circulation.'

I stared at the bag at my feet. 'So what is expected of me, and this pistol? Am I to barge in through the servants' quarters, waving it like some idiot highwayman of old, shouting "Your money or your life!"?'

Alexander smiled. '*No*. They can keep their money, and

if you are smart, also their lives. As I have just explained, there is only one thing that needs to be stolen. And you will have good help in doing so.'

'From whom and how?'

'None other than Monsieur de Breton. Otherwise known to you as Mr Sirius Gunn.' He raised an eyebrow at the revelation. 'Like a loyal hound, our good friend has been *nuzzling* Lady Victoria for almost a year. Now is his time. You will knock on the front door and say you have come directly from his home in London, where a French messenger delivered those sealed papers for his immediate attention.' He gestured towards the sack. 'They inform him of his father's illness and the need to return as soon as possible to the French estate. Sirius will ask the lord for a moment to compose both himself and a reply. You will be shown to a study where, once privacy has been assured, Sirius will pass you the tiara. You will put it in the messenger's sack and leave.'

'And that is all?'

'It is.'

'So why the weapon?'

'The simplest of plans often births the most complex of disasters. It is better to be prepared for such an eventuality.'

It seemed I had no alternative but to do what was asked of me. The choice of using or not using the weapon would ultimately be mine. Besides, the caper might present the opportunity I had hoped for. I could steal the jewels and then run for the hills.

'I am just wondering,' I asked, 'if you also have no option but to do as the professor says?'

'There is always an option.' His head turned to the window and the blur of the passing night. 'If you wish me to stop the carriage so that you may run, I can do so.'

'And then what?'

He shrugged. 'I could buy you a minute or two under the pretence you told me you needed to relieve yourself. Then I would have to raise the alarm, or else the coachman would do it, and of course you would be hunted down and found.'

My eyes fell on his leg. 'Would you run, if you could?'

'No. I have no desire to. The professor looks after me. Bestows on me a lifestyle and a manner of respect I have not found elsewhere.'

'And in return, you handle things like this for him?'

'Like this and other very different tasks. I am a qualified lawyer, but no practice in New York or London craves a cripple as counsel. As a result, the professor benefits from the services of a professional who not only knows the law here and in America but is happy to help him break it.'

'So, do you have the tattoo?'

'Tattoo?' He looked at me suspiciously. 'To which tattoo do you refer?'

'You know of what I speak.' I put my hand to my bicep, the place where I saw Brannigan's. 'The triangle. The droplet of blood.'

He looked angry. 'If you know of that, then you realise I do not. Cannot. So *why* do you ask?' He put a hand on his stump. 'Is it to belittle me? To mock my affliction?'

'No. I meant no offence.'

'Then I conclude that while you know of the symbol you do not understand what it represents. Is that the case?'

'I saw it on Brannigan's arm. He said it represents some brotherhood and he almost killed me when I made light of it.'

He fought back a laugh. 'Did he, indeed? Well, I suppose that would be appropriate, given all the circumstances.'

'Circumstances?'

His lightness of mood disappeared. 'You should take your clues from both the triangle and the blood. I have said enough. Now back to the matter in hand – the one with which we are both charged. Are you willing to participate in this venture? Or, would you prefer me to stop the horses, so you may make an excuse about the weakness of your bladder and run for the hills?'

NINE DAYS TO EXECUTION

NEWGATE, 9 JANUARY 1900

There was a hanging this morning. One conducted by James Billington, Johncock's favourite to execute me.

Louise Masset – that was her name. *Child killer* – that was her epithet.

Murder is probably all she will ever be remembered for. Not as a bonny baby held and cooed over in the arms of her mother. Nor as a sweet child, big eyes full of hope and dreams. Not even as a romantic teenager, hoping to land herself a kind man who would take her as his wife and raise a family with her. But solely as the child killer she became.

News of the execution was relayed via Boardman and Baker, two of Johncock's most trusted cronies. They entered my cell mid-morning, snapped on my walking chains and cuffed my hands behind my back.

'Mr Billington did a real neat job on the bitch,' beamed Boardman then scratched at his red beard as though he had lice. 'An artist, that's what Mr Billington is. An artist.'

'Pleasure to watch a drop like that,' added Baker. 'Real pleasure.'

Foolishly, I imagined I was being taken to the Press Yard for my first spell of open-air exercise since incarceration but as we turned a corner and they opened a gate it became apparent something more sinister was planned.

'Welcome to the execution shed,' announced Boardman with a flourish. 'What do you think of that scaffold then? It's the finest in Britain.'

I stared at a raised platform of light wooden boards. Above it stood the ghastly frame of the single-beamed gallows. The rope had gone but I could see the iron rings through which it had been woven. There was an area of flooring marked off with broad white lines, beyond which darkly stained trapdoors hung ominously open. Beneath them, blocks of straw, broken by the fall of Louise's dead body.

To the side of the bales stood a large, tightly packed sack of sand, not unlike ones I had driven my fists into while learning to box. Only this served a different purpose. It had been hung from the rope beforehand to take all the stretch out of it.

There are not many sights in life that have rendered me speechless but this was one. Here was the place I would die. Few people know the exact location, the precise time and full nature of their death. Even fewer are shown it in advance or are made aware of what will be said to them in that final minute of existence.

'Billington left 'er 'angin' for close to forty-five minutes,' added the leathery youth.

'Standard time,' remarked the older man, glad of the chance to demonstrate his experience. 'Though lately, I've seen 'em cut down after fifteen. Unless of course their 'eads come off, then they're down much sooner.' They both laughed.

Baker nudged me as though we were great pals. 'Looked pretty as a picture she did, when she were stood up there. Sweet as a peach in her newly laundered dress.'

'Like she wanted to dance,' joked Boardman, waggling two fingers to mimic how her legs kicked when she was hanged. 'But not so pretty when she turned purple an' shit 'erself though.'

Amid another peel of laughter, Baker pointed to a handcart in the corner. 'Once she'd done her little jig, *mademoiselle* departed in that there carriage. Proper *ooh la la* it was.'

'Though we took 'er to the coroner, not to that French lover wot she killed 'er kiddie for.' Boardman shoved me at the cart. 'Why don't you try it for size, Lynch? It's same one we'll be layin' you out in.'

I broke my silence. 'I've rested in worse places. And I'll wager your wife would rather stretch out in there with me than in bed with you.'

'Watch your tongue,' he snapped. 'Or I might just forget I'm responsible for your 'ealth an' welfare, an' do you some mortal 'arm.'

I squared up to him. 'Try it.'

He gave me a hard stare. The look of a bully. The glare of a man wanting to do something he could brag about.

'Go on. *Do* it. My legs and arms are chained, so if you are aching to hurt me then chance your arm and see what happens.'

He swallowed. A lump of doubt slid like a chunk of apple down his throat.

'I didn't think so. Now what about my exercise?'

Young Baker yanked my wrist chains. 'You'll get your exercise all right.' He spun me around, pulled me backwards, down a long landing. We turned a corner and he pressed me tight against a wall. Keys rattled. A cell door was unlocked.

Boardman swung it open. 'This was 'ers, Lynch. That bitch's pit.'

It was bleak and empty. The single blanket that had given her comfort during her last night lay crumpled on the floor. It was easy to imagine Louise Masset holding it. Letting go of it for the last time as she stood and walked out.

'Can you smell 'er fear?' asked Baker. '*Can you*?' His face contorted with a sickening pleasure. '*I* can smell it. The whiff of dyin' is as pungent as piss. It's so thick an' nasty we won't never be able to scrub it away.'

Boardman drew my wrist chains high up my back. 'Suck it in!' he demanded. 'Pigs like sniffin' other pigs' shit, so go on, you murderin' swine, get a snout full of 'er stink.'

He had said too much. I smashed the back of my head into the bridge of his nose.

He let out a grunt of pain, spat blood, then smiled. 'Thank you, Lynch. You've just given me the excuse I needed.'

I kicked my heel hard against his shinbone but didn't catch him hard enough.

Boardman punched the side of my head. A meaty blow that set my ear ringing. I soaked up the pain and shuffled backwards into him until he toppled over.

'Man down!' shouted Baker, 'man down!' He blew hard on his whistle.

150

I turned.

Boardman got to his feet and started to come for me.

I kneed him between the legs.

Air whooshed from his mouth.

I tried to kick out but the irons snagged my ankle.

He backed up against the outer wall of the cell, his hands protecting his groin. It was a stupid move – it left his face unguarded.

I butted him again. Teeth snapped and stuck in my forehead.

Boardman fell, moaning, to the stone floor and I dropped alongside him. Quickly, I slid my legs either side of his neck.

He grabbed at my ankles, but it was too late – I had already trapped his head.

I shifted my hips and started a move that would at its worst render him unconscious and at best kill him.

A baton smashed my head. Hands snatched at me. Fingers grabbed my chin and hair, twisted my neck, hauled me off him. I was forced upright and pushed into Louise's cell. Leg chains snapped my ankles and I fell. My chin cracked the floor and I bit through my bottom lip.

Pain pinned me to the ground. Beyond me, noises simmered then came to a shouting, whistling boil. Angry voices raged at each other and called for reinforcements.

Then silence.

Delicious, hear-a-pin-drop silence.

Someone had taken charge. Wiser ones had discovered

Baker and Boardman had not been given the governor's permission for our little walkabout, and now there would be hell to pay. Old heads were fathoming out how they could exonerate themselves from this debacle and cover up everything that had just happened.

I managed, in great pain, to roll over and rest against the wall. Opposite me was Louise's bunk.

The sight of it made me wonder what her last night had been like. Had she slept a wink? Prayed all night? What had been her final thoughts when they had come for her and marched her to the scaffold?

I pressed my back hard against the wall and managed to stand up. Blood trickled down my forehead and touched my lips. I thought of Boardman's broken teeth and spat. I straightened up and took several deep breaths to steady myself.

Then it happened. The most unexpected thing.

I heard a key slip into the lock of the cell door but I did not turn. A diaphanous movement across the room held my attention. A young woman in a long white dress was sat on the bunk. She clutched a blanket tightly to her bosom. I understood why she held it close. The tatter of cloth was the last softness she was afforded. The only thing that embraced her without revulsion, that brought a modicum of warmth and comfort to her skin and bones.

'We're coming in, Lynch,' shouted a gaoler.

'We don't want any trouble,' cried another.

My attention stayed with the woman. Her face was white

and her eyes full of tears, but she smiled at me. A smile of sympathy and understanding.

'Come quietly and we won't hurt you,' said the turnkey. 'There'll be no recriminations. We only want to return you to your cell.'

The woman dropped the blanket, rose like a balloon and vanished. There was a rush of cold wind.

Heavy hands grabbed my shoulders and forearms. Men dragged me from her cell. Amid this mass of hot and heaving gaolers, I felt only the shuddering chill of the apparition.

A corridor away from the women's block, the turnkeys grew less rough and let me walk more freely between them. 'Louise ...' I asked a young gaoler whom I had not seen before, 'how did she behave on the gallows?'

'Shut the fuck up!' the man shouted in my ear.

An older and calmer voice said, 'She stood tall. Had her chin up. I think she had accepted who she was and had made her peace with the Lord.'

WARWICKSHIRE, NOVEMBER 1885

Cab wheels crunched gravel. In a cold night sky the waning moon seemed to glisten with ice. We stopped in front of a gaslit front door. I glanced at Alex then hopped down from the carriage. Beside me, horses steamed from their exertion and snorted white breath into the blackness.

Within two pounds of the brass doorknocker, a plump and surly butler opened up. Warm light and aromas of roasted meats spilled from the wainscoted space behind him.

'Can I help you?' His tone suggested I should have been at the tradesman's entrance.

'I am here for Monsieur de Breton.' I dipped into the sack given to me and produced the bogus letter. 'An important message for his *immediate* attention.'

'Wait here,' he commanded and closed the door in my face.

Several minutes passed before the door reopened. 'You may enter,' announced the butler.

Across a floor of chequered white and grey marble, I saw Sirius Gunn in a dinner suit. Alongside him was a young brunette with a hooked nose reminiscent of a vulture. Opposite was an older version of her and a white-haired, corpulent man in his sixties.

I raised my voice and spoke to Sirius from the doorstep. 'I have a letter from your house in London, sir. It came today via France. The messenger was too exhausted to take directions here.'

Sirius looked to the lord in what I presume was a passable French accent. 'Please excuse this untimely interruption; I will deal with it as quickly as possible.'

The old man nodded and Gunn advanced. I handed him the sealed parchment; he broke the wax and opened it.

'*Non! Non! Non!*' he exclaimed. '*Mon papa!*' He held the paper to his breast and seemed distraught.

'What is it, Thierry?' The young vulture flew to him.

He passed her the letter and stayed slumped in grief.

'Oh, my dear!' she exclaimed and fluttered back to her parents. They crowded her as she translated from French:

My precious son and heir,

I know you are with your darling Victoria and I hate to interrupt your important visit but I am in dire need of your presence.

It seems the illness that had been but a rattle in my chest this last year, has grown in boldness and shown itself to be a killer of tissue and choker of breath. I am to be admitted to the sanatorium as a matter of urgency and have been advised to call you to my bedside.

I pray we are reunited one last time.

Your loving papa,
Bertrand de Breton

Victoria was close to tears when she finished. Her mother gathered her close. Her father took the letter and solemnly reread it.

Sirius gradually stirred from his shock. As though remembering his manners, he turned to the master of the house. 'My lord, please excuse me. I need to take the messenger outside so I can compose an answer for him to rush back. Then perhaps you and I may conclude our *private* discussions.' He looked pained. 'I still have much I wish to say to you, and hopefully, with your blessing, to Lady Victoria.'

'Most proper of you,' concluded the lord. 'But you and your man must not stand outside in the elements.' He gestured to a passage on his left. 'Take a moment in my study to compose both yourself and your reply. Giles will show you the way.'

We followed the butler to a room of panelled oak and the smell of old cigars. The servant checked Lord Graftbury's desk to ensure we would not have sight of any confidential papers. He removed several documents and the family seal, then commented, 'You will find pen, ink and paper there, sir. I will wait outside until you require my services.'

'*Merci*,' said Sirius. He waited until Giles had left, then checked the door had been firmly closed. 'Get your sack open. Quickly.'

I loosened the drawstring and Sirius unfastened his jacket. From a voluminous inside pocket, he produced a small tiara that glinted brightly. I only saw it briefly, as he put it into the sack, but it was strikingly beautiful. A glorious glittering of silver, diamonds, pearls and rubies.

'How much is that worth?' I whispered as I secured the drawstring.

'More than your life is, so be careful.' He left me and hurried to the desk. There, with quill, ink and paper, he deftly fashioned a note to his dying father. When completed, he blotted the paper, nodded to me and said quietly, 'Open the door; we are ready.'

As Sirius had anticipated, the others had already gathered in the corridor and they witnessed him passing the note to me and the instruction, 'Go quickly and safely, for you carry the most precious of messages.'

'I shall,' I promised and headed for the door.

'Wait,' commanded Lord Graftbury.

I halted, mid-step.

'Give your sack to Giles.'

My heart froze.

'Give it me, boy, come on.' The butler held out his hand impatiently.

My eyes found Sirius and I saw that he shared my nervousness.

Giles half-turned. From a narrow hall table, he lifted a small cloth parcel. 'Cook has wrapped some cold meat for you; let me put it in there for your long journey back.'

'I have no time, sir,' I said and dashed for the door.

As I opened it and stepped into the night, I heard Sirius apologising for my discourtesy.

The coach had been drawn rudely close to the house and there was no opportunity to run away, had I still harboured the notion. Indeed, it seemed to me that the coachman might well have been carrying a shotgun beneath the black cape that covered his hands and knees.

Once inside the carriage, I exhaled an enormous sigh of relief as the horses pulled away.

'Did you get it?' asked Alexander.

'In there.' I gestured to the sack.

He lifted it from the floor and undid the string. 'Damnation! *Where* is it?' he shook the sack. 'It *isn't* in here.'

I grabbed it from him. He was right – there was no jewellery. I lifted out the gun. *No tiara.* I began to panic.

'It must have fallen out. We have to stop!' My hand frantically searched the sack for a hole that it might have slipped through. Nothing. 'Stop, I said!'

Alexander sat back and shook his head. 'You have failed your first test, Simeon.' His voice was cold with disappointment. 'There was no theft. No royal tiara. The jewellery you saw in the house already belongs to the professor.'

'I don't understand.'

'You have been tricked, my friend. Fooled from the moment he asked for your help until this very second.'

Events flashed through my mind. I held open the sack. 'But *I saw* Sirius place the jewellery in here.'

'No, you didn't.' He leaned forward and grabbed it from me. 'He made an exterior fold in the cloth, like this. Sirius slid the tiara into the fold and lifted the sack as he handed it to you, so you couldn't look inside. As you lowered it and pulled the drawstring, he palmed the tiara and returned it to his jacket. You should have checked. You really should have checked.'

My mind filled with doubt. 'And the revolver?'

'Packed with dust, not gunpowder. Just in case you

thought about using it on me and stealing the coach to make a getaway.'

'I had *not* thought of that.'

'Then be grateful for your lack of imagination. It would have been the death of you.'

'And the posh nobs in the house, Lord and Lady Graftbury?'

'Oh, *they* are genuine. But they are friends of the professor's and like to play along with him.'

'Bastards.'

'He rewards them with the odd piece of stolen art and Sirius is not averse to fucking their daughter, so it works well for everyone.'

I sank into the corner of the cab and wished I could disappear. 'What was this all about?' I shrugged in despair. 'Why was I ridiculed so elaborately?'

'It is not ridicule; it is the making of you. The professor wishes to test your mental faculties and your progress, that is all. He wants to see if you are ready.'

'For what?'

'For whatever he has in mind.' He smiled in a way that intimated he could say more but chose not to.

We settled into our seats and mulled over respective thoughts before the motions of the brougham and the darkness of night lured us into slumber.

It was exceptionally late and dangerously icy when we arrived back at the house. I stuck close to Alexander as we headed indoors, but he insisted he didn't need my help. I bade him good night in the main hallway and went straight to bed but could not get another wink of sleep.

I had failed my test.

Failed it miserably and in the morning I would have to face the wrath of the professor. The thought was too much to bear.

After several restless hours, I got dressed and went downstairs to the kitchen. It was cloaked in darkness save the faint flicker of a fire in the range. I headed there to warm my hands and stir the embers. To one side, I saw a lamp and decided to light it and at least comfort myself with some bread and cheese.

'Simeon? Is that you?'

Surrey was sat on the floor, cowering in the corner of the room.

'What is wrong? Are you all right?'

She did not answer. From my light, I could see she was dressed as the raggedy boy I had first encountered in Manchester. The brightness of the lamp caused her to blink and shield her eyes as I approached.

I saw other things now. A tied sack on the floor. Her hands caked in dried blood. Red-stained gloves between her legs, as though dropped there. And a knife.

I went to the big, deep, oblong sink, put in a plug and ran water. 'Come here – bring that blade and gloves.'

She didn't move.

I returned, grabbed her by the wrist and hauled her to the sink. 'You have to clean up.' There were spatters of

160

blood on her forehead and smears on her cheek, where she had wiped herself with a hand or forearm.

Surrey stood shaking. She stared blankly at the wall while I cleaned her up as best I could. I dipped her hands in the water, mopped her face with a cloth and dried her with a towel. But I had barely scratched the surface of what was necessary. 'Surrey, there's blood all over your waistcoat, your shirt and pants. Even your shoes.'

'I'll change and burn them.' These were the first words she had spoken since saying my name. 'Change and burn,' she repeated as though drilling herself. 'Change and burn.'

I went to get the hessian sack. 'This will need dealing with as well.'

'Don't touch it!' She looked angry. 'Please, *don't*, Simeon.'

'I am trying to help you.'

'I know you are. And you have. You helped a great deal.' She put herself between me and the sack. 'But leave me now. I am fine.'

'I am not sure you are.'

'Go! *Please*, just go.'

I dried my hands on the towel and looked at the bloody stains. 'Make sure you burn this as well.' I threw it down and headed to the door.

'Simeon!'

I turned to her. 'What?'

'Don't tell the professor you saw me. Whatever you do,

don't tell him. It would not be good for either of us to speak of this. '

NINE DAYS TO EXECUTION

The visit to Louise Masset's cell left a profound and painful impression on me, one far deeper than Boardman's splintered teeth and oafish fists had done. *Her* ordeal was *my* ordeal. I had glimpsed my own death. Felt the hangman's clammy hand on my neck.

I spent the next hours wondering if my imagination, perhaps even my conscience, had conjured up the chilling vision of her. Had the ghost of an executed child killer really appeared to me? Was it possible that after being hanged, your spirit stayed trapped in the place where you ended your life? Were all cells and gallows haunted by the ghosts of those who had died there?

This was what awaited me – a form of purgatory. I would be killed and buried, but every night my restless soul would roam the death cell.

I had to escape. Had to use that inconsequential nail to break apart every brick of my damned cell and claim my freedom. Anger boiled inside me. Anger at my helplessness and at those responsible for my imprisonment.

My rage was curtailed by a visit from Huntley and a sandy-haired turnkey with a twitch in his left eye. 'Routine cell search, Lynch. Stand up, place your hands on the wall – you know the drill.'

I did indeed. Huntley patted me down while his twitching accomplice walked the slim space between bunk and window. He shook out my mattress and checked my pot before declaring, 'All in order, sir.'

'Pleased to hear it. Now wait outside, while I talk to the prisoner.'

'Sir, it is protocol that there are always two of us with prisoners—'

'I know the protocol; now wait *outside*, I said.'

'Yes, sir.'

The twitcher left. Huntley watched the door click shut then turned to me. 'I need to speak in privacy, Lynch.'

I eyed him suspiciously. We had not talked since before my visit to chapel. 'Talk away, Mr Huntley. As you can see, privacy is something I have an abundance of.' I looked beyond him. My gaze fixed on the nail that nestled in the gap in the masonry and I wondered if he had been responsible for it coming my way.

'I am part of a new breed of graduate officers,' he said, 'sent to old places like this to clean up the prison service. That means at times I am even less popular than you.'

'Ha! People want to hang you, do they, Mr Huntley?'

'Some would. Gaols like this are either being cleaned up or closed down. Newgate is rotten to the core. Built

163

on bribery and corruption, it will be gone within half a decade. Probably sooner.'

'A pity it won't close in a few days.'

'You will not be that fortunate. Still, as one of the officers supervising this unit, I have the means to make your life more comfortable.'

'More comfortable? That sounds an impossible task to me.' I waved a hand sarcastically across the cell. 'As you can see, I already have all the luxuries a man could wish for — just look at that fine shit pot in the corner.'

'The prison is overcrowded, so you cannot be moved. I understand this cell was a storeroom just six months ago, such is the pressure on the building.'

'I weep for it. Poor building.'

'Lynch, I am trying to be kind. I cannot relocate you, but I may be able to arrange some *company* in here for you, if you wish.'

'I do *not* wish. I have never been with a whore and never will.'

'Many of our female prisoners are also in need of comfort.'

'No, thank you.'

'I noticed from the record books that you have not yet been given access to the exercise yard. From now on, you will be regularly afforded that privilege. It is important for the mind that the body is exercised.'

'And my soul, is that to be attended to as well?'

'I was pleased to see that you went to chapel. I knew

you were a Catholic but I thought you might find comfort there.'

'Comfort in the crucifixion, the pain of Christ and the *nails* of the cross?' I stressed the word to see if he reacted.

He didn't.

'We all carry a cross of sorts, Lynch.'

'Do we really? Then please tell me what is your cross, Mr Huntley.'

'I believe it is to serve inside institutions like this and extend humanity to men like you.'

'Humanity? Let's not dress this up to appear better than it is. Execution is no grander than murder in the name of the Crown.'

'It is the will of the people.'

'In my experience, the will of the people is determined by whoever pays them or whatever gin or strong ale they've been drinking.'

'There is truth in that.' Huntley smiled and knocked on the door for it to be opened.

'Which are you?' I asked.

'What do you mean?' He looked at me quizzically.

'Friend or foe, Mr Huntley? Which one are you?'

'I am just doing my duty, Lynch. Just doing my duty.' He knocked on the door for it to be opened.

I retired to bed immediately after leaving Surrey in the kitchen, but still could not sleep. I lay on my back in the blackness of the room and remembered the fear on her face, the blood on her hands and that mysterious sack on the floor.

What jewels or goods had it contained that were worth spilling blood for?

Most probably killing for. Why had she been so anxious that I did not talk about seeing her? Was it because she wasn't supposed to have been seen by anyone? Or was it simply because she was ashamed of the state she was in?

A bigger question came to mind. Had I just experienced a glimpse of what would be my own future? Killing to order. Murder at Moriarty's behest. And all the anguish that went with it.

I was still struggling for answers when a servant knocked on my door and informed me that my morning session with Mr Brannigan had been cancelled. Instead, I was to join the professor in the orangery as soon as possible.

As I entered that cold glass room, I saw him sitting by a frosted window overlooking the snow-covered lawn. He was in only his shirtsleeves and seemed oblivious to the chill. A copy of a newspaper called the *New York Times* was spread on his table. Next to it was a silver coffee pot, the long spout arched gracefully like the neck of a swan, and a white cup.

I approached his table. 'Good morning, sir.'

He looked up. 'Good morning, Simeon. Come and sit. I have ordered eggs and ham for us both. A breakfast I grew fond of while in New York.' He folded up his paper and put it to one side. 'My mother was American, God bless her soul, and when my father was away on business, she would sometimes instruct the kitchen to cook up meals that reminded her of home.'

'Like ham and eggs, sir?'

'And waffles, and grits, and apple pie.' His eyes softened with nostalgia then in a blink hardened again as he asked, 'What did you make of your performance at Lord Graftbury's yesterday?'

'Not a great deal, sir. I know that I failed. Most miserably.'

'You did. But the odds were somewhat unfair. Let me see, there was Alex, myself, Lord and Lady Graftbury, their pug of a daughter, and Sirius; that's six against one. Oh, and of course the butler, Giles; that's seven. Furthermore, we all knew exactly what you were going to do and when you were going to do it.'

I felt heartened by his words. 'I take some comfort from that observation.'

'You should. But only a little. To survive in life, you will often face greater odds and opponents with more knowledge of a situation than you have. The lesson, Simeon, is to always check that what *appears* to be so, really *is* so.'

'I will, sir. I will.'

167

'Remember, Truth is not a friend, he is a deceitful enemy.'

'I will.'

A maid arrived and put down plates laden with heavy slabs of tangy, salted gammon and huge, fried duck eggs. Moriarty punctured one of the deep yellow yolks and watched with satisfaction as it flooded his plate. 'Eat,' he urged. 'We will continue our discussion when you are nourished.'

I was grateful for the chance to do so because I had missed two meals yesterday. So good was the smell and taste of the food that it was a struggle to remember my manners and not to wolf it all down.

Despite my efforts at self-restraint, I finished long before Moriarty did.

He picked up his napkin, wiped his mouth and put the egg-yellowed square of cotton to one side. 'It is time for us to speak openly. About you and about why I have brought you here.'

'I am eager to know, sir.'

'I am sure you are. You were chosen, Simeon, by me and by no one else. I saw you box as a young workhouse boy and noticed a spark of innate savagery in you. I even won some good money on your fists. As a result, I made enquiries and my men traced you to your last abode in Manchester.'

'But why? For what purpose, sir?'

'For the brotherhood, an organisation that has existed for

many generations.' He paused then added, 'I know you have seen its symbol, the tattoo on Mr Brannigan's not inconsiderable bicep, and have asked about it, so let me illuminate you. The name of the brotherhood is the Trinity, hence the triangle. Those swearing allegiance are bound in blood to shed blood. Not only their *own*, if the cause necessitates, but primarily, that of my enemies. In short, they are sworn to kill, Simeon, to take the lives of other people.'

'What kind of people, sir?'

'Evil people. Truly evil people. The kind that would endanger you, me and all those we hold dear. People who deserve to roast in the fires of hell.'

His face told me he believed what he said. That despite the probability that every murder committed in his name grew his empire, he saw the killing as justified.

'Mr Brannigan,' he continued, 'Mr Gunn and Miss Breed are killers. *Assassins*. Highly trained murderers who do my bidding. They are my power of three. My Trinity.'

The enormity of his statement rendered me silent. Of Brannigan, I could believe it. But not Gunn – he looked far too much like a pixie. And until the early hours of this morning, not Surrey.

The professor sensed my doubt. 'There's more to murder than brawn or savagery,' he pointed out. 'Take Miss Breed. She is a true virago. Her bravery is unbounded. Her slightness of size and flatness of form allows her to convincingly act as either a boy or girl. Urchin, housemaid, barrow boy or courtesan, she can play any part with distinction. Her

169

litheness allows her to slip through spaces that butterflies would become lodged in. And once she is where she wishes to be, then she strikes, like a crack of lightning.'

Again, I pictured Surrey in the half-light of the kitchen, hands shaking, fighting to gain her composure. I had seen her spirit broken, and then I had witnessed her determination to become whole again. 'You mentioned yesterday that she was dealing with a Chinese "problem". Did she . . .'

'Did she what?' His eyes sparkled with excitement. 'Resolve it? Yes, she most certainly did.' He poured himself more coffee. 'Usually, Miss Breed favours poison. In drinks such as this.' He lifted his cup and smiled. 'Sometimes she is more physical. A hatpin, through the heart or throat. Occasionally a blade, though I have to say this is not her forte; she tends to be somewhat untidy when it comes to the shedding of blood.'

'And Mr Gunn?' I asked. 'What is *his* expertise?'

'Treachery,' he answered, proudly. 'Sirius has a consummate charm that wins the admiration of men and a handsome look that hobbles even the most intelligent of women. Once he pays his victim the attention they crave, then they are his. From that moment forth, it is only a matter of him timing his great betrayal and seizing the moment in which to despatch them.'

Moriarty took out a small silver snuff box, laid a pinch on the back of his hand and took it before continuing, 'Mr Brannigan is the longest-serving and final member of my Trinity. He kills quickly, unquestioningly and

170

without remorse.' The box was closed and he returned it to his jacket pocket. 'Recently, he had to despatch an eleven-year-old boy. Not for one second did this trouble him.'

'A *child?*' I regretted saying the word aloud, but my conscience back then was not as corrupted as it is now.

'Yes, a child, Simeon. Evil is not confined to maturity – you of all people must know that. Pre-pubescent assassins are plentiful among the ranks of street Arabs that populate both London and New York. And there are moments when these deadly delinquents need disposing of, just as much as evil adults do. Just as much as evil *women* do.' He paused briefly to take stock of my reactions, then added, 'Whether at home or abroad, I run my enterprises in ways that do not require anyone to be murdered, but sometimes those I deal with force my hand. Or to be more precise, the hands of those in my service.'

'And Mr Brannigan, I suppose his hands contain an expertise for ...' I struggled to find a delicate way of expressing it, 'for strangling?'

'Yes, you are correct. As he has no doubt taught you, he is particularly adept at creating ligatures from whatever environment he finds himself in. His favourites include silk belts from ladies' gowns or piano wire plucked straight from the ribs of a grand or baby piano in a fine gentleman's home. Out in the wilds of the country, he once despatched a fellow with a garrotte fashioned from his own bootlaces and some oak twigs. Michael is most inventive.'

171

'And *they* are the three members of your "Trinity"?' I asked. 'Sirius, Surrey and Brannigan.'

'Yes, they are.'

'And am I to be some form of assistant? An errand boy to fetch and carry for them?' I thought once more of Surrey in the kitchen. 'To wipe up after them, to clean their bloodied hands and garments?'

'You have not been brought here to provide such meagre service.' He paused for a moment then added more solemnly, 'Unfortunately, Mr Brannigan has a terminal growth on his lungs. One that the best doctors in Harley Street say is inoperable.'

I was shocked. 'I'm sorry, I had no idea . . .'

'How could you have known? You are not a medical man, are you?'

'No, sir, you know that I am not.'

'If you had been, then you would have been aware that an insidious parasite is relentlessly devouring parts of his inner self and causing him immense pain.'

'Poor man.'

'Poor man, indeed. But do not let him hear you say such a thing, or you will be the one needing pity. Pity and a basket of bandages.'

I shared a smile with him.

'The growth will kill him shortly,' continued Moriarty. 'We do not know if that tragedy will play out within days, weeks or months. But play out it will.'

'And then there will be two,' I said, recalling the

brutality of my terrible fight with Brannigan and the agony he must have secretly endured.

'No, Simeon, by then there will be three. *You* will be the third. That is the purpose of all this training and testing. It is to ready you for the moment when you will fill the void left by Michael.'

The enormity of what he was saying began to sink in. I was being trained to kill at Moriarty's bidding, to earn my way in life by ending the lives of others.

'I don't think that is something I will be able to do, sir.'

'Not now. But in time you will learn. You have the anger to kill. It is in your blood. I see it flare up in your eyes. Michael says rage is rooted deep in your soul. When we have added brains and subtlety to your savagery, then you will be ready.'

'And what, sir, if I don't want to be ready?'

'That is not an option, Simeon—'

'Sir—'

'Do not interrupt me! You have killed already. Taken the life of a good and honest person, by all accounts.'

I hung my head in shame.

'The die is cast. You are what you are. Only instead of being stretched on some gallows, you will be educated. I will protect you and reward you with money and luxuries that a runaway urchin could never have imagined.'

Still my conscience prevailed. 'But, sir, what if I am unable to do what you ask of me?'

'You will be able.' Moriarty rose from his seat. 'And if you are not, then as you say, there will be only two.'

'What do you mean, sir?'

His stare hardened. 'You clearly need me to be blunt. So I will oblige. You will be killed, Simeon. You know too much to walk away from here as a free man. A grave will be dug, your life will be taken, and you will fill it.' A thin smile ended his sentence. 'Do you have any other questions?'

PART THREE

Ale-glasses and jugs,
And rummers and mugs,
And sand on the floor, without carpets or rugs;
Cold fowls and cigars,
Pickled onions in jars,
Welsh rabbits and kidneys – rare work for the jaws! –
And very large lobsters, with very large claws;
And there is M'Fuze,
And Lieutenant Tregooze;
And there is Sir Carnaby Jenks of the Blues,
All come to see a man 'die in his shoes!'

The Ingoldsby Legends; or, Mirth and Marvels,
Thomas Ingoldsby

DERBYSHIRE, MARCH 1886

Winter thawed into a new spring and with it melted much of the ice wall that Elizabeth had constructed between us. I suppose my educational and cultural improvement made her warm to me.

Paradoxically, as my feelings and optimism grew, Brannigan's strength and general health ebbed away. By the time the cherry blossoms flowered, the hacking cough that he had initially dismissed so lightly rendered him permanently bedbound.

Every morning, I made time to sit with him and stayed for the same duration we used to devote to training, sparring, and more latterly sharing stories. He would tell me of his journeys with the professor to America – to Boston, New York and New England. He enjoyed talking about their funny ways and accents. 'I'd been sent to teach this crooked businessman a lesson,' he told me. 'The fella was a proper Charlie from Harvard who'd messed up some investments. When I said the professor wanted things put right he told me 'Go fry an egg!' Can you believe that? *Go fry an egg!* Michael laughed so hard it caused him to cough.

I smiled. 'What did you do to him?'

'I'll tell you what I did. I fried him. I heated the stove in his shitty room and cooked his hand. I said that unless he made good on the money he owed then I'd come back and boil his head.'

'And he did?'

'Within two days. He paid in full and with interest. The professor loves the Yanks but I can't stand them.'

I plumped up his pillow. 'You need to rest. I'll see you tomorrow.'

'And you need to train harder. You're going weak in the arms and stomach. Just because I'm not able to crack the whip, doesn't mean you can grow soft.'

'I am not *soft*. I train daily.'

'When? When do you do this?'

'Right after I've seen you. I go through all the drills you gave me. I do them as though you are watching over my shoulder.'

He seemed pleased. 'Good. But don't cheat, Simeon. Cheat in training and you cheat yourself.'

'I know. I've been taught by the best.' I patted his arm.

'That you have.' He coughed painfully. I passed him a bowl and he retched more of the dark matter that was killing him, then he lay back and looked exhausted.

'Would you like me to get you some water before I go?'

'No. Any more water and I'll bleedin' drown. I want whisky.'

'You know I can't give you that. Doctor's orders.'

'Fuck the doctor. I am dying, aren't I? Not having whisky isn't going to cure me.'

'I'm still not getting you any.'

'Bastard.'

'You are a bigger bastard. Bigger and uglier.' I raised a pretend fist.

He rasped out a laugh. Gripped my arm. 'Be useful then, before you go running after the few skirts that work around here; distract me with a story.'

'About what?'

'Anything. Just take my mind off this room and the damned pain in me gut. I know; tell me about this other trainer you had. The one half as good as me.'

I laughed. 'Twice as good as you and only half the trouble, that's what he was.'

'Then speak of him.'

So I did. And because I knew he wanted companionship even more than whisky, I began right at the beginning. Back in the days when I was in transition. Changing from a meek child, bullied and chided, to a wild animal, fuelled by a savage rage that once unleashed could not be controlled.

LONDON'S EAST END, 1875

When I was eleven years old I was a workhouse kid, quite a different character from the one destined to walk to the gallows. The young Simeon was as timid as a mouse, wouldn't hurt a fly, let alone another human being.

But all that changed. Not as the result of a single event, but because of a series of experiences layered upon me like suffocating blanket after suffocating blanket. Humiliation by bullies, fear of being beaten and ridiculed, loneliness and desperation.

Buried inside me, beneath my cowardice and isolation, was a terrible anger that could not escape, that was unable to kick off those psychological blankets and allow me to breathe easily and free.

Until one morning.

Instead of running and crying, as was my wont, I had lashed out at two boys who had been making my life a misery and, foolishly, I did so under the noses of our masters, ensuring we were all soundly punished.

I was caned and locked overnight in a coal cellar. The man who released me was memorably horrible. Brandon Timms was the only supervisor more lice-ridden and filthier than any of the wretches he oversaw. He was bald, save lank, greasy hair that sprouted just above his ears and fell beyond his shoulders. His hands were covered in crops of warts that he would rub in our faces. His old brown woollen suit was short in the legs and stank of every belly-load of beer he'd vomited and every careless piss he'd taken.

Timms clipped my head as he pushed me through the boardroom door and commanded, 'Git over there, boy! And be sure you're seen and not heard.'

I remember that the room had a cavernous fireplace that burned a mineful of coal. That day, the blaze warmed a gathering of stout men hunched around a dark, highly polished table that supported lazy arms, fat cigars and numerous cups of tea and plates of biscuits and cakes.

'Stand straight! No slouching, mind,' ordered Timms as he positioned me for consideration.

The governors talked of the classroom altercation, then fell silent as they waited for Jeremiah Beamish, the workhouse master, to make an entry in a ledger spread beneath his podgy fingers.

Eventually Beamish downed his pen, thumped hefty forearms onto the table and cleared his throat.

'It is my *job*,' he announced, 'to raise you in a manner that society might approve of you. It is my *duty* to ensure that everything and everyone within these walls is governed by fairness, equality and transparency. It is therefore my *decision* that you and the boys you were fighting, Charles and James Connor, will settle your differences in public.'

He picked up a cigar glowing in an ashtray at his elbow, drew on it, and amid a cloud of smoke announced, 'The three of you seem to have a taste for violence, so my colleagues and I think it just that violence itself will tutor you.'

He could tell from the vacancy in my eyes that I was none the wiser.

'You are to *box*, child.'

My brain filled with fear and I struggled not to shake or even soil myself.

'Whichever brother chooses to face you, you will fight him. It will serve as a lesson for you all, and who knows, it might even produce some extra income for the workhouse through ringside wagers.'

The mention of money prompted mumbles of appreciation from the other men at the table.

'In preparation,' continued Beamish, 'the three of you will be trained in the fine art of pugilism. And I hope that in so doing, you discover some dignity for yourselves and respect for this fine establishment.' He leaned on the table and it creaked under his weight as he spoke to the governors. 'I will have Blackson and Miller tutor them; they both have a sense of what is required to make silk purses out of sows' ears.'

They made more appreciative murmurs. Beamish listened and then turned back to me. 'There must be no physical contact of any kind between the three of you until the day of the bouts. No kicking, hitting, poking, tearing of hair or even spitting. Any child not heeding my words will be reminded of them by a merciless flogging.'

I was fascinated by a trickle of sweat that dripped from his chin. It hit the table top. Glistened on the polish and formed a tiny, greasy bead.

'Look at me!' he shouted.

I lifted my gaze.

'Do I make myself unmistakably clear, boy?'

I was almost too frightened to speak. 'Yes, sir.'

'Good.' He turned to Timms. 'Get him out of here. Have

Matron check the mite over. See that he is bathed and dis-infected before being returned to the others.'

With a wave of his hand I was dismissed.

Despite the master's urgency to be rid of me and to start his boxing caper, it was not until the early hours of the following morning that I met the man who would train me.

I was asleep in the cold, overcrowded dormitory when a voice ended the safety of my dreams. 'Get up!' it boomed. 'Get the fuck *up*! Right this moment!'

I woke with fright. A large, black man was by my bed. The first I had ever encountered. He tore the blanket away and bellowed, 'GET UP!'

I swung my legs to the floor.

'People call me Blackson,' he declared. 'But to you, I am *Mister* Blackson.'

He pushed his face intimidatingly close to mine. Grabbed my arms. Squeezed them until I squeaked in pain. 'Does that hurt?' He squeezed some more. 'It must, because I have felt string with more muscle than you have.'

'Let go. You are—'

'Be quiet and listen. From now on, I own this puny shoe-lace of a body of yours. The breath in your tiny lungs and the pansy pink blood in your weedy veins, they are mine.'

He let go and my biceps burned where he had gripped them.

'Put your daddles up,' he demanded.

Other boys were stirring now, shifting in their bunks, curious to see what was happening.

183

'Daddles up!' shouted Blackson and slapped my left cheek for good measure.

I lifted my left hand and touched the stinging flesh. He slapped my right cheek.

Sniggering broke out in the dorm.

My right hand rose protectively and he jabbed me hard in the stomach. The spluttering I made created another wave of laughter.

'Next boy that makes a noise feels my fists,' warned Blackson. 'So get back to sleeping or playing with yourselves.'

I straightened up and struggled to breathe.

'At least you're not cryin', that's a start. I hate criers.' He cupped my chin in one of his giant palms. 'You want to hit me, don't you? I see it in your eyes and your balled-up baby fists.'

He put his hands behind his back. Leaned forward. Stuck out his chin. 'Go on then, lad. Land your best blow.'

I clenched my fist even tighter and threw my hardest punch.

Blackson's hidden right hand reappeared and caught my fist mid-air. He held it like it was a small ball tossed by an infant and tightened his grip so painfully I thought he might grind my bones to dust.

I danced in pain. Felt water flood my eyes. Pushed my teeth together to halt a scream that would have shamed me for ever.

Finally, he let go. 'You need to be less *pree-dick-table*.'

He pointed at my heaped clothes on the floor. 'Now get dressed, we have work to do. And lots of it, judging by the poor shape you are in.'

And work we did. That morning and every morning, *Mister* Blackson came for me. His thin form appeared like a spectre at my bed, usually materialising only minutes before Miller came for the Connor brothers.

Day by day he would slap me awake. Grind my soft fists in the pestles of his palms. Laugh at every punch I threw at him.

'You must learn to bob 'n' weave,' he told me. 'Stay on your toes. The floor should never feel your heels.' He would dance forward and sideways to demonstrate. 'A boxer's feet are his leading fists. They strike the first blows by moving you away from the knuckles of your enemy.'

Gradually, the training became easier. My body and mind adjusted to each extra notch of torture. Soon, I could take a slap without flinching. Sometimes, I could even counter with a punch that found its target.

One morning, he stopped the sparring and said, 'I'm going to show you something now, something you'll never forget.' He held his big right hand high in the air. 'This is called the rabbit punch and it's a great favourite of Mr Miller. So you can be assured the Connor boys will be instructed to execute this on you.'

He feigned a blow to my stomach with his left hand and then, as I dipped my head and backed away, he hit me hard across the back of the neck with his straight right hand.

I instantly went dizzy, lost my footing and fell to my knees.

'It's called a rabbit punch,' he explained as he hauled me to my feet, 'because it is used to break the neck of rabbits.'

He left me to wheeze, then added, 'You will have but thirty seconds to recover if that happens when you're in the ring. Now, breathe slowly through your nose and out slowly through your mouth. Breathing like that calms your heart and stops you pissing yourself.'

I did as I was told and from that day forth during every training session I kept a vigilant watch for the rabbit punch. Only once more did he catch me with it, and that was during the culmination of a particularly brutal session that involved his newly introduced combination of uppercuts and jabs.

Day by day, I became not only fitter but also more skilled. During an intensive boxing session I found myself wrong-footed but managed opportunistically to throw a strong left jab that caught Blackson under the ribcage and left him coughing.

'I'm sorry,' I said quickly, afraid of the retribution that might follow.

Still slightly winded, he asked, 'Which hand did you hit me with?'

I shied away from him; afraid he might crush it, or worse.

'I'm not going to hurt you. Which daddle?'

I held up my left.

He straightened up and examined it. Raised both his

palms as targets. 'Punch me. As hard as you can, but with only that fist.'

I followed his orders.

'Harder.'

I complied.

'Now with your right.'

Again I obeyed.

'I thought so!' He sounded delighted. 'You're a *southpaw*.'

'I am? What's a southpaw?'

'A person who punches hardest with their left. I've been teaching you all wrong. I should have known.' His voice grew excited. 'Only I have never come across a southpaw before. Never fought one. Never trained one. Fancy that.' He shook his head in disbelief. 'You keep this to yourself, mind. It's a secret that will serve you well when you fight one of the Connor boys.'

And keep the secret I did. Though at the time, I failed to see what difference using a left hand could have over a right.

Blackson held a different view and, true to his word, he changed things from that moment onwards. Not only did he make me lead with my right, he had me concentrate so much on my foot movements that at times I felt I was being taught to dance rather than box.

Our daily sessions finished in the biggest of the yards, the one that separated the chapel, dining halls, admin block and machinery shed. Our routine was always the same. He would sit and smoke his clay pipe, and I would have to run until his tobacco had gone up in smoke. By the time he tapped the black ash out on the stone floor, I would be bathed in sweat and unable to speak.

Before we parted, he would always open a roll of cloth and give me chunks of cold chicken and bread to eat as a reward. 'Food and sleep are your secret trainers,' he would tell me, 'they work while you rest. Along with that mighty left daddle of yours, they are what will win those fights for us.'

When the day of the big fight came, it started most strangely, for Blackson took me for a good breakfast instead of a workout and we talked. Just talked. Not about the fight. Not even about boxing. Just about life.

'You know,' he said, warming up to tell me something of importance, 'you think you've got it rough. No momma, no father, no home and a fight, in which you might get badly hurt. But that's just life, boy. Life hurts almost everyone you will ever meet. As you grow up, you'll always be fightin'. If not with your hands, it'll be with your head or your heart.'

'Is that how it's been for you – one long scrap?'

He laughed. 'What do *you* think? Here I am, the only black face in the workhouse; do you imagine I've had things easy since my family came here?'

'You weren't born in London?'

'Norwich. My grandparents came from Sierra Leone.'

'Is that *near* Norwich?'

He laughed again. 'No, it is in Africa. That's a whole

world away from here. My parents came on a ship and nearly died during the voyage. They made their way as servants in fine houses. And for their crippling labours they got treated no better than dogs. Our name wasn't Blackson, not back then.'

'It wasn't?'

'Blackson was the name ignorant white men gave my father. To them he was just the black's son. Bosede Bangura is my real name.'

I pulled a face. 'That's a strange name.'

'Only to you. To me, it is a very *precious* name.'

'Then I shall call you by it. At least for today.'

He scratched at his head. 'Remember, when you fight, you defend both *your* family's honour and *mine*, as I am the one who has trained you.'

'I'll remember, I promise.'

'My father,' he went on, 'became a performer in a circus. Many years before, he had heard of a great countryman called Pablo Fanque who became a famous showman. My father decided that if he was going to be pointed out and laughed at for not being white, he might as well get paid for it.'

'What did your father do?' My imagination ran away with me. 'Was he a lion tamer? An acrobat, or—'

'He was a prize fighter.'

'A boxer?'

'An excellent one. A fine trainer, too. He taught me all I know. At the fairgrounds, people would pay to fight my

189

father, on the promise they'd win a guinea if they knocked him down. No one ever did.' He looked sad and added, 'One day he beat a gypsy from a rival circus. Much money had been bet on the pikey and the loss wasn't suffered well. The following night, my mother and father were clubbed to death in their caravan. I only survived because I had been out playing with a friend.'

I didn't know what to say, or do, to make him feel better. I just sat close and leaned against him, to let him know I was on his side.

'Come on,' he said, vigorously ruffling my hair. 'The talking is over. Now it is time for you to honour yourself, and cost Beamish a bob or two, for he's sure to have bet on a Connor boy giving you a hiding.'

I got up and followed him out of the room. We walked long corridors towards the quadrangle where the bout was due to be held, past the pungent smells of the kitchens and steam of the laundry. Miller and the Connor brothers appeared from a side door in front of us. They glanced our way. Swaggered on ahead and I had my first pang of nerves.

As we neared the end, Bosede put an arm around me. 'Remember to hit, hit and hit again. Do not let pain stop you from punching them. Ignore it. Swallow it like water and spit out fire.'

Miller pushed open the double exit doors into the quadrangle and the roar of a crowd deafened me. Workhouse inmates jostled to see us as we walked out. They were packed deep. People at the back were standing on crates or balancing on each other's shoulders. Towards the front, men in suits and hats were seated on benches and chairs. Most were smoking and placing bets.

Eight posts marked out a rectangle of tattered turf and two thick ropes ran around it all. Across the centre of the patch of grass was a short, newly painted white line, known as 'the scratch'. This was where the referee gathered fighters when he wished to commence or conclude the boxing. A couple of three-legged stools stood in diagonally opposite corners.

My teeth chattered in the cold as we ducked the ropes and entered the arena. Bosede slapped my biceps to warm me up. When his eyes caught mine I could see encouragement in them. I wanted to do him proud but feared I lacked the courage.

'Stand up straight and don't be frightened.' He forced my shoulders back and stared intently into my eyes. 'You won't notice the crowd. Not when one of the twins hits your face or body.'

Charlie Connor and Miller stayed outside the ropes while Jimmy slipped inside. So he was the one – the best of the Connor boys. The devil I had to beat.

Jeremiah Beamish raised his hands and voice to address the crowd. 'Gentlemen, gentlemen! I seek your silence and your keenest attention.' The master paused until they quietened. 'A great grievance is about to be settled between Simeon Lynch and the brothers James Arthur and Charles Arthur Connor, who I am told have been in a state of

mutual animosity since first clapping eyes on each other.'
Beamish took a couple of paces to his right and clasped the
shoulder of a burly white-shirted man with a stern face and
a large black moustache that appeared freshly waxed and
curled. 'I am privileged to introduce to you Jonathan J.
Clark, a most distinguished official from the London Prize
Ring.'

Cheering rang out.

'Mr Clark,' continued Beamish, 'has graciously con-
sented to oversee our match, fought under a most agreeable
adaptation of the Broughton Rules. Along with him are
two impartial umpires, Mr Gray and Mr Southgate, who
will help keep time and rule on the outcome of this fight.'
He paused while the aforementioned gentlemen rose
slightly from their ringside seats so they could be identified.
'I am sure you understand that their decision on the winner
and the subsequent allocation of associated battle monies
will be final.' This comment resulted in a mixture of boos
and cheers.

'Come 'ere, boys,' demanded Clark gruffly as he beckoned both Jimmy and myself. 'I want a fair stand-up fight.
Fifteen rounds of three minutes apiece. No gouging, no
butting, no punching beneath the belt.' He motioned to our
feet. 'Show me your boots. I told your master this 'ad to be
a fight without spikes.'

I raised my footwear one at a time and he checked both
the toes and heels before doing the same with Jimmy.

'That's agreeable.' He dusted his hands together. 'Now

listen closely; from debilitating blows, you will have thirty seconds' respite. Time must be spent on one bended knee, this being a signal to your opponent that you may *not* be struck by him until you once again stand fully upright. Hitting an opponent when he is down will immediately result in disqualification.'

He took my right hand and Jimmy's. Pulled us knuckle to knuckle. In a lower voice, almost a whisper, he told us, 'You do as I say, when I say, or so help me God, afterwards I'll hurt you twice as hard as you've managed to hurt each other.'

With that remark, he stepped back and lifted his voice to its original volume. 'You must start to fight upon hearing the command "Box!" and you must desist on hearing the shout "Time!" Now shake hands, go to your corners and be prepared by your seconds.'

I was unsure what a 'second' was but I headed to the stool where Bosede awaited me. 'Shut your eyes,' he commanded. I did so and immediately he covered my face with his palms and rubbed into it some foul-smelling substance. 'Animal fat,' he explained. 'It will slick away any punches that get around your guard.' He wiped his greasy hands on the towel. 'Are you ready, Simeon?'

It was a fine question. One that dredged up all my fears. He slapped me hard across my left cheek. 'I asked, are you *ready*?'

'Yes!' I answered.

'Good, then *fight*. Fight for our honour.'

I took a deep breath and walked to the scratch. The moustachioed official stepped back, made a downward gesture with his hand and shouted 'Box!'

Jimmy swiped wildly. Swung with his left and then his right. His arms wheeled through the air like blades of a windmill in a hurricane.

I stepped to one side, left him flailing on a top rope. From down below, a man with a ginger beard shouted, 'Hit him, Connor! Kill the little bleeder.' Bosede had been wrong; I heard every sound. Saw every face.

Jimmy punched again; landed a blow – a right-hander that stung my left ear. Sent a ball of humming pain bouncing through my skull. My head was down, vision blurred, knees weakened.

I saw his silhouette across the grass, already stepping a triumphant dance, a victory jig.

I heard the crowd cheering him on.

'Kill 'im!'

'Go on, lad! Get the bleedin' little chicken!'

'Lay 'im out!'

Jimmy hit my other ear. The ball of pain bounced again. The crowd tasted blood.

'Hit the fucker!'

'Get stuck in there!'

'Give 'im wot for!'

Jimmy's jubilant silhouette danced across me.

That was when it happened. The terrible rage that had tormented me broke free of those layered blankets of fear.

It possessed me. Raised my head. Bounced me on my toes. I smashed my right fist into Jimmy's face. The exhilaration was sublime, beyond anything imaginable.

He threw a counterpunch. I blocked it. Thumped his stomach. Again came a rush of joy.

His shadow scurried away from me, and my anger chased it, hunted it down. Slammed a hard left into his nose. Followed by crisp combination punches.

Left, left, right, right. Anger knew what to do. Anger was merciless.

Jimmy dropped like a rock. His legs twitched.

Anger stood over my tormentor. 'Get up!'

The referee forced himself in front of me. Pushed me backwards and counted, ' ... seven, eight, nine ...'

'Get up!' I screamed.

But Jimmy didn't.

They threw water on him. Carried him to his corner.

I sat on the wobbly stool and watched the blurred eyes in his pale face search for explanations. There was pandemonium now. Clark, the referee, Beamish, and I think a doctor too, were all leaning over Jimmy.

My bully was spluttering, moaning and whimpering. His brother Charlie shouted something and pushed Miller in the chest, then his eyes caught mine. They blazed with hatred.

Anger made me smile at him across the ring. Charlie broke from the melee and before I could get from my stool, he was on me. He grabbed my shoulders, headbutted my nose.

I fell backwards into the ropes, snorting blood. Pain

burned in my forehead, but there was no fear. Only anger. Anger twice as big and powerful as before.

I hurled Charlie off me. Hammered a fist into his nose. Broke it. Burst it. Bloodied it. He rushed me again and I dodged. He hit the ropes – was still off-balance when I cracked my forearm across the already broken bridge of his nose.

Agony sank him to the floor, pulled screams from him that silenced the entire crowd. Blood gushed between his outstretched hands.

Then I saw it. The exposed back of his head. The neck of the rabbit. My left came down like a guillotine and Charlie collapsed face first. Sprawled out.

But still Anger wasn't finished. I dropped to the ground, turned him and drew back my fist.

Clark's hand snagged my wrist. 'Stop, boy! Stop now!' He pulled me up and off him. 'Get to your corner!' He pushed me away.

Charlie was getting up. I turned and tried to get at him again. Bosede held me back. 'I'm going to kill you!' I screamed. 'I am going to fucking kill you!'

Bosede lifted me clean off the ground. My legs kicked the air as he carried me away. My mouth was open but I wasn't shouting – I was roaring. Wild, animal noises stampeded from my throat. The beasts of loss and sorrow had been freed.

Bosede held me tightly so I couldn't breathe. 'Easy now, easy! You've won. You can calm yourself.'

But I couldn't. Beating Charlie had been like beating everything that had ever hurt me. And in that very moment I knew that Anger and Violence were my new friends. My protectors. My guides to survive and to prosper.

DERBYSHIRE, MARCH 1886

Michael Brannigan's eyes had closed several times during my recollections of Bosede and the Connor brothers, but every time I stopped, one lid would flicker open and his frail hand or hoarse voice would urge me to continue.

Finally, I was certain that he was asleep, for he was snoring and his chest rattled with every exhalation of breath. I pulled the bed sheets up and over his big arms then crept out of the bedroom.

The old wrestler's rapid decline had a visibly saddening effect on everyone in the house but in particular on the professor. His mood blackened by the week, and after each examination by Brannigan's doctor, Moriarty would withdraw for several hours. One night, after such a call, he took me to one side and insisted I walk with him to a wing of the house that I had not previously seen.

'I am touched by the peace you have made with Michael,' he said. 'It shows you have learned both humility and respect. It pleases me that he speaks fondly of you.'

'He need not have been so generous with his words.'

'No, indeed he did not, but he has been. Sadly, Dr Reuss tells me he is nearing the end.'

'I am truly sorry to hear that.'

'It may only be days now. The practitioner says a lesser man would have passed months ago.'

'Mr Brannigan is no lesser man; he is a natural fighter.'

'He is, but this is an unfair battle and one he cannot win. Which means it is imperative that you are properly prepared to fill his place.'

'I will do my best.'

'And I must ensure that your best is good enough.' He unlocked a dark oak door and we entered a cold room that smelled of strange chemicals and a burned-out fire.

Candles flickered. Wooden boards bowed and creaked beneath our feet. My eyes adjusted to the low light and it seemed at first that I had entered a private museum. A most macabre one, for on a series of small, circular tables, I saw more than a dozen severed heads. The skulls had been boiled free of flesh and rendered off-white by some chemical treatment.

'They are real,' Moriarty remarked, mildly amused by the shock on my face. 'I have them for academic reasons. I harbour an interest in phrenology; do you know what that is?'

'Collecting heads?'

He laughed. 'No, it is the study of the brain. The brain and the craters of the cranium that control thought and emotion.' He pointed past me. 'There is a fine skull to your left. That one came from the medical school in Edinburgh.'

I focused on a large head, ivory white with black holes where a nose, mouth, ears and pupils had once been.

'Close your eyes and run your hands slowly over the top of it.'

I hesitated.

'Go on. It cannot bite you.'

I shut my lids and reluctantly rested my hand on the skull.

'Do you feel the indentations, the edges that signify the end of one section of the mind and the beginning of another?'

At first, everything felt uniformly smooth. Then I discerned distinctive peaks and troughs, ridges and bumps. 'Yes,' I confessed. 'I feel what you mean. It's like running through a field of grass. It looks flat but then your feet find it's really uneven.'

'You are correct. And your simile is actually most apposite, because the brain is simply a collection of fields, each one responsible for a different activity. Open your eyes and look.'

I took off my hand and did as he asked. Areas of the skull had been marked in pen and labelled CONCEN-TRATIVENESS, SECRETIVENESS, CONSTRUCTIVENESS, SELF-ESTEEM, CAUSALITY and CAUTIOUSNESS.

Moriarty walked over and put his hand on the skull. 'It is all obvious, really. The human skull fits over the brain, like a glove fits over a hand. If you saw a glove you'd be able to identify the fingers, thumbs, palms and knuckles and describe in full their functions – writing, feeling, carrying, punching, stroking, et cetera. Look at the skull as a cranial glove and it is the same. We can identify feelings, fears, hopes and dreams and mark them down as easily as we could a finger or thumb.'

It seemed to make sense. Certainly all those thoughts and powers had to be kept somewhere and I supposed it was the work of smart men like the professor to determine *where*.

'Hippocrates started phrenology. Then it was continued by the Romans and most latterly the American publisher and lecturer Lorenzo Fowler, with whom I have had some discussions about starting a British Phrenological Society.'

He rounded an exhibit in front of us and placed his hands on another to his right. 'This is the head of John Bellingham. I had it stolen from Barts Pathology Museum and replaced with that of a lesser mortal.' He caressed the cranium. 'Do you know who Bellingham was?'

'I am afraid I do not.'

'He assassinated Prime Minister Spencer Perceval. Shot him in the heart because Perceval had introduced governmental policy that Bellingham said ruined him. Feel his skull, Simeon. Feel it with one hand while you compare your own. Tell me if you discern certain similarities.'

I had no desire to do so and simply stared at the skull.

'Do it!' barked Moriarty.

Reluctantly, I stretched out one hand and placed the

other on my own head. My eyes were magnetised by Moriarty's stare.

'Well?' he said. 'Is there anything?'

'I don't know. I can't really tell.'

'Try harder.'

'Maybe a bump? A ridge?' I speculated, desperate to please him.

'Where?'

'Here?' I fingered a vague point above my right ear.

His eyes glowed with excitement. 'That convex area above the ear is responsible for our dynamic energy. It is the source of fighting spirit, revenge and even violence. It is what we phrenologists call the Well of Destructiveness; it is from here that we draw our rage and anger.'

I put both my hands to my head and felt the swell in the bone. 'What does all that mean, for me?'

'For you? It means everything, Simeon. It means that, like Bellingham, you were born to kill. But let's hope you avoid his fate – he was captured and hanged.'

I must have looked shaken by his comments, for he added, 'Do not worry. Bellingham did not have *me* or any other members of the Trinity to protect him.'

'All these heads,' I said, keen to move away from observations about me, 'have they also come from museums and medical schools?'

He laughed. 'No, only those two.'

'And all the others?'

'They are the heads of my enemies.' His eyes lingered

201

on them with malicious nostalgia, before he added, 'This is my trophy room and my laboratory. I have here, at my fingertips, the skulls of politicians, policemen, judges and members of every major criminal family in the country.'

He passed from skull to skull and touched each one like a wine merchant might fondly caress bottles of valuable vintages. 'I also have heads from palmers, nobblers, duffers, snoozers, cracksmen, macers and broadsmen. Every type of lowly felon you could imagine. From phrenology, I know what makes the broadsman a good card sharp, the macer an excellent cheat and the nobbler such a violent punisher of men.'

I noticed all the skulls were unnamed and not even identified by numbers or codes. 'There are so many – how do you know which head is which?'

'Oh, I know them all. Know them intimately. I need no records or *aide memoires*. I remember each and every head, as it was when it was full of flesh and hair, when brains pulsed beneath these foolish foreheads and plotted against me. I even remember the foul words spoken by many of these gaping, silent mouths.'

He turned slowly. 'They were monsters who preyed on society and when my path crossed theirs they threatened me or my family to such a degree that they had to die.'

I counted more than thirty heads in the room. Thirty lives taken. 'Is this everyone you have had killed?'

'Good Lord, no. These are only the ones that mattered. The instigators. The leaders. The truly troublesome.'

'Why are you showing me these things, telling me about all this?'

He put a hand on my shoulder. 'So you understand me. What my life is about and the cause that drives us all.'

'Cause?'

'Every life must have direction. Purpose. I spoke some time ago to Mr Herbert Spencer, a man from these Derbyshire hills and a great biologist. Like Mr Charles Darwin and myself, Herbert is fascinated by the evolution of mankind and I proposed to him my theory that life is about "the survival of the fittest". He was quite taken by the phrase. I saw all expression on his face freeze at the thought. To survive, Simeon, we must eliminate our enemies, especially the most evil of them.'

Moriarty walked towards the door, where one skull stood alone against a wall. 'That specimen was from a particularly evil strain of mankind. It was harvested very recently by the talented Miss Breed. By the time the whole strain is wiped out, that entire wall will be filled with plinths and specimens.'

He slapped his hand on the middle of the skull bone and a smile lit up his face. 'Come now. We are late for dinner.'

'Whose head is it?' I asked as we left the room.

'Not the one I truly wish for,' he said as he closed the door and put his arm around my shoulders. 'In time, I will tell you more, Simeon, much more. But not now. The duration of such a revelation would ruin what I hope is a very good meal.'

EIGHT DAYS TO EXECUTION

I know not how the days in gaol passed so quickly, only that they were gone.

One hundred and ninety-two hours. This was the sum of time I had left upon God's earth. Holmes was being proved right; each passing second brought me closer to insanity. I had scraped every bar and brick with that damned nail and had not loosened anything except my mind.

Was escape still possible? It had to be. One of these ancient bricks would loosen. One of those idiot young turnkeys would make a mistake. My chance would come; I just had to remain vigilant.

Noises gathered outside my cell. Perhaps this was the moment. Keys jangled, bolts slid, locks turned and the door creaked open.

A rakish turnkey with a grey beard stood in the entrance. His eyes checked my chains. Satisfied himself that I was not a danger before he even spoke. 'Time to get you weighed and measured. The 'angman, Mr Warbrick, wants to know your details, so he can prepare good an' proper.'

'You mean Billington?'

'Warbrick. Billington has stepped aside, so his friend can have you.' Greybeard slapped a baton in the palm of his hand while two other screws fitted walking chains to me.

'Most generous of him,' I said. 'Who would have thought hangmen had hearts?'

'He's safe,' declared a younger one, pulling at my links then standing clear.

'Then get 'im movin'.'

They marched me to a room near the kitchens. Jostled me onto a cast-iron beam-scale that more regularly measured sacks of food sent from the merchants.

'We got ourselves a meaty one, here,' said a pimply young screw, as he gripped my biceps and held me still.

'Meat to be tightly strung,' quipped another, 'like brisket or pork.'

'Get on with it,' demanded their master.

His minions struggled to select the correct weights that would determine my measure.

'Sort yourselves out!' demanded Greybeard. He looked to me and added, 'An' you, stand still. Mr Warbrick says he needs precise measurements so he can despatch you humanely, so don't you move none.'

'Twelve stones, nine pounds and three ounces,' announced a third man.

''appen the executioner doesn't want you *'anging around* unnecessarily,' added Pimples.

Once they had their measure, I was bundled back to the cell and pushed to the floor. My arms were yanked high behind my back while they undid the walking chains and secured me again to the cold iron ring sunk in the stone.

Greybeard stayed just out of my reach, staring at me. 'I

know what you done, Lynch. Who you killed.' He spat on the ground. 'I hope your visit to the scales has got you thinkin' what it'll be like.' He put a hand to his throat. 'The jerk of the rope. Your body fallin' like a sack of rocks. You swingin' an' stranglin', while your legs dance, an' your rotten 'eart jumps clean out its ribcage.' He stepped back into the doorway. 'Think on it now, Lynch.'

He was about to shut the door when Huntley appeared over his shoulder.

'Move aside, man. I need to talk to the prisoner.'

Greybeard looked startled and stepped into the corridor.

'Close the door.'

The turnkey hesitated then did as instructed.

Huntley looked to me. 'Unpleasant fellow. I hope he didn't behave in an unchristian way?'

'Unchristian?' I smiled. 'That fellow would have sold tickets to the crucifixion. He's the type that thinks executions are entertainment.'

'I don't believe the taking of *any* life to be correct. Either by a criminal such as yourself or for that matter by the Crown.'

'A radical view.'

'I like to think of myself as a reformer, not a radical. Though when I look at the penal system I see precious little evidence of reformation.'

'Perhaps in time you will. I hear that, thanks to the reformists, Tyburn Tree is now a place of free speech. All kinds of imbeciles assemble there and spout whatever non-sense has been brewing in their brains.'

'That much is true. Speaker's Corner lies close to the old Tree. Though talking treason will still get you stretched.'

'And rightly so.'

I considered taking him prisoner. He was a young and able man but no match for me. Michael Brannigan had taught me a dozen ways to incapacitate a fellow like him. I could do it easily. Grab the nail from its resting place and hold it to his throat. But then what?

'I have been asked by your lawyer,' said Huntley, 'to assure you that he has been doing all he can from a legal perspective.'

I glanced at the window. 'There is more chance of me escaping through those bars than Levine walking me out of here as a free man. And both you and I know there is no chance of that.'

'Not any more, but there have been escapes. You've heard of Jack Sheppard?'

'A figure of folk stories and exaggerations.'

'Undeniably, but he was also a real person and many of the tales are true. Sheppard was a burglar, the best in London many said, and he did escape from here, twice.'

'*Twice?*'

'Once through a barred window like yours and once up a chimney.' He raised an eyebrow. 'He even helped his lover escape.'

'And how did he do that?'

207

'He cut through the window bars, dangled a sheet over the outer wall and helped her down.'

'And they both got clean away?'

'They did, but Sheppard was recaptured and hanged.'

'A good story with a bad ending.'

'Most stories of the condemned are.' Huntley must have feared his quip depressed me, for he added, 'But I do understand that Mr Theodore Levine is quite one of the finest legal minds in the city. If there are grounds for appeal, I am certain he will find them. Or invent them.'

'I will try to draw comfort from that remark.'

'I have arranged exercise for you. My men will come shortly and take you to the yard. The day is cold but clear. Some fresh air will do you good.'

I was about to thank him when keys turned in the lock.

The door opened and Johncock stormed in, followed as usual by several of his men.

'Mr Huntley, I am informed you have arranged for Lynch to be given access to the yard – is that right?'

'It is, sir.'

'I have cancelled the order.'

'With respect, sir, I have full authority when it comes to the welfare of this inmate. He is entitled to exercise and—'

'Fuck your "authority", Newgate is my gaol.' Johncock slapped a hand on Huntley's chest and pushed him back a pace. 'Outside, Mr Huntley. You and I need to have a private word.'

They exited, followed by Johncock's cronies and through the viciously slammed door, I briefly heard shouting.

Silence followed.

Silence that stretched from seconds to minutes and then hours.

Apparently, I wasn't to be exercised after all.

More importantly, Mr Huntley's star was no longer in the ascendency and Johncock was once more master of what was left of my life.

DERBYSHIRE, APRIL 1886

I took a morning off from sitting with Brannigan and spent it running errands for the professor.

Firstly, I delivered a handsome amount of money to a judge staying at Tissington Hall, a fine Jacobean mansion located only a few miles away from Moriarty's abode, then picked up a hefty envelope of documents from a senior police officer in Matlock Bath.

Thackeray, the coachman who had taken me on the deceptive mission to 'steal' the King John tiara from Lord Graftbury's estate, drove me hither and thither. It made an agreeable change to ride up on the box with him, and he delighted in pointing out homes and areas of note, including businesses established to charge people to bathe in the county's natural waters. 'They's mad in the 'ead, they is,' he proclaimed in his gruff Lancashire accent. 'Pays good money to drink rain and an' sit in it till their knackers freeze off. Pays even more for the same bleedin' water to be 'eated in baths so theys can *steam themselves*. Who knows wot the world's comin' to.'

I thought back to the squalor I had endured as a child. 'There are times when I would have gladly paid for a hot bath.'

He was not deterred by my interruption. 'I reckons all the water round 'ere's what gived the professor ideas for them baths back at the big 'ouse. More money than sense, the lot of 'em. Even our prof.'

When we got back, I helped Thackeray rub down the horses and put away the carriage in the big barn where all the vehicles were kept – broughams, landaus and all manner of char-a-bancs, curricles, floats and gigs.

He ran a hand lovingly over the black lacquer of a nearby vehicle. 'A curricle like this is light 'n' fast. But it leaves you out on show. Draws eyes from all round. So, when you is wantin' to go *in-cog-nito* as Mr Gunn calls it, this old beaut' is your best bet.' He slapped his hand on the back of the most familiar type of carriage in the country.

'It's a Hackney, isn't it?'

'An, 'ackney, indeed.'

'I grew up in London and saw plenty of them.'

'I bet you did. There's more than four thousand 'ackneys down there. But none like this. We rebuilt 'er. Made 'er lighter. Lowered an' stiffened the suspension. Now she's easy for two good animals to pull, fast an' nimble.'

He was about to go into greater detail, when we were interrupted by Jane, the young maid who had taken me to the bathhouse after my first encounter with Brannigan.

'Hello!' she shouted from the doorway. 'Is anyone in there?'

'Thackeray's 'ere – wot d'you want?'

She headed towards us. 'Is Mr Lynch with you?'

'Yes. I am here.' I came out from behind the Hackney.

'I've come from Mr Brannigan, sir. He's been asking for you.'

I was distressed to hear of this. 'I told him last night that I was going on some errands this morning.'

'I only know that he's asking, sir. Shoutin' your name every time he can get a breath.'

'I'll come straight away.' Even though Brannigan had plainly forgotten what I'd told him, I felt guilty about not having been there for him.

I followed Jane across the courtyard. She left me at a side door and went to the kitchen, while I made my own way to Brannigan's bedroom.

His curtains were closed but the sun was at its brightest and a warm lemony light forced its way over the rails and around the edges of the fabric.

Michael was propped up on a pillow. His eyes were half-shut and there was a terrible rattling in his breathing. The suggestion of a smile came to his dried lips when he saw me and he lifted a hand from his bed. 'Some water.' He had not the strength to add a 'please'.

'Of course.' I hurried to a rough wooden table set against a wall and from a large pitcher poured him a glass. I returned to the bed and held it out for him. His hand came up again but not high enough to take the glass. I put it to his lips and gently tilted it so he could drink. He shut his mouth when he had had enough. I put the drink down on a table by the bed. 'Tell me if you'd like some more.'

'Pipe,' he answered, feebly.

'No.' I smiled at him. 'You know what Dr Reuss said. No smoking. It's not good for you.'

'Fuck him!' He took a breath. 'Pipe. A *last* smoke, Simeon.'

It hurt me to hear him say that. It was as though he was dying this very minute. Maybe I'd read too much into it.

'Pipe,' he pleaded.

I looked across the room. Many of his belongings were on a shelf, along with a photograph of him as a young wrestler. I brought his tobacco pouch, matches and pipe. It was a vintage piece made of clay, the bowl engraved with Romany caravans and horses.

Michael was incapable of putting together the smoke, so I tapped the bowl on the bedside table, took a pinch of leaves from the pouch and packed the pipe. I lit it and raised smoke before holding it to his lips.

The old wrestler struggled to draw down the tobacco. His lungs fought back and forced him to cough. It made his chest tighten. His face corrugated with pain.

I pulled the stem from his lips. His eyes looked at me

accusingly and I let him try again. This time he did better. Took short draws, held down the smoke until his body surrendered to the fumes.

Several silent minutes passed – me holding the pipe to his mouth, him lying back, his throat rasping from poisonous inhalation and painful expiration. I had no idea what thoughts passed through his mind, but I was recalling our first fight. How comprehensively he had defeated me. This dying man seemed an entirely different person.

The lips stopped sucking. The rasping ceased. For a split second, I saw a hint of contentment in his eyes.

'Are you finished?'

Slowly, he tilted his head my way. 'Finished. Yes, *I am finished*.'

I took the pipe and placed it on the table by his bed. Went to pull the top sheet up over his arms.

He grabbed my wrist. 'Simeon.'

'What?'

His eyes looked pained again. 'Please, help me.'

I smiled. 'I am not getting you whisky, so don't be asking me to—'

'End me.'

I took my hands off the sheet. 'What did you say?'

'Finish me off, lad.'

The remark made me shudder. 'You're talking nonsense.' I pulled up the white sheet.

He pushed it down again. '*Please.*' Another cough rose, scratching its way up from his lungs and watering his eyes.

I reached over and passed him a bowl to spit into. Brannigan spattered it with black and bloody phlegm then fell back to his pillow, exhausted.

I put the bowl down and listened to him wheeze. The breathing seemed to rattle every bone in his wasted frame.

His face twisted again in pain. Then there was a smell. An awful stench. He had fouled himself.

I looked at him and he stared back into my eyes and then away in shame.

'Don't worry. I'll get a maid and we will clean you up. Make you comfortable again.'

His head turned my way. 'For God's sake, save me from this.'

He was crying. The most powerful person I had ever fought was in tears.

I felt myself well up. Felt all his shame and hopelessness. 'Shall I call the professor? Dr Reuss?'

His hand searched for mine. I took his fingers, squeezed them, gave him courage. 'The doctor will give you opium. He'll be able to—'

'*Do it!*' he pleaded. 'Do it now.'

I felt his hand tighten around mine. My heart jumped in fear. I glanced to the open door, hoping someone would come in and break this moment.

He coughed again. Retched over the sheet beneath his chin.

I pulled away and walked to the door, shut it and slowly walked back. I tried not to look at him. My left hand covered his mouth. My right pinched his nose before he could take a breath.

Michael grabbed at my left arm with both hands, and I thought he was going to fight me. But he didn't. His demeanour was of someone lost, not frightened.

I began to pull my hand from his mouth, but he kept it there and shut his eyes. I held on and pushed down, pinched more tightly. Michael's legs kicked. His back arched. Knees raised. Heels scuffed at the sheets.

Then the kicking stopped and his hands fell from my arm. There was a final awful rattling in his chest but I kept my hand across his mouth, still held his nose. Made sure it was done.

Then I just stood there and stared. Listened for the silence. Watched for the lack of movement. Birds called in the trees outside his window. Floorboards creaked beyond his room.

The door opened noisily and startled me. Surrey held onto the handle as she entered. 'My goodness,' she said, making light of the smell, 'has someone—'

She saw Michael and her eyes found mine, questioningly.

I confirmed her thoughts. 'He's dead.'

She let go of the door and rushed to him. Put her fingers to his neck, feeling for a pulse – something I hadn't thought of doing. Then she looked up at me.

'Did you find him like this?'

I didn't answer. Didn't know what to say or how to behave.

She looked at Michael again. Saw how the sheets had

been soiled and kicked up, how his spitting bowl had been knocked over. She touched the warm pipe on the table.

Surrey stepped away from the bed and put her hands on my arms. 'Are you all right?'

I couldn't speak.

She put a finger across my lips. 'You found him like this. You came in and found him like this. Didn't you?'

I nodded.

She embraced me. Held me tight for a moment. It was good that she was here. That she understood.

'Go downstairs,' she said. 'Find the professor and tell him Michael has passed. That I am with him and I need some assistance. He will take care of everything.'

I turned to leave.

'Simeon,' she called.

I turned.

'I know this is what Michael wanted. He had asked me to . . . ' her eyes filled with tears, 'to *help* him . . . but I couldn't.'

EIGHT DAYS TO EXECUTION

NEWGATE, 10 JANUARY 1900

It was Johncock who next opened my cell door. His lackeys closed it after him and stood by the lock as he advanced on me. 'Get up off your bunk, Lynch.' His face was still reddened from his earlier anger at Huntley.

I rose with my customary slowness.

He stood so close to me, his boots touched the ends of my toes. My heels were backed against the bunk. I could see nothing but his eyes and the triumph that burned there.

'If you think toads like 'untley can disrupt my gaol and make life soft for you, then you are mistaken. Newgate is *mine*. What 'appens 'ere is down to me. Me! Not the blessed keeper and 'is committees. Not this wretched government of no-good do-gooders. And certainly not Mr 'arrison Fucking 'untley.' His rage caused him to pant for breath before he added, 'Do you understand me, Lynch? *Do you?* You murderous piece of shit, DO YOU UNDERSTAND?'

He shouted so loud that my eardrums buzzed like a thousand bees inside a clouted hive.

I didn't shout back at him. To the contrary, I whispered, 'I think the whole gaol heard you, Mr Johncock. Most of London, too.'

He stepped back a stride, and told his men. 'I'm finished with 'im.'

A crony banged on the door for it to be opened.

Johncock jabbed a finger at me. 'Huntley doesn't really care, you fool. He doesn't give a damn about you or your so-called *welfare*. Not one jot. This is all about 'im. What's good for 'im and 'is career, that's all. You're just a pawn in 'is game.'

He walked over to his men. 'The prisoner wants exercise, so give it 'im. Make this monster walk until 'e falls to 'is knees and begs to crawl back into this cell as though it's a palace.'

DERBYSHIRE, APRIL 1886

Sick to the pit of my stomach, I carried my grief down the grand staircase to the main hall, where the enormity of my actions sank in and overwhelmed me. I'd grown closer to Michael than I'd realised. He'd won me over. Shaped me. Influenced me. Now, I had ended his life.

In a daze, I wandered the corridors until I came to Moriarty's study. To my relief, I heard him in conversation with Cornwell, the butler, a man I knew was certain to take charge.

I knocked and opened the door.

They looked surprised to see me.

'Mr Brannigan has passed away,' I said from the doorway.

Moriarty's face creased up in pain.

I stepped closer and knew I had to lie about what had happened. 'Sir, I had been called in to see him by one of the maids, and I am afraid he was gone by the time I arrived. Surrey, Miss Breed, is with him now.'

The professor's head slumped to his chest.

'I will attend to him, sir,' said Cornwell. 'Once I have ensured that we have done what needs to be done then I

shall come back to you and see if you wish to visit him.'
Without another word he left and set about his duties.

I stayed, expecting Moriarty to ask questions. Awkward
questions that might force me to confess my lie. But the
professor's head remained sunk in his hands. A full minute
passed before he looked up. His eyes were glassy and grief
had already corrugated his brow. 'Leave me now, please,
Simeon. I would like to be alone with my thoughts and you
are a distraction to me.'

'As you wish, sir.' I nodded respectfully and left.

Once I shut his door, I found myself stranded. I could
not return to the bedroom. Could not simply walk in there
and innocently 'help out' in the aftermath of the murder I
had committed.

I found my way into the garden and sought sanctuary
in the maze. Here I had privacy. A place to hide from the
snarling dogs of anger, loss and shame that were snapping
at my heels.

With trembling hands I lit a cigarette and tried to justify
what I had done. It had been what he wanted. I told myself
this a hundred times. I had only done what he had wanted.

As I walked back, I realised I would never walk the gardens again with my old mentor, never feel the grip of his
coarse, crocodile-skin hands as he trained me. Nor see that
grudging smile he always gave me at the end of a tough
workout – his gesture of approval. One that had helped form
a brief but strangely meaningful friendship between us.

The house had become eerily silent during my brief

absence. All clocks had been stopped to mark the moment of Michael's passing. Male servants had begun to wash the body. Maids had already changed bed sheets and opened windows to air the room. Moriarty's groom stood ready to dress the old wrestler in his one good suit and a photographer had been sent for.

For the next two hours, Sirius and Cornwell orchestrated the movement of the corpse around the house and grounds so that it might be photographed in memorable poses with all manner of acquaintances. I was even required to pose with him by the ring. I confess that holding Michael's cold flesh close to me was a distasteful experience and I am sure it made for quite terrible pictures.

A wreath of laurel with black crepe ribbons was hung on the front door and not until nightfall were the gentlemen of Lymms the Undertaker allowed to take possession of his body and make all the necessary preparations for the burial.

A downstairs room at the rear of the house was prepared for visits and festooned with sweet-smelling candles to mask whatever odours might be given off. Mourning cards were rushed to Ireland where there were many Brannigan cousins, nephews and nieces. During all this, Moriarty barely spoke to any of us. He gathered his heavy grief and, along with a large bottle of whisky, retreated to his study.

I was about to ascend the stairs and retire to bed when Sirius called from behind me.

'What do you want?' My temper instantly boiled. 'I warn you, I am in no mood to be aggravated.'

'I wish no such thing. To the contrary.' He walked up to me, then added, 'I simply wanted to say that I thought it was a fine thing that you did today. An honourable thing.'

I was surprised by his comment. 'I don't know what you mean.'

'I know you do. We all do.'

I felt a flush of terror.

'Do not worry. No one disapproves.' He extended his hand. 'I wanted to say thank you. Michael was close to me. To us all. And none of us were able to do what you did.'

I shook his hand but still made no admission.

'We will never talk of it,' said Sirius, 'but we are all grateful for what you did.' He tipped his hat. 'Goodnight to you.'

'And to you.'

I climbed the stairs and realised that I had probably misjudged Sirius. Deep down, it seemed he did care for someone other than himself.

EIGHT DAYS TO EXECUTION

NEWGATE, 10 JANUARY 1900

The stink of the prison even permeated the Press Yard, where supposedly we prisoners benefited from a dose of good old fresh air.

'Get moving, Lynch,' demanded one of Johncock's men, before adding a hearty shove that sent me staggering in my chains.

I regained my balance and greedily surveyed the new landscape. There was only one door, locked and guarded on both sides. That meant the gaolers realised this spot was vulnerable. Escape was possible, but difficult. My heart skipped a beat in excitement.

'Walk!'

I shuffled my feet as my eyes continued to roam. The yard's outer walls were very high and sheer. I spotted no easy hand or footholds to begin a climb and even if I were unchained, the screws would be on me before I could scale a fraction of them.

'Walk, I said!' A turnkey cracked my back with a baton.

I lurched forward and began a ponderous loop of the small exercise area. Half a dozen other men were walking in pairs, clockwise. I took the other direction. Not because I wanted to register some pointless individuality but because I wanted to face them. Years of murdering and hurting people teaches you not to allow six hardened criminals free access to your back.

The first two convicts were more boys than men – skinny teenagers who looked as though they should have been starting apprenticeships, not gaol terms. Behind them lumbered two men of my age. Their heads were bent in conversation, their hot breath frosting in the crisp air as they trudged. Bringing up the rear were two old-timers.

They lagged a good six yards behind the others and didn't speak or look up.

As the prisoners passed me our eyes briefly met. The young boys looked away, partly in shame at their own wasted lives and partly out of respect for an older, more hardened felon. Respect was everything in gaol. Show it and you were left alone. Deny it and you could end up dead.

The next two men held my gaze a little and weighed me up as they passed. I guessed in that fleeting moment they came to recognise me and remember what I had done.

Finally, the old men stepped up. Neither gave me a glance, nor broke their stride. Their minds were elsewhere – most probably reliving the past, remembering old loves, nights of ale and pockets of cash. I was beyond their cares. Like me, they were just counting down their final days and taking some comfort from memories.

Lap by lap, I built up a picture of the yard and committed it to memory. If any part could be climbed, it would be the corner furthest from the gate, but I would have to unchain myself and be fast across the ground before the screws came for me.

The nail might afford me that break. If I could learn to use it to pick the manacle locks quickly, perhaps fooling the gaolers by pretending to fall, then I might have a chance of fighting them off and hitting that wall with enough power to leap up and grab at something.

I knew it was a desperate plan, but surely desperation was the platform for every escape from incarceration.

Johncock's men followed his orders assiduously. They gave me no rest. Walked me to the point of exhaustion and beyond. I distracted myself by remembering and imagining the earliest days of my life, right back to my birth in 1864. As Moriarty had mentioned when we first met, I had been born in a tavern of ill repute to a woman of even lower standing. Apparently, I appeared in her pooling blood and presented to a room full of drunkards the dilemma of whose life to save.

The jury of inebriates chose badly. They saved *me*. And in so doing they sentenced my birth mother to death. After which, the enterprising landlord of that thief-infested flash house arranged, in return for several pounds and a basket of goods, to have me delivered into the care of Cyril and Philomena Lynch, an ageing baker and his childless young wife.

Along with their good name, they gave me the comforts of the tiny lodgings attached to the bakery and shop that they ran. Theirs was a home of little money but abundant love. They raised me the best they could. Philomena taught me to read and write, to experience what she called 'the miracles of language and words'.

Cyril showed me how young boys should behave in order to become good men. How to demonstrate respect and earn it back. 'Manners maketh the man,' he used to impress upon me. Had his bakery done better, then undoubtedly he and Philomena would have raised me as well as they did their wholesome breads and cakes. But it was not to be.

When I was eight years old, the man I had grown to call father worked himself to death during the London Season. While the society debutantes and moneyed politicians flirted and dined upon his produce, my mother wept her eyes red and buried him in a pauper's grave.

Less than a week later, his creditors came knocking. The lease was surrendered, hired equipment returned and all stock sold. Still she could not make the frayed ends of our lives meet.

We were for the workhouse. And in truth, once the tears had been dried, we knew we were lucky to be so destined. Had father not been a friend of Mr Potts, the harness maker, and had he not been a cousin of Mr Flanders, treasurer on the board of governors, then our beds would have been the cobbles of an alley and the roof over our heads nothing more than the sulphurous skies of London.

Within moments of stepping into the dark entrance of that awful place we were separated. Still in her black widow's cap, she was taken to the women's ward, while I was clipped around the ear and hurried to the children's house.

We had each taken with us one of her smaller shades, removed from their rough wooden frames but kept close to our hearts. Mine was that of a beautiful lady, hers that of a well-groomed young boy. It comforted me to know that in her bunk at night she would kiss her picture and I would kiss mine. There and then, at least in our hearts and minds, we were together.

Every day, my young hands were bloodied by picking

clean threads from tarred sailing rope, breaking stones in the yard or, when the stench of the privies got too much, washing down walls with chemicals and vinegar.

Work was a distraction from the pain of separation but it was also exhausting. Frequently, I was beaten for leaving my bed and trying to make my way to her. The slash of the cane left raw scars on my flesh, but still my aching spirit would drag me down those forbidden corridors. One touch of my mother's hand was worth a dozen lashes of that cane.

When my daily labours were over I foolishly asked for books to read. This caused me to be mocked by masters and boys alike. When I complained about pain or hunger, I was beaten into silence. In time, I learned that it is the nature of boys to find someone weak to bully so that they themselves might appear stronger.

So lost was I in my thoughts of my upbringing that I meandered off my circuit in the prison yard and bumped into the two young men circling in the other direction.

'Lynch!' One of the screws shouted out as we collectively collapsed on account of our tiredness and the restriction of the leg irons.

Other turnkeys, fearing some fight had broken out, rushed across the yard and halted the progress of the other circling men.

As I got to my knees, I saw that the teenager had fallen flat on his face and cut his eye. Blood seeped through the fingers of the hand he put protectively to his face.

A screw pulled me away and pinned me to the Press Yard wall while they tended the injured inmate. The young man who had been walking with him shouted to me, 'You stupid bastard, you've nearly 'ad his eye out.'

It was his brother. I saw it now. They were twins, but not identical. The shouter was a little thinner, taller, more angular in the face. But they were twins.

The screws got the man to his feet and, with head bent and blood still dripping, they escorted him out of the yard.

The other prisoners were moved out with him and I was left alone. The gaoler at my side gave me a push. 'Off you go again, Lynch. You've had rest enough.'

I was cold and welcomed the chance to walk a little. The yard reminded me of the one at the workhouse where, whatever the weather, we children were turned out 'for fresh air' and often returned so frozen that our bones would ache and our fingers and toes burn from chilblains.

One such day, I had been keeping a safe distance from the Connor twins when the workhouse matron, a rotund, red-faced woman with a thick Irish accent came for me.

'So this is where y'ave bin 'idin',' she'd said with great annoyance. 'Oi've been walkin' me feet off looking far ya.' She grabbed my arm and marched me into a building I had never been in before. It was dimly lit and full of strange smells and noises. Through the gloom, I spied rows upon rows of single beds. Flames flickered in two soot-stained fireplaces but the spitting heat was insufficient to warm anyone more than a few feet away.

The beds were jammed tighter than East End terraces, each cot occupied by a crumpled figure either sleeping or moaning.

'Why are we here?' I asked fearfully.

Matron didn't answer. Her grip on my wrist tightened. She pulled me past bed after bed. At the far corner, she stopped in front of a drawn curtain. 'Prepare yourself, child. It is time for you to be a man.' She pulled back the dusty drape.

My eyes fell on a creature so pale and still that I did not at first recognise her.

'*Mother!*'

She was unnervingly white and utterly emaciated. A raw red graze glistened on her left temple. Streaks of wiped blood crusted her beautiful cheeks. There were pennies on her eyes – cold brown metal where there had once been blue as bright as a summer sky.

'Take them off!' I shouted and made for the bed. 'Wake her up. Take those *things* off her eyes.'

Matron grabbed me. Pulled me back. 'She's dead, child. Behave yerself an' accept what's 'appened. She's dead 'n' gone.'

'Lynch!'

The voice came from the present, not the past.

'Get walkin' again, or you'll be gettin' a beatin'!' A screw had his yardstick raised and in line with the centre of my skull.

Only as I looked up at him did I realise I had stopped

moving and had been cowering in a corner of the yard. Memories had stranded me there, left me childlike. Small and frightened. Afraid of what the motherless future held.

DERBYSHIRE, APRIL 1886

The three days that followed Michael's death were lost in sombre preparations for what the professor vowed would be 'a funeral fit to grace the Père Lachaise cemetery in Paris'. I had to wait until the morning of the fourth day to understand what he meant.

Thackeray arrived with the hearse and six black horses, followed by two velvet-lined mourning coaches drawn by four immaculately groomed animals. The sun glinted off the polished wood and brass of the carriages and enriched the myriad colours shimmering in the ostrich feathers that had been fixed high and proud.

The coffin itself was of solid oak and bore gleaming brass handles and a plate with the inscription 'Never Beaten by Mortal Man'. Six pall-bearers shouldered the box from house to hearse, accompanied by two black-gowned mutes, twenty pages and six feathermen.

The chief funeral attendant signalled to the coachmen and with a collective groan from the idling horses the grand procession began.

No one spoke. The clop of hooves on cobbles was all that could be heard as I walked at the front, along with the professor, Sirius, Surrey and Lady Elizabeth. Three of Michael's cousins, each as broad and burly as him, had journeyed from Dublin and Cork, and with them were two young nieces, not yet ten years old. Both of the girls constantly shivered from the cold, a lack of sleep and what I imagine was a fear engendered by the horrors of the day.

The route was hilly and circular, passing through the small village of stone cottages where most inhabitants had the common sense to turn out and pay their respects. After about a mile, the procession returned to the southern gates of the Moriarty estate, where the private chapel and grave-yard lay.

The startling white headstones and tombs contrasted with the black crepe and silk of the mourners with their long dresses, coats and tall hats, and set against the endless rolling green of the Derbyshire countryside made for a memorable and moving sight.

Once the casket had been lowered on ropes into the freshly dug grave, we all threw earth onto it and said our private goodbyes. As I dropped my handful of soil, I heard Michael's voice pleading with me to help him die and I struggled to block out the images of him fighting for breath beneath the clasp of my murderous hands.

I walked away, wondering how many people knew I had killed him. How many of them condemned me, or praised me for it.

Back at the house, there was a plentiful supply of ale

and cider. A lavish banquet that included ham, pork, beef, pies, cakes and cheeses was laid out in the ballroom, where Christmas functions and summer dances were held.

I ate and drank like this might have been my last night alive, and I was not alone in doing so. The house was filled with those who had known the old wrestler but had been parted over the years.

Among them I found Sebastian the Jew, who had given me shelter back in Manchester. He embraced me warmly and introduced me to others who performed similar roles for the professor. 'We are all lowly recruits in Moriarty's great army of criminality,' he boasted as he raised his tankard and knocked it drunkenly against mine.

Although the ale and wine continued to flow, I found that once we were alone, our conversation evaporated and my old acquaintance even had trouble holding eye contact with me. 'You don't seem relaxed in my company, Sebastian – why would that be?'

'I am sorry. It has been a difficult and emotional day.'

'For some more than others.'

'You have my sympathies.' He raised his tankard respectfully and sought more solace in its contents.

'Did you know Michael well?'

'Well enough.' He wiped ale from his moustache and beard. 'I was one of the few who were aware of what he did for the professor.'

I saw great nervousness on his face. 'I sense you have more to say, Sebastian. If that is the case then speak now, or I will remember this moment as the time you chose not to.'

He took another swig of his drink and wiped his beard again. 'Myself and some "chosen" others, *area lieutenants* as Moriarty calls us, knew of Mr Brannigan's illness and the professor's hunt for a replacement. He had alerted us to be on the lookout for you.'

I was thrown by the comment. 'What do you mean?'

His eyes showed a reluctance to continue.

'Tell me, what did you mean, "on the lookout"?'

'We were told there was a boy from London whom the professor considered *special*. He was said to be on the run following a murder. We were given your description and your name.'

'But when we first met, still you allowed me to call myself Terry and live a lie.'

'It was your lie to live.'

'Was it you who led the professor to me?'

'It was. I had no choice. After that, he had you watched most closely. Indeed, he and Alexander were in attendance during that country-house burglary we carried out. Sirius even rode with one of your drivers.'

The news that Moriarty had found me in such a fashion and had gone to far greater lengths to insinuate himself into my life than I had realised was disturbing.

'Simeon . . . '

I didn't let him continue. 'I thank you for your openness. Now I am sorry, I really have to be elsewhere.'

232

Sebastian caught my sleeve. 'If you ever need to come back, for whatever reason, I can hide you. You can trust me with your secrets.'

I shook him off. 'You make such an offer only because you fear me. You are not my friend, Sebastian, so don't pretend to be. You are just frightened I might turn on you because you gave me up to Moriarty.'

'No, Simeon, I—'

I did not listen to whatever lie he was constructing. Instead, I headed towards the door determined to take some air and shake off my rising anger. I never reached the doorway because Surrey came into view, demurely clad in a long black mourning dress, hat and pulled-back veil.

'So there you are!' she said with relief. 'I have been searching for you.'

'Am I really so elusive?'

'I hope so. Being difficult to find may save your life one day.' She put her arm through mine and forced a thin smile. 'You must come now; it is time.'

I knew what she alluded to. The thing that had been decided upon before I knew her or Moriarty, before even Sebastian knew of me.

I allowed Surrey to guide me to a small reception room in the east wing. The curtains were drawn and Alexander and Sirius stood at the far end of a large rosewood table. On it were variously sized surgical knives, a collection of bottles of coloured inks, several pads of cotton, a bowl of water, two white towels and some lengths of bandages.

'I shall wait outside.' Alex hobbled up to me and gripped my arm reassuringly. 'The professor has asked me to say he is proud of you. As you've seen, he is unfortunately tied up with other mourners, but he sends his best wishes and his thoughts are with you.'

'Thank you.'

He nodded. 'I will notify him the moment it is done. Good luck, Simeon.'

The three of us watched the door close after he exited. I heard the turn of a key in the lock and wondered whether this was to keep people out or keep me in.

'We do it the old-fashioned way,' announced Sirius. He picked up a small silver knife. 'A wound is opened and indelible ink rubbed into the incision to provide a permanent reminder of our mutual allegiance.' He put down the double-bladed instrument, took off his jacket and rolled up his sleeves. 'Where is it to be, Simeon? Bicep or shoulder? Forearm or ankle?'

I slipped my own jacket off. 'Across my heart.'

'Bravo!' He clapped sarcastically. 'Always tougher, braver and infinitely more foolish than those around you. So be it. Take off your shirt and lie on the table.'

I watched him select the coloured inks as I finished undressing, then I lifted myself up onto the table and lay down. The wood was cold on my back and the brightness of the great chandelier over my head forced me to close my eyes.

I heard both Sirius and Surrey talking. Felt their hands on my chest. The nip of hot steel cutting my warm flesh.

'Open your eyes,' said Sirius.

Surrey stared down at me. 'I hope you have learned the words the professor gave you, for you have to respond to this part.'

'I have.'

'Good.' She lifted a knife into view, cut her own finger and passed it to Sirius. He followed suit, then they jointly declared, 'We bleed for you, brother, as we hope you will bleed for us. In giving of our blood, we swear an oath of loyalty to you and to the Trinity, to all it stands for, even if such loyalty costs every drop of our blood and your blood. Do you so swear?'

It was time for my lines. 'I do so swear. And I swear that I will shed my blood without hesitation and without reservation for you, the Trinity and for all we stand for.'

They squeezed blood from their cuts and rubbed it into the droplet-shaped wound that Sirius had carved on my left breast. Surrey kept her finger there as she kissed my forehead and both my cheeks, then she stepped away.

Sirius did the same. He helped me upright. Embraced me. 'It is done, brother. You are to us in equal measure and dependency as we are to you. May God protect us all.'

Surrey held a pad of cotton to the raw tattoo and as my blood flowed I thought of that I would have to spill from the veins of other people. Would they all be as bad, as *evil* as Moriarty had assured me they would be? I knew that this could be more than a nagging doubt. It could be the ruin of me. The professor had spoken plainly enough. Kill or be killed. The survival of the fittest. I knew also that I was in too deep to ever get out.

Sirius left briefly, to tell Alex that the ceremony had been completed.

He returned with a decanter of whisky, poured us all a measure two fingers deep and raised his glass. 'To Michael Brannigan; may he have a hell of a time in heaven, or a heavenly time in hell.' We clinked our tumblers and downed our drinks.

Toast followed toast, and I buried those remaining doubts about my conviction to the cause – buried them so deep I barely remembered I had harboured them.

When the decanter was empty we left the room arm in arm. Amid the shedding of blood, swearing of oaths and downing of drinks the three of us had bonded. A new Trinity was forged and I truly felt closer to them than anyone else in the world.

Moriarty smiled at us from across the grand dining room and raised a glass of red wine in our honour.

'Goodnight, brother.' Sirius drunkenly embraced me before heading off after the professor.

'G'night!' I called after him. Then lost my footing on the first tread of the stairs.

'Oops!' said Surrey. 'Steady on there.' She slipped her left arm around my waist and moved my right arm over her shoulder. We giggled our way up the stairs and collapsed laughing on my bed. The drink had gone to my head and my world rocked like a bumped cradle.

Surrey took my hand and leaned over me. 'Can I sleep here tonight? I don't want to be alone. Not tonight.'

I made a noise. It wasn't a yes. Nor was it a no. It was a sigh.

Surrey extinguished the lamp. Moonlight shone through the window but my eyes had not yet adjusted. In the dark I heard the rustle of her falling dress and petticoats, her groans as she struggled out of her corset, then the creak of boards as she crossed the room and hung garments over a chair. I saw her standing and stretching, while I clumsily undressed and let my clothes fall to the floor.

Sleep was fast overcoming me. Its velvet ropes pulled me into that soft world where there is no pain and no hate. I lay down and felt Surrey climb up behind me onto the mattress. Her hand came to rest protectively over the wound on my chest. She pressed her knees and thighs against the back of my legs and kissed my neck and shoulders. Her flesh on mine created an exquisite sensation that even overwhelmed my drunkenness.

My heart was drumming fast as she put a hand on my shoulder and rolled me over so I rested on my back and faced her.

'It's going to be all right,' she said. 'Trust me, I know how to make everything all right.'

And she did. Slowly and patiently, she took away part of a great hurt that I had carried for so long that I had become unaware of what it would be like to be free of it.

EIGHT DAYS TO EXECUTION

My feet had blistered and burst. But still the gaolers made me trudge around the Press Yard. The envelope of grey above my head was smudged with the darkness of incoming night. Freedom was so visibly near, and yet still beyond reach.

Through the door of the yard strode Huntley. A step behind him came Johncock, followed by several new turnkeys who stopped and mingled with the old guard. As I continued my slow circuit, Johncock jabbed a finger into Huntley's chest before storming out, closely followed by his cronies.

Huntley watched them go and then walked over to me. There was triumph in his eyes. 'You can stop walking, Lynch,' he called from a few yards away. 'Johncock has been given his own marching orders – all the way to the governor's office.'

The pendulum of prison power had swung back in the younger man's favour. Not that I had the strength to care. I fell onto my knees and almost collapsed completely.

Huntley bent down to aid me. 'Good God, man, you look dead on your feet.'

'A bad choice of words,' I said through a mouth as dry as a desert.

'Let's get you back inside and give you some water and

food.' He shouted to two of the screws who had accompanied him into the yard. 'Leadbetter, Reece, come here.' They crossed the yard quickly. 'Support him under his arms. Get him back to his cell and see he has water and food.'

They took my weight and I extended an arm over the shoulder of each screw. Within minutes I was back in the warmth and stink of my cell. The assistant keeper had been right about one thing: I was strangely pleased to be back inside its four walls. Lukewarm tea and a bowl of cold, hard gruel was all that could be mustered but I finished every mouthful.

About an hour passed before Huntley was let in. Again he had his men wait outside.

'Mr Johncock overstepped the mark today. You should not have been treated so primitively.'

I looked up from the blistered skin I was inspecting on my feet. 'Is that an apology, Mr Huntley?'

'Not officially, no. But I am personally sorry that you were treated in such a fashion. The governor was not in his office today, so I could not have Mr Johncock's intervention immediately countermanded. Indeed, I had to go to the governor's home to seek it.'

I raised an eyebrow in mock approval. 'Then I am indeed honoured. But you know, Mr Huntley, one way or another, I will be gone in a little over a week, and Johncock will still be here. Though unable to collect my winnings, I would safely wager that he will make your life hell.'

'I have met many Johncocks in my life. He is in every prison I have worked in. Cold Bath Fields, Holloway, Strangeways, they all have their Johncocks, but in time they are replaced by better men.'

'Is that what you are, a better man?'

'I hope I am.'

'Then you should do better than work here.'

'And I shall. After a little more experience, I will be in contention to be governor of a new prison. Until then, Newgate is vital to me. It has history and profile, both advantageous for a man of ambition.'

'Newgate is no better than a broken privy.'

He nodded. 'Sadly, you are correct, but nonetheless, it remains an important place for me to make my mark. It constantly has the attention of both the public and the government. Many famous people have passed through its gates: the great lover, Casanova; the pirate Captain Kidd; and Lord Gordon – he of the Gordon Riots.'

'Please save me your roll call of the famous and fallen; it is of no comfort to me.'

'Of course not, and I must leave you. Be on your guard, Lynch. Johncock has been put in his place today, but my experience is that old dogs like him cannot be taught new tricks. He will wander out of his place and want to bite you every bit as badly as he wishes to sink his teeth into me.'

Surrey raised her head from my pillow and squinted through the shafts of morning sunlight that bisected the room. 'What are you doing?' she asked in a voice softened by sleep. 'Come and lie down.'

Sweat poured from me as I perched on the edge of the bed, shaking off the last vestiges of a nightmare. 'I was remembering my early life.'

'What about it?' Surrey was naked, save for the bed sheet around her. She edged nearer to me and draped a part of it over my bare shoulders.

'I was dreaming about Philomena.'

'*Philomena?*' she said suspiciously. 'Who was she? A lover?'

'Philomena was the generous lady who cared for me after my mother died.'

'I am sorry . . .'

'You weren't to know. She and her husband Cyril, a baker, took me in for a while, taught me what little I know. When Cyril died, the debts were too great and she and I were for the spike.'

'A common enough tale.'

'I know. That's where Philomena died. Where my life really changed.' I felt emotional. 'This is not something I have ever spoken of.'

She kissed the back of my neck. 'Then tell me. Let the demon out, so it cannot torment you.'

I stared straight ahead. Set my eyes on the sunlight

beyond the window, remembered the smoke from the workhouse chimneys, the stink of its corridors and bedrooms, the whimpers of the child that I had once been.

'Matron came and told me that Philomena was dead. Showed me her corpse. It frightened me, her being so white and cold. It terrified me. I was still in shock when I was dragged into a classroom full of children and everyone was told she was dead.'

'How awful for you.'

'"He's been told." That's what Matron said to the teacher. "He's been told. Best thing for him now is to go on as normal." I will never forget her words. *Normal?* Nothing was ever normal again.'

'She sounds a proper bitch,' said Surrey.

'She was. I made my way to my desk. Past all those staring eyes. Carrying my loss like I had soiled myself.'

'You poor darling.' She leaned her head against me.

'Laid out on my desk were all the things we worked with. A rough slate. A small cloth. Some cheap chalk. Things to copy down stupid words scrawled upon a wallboard. I was so shaken by the news that I couldn't wipe the slate clean. I fumbled it. Dropped it. The thing fell to the floor and broke into pieces. One child, a boy called Jimmy, who used to bully me, shouted "Idiot! You're a right *flat,* Simeon Lynch." Then his brother Charlie joined in, "Mummy's boy broke his toy, broke his toy, broke his toy. Mummy's boy—"'

I couldn't continue.

Surrey rubbed my arms comfortingly, kissed me. 'You don't have to go on. Lie down and rest.'

'I want to go on. I have to. If I don't speak of it now, then I never will.'

It took me a few more seconds to compose myself.

'I had intended to bend down, to pick up the pieces of the broken slate, apologise to Mr Addison, the teacher, for my clumsiness. But the teasing changed all that. Something inside me snapped – the thing that had held together all my fear, my restraint, my goodness. I picked up a sliver of slate, turned and slashed Charlie Connor in his face. Straight into his cheek. Almost put it through his eye.'

'He deserved it.'

'Maybe. It doesn't matter if he did or not. I remember feeling a surge of relief. It was like crying an hour's worth of tears in a split second and feeling stronger for it.'

'You were letting out your pain.'

'I was. And once Charlie went down screaming, his brother came for me. Rushed straight at me. I didn't think how to react; I just stuck that same piece of slate in his stomach. And when I did, my dearest Surrey, I cannot describe to you how happy I felt.'

'What happened to the boy? Was he badly injured?'

I shook my head. 'Neither of them were. The wounds were shallow but the shock was great.' I turned to face her. 'What I did that day changed me. The workhouse master made me fight the boys as a punishment, box them. He said it was to teach us a lesson. And it did. It taught me how to sharpen my anger and wield it like a sword.'

She put a hand to my face. 'I have anger similar to yours, so I understand your pain.'

'What do you mean?'

'My parents were not good people, not like those who tried to raise you. They taught me to kill. Or at least my father did.'

'I am not sure that I understand.'

'There has always been a Breed in the Trinity. My family has served the Moriartys for generations and my father was a close aide to Brogan's father. With no sons in the family line, he wanted to prove his loyalty by making sure I could fill the gap he would leave.'

'I am sorry to hear it,' I said. 'This is no life for a lady.'

'A *lady*,' she laughed. 'Is that how you see me now?'

I laughed as well. 'I do. I do indeed. Now can we please stop talking?'

'We can.' Surrey pushed me back on the bed. 'Consider our *talking* well and truly stopped.'

244

ONE WEEK TO EXECUTION

My feet were swollen and sore from the six hours that Johncock made me walk the yard. I had no more water with which to soothe them or to quench my thirst. My stomach grumbled from hunger and there seemed not a part of me that did not ache from some brutality or other.

I sat in the darkness of the cell and listened to the turn-keys settling down. It was gone midnight and I knew their habits well. All doors had been checked, names called and the gallery gates secured. No mistakes had been made, no opportunity afforded me to escape. No gaoler would now walk the landings again until about an hour before day-break. Despite another day passing, my resolve to be free burned brightly.

In my hands was the nail some mystery helper had given to me. Although I had no proof, I was all but certain it had come from Huntley. He had sent men to take me to chapel and had been in the room when the orderly had passed the bible to me. He had fought for my right to fresh air and exercise and was the only man within this place of damnation who appeared to have any spark of humanity in him.

I manipulated the nail in the lock of the leg manacles and counted until I managed to open it. Two minutes.

I tried again. A hundred seconds.

A third attempt reduced the time to eighty seconds.

For the next two hours, I practised but could not improve beyond the one-minute mark. It was too long a time to free myself in the Press Yard if I ever had the chance. I threw the nail to the floor in anger, roared like a wounded animal and banged my fists against the walls to vent my building frustration.

My knuckles were grazed. Blood seeped into the tears of skin. I licked the wounds.

'Quiet back there!' boomed a turnkey's voice. Feet slapped the floor towards my cell. I grabbed the nail and plunged it back into the recess by the door, snapped the leg irons shut and lay back down on the bunk.

The door opened. Greybeard and two of his men rushed in, wielding sticks. A flurry of blows followed to my legs and torso but I kept my knees bent to protect my testicles and my hands across my face to avoid major injury.

When they were done, Greybeard grabbed my hair and lifted my head. 'That's for who you killed. For what you did and who you are, you offspring of Satan's whore.' He spat in my face and banged my head down on the bunk. 'Now shut up, or we'll shut you up for ever.'

The door slammed and I heard the locks turn and men march off. Oddly enough, I understood their anger. Like me, they wanted to avenge what they understood to be a terrible murder. My first. One I had committed as a young man. The one that had haunted me all the way to the gates of Newgate.

The year had been 1878 and following my brutal boxing

encounter with the Connor brothers, Jeremiah Beamish decided good money could be earned by having the three of us fight children from neighbouring establishments. It was what he called his 'academy' project. In truth, it was merely a way to sell tickets and take bets on which work-house boy might beat the other.

Bosede and Miller continued to train the twins and me; over the next few years, because of our common plight and a mutual hatred of being exploited, we actually grew to be friends.

I fought more than forty times and never lost. Jimmy had a similar record and Charlie was not so far behind. Our victories, and occasional losses, all made Beamish and his cronies a small fortune. But not us. We got the odd copper, some extra food and occasional jug of ale, but nothing more. We were told we had a debt to pay to the workhouse for taking us in and should be grateful for the chance to do it so easily. And we were warned that we'd be unable to discharge ourselves from that hellhole until Beamish con-sidered the debt settled.

Three days past my fourteenth birthday we decided we'd had enough. In the dead of night we made a run for it. The Connors had an older cousin who ran a gang in Southwark, so we made our way there. His name was Hoolihan, Patrick Hoolihan, and he was famous in the East End, or at least he was about to be.

Hoolihan already had a reputation as a fellow you didn't mess with, someone who always had a plate of hot food and a place to rest for strong young men who could provide muscle for his criminal activities.

When the three of us joined, there were no more than thirty in total. But as time passed numbers grew. Eventually, the Hoolihan group gained notoriety as the Hooli gang or more commonly, the 'Hooligans'.

Paddy had access to innumerable run-down old buildings on the south side of the river and he used these to store whatever could be stolen from ships mooring on the Thames.

Around ten of us ended up living with him in a large slum in Southwark, mainly to guard the stolen goods that got stored there. He had done a deal with the landlord, collecting rents on his behalf in return for the use of the three-storey end terrace and several cellars that he stacked with poke from his street gangs. There was a brazier down there as well and once a month a fellow called The Fireman would roll up and get it roaring so he might melt down stolen coins, cutlery and jewellery into bars of gold and silver.

Several of the gang were dippers – pickpockets – more accustomed to using their hands to lift the wallets and purses of London's richer citizens than fight for a living. Their clothes fascinated me, especially the secret pockets sewn into slits in their shirts, pants and coats. They could take a coin from your palm and make it disappear without you even knowing you'd lost it.

There was also a handful of brawny dragsmen, loutish

youths who preyed on carriages. They simply pounced on the vehicles and dragged off whatever goods they could get their grubby hands on. Three of the others were seasoned cracksmen. Almost nightly, they crossed the Thames to tiptoe in and out of moneyed cribs in Marylebone and Mayfair.

As the years passed, Jimmy, Charlie and me settled comfortably into this motley crew and as a result we had more clink in our pockets than we had ever dreamed of. We stole from houses and from shops, from rich folk rolling home drunk in their carriages and from pretty much anyone who had anything worth stealing. At night we spread out our haul for Hoolihan, got paid a fair whack for our work and drank and ate like kings.

But all good things come to an end, and our run halted in the middle of a night when everyone was fast asleep in their cribs.

The coppers came – a raid that caught us all by surprise.

I was bunked upstairs with the twins when the front door was broken down and the fighting broke out. We bolted for a window and almost made it, but a rozzer with a stick started to beat Jimmy and another pulled a knife on Charlie. At first I thought he was bluffing, just trying to frighten him into surrendering, then he stabbed him.

I had no choice but to wade in. Filled with rage, I grabbed the knife, forced the copper flat and stuck it through his neck.

I had killed him. It was as simple and terrible as that. In

a single second, a spontaneous action with a knife changed my life. Made me a murderer. Forced me to flee London and brought me under the influence of Moriarty. And in prison I was marked out as a cop-killer, the kind of convict gaolers liked to kill because policemen were their brothers-in-arms.

I rose from my bunk and touched the many places where the gaolers' sticks had found flesh. There were no breaks, just bruises to count. The moon had moved in the night sky and now caught the wall by the door and the head of the nail I had hidden in the brickwork. It was my only tool. Aside from my hands, my only protection. Tomorrow I would take the nail into my murderous fingers and try again to escape.

DERBYSHIRE, MAY 1886

Surrey and I spent almost every night together following Michael's funeral and although I felt something more than just a sexual attraction to her, I did not believe it to be love. And in truth, I suspect she felt the same. Her passion and desire exceeded mine and that discrepancy became increasingly noticeable as time passed.

One day, as we walked in the garden before she went off on a job, she asked out of the blue, 'Are you growing bored of me, Simeon?'

'What?'

'Nothing I say or do seems to amuse you or please you any more.'

'That isn't true.'

'I feel it is. In fact I have a feeling that you would rather be somewhere else. Perhaps with someone else?'

'You are being silly. What makes you say such a thing?'

'I don't know. Female intuition, I suppose.'

'And what exactly is that?'

'It is a sense. Like smell, or touch.'

'And only females have it?'

'No. Men have it, too. Masculine intuition, but it is not as finely honed. It cannot sense emotional and sexual nuances nearly as acutely as feminine intuition can.'

'For example . . .'

'It doesn't matter.'

'It does. Give me an example to prove your point.'

'Very well.' She let out a sigh, then continued, 'I think you still nurture passionate thoughts for Elizabeth, even though the woman is old enough to be your mother.'

'She is not *that* old!' I protested, perhaps a little too strongly. 'And no, I do not *nurture* any such thoughts.'

She burst out laughing. 'You are a liar, Simeon Lynch, and a very bad one at that.'

I turned away, partly out of embarrassment and partly because I feared further interrogation.

'Are you sulking now?' she teased.

'This subject is closed, Surrey. I do not wish to discuss it any further.' I quickened my step to get ahead of her.

She grabbed my coat-tail. 'Wait.'

I turned. 'What now?'

'Just tell me this. Did you get more excited kissing *Elizabeth* in the drawing room than sleeping with me?'

I was speechless with shock.

Surrey saw that she had drawn blood. 'I saw the whole thing, my love. We *all* did.'

My blood ran cold. I felt a terrible vulnerability. 'How? How could you have seen anything?'

'Sirius and I were with the professor, when you went through to the drawing room. He called us through to watch.'

'You watched? From where?'

'Through the wall.' She paused and then explained. 'There are false walls throughout the house. Secret passages big enough to walk through, all with spy holes. They run everywhere and allow the professor to watch us and any guests that visit.'

'In God's name! That is terrible. He cannot do that!'

'Of course he can,' she laughed. 'This is the house of Moriarty, so he can do what he jolly well likes.'

A dreadful thought occurred to me. 'And us? Has he watched us, in bed together?'

'Most probably.' She did not sound concerned.

'Sweet Lord! That first night – did he watch us then?'

'I don't know. Most likely.' She shrugged. 'If it is any consolation, neither Sirius nor I were aware of this practice until *after* our initiations. It was only then that Michael told us.'

'Did the professor know you were going to tell me?'

'Yes. Actually, it was his suggestion. He said that given our *closeness*, I really should.'

I shook my head. 'Then he *has* watched us.'

'Undoubtedly.' She sounded bored. 'Perhaps he did so with Elizabeth.'

'What?'

Surrey laughed again. 'You are so easy to provoke. You know they are lovers, don't you?'

'No.' I couldn't help but sound aghast. 'Such a thing never crossed my mind.'

'Then you are even more naive than I took you to be. Your precious Elizabeth has been fucking him for years and is no more a lady than I am.'

'Watch what you say!'

'I'll do nothing of the kind. No one but the professor tells me what to say or do.' She slapped her hands into my chest and pushed me away. 'Certainly not you.'

'Surrey, be careful what you say.'

'You are a fool, Simeon Lynch. Before she began calling herself *Lady* Elizabeth Audsley, she was plain Lizzie MacIntosh. You should ask *her* about *that,* when you are next drinking tea and being her puppy dog.'

'I'll ask her no such thing.'

We stared angrily at each other and in the midst of that cold and silent moment it felt like all the warmth we had built up between us with every naked kiss and personal truth had suddenly been frozen.

'I have to leave tonight on business for the professor, so I will bid you good day,' she said frostily.

'And I, you.' I did not even tell her to be careful, though I wished to.

Surrey walked away, then stopped and turned. For a second, I thought she was going to shout at me. Then I saw she was crying. But before I could say a word, she turned again and ran towards the house.

I watched her go and felt sad and guilty. Surrey did not deserve to be hurt or disappointed by me. But in time she would be. Because she was right.

My heart belonged to Elizabeth.

The following morning, Sirius caught me en route to the library, where I was hopeful I would find Elizabeth and be able to steal a private minute or two with her. If indeed anything approaching privacy was possible in that damned house.

'Simeon, the professor wishes us to accompany him to London for a business dinner. We must leave within the hour and take a locomotive from Derby to St Pancras. In the capital, a carriage will take us to his residence in Primrose Hill, where we will spend the night.'

London.

I had not been back since fleeing the capital with blood on my hands and fear in my heart.

'Is there a problem?' he asked.

'Not at all. It will be a pleasure to go there.'

'There will be no *pleasure* in this venture. We are to dine with that creature Chan, along with members of his dreadful clan and their ghastly cohorts, so we will have to be on our mettle.'

'Is Surrey joining us?' I asked disingenuously, for I knew she had departed the night before.

'No,' he answered, 'the professor has another assignment for her.' He half-turned to leave, then added, 'I meant to enquire, Simeon, do you not find her somewhat boyish between the sheets?'

'I thought you were a gentleman, Sirius, and would not be inclined to ask such a thing.'

'Touché. By the way, if I were you, I would beware her temper. Woe betide the man who finds himself out of favour with Miss Breed.'

I brushed off his jocularity and entered the library. Wide wooden boards gave way to seven rows of vast shelves that stretched upwards to the carved bannisters of an upper gallery that encompassed the room. Much as I had expected, Lady Elizabeth was at a table that afforded her views of the gardens, should she wish to lift her divine head from the book she was engrossed in.

'Good morning,' I said as I approached.

'Simeon?' She sounded surprised as she looked up over the edge of her volume. 'How are you?'

'Very well, thank you.' Without asking permission, I took the seat opposite her. 'I have something important to ask you.'

She put down her book. 'Then ask.'

'Is your real name Lizzie MacIntosh?'

Her blue eyes widened with concern. Her lips pressed together to suppress a quick reaction. She closed her novel with a thud of pages and stood up. 'I came to choose some reading matter for our journey. This will suffice. I will see you a little later.'

As she walked past me I caught her wrist.

Fury flared from brow to lips as she tried to pull away, 'Let me go!'

I held on as I got to my feet. 'Not until you tell me.'

'There is nothing to tell.' Elizabeth shook me off and rubbed her wrist.

'Are you afraid the professor is watching us?' I motioned to the gallery above. 'Does he this very second gaze down upon us like some prying God?'

'Don't be ridiculous!' She hastened to the door.

I followed quickly and stopped her opening it.

'Simeon! Let me pass.'

'Not until you answer my question.'

Her face glowed red with anger. 'No, the professor is not watching us.'

'How can you be so sure? Surrey told me all about his world within the walls.'

'*World within the walls?*' Her expression turned to one of bitter mockery. 'That is most surely *your* phrase, not hers; that poisonous slip of a girl is not so imaginative.'

Elizabeth stared me down but I could see her bosom

rise and fall from the anger and nervousness she sought to conceal.

I don't know what possessed me. Perhaps it was her defiance. Or the excitement of being so close to her and us both in such high dudgeon, but I felt emboldened enough to kiss her.

At first, it seemed as though she offered no resistance, then she pushed me back and slapped my face. Her blue eyes regarded me for a split second, then she grabbed the door handle. I let her open it and leave.

My face no doubt bore the imprint of her hand but all I could feel was the exhilarating touch of her lips. For close to a minute, I stood petrified and mesmerised, before reluctantly making my way to my room.

It did not take me long to pack. I needed only a few items. Casual garments to travel in. Smart ones for dinner. A gun for noisy despatches, a knife for quieter ones and Michael's garrottes for absolutely silent ones.

Outside, in the courtyard, I smoked a rollup with Thackeray while we waited for the others. They finally appeared, with servants in tow, carrying their many bags. Alex and the professor remained in conversation but lifted their hats to me as they got into their own carriage, the lavishly furnished former mail coach. I thought about Moriarty surreptitiously watching me and felt resentful. There would come a time when I would confront him about it, and many other things.

I rode out front on a brougham with Thackeray, leaving

Lady Elizabeth and Sirius to travel inside. I was in no mood to sit awkwardly among them and be exposed to any unpleasantness.

Thackeray and I passed time speaking of women and their strangeness. My northern friend, far more experienced with the fairer sex than I, shared many confidences on the difficulties he had encountered in understanding their ways and predicting their behaviour.

There was much bustle and business when we reached Derby, especially at the approach to what was one of the busiest train stations in the country. Carriages jostled for positions close to the entrance and Thackeray got into a verbal confrontation with another coachman who was intent on pulling to a halt in the same space as he did, at exactly the same time.

The inside of the station had quite an effect on me, as I had never even travelled on a train before. The collision of sights, sounds and smells was mesmerising. Oil, grease, coal. Hissing steam, shrill whistles, slamming doors, shouting conductors. Excited children, uniformed staff, parting couples. Everywhere there was vibrancy.

We boarded a Midlands Express and I hung out of the window of a first-class carriage and marvelled at the gigantic drive wheels grinding slowly on the rails, while plumes of smoke chugged from the front of the train and washed back over my face and windswept hair.

The professor secured the door and addressed Alexander. 'Be so kind as to commence the briefing. Perhaps it is wise to begin with a little background on Mr Chan, so young Simeon understands the situation.'

Alex unbuckled the clasp of an old Gladstone bag that he was seldom parted from and produced a buff-coloured envelope. Inside were several photographs. He handed them to me. 'The first is of Huiwi Chan. He is a Chinese immigrant who came to these shores with his brothers more than forty years ago. He is now in his eighties and apparently neither speaks nor understands any English. Fortunately, the professor *does* speak very passable Mandarin. Nonetheless, Chan insists all business communications include his grandson Lee, who is fluent in both tongues. His is the second photograph in your possession. Lee is an extremely dangerous man. We understand he has killed three, perhaps four people who were foolish enough to displease his grandfather.'

I looked at the portrait, as did Sirius and Elizabeth who were now either side of me. It showed the face of a fellow in his thirties with chiselled cheekbones and a strong jaw. What was most noticeable was the look in his eyes. He wasn't posing for the photographer; he was staring challengingly at the lens, like a lion weighing up his prey.

'You will be in the company of many violent criminals tonight,' continued Alex, 'but none are as ruthless and brutal as Lee, and none, including him, dare act without Huiwi's instruction. Old he might be, but he still has absolute control of those who follow him.'

The professor added to the background. 'Initially, the

Chans settled in the East End and at first appeared to be solely concerned with their traditional businesses of tailoring, laundry and distribution of herbal medicines. But appearances are deceptive. In reality, the old man and his son Bai, Lee's father, were secretly building a varied criminal enterprise. Bai was killed in a dockland battle – one the Chans subsequently won. They now control a great number of opportunities within the port of London, including the importation of undesirables from his homeland and the shipment and distribution of opium. Had they confined themselves to these activities then perhaps our paths could still have crossed as safely as country roads conjoin in remote corners of Cornwall or Cheshire. But sadly they did not.'

Alexander continued the account. 'They have become increasingly meddlesome in matters of our interest, especially horse racing and the lucrative betting that accompanies it. One of their associates, an equestrian veterinarian, doped a horse we needed to win. Opium was put in its water. We lost a lot of money on that outing.'

'And the meddler lost his head,' added the professor. 'You saw the acquisition in my laboratory gallery, Simeon. It is also partly the reason I did not wish to have Miss Breed attend the dinner with us. One never knows whose memory might be jogged by her presence, even if she does currently look very different.'

I understood now why Surrey had been so shaken that night I had discovered her soaked in blood and sitting alone in the darkened kitchen, with a hessian sack tightly bundled up. Decapitating the veterinarian must have been a gruesome and traumatic task.

'So, now both sides must speak?' surmised Sirius. 'And I take it that our gathering is devised for us to deliver a final warning?'

The professor smiled. 'Mr Chan does not take notice of warnings. Tonight is about me making him, his grandson and his business partners, a proposition that hopefully they will see as impossible not to accept.'

Alex took his cue to elaborate. 'They will be asked to withdraw, forthwith, from all racecourse and gambling activities. In return, we will grant them a share of revenues from the courses that they are currently trying to exploit. In short, they get paid for doing nothing.'

'And if they don't agree?'

'Then there will be bloodshed,' Moriarty replied. 'If they force our hand then we will embark upon a spree of beheading that would shock Vlad the Impaler.'

I handed the photographs back and asked with some trepidation, 'What part am I expected to play?'

Alex returned the pictures to his envelope. 'After dinner, the professor and I will retire with Chan and his grandson. The Chinaman has also demanded a 'virtuous exchange', to ensure no foul play takes place. This means Lady Elizabeth will sit in one room with a member of his family, while Lee's wife Wu will sit in another with Simeon. Sirius will stand on guard with one of the Chan men in the corridor that separates the two rooms.'

261

We progressed into St Pancras and disembarked at what was a breathtaking cathedral of a station. Porters moved our luggage, and Moriarty and Elizabeth walked off together.

As we ventured into the London fog and busy streets, I realised I had quite forgotten how the smoke and dirt clung to the clouds and leached away all colour from the day. We hailed two hackneys and made excellent progress to the professor's house. It held a good position on Albert Road, close to Primrose Hill and the Zoological Gardens. Strong gates and high walls kept out prying eyes and uninvited visitors. The grounds were patrolled front and back by armed men, many of them ex-militia.

Once settled, I was introduced to the house servants and then shown around, so that I might familiarise myself with the building. It was a third of the size of Moriarty's mansion in Derbyshire but still generous in dimension and lavish in furnishings.

I was admiring the dining room, resplendent with cherry-wood panelling, a matching long table and chairs sited under crystal chandeliers, when Sirius came to the door. His face was lit up with excitement. 'They are here,' he announced. 'Let the games begin.'

The professor had described old man Chan as 'a reptile' and once he walked into the house in Albert Road I understood why. Small, thin and wheezing, he shuffled in a slow, hunched manner that gave the impression of a prowling lizard. His face was saggy and spotted with dark brown age patches that looked from a distance like scales. Flesh hung in folds from his neck like turkey wattle.

He took a seat at the middle of the table, next to his grandson. On his other side sat the professor and then Elizabeth. I was positioned directly opposite him, near Sirius. The rest of the party consisted of half a dozen men from Moriarty's London contingent and a corresponding number from Chan's organisation, out of which only half appeared to be Chinese.

Dinner was deliberately an excellent and refined affair, designed to lower the tensions on both sides and eliminate any chance of violence breaking out. A rich julienne soup followed by broiled salmon, then a trio of roasted beef, lamb and chicken. Finally, vast plates of cakes and éclairs were laid out, along with mountains of strawberries and cherries. Along with this feast came a plentiful supply of white, red and dessert wines but both Lee Chan and I abstained. Our eyes locked several times during the courses. The stare that had scorched the lens of the portrait camera burned a path across the table to me.

I returned it with icy disdain. We both recognised each other for what we were. Killers know other killers. It is a haunted look that no one else has. One that says a line has been crossed and will if occasion demands be crossed again.

The moment came for us all to leave the table and fulfil our respective duties. The younger Chan rose and half-smiled at me. That old familiar tingle, that exciting chemical precursor to violence, rushed through my blood.

It would give me great pleasure to test myself against him and I am sure he felt exactly the same.

The room emptied and I went to sit with Lee's wife. Wu Chan was more mouse than woman. Slight of size and weight, small black eyes, tiny hands and quieter than any human I have ever met. She moved silently in a long red and gold one-piece dress and did not speak a word. Indeed, such was her silence, I wondered whether she understood any English.

Three silent hours and the chimes of midnight passed before the tense and awkward wait was terminated. Doors opened down corridors, feet clattered on wood and marble floors, servants' bells rang and voices chattered. A sharp knock on the door startled me. Wu looked up and I saw fear in her eyes.

'There is no need to be afraid of anyone who knocks,' I said, more to myself than my companion. 'It is those who do not that must be feared.'

Sirius entered, nodded at the lady and informed me quietly, 'Business has been successfully concluded. Elizabeth is with the professor and your guest can be reunited with her family.'

I thanked Sirius and as he left I spoke slowly and a little more loudly than necessary to Wu, ignorantly imagining that slowness and loudness would somehow help her understand a foreign language, 'They are finished. You and I may now rejoin the others.'

'Thank you, sir,' she said in perfect English, then rose

without emotion, put her hands together, bowed slightly and shuffled out of the room as quickly as her long, tight dress would allow.

I walked behind her to the main hall where everyone else had already gathered. Elizabeth was next to Moriarty and still seemed tense. Sirius was vigilantly watching the Englishmen in Chan's party. They were tall and broad, dressed smartly in dark suits and were lighting cigarettes. 'Who are *they*?' I asked him.

'I don't know,' he replied in a hushed voice. 'They are from London and the Midlands and run illegal betting rings for the Chans. They put up the cash, while those lackeys provide the muscle and take the risks.'

I was about to take a closer look at them when I heard the professor laughing. I turned and saw him and the old Chinaman shaking hands. Lee Chan was close by, his eyes taking in everyone and everything.

Servants descended upon the visitors with coats, and we soon passed through the front door and into the crisp night air. As our guests' carriages approached my attention turned again to Chan's men. I recognised two of them. A large fellow and a smaller, stouter one. They were Brummies. Blinders.

In the same moment, the big man also recognised me, and he declared loudly to his friend, 'It's 'im! 'im wot done 'enry and Billy in that alley.'

The smaller man squinted across at me. 'You're fuckin' right!' He threw down his cigarette and moved quickly towards me. I saw the glint of a blade slip from his sleeve to his hand.

He lunged and swept it at me. I dodged to the side and he missed, bumped shoulder first into a wall.

Before I could make my next move, Lee Chan stepped forward. He spun on his left foot and sank the sole of his right shoe into the middle of the man's head.

The Brummie went down in an unconscious sprawl.

Lee shouted something in Chinese. Several of his countrymen rushed forward, lifted the knifeman from the floor and carried him away.

Lee straightened his dinner suit and walked over to me. 'Please forgive such intolerable rudeness. I apologise for my man's actions. I assure you he will be severely dealt with.'

'It looks like he already has been,' I answered.

'He will be *properly* disciplined.' He nodded courteously, then added, 'Please tell me, why did he so urgently seek to harm you?'

'I think he mistook me for someone. I suspect he drank too much of the wine that you and I avoided,' I added lightly. 'Some Englishmen get confused and do stupid things when they are drunk.'

He could tell I was lying. 'And some do stupid things when they are sober. Like beheading a man I was fond of.' He stepped closer to me. 'Do you know of what I speak?'

My eyes held his and I remembered Surrey and her bloodied hessian sack in the kitchen back in Derbyshire.

The professor stopped the conversation. 'Lee, your

grandfather is calling for you. I think he is very tired and wishes to go home.'

Chan could not refuse such a request. But still his eyes held mine. 'We are strangers,' he said directly to me, 'but I *know* you. Know what you are and what you do. We will meet again, of that I am certain.' He nodded ominously then strode away.

After the visitors boarded their carriages and left, Moriarty gathered everyone and summarised the outcome of the meeting. 'We have tonight laid the basis of a cooperation that will serve us well for the next half-decade. Between the Chans and ourselves we have the most lucrative business infrastructures inside and outside of London. Now we must take full advantage of what is at our disposal.'

Once the applause had died down Elizabeth declared she was weary and retired for the night. The professor, Alexander, Sirius and I stayed up until dawn, mainly drinking and talking about the future.

I learned that Moriarty's British and overseas businesses were booming and that his family was now heavily invested in every major legitimate and illegitimate enterprise imaginable. Somewhat in his cups, he mentioned the family's heads of shipping, pharmaceuticals, transportation and 'entertainment' based in cities all across the world. It struck me that what he forgot to mention was the great pains he and his kin went to in order to remain far removed from the criminality but closely protected, by the likes of us.

*

The following day, we rose late and headed back to Derbyshire. I was informed that Elizabeth and Sirius had already left on an early train as they had other business to attend to, and I found myself returning with only the professor and Alex.

On arrival in Derby, we were met by Thackeray. To his disappointment, I explained that I was too tired to ride up top with him. Instead, I climbed inside and within minutes was asleep.

When I awoke we were in the countryside. The carriage had halted and from outside, I heard voices. Men, shouting loudly.

'Get out! Out with your hands up!'

The professor's face showed a mixture of surprise and interest, but certainly not shock. He spoke to me in a calm and unworried voice. 'This is not a trick, Simeon. It seems we are about to be subjected to robbery and no doubt a hideous delay as well.'

We had been stopped at a remote junction on the Derbyshire–Staffordshire border. Two armed men had fallen upon us. One had climbed up the carriage steps and put a gun to Thackeray's head. The other pulled open the carriage door, and at pistol point, ordered us out.

I am sure that in the haze of that heated moment the thieves had both felt in complete control of that situation. I am equally certain that, out of the four of us, they believed Thackeray, with his weathered looks and broad shoulders, presented a greater danger than the middle-aged man, his disabled companion and their youthful servant.

It would, then, have come as a complete surprise to them when I knocked away the pistol of the assailant nearest me, grabbed his arm and broke it with a twisting move that Michael Brannigan would have been proud of.

The man was still yelping when I picked up his weapon, pressed it against his head and shouted to the accomplice, 'Put your pistol down, or I will shoot your friend.'

His friend pushed his gun to Thackeray's skull. 'You do that, young mister, and I'll off your coachman.'

'Put it down,' I shouted again, 'or in three seconds, I pull the trigger.'

He shifted the gun again. 'I mean it, mister.'

Across the ground, I saw my shadow and the robber's, fused by the gun I held to his head.

'One!' I shouted.

There was no call of two, or three. A familiar feeling filled me. Flushed every atom of my body. It was anger, but not as I had known it before. Not wild and raw, not hot and snarling. It was as cool, soft and comforting as a freshly laundered bed sheet.

I pulled the trigger. The shot echoed across the countryside.

Thackeray made a grab at the shocked man by his side and pushed the pistol skyward. Another roar entered the clouds.

Anger catapulted me onto the driver's boards. I knocked Thackeray aside, grabbed the robber around his neck and leapt from the carriage. I saw my shadow land and crumple, separating from the man whose neck I knew I had just broken as easily as a trapped rabbit.

And then that coolness went, emptying from me like a plug had been pulled. Within a second, I felt drained. Felt nothing.

'You really must learn to count, Simeon,' remarked the professor, as he moved from the carriage to inspect the bodies. 'My, what a mess. Thackeray, bury these fools in the undergrowth.' He waved a hand to his left. 'And make sure you empty their pockets; we should at least profit from their impertinence and our inconvenience.'

The coachman walked around the back of the brougham and unclipped a shovel that he used whenever wheels needed digging out of ruts – or apparently, a corpse needed burying.

'Give me a little time, sir,' he called as he headed into the thicket. 'I'll soon 'ave two nice graves for these bastards to slip into.'

ONE WEEK TO EXECUTION

NEWGATE, 11 JANUARY 1900

Despite the torture of my walking marathon, I slept little that night. My mind was in torment and I only fell asleep when the soft light of dawn began to illuminate my cell.

I was fuzzy headed and still chasing off nightmares when two gaolers shook my bones and announced that Levine was at the gate and wished to see me as a matter of urgency.

Walking chains were fitted and I was taken to a room where my peacock lawyer strutted from wall to wall in a suit of blue, shirt of pink and tie of red.

'I hope you have good news,' I said as the screws fastened down my chains at a table and pushed me into a chair.

'I have lodged intent of appeal with the Crown,' he said as soon as we were alone. 'And I have found men of straw to bolster our case.'

'Men *of straw*? We have to rely on scoundrels who stalk the Old Bailey offering to lie for any solicitor with coin enough to buy their oaths? I would beseech you, sir, to—'

He flapped a hand to cut me off. 'No, no! These are stronger *straws* than the court has ever seen. Do not worry about their veracity or believability.'

'And what will they say?'

'Whatever we wish. But to put the right words in their mouths, I must know more than is on your file, more than you said at the trial – hence the urgency of my visit.'

'I have held nothing back.'

'Then we must go over everything in meticulous detail and see if we have missed something.'

Levine fished a gold pocket watch from inside his jacket and examined it. 'Neither of us has an abundance of time, Mr Lynch. Your story, please?'

'Very well. You know that I resided in a flash house run by Paddy Hoolihan.'

'I do.'

'That I had intended to leave the following morning with two companions, Jimmy and Charlie Connor—'

'This I know. Go on. Go on!'

His impatience irritated me. I closed my eyes so I could not see him. Let my mind drift back to that night. 'I had fallen asleep, when there was a noise. Charlie, Jimmy and I were bunked at the top of the house, crammed into the roof space just beneath the rafters. It had been the worst spot to lodge, until we heard the sound of the Old Bill breaking down the door.'

'What did you do?' He dabbed his nose with a handkerchief.

'I remember Jimmy dropped to the floor, peered through a crack in the boards to see what was the cause of all the noise. "Coppers!" he said. "They're downstairs." I pulled on my boots. Charlie opened the loft hatch and said there were lanterns moving near the foot of the stairs, so we decided to chance it.'

Levine had produced a small pocketbook and made notes with a pencil as I continued: 'Charlie was first down the ladder, then Jimmy, then me. No sooner had we reached the landing than the coppers were almost up the stairs.'

'How many?'

'Four.'

'You are certain?'

272

'I am. It is the same four I mentioned in my statement.'

'Proceed.'

'The twins headed for a bedroom and two of the coppers followed. I planted a boot in the chest of a third and he fell backwards, taking the fourth copper down the stairs.'

'Was he badly hurt?'

'I don't think so. I don't truly know.'

The lawyer grew thoughtful. 'As far as I can recall, there was no evidence of his injuries.' His pencil hovered in mid-air. 'Continue.'

'I ran into the bedroom and saw Jimmy and Charlie over at a window that had been pulled open. Close to them was a young copper, hitting out with a police stick. And, more dangerously, there was a bearded brute of a bobby, the one that had the knife.'

'This would be Mr Jackson?'

'It would. But I did not know his name. Not then.'

'Was a knife in *his* hand when you entered the room?'

'I didn't see it straight away. He was shouting at the Connors to give themselves up.'

'And the other policeman?'

'The younger one stepped forward and struck Jimmy across the knees with his stick. Charlie went to his defence. That's when I saw the bearded man raise his voice and flash the knife.'

Levine looked up from his notebook. 'This was Jackson?'

'Yes, Jackson. He stabbed Charlie. Sank the blade into his abdomen.'

The lawyer finished writing then drew a line under some words. 'You are certain you saw the knife enter Charlie Connor's body?'

'I am.' I put a hand on my stomach. 'Just here, below the ribs but above the waist and to his left. Charlie screamed and fell to his knees. There was blood everywhere. You could see instantly that it was a very bad wound.'

'And what were you doing at this moment?'

'At first, I was in shock. Then I joined in.'

'How?'

'I punched Jackson.'

'In what part of his body?'

'In the face. Right on the jaw. It was like hitting a wall. He took the blow and came for me.'

'With the knife?'

'Yes. He swiped wildly. Almost cut my nose off. I dodged the blade, grabbed his wrist and ran him into a wall.'

'Did he drop the weapon?'

'No. He held on. Smashed his head against my nose. Shouldered me away.'

I closed my eyes again to relive the encounter, 'I clung to his wrist, kept my balance and pushed back. He lashed out with his free hand. I lost my grip and grabbed again. He flung up a knee between my legs. I rode the pain and grabbed his knife hand again. The best I could do was wrestle it up above my head. I jammed my body against his so there could be no more kneeing or butting. That's when Jimmy and the other bobby banged into us.'

274

'What happened then?'

'Well, the sudden weight of their impact seemed to glue us together. We barrelled across the room and bounced off a wall. Our legs entwined and we fell.'

'Please describe precisely what you did after the fall.'

'I pulled myself out from under the crush of bodies and rolled onto my side. Got quickly to my knees and feet. That's when I saw that Charlie was dead.'

'When?'

'As soon as I got up. I saw it straight away.'

'How? How did you know the Connor boy had expired?'

'He was motionless. Eyes blank. There was a pool of blood next to him, dark and spread out like spilled oil. Then I saw the knife.'

'Officer Jackson's knife?'

I nodded. 'Only it wasn't stuck in Charlie. Nor was it on the floor.'

'It was in Jackson?'

'That's right.'

'Be more precise.'

I put my hand to my throat and felt for the place. 'Here, just below the Adam's apple. The point of the blade had gone all the way through Jackson's neck, into the wooden boards he was lying on.'

Levine raised an eyebrow. 'And how had it got there?'

There was no point lying. 'From my hand. I had wrestled him for it and when we fell I must have driven it through his flesh.'

He closed his notebook. 'And Jackson, did you see him die, or just learn of it later?'

I felt like a cannon had exploded in my head. 'I saw him in his death throes, twitching uncontrollably, like his arms and legs were on invisible strings being pulled by invisible men. Then he lay still. I panicked and bolted through the open window.'

Levine took a moment to complete his notes. He turned a page before continuing, 'We are done with Jackson, now tell me of the other murder, the latest one.'

'You know me to be innocent of that.'

'What one knows, and what one can prove or disprove, are entirely different things.'

'I will not speak of it.'

'You must.'

'I *must* do nothing of the sort, Mr Levine. My lips are sealed on this matter and I am certain you understand that I have good reason for not wishing to elaborate.'

'Then we are done, Mr Lynch. For now at least.' He put away his notebook and pencil. 'It seems that on the first count I must fashion some fiction rather than rely on fact. While on the second,' he shrugged, 'I am powerless until you deign to be more forthcoming.' He gave me a pointed look.

'Mr Levine, what would you have me say that doesn't cast aspersions on our mutual employer and his family? If I ventured down that path then I might as well break my oath and accept Mr Holmes's offer.'

Levine summoned the gaolers with a knock on the door. 'Then indeed we are done.'

I watched him go and wondered whether this dapper man really had the wherewithal to secure my liberty. If not, then I would be solely dependent upon that hidden iron nail in my cell, if not to secure my freedom, then at least to bring a dignified end to my agony and deny the hangman his fee for taking my life.

DERBYSHIRE, MAY 1886

In the days following the attack on our carriage, there was much speculation as to whether it had been as random as it seemed. Alexander supposed that it might have been the work of the Chans. Moriarty dismissed this as unlikely because of its amateurish qualities and the demand for money. 'Had the Chinese been involved, they would have just killed us,' he insisted.

The professor paid me handsomely for my work in London, and for my part in extricating us from the troubles on the journey home. I had crossed a Rubicon and drawn my first blood as a member of the Trinity. The professor said Michael would have been proud of me and such praise was sufficient to chase off any doubt about what I had done.

The following month I was given my first 'official' task, the offing of a man in Lincoln. Most unwisely, he had stolen from one of Moriarty's betting syndicates and gone on the run.

His name was Isaac Pickering and he was a big and foolish fellow. Big made him conspicuous in the small eastern city where outsiders were rare. Foolish made him throw his money around in flash taverns and feral whorehouses where such things attract undue attention and unbridled gossip.

I found him drunk as a lord in the bed of a whore older than Noah's grandmother. The dollymop's years of experience saw her take to the hills as soon as I kicked open the bedroom door.

Candlelight made Pickering's silhouette so large that it filled a wall and folded across the ceiling. I watched it shrink as my knife pierced his greedy gut. I covered his mouth to prevent too much noise bellowing forth. Once his strength ebbed away, I manoeuvred him to a window and pushed the fool into the street below for Thackeray to haul away in a cart.

I felt no pangs of regret. He had chosen a life of crime and knew the dangers. Moriarty assured me there was justification in what I had done.

Justification. It was a word I would use many times to fool myself. That and the fact that I had no choice. Moriarty's threat to expose my earlier crimes meant the shadow of the gallows always hung over me.

Fate had decided my future. Murder had become my trade.

After Pickering's death, I became regularly deployed

by the professor to vanquish enemies who had flourished during the last days of Brannigan's illness. Killings followed killings. With each one, I felt that soft comfort of my inner anger and I became less concerned about the reasons why the individual had been singled out to die. Moriarty had been right. I did not need to know these things. It was enough for me that he considered them evil.

The first assignment that Surrey and I worked together was a banker whom she, at Moriarty's request, had befriended and beguiled.

The man had handled many of the professor's dubious business accounts and over the years had fallen into the habit of demanding increasingly larger fees for his services. The professor had tolerated this, until Alexander inspected the accounts and found a great deal of money had gone missing. A second audit confirmed the thefts had gone on for years and this sealed the banker's fate.

Dressed in her prettiest of outfits, Surrey lured him to a house he had been renting for his recent assignations with her. I lurked in the shadows of the entrance hall, hidden behind a cluster of coats and cloaks that hung from a large wooden stand. Patiently, I waited for the sound of the door closing, his feet crossing the floor and his lustful call to Surrey that he had arrived.

When he passed me, I sprang out and hooked his throat. He was smaller than me, so I was able to lift him off the ground and choke him in the crook of my arm.

I confess, I could have despatched him quicker but found

myself absorbed by the shadow puppetry his struggling body made on the floor and wall. The multiple 'shades' of a dying man were unique works of art. Innocent childhood memories of silhouettes and maternal comfort had, through the cataclysm of murder, formed an addictive relief in my troubled mind.

Thackeray and I disposed of the body, while Surrey used the banker's keys and codes to empty the contents of the nearby vaults. Come Monday morning, it surely looked to the world as though he had stolen the money himself and done a runner.

Moriarty was exceptionally pleased with us. He paid bonuses of five hundred pounds each into our respective Trinity accounts. I was gradually becoming richer and wiser. In the process, I realised that money was the only thing the professor craved more than power.

While my professional life was flourishing, my romantic aspirations were not. Elizabeth continued to avoid me. Conversely, Surrey made it abundantly clear that she could forgive and forget. Inevitably, in a moment of weakness, I found myself inviting her back into my bed and we fell into our old ways. For me, it was born more out of desire for companionship than sex. There was no expectation of each other. No words of commitment uttered or asked for. But there was *something* between us. Something more than mutual kindness, something I couldn't quite describe. Perhaps it was simply the joint peculiarity of our situation. We were, after all, just murderous lone spirits thrown together, living together, not judging each other on immorality or sinfulness.

Many mornings, Surrey rose before I did and was gone before my eyes had properly opened. On those days, she would betray her tough exterior by leaving a flower or leaf on the table by the window. She did it because she knew it reminded me of her love of the outdoors and would make me smile. 'Wake with sweetness and you can face the sourness of any day,' she would say.

I confess that I began to miss her when she was not around. Worse still, when she went away on jobs for the professor, I found myself hating the thought that she might get hurt or even spend the night with someone else. I never asked her if she had, but I could always tell. She either wouldn't come to my bed that evening, or if she did, she would turn away from me and complain of feeling tired or ill.

Alone, in the gardens one morning, she surprised me by asking, 'Do you ever think of running away from all this?'

'To where?'

'To anywhere. Just you and me. Starting afresh. We both have money now. If we combined it then we could buy a cottage in the countryside somewhere and—'

'Moriarty would never let us leave.'

'We wouldn't ask his permission. We'd just take the money—'

'Surrey, we buried the last person who took his money and left. I have run from many people in my life, from the police and from the hangman, but we could never leave Moriarty without his blessing.'

She looked depressed. 'I know. I was just dreaming.'

'Then don't. You and I are not allowed dreams.'

'Are we not?'

'No. The closest to dreams we are permitted is the way we live right now. When we have full stomachs, a warm place to sleep and the energy to make love. Those are our dreams.'

'It is not enough,' she said, almost underneath her breath. 'Not nearly enough.'

'For now, it has to be. Things change. Opportunities may arise. And I promise you, Surrey, if such a chance came to escape and be free, then I would seize it and never let go.'

One Week to Execution

NEWGATE, 11 JANUARY 1900

Levine's plans for lodging appeals filled me with some degree of optimism. Judges and lords were among the most corrupt of men. I would be freed, and once at large again, I would be able to settle old scores. Such thoughts made me realise that I had grown idle since the first hours of my imprisonment; now I needed to build strength along with belief.

I lay on the floor and did slow sit-ups until my stomach felt like it had been beaten with bars. I rolled on to my hands and performed press-ups until my wrists and shoulders collapsed.

I was still slathered in sweat when Johncock opened the cell door with two of his men. 'My, you do look flushed, Lynch. Have you been playing with yourself?'

I didn't waste what little breath I had by answering him.

'Mr Sherlock Holmes, the great detective himself, is here to see you.'

'I am busy perspiring and do not wish to have any visitors.'

'You are busy being scum, and scum has no say in the matter.' Johncock opened the door so Holmes could enter. 'Be respectful, Lynch, or you'll have me to answer to.'

I shrugged and sat on the floor near the ring to which my leg chains had been fixed.

Holmes was wearing a top hat, a white collared shirt with brown silk tie and chequered brown suit beneath a double-breasted frock coat. The shadow he cast across the cell was uniquely his. I would recognise it anywhere in the world.

He removed his coat and laid it over the end of my bunk then took the liberty of sitting there. 'There is the matter of the wager between Dr Watson and myself,' he said, removing his leather gloves. 'I have come to see which of us is nearer being declared a winner.' He glanced towards Johncock. 'You can leave us now, gaoler. Mr Lynch will do me no ill.'

'Are you sure, Mr Holm—'

'Quite certain. Now, please go about your duties.'

Reluctantly, Johncock left with his men.

I wiped sweat from my forehead and rubbed my face with my shirt. 'Unfortunately, you will soon be obliged to pay your companion twenty pounds, Mr Holmes. I have no intention of turning Queen's Evidence. Not now, or in the future.'

'That remains to be seen.' He laid down the gloves. 'The future is never as you expect it to be. Not until it has been rendered into the present and then pressed like a leaf into the volumes that form our past.'

'How poetic.'

'Our future perspective alters from day to day, so what today is unbearable or unimaginable, mostly with the passage of time becomes acceptable. I still believe my twenty pounds to be safer than the good doctor's.'

'You have my answer, Holmes. May I be left to exercise?'

He studied me with interest. 'Your lawyer has raised your expectations unfairly. The use of dirty money to bribe people into bearing false witness will hold no sway with this government.'

'Who told you of new witnesses?'

'You did.'

'I said no such thing.'

'My dear fellow, you all but *shouted* it at me. Your demeanour has completely changed since our last discussion.

There is vigour to you and previously there wasn't. And what would be the point of you exercising if there was not hope? In your case, hope could only come in the form of an appeal to the home secretary, which in turn would not be possible without either new evidence or new witnesses. And of course we both know that such fresh testimonies at this stage of your incarceration would undoubtedly have been purchased.'

Even though his deduction impressed me, I said nothing.

Holmes rose from my bunk, took several paces to the window then walked back towards me. 'I must confess,' he continued, 'there are some aspects of your case that both interest and concern me.'

I half-laughed. 'Neither your interest nor your concern are actually of any interest or concern to me.' I looked up at him. 'I hear you are a busy man, best not waste any more time on me.'

'Oh, it is not wasted. Not yet, at least. I am curious to know who you were with on the day that PC Jackson was killed in that den of thieves in Southwark.'

I lowered my head again. 'All the detail I wish to disclose has been recorded in my statement to the police.'

'I have seen the statement. It is flimsy and inadequate, containing no names of individuals, so please tell me, who were the other gang members embroiled in that encounter with you?'

'I cannot remember their names.'

'Cannot, or will not?'

'I choose my words carefully.'

'As do I.'

'They were members of the gang I was running with.'

'I am aware of that. The Hoolihans.'

I did not confirm or deny anything.

Holmes paced again. 'Patrick Hoolihan is almost as complete a fool as his half-wit cousin Andrew O'Connell. Although the latter can be forgiven as nature dealt him a most unfortunate set of cards.'

I wanted to ask what had become of them both but held my silence.

'They're both still at large,' said the shadow passing by me. 'Fittingly, they are said to be as thick as thieves. Although, as you would expect, many of Hoolihan's original gang have gone.' He stepped closer and added, 'Several of them have been hanged. Some have been killed while at large. Others have simply *disappeared*.'

He reached into his jacket and produced a document marked with a red wax seal. 'This is official confirmation that, should you provide a full and honest account of your years of criminal activity in the employ of James Moriarty, then you will *not* be executed. Furthermore, should your testimony result in a successful prosecution of Moriarty then you will be pardoned.' He stepped forward and pushed the letter against my chest.

I let it drop to the floor. 'I said I have given my answer.'

'That document is signed by Sir Matthew White Ridley, the home secretary.'

'Had Lord Salisbury himself signed it, it would still be on the stone and my answer would remain the same.'

'With a pardon, you could start a new life. I would personally see to it that you were resettled a long way from the reach of that octopus Moriarty.'

I confess that Holmes's words woke in me my sleeping worms of doubt. I itched to accept his offer, to be done with the relentless frustration of being unable to escape.

I picked up the official document. His eyes widened in victory, and in that distasteful moment of presumed triumph he sparked in me a resolve not to give in. Not yet, at least. I handed it back to him.

'My answer remains a firm "No", Mr Holmes. I am now bereft of further ways to phrase the rejection.'

'Stubbornness is an impediment, not a virtue, Lynch. You need to overcome it.'

'And *you* need to leave, Mr Holmes. You have worn out my patience. And as I am sure you are aware, beneath this awfully thin veneer of politeness lies the essence of a murderous man.'

'I am sure that is true. Very well, I shall go, but remember this. My offer is not without limit. You have three days, including today, in which to accept it. After that, consider it withdrawn.'

'I wish to use the lavatory, Mr Holmes, and would greatly appreciate some privacy, if you please.'

He looked to me again. Searched for some sign of weakness that would allow him to negotiate further.

I undid my trousers and dropped them. 'You could leave me that offer if you wish. The paper upon which it is written looks soft and clean; I may have use for it after all.'

'Gaoler!' shouted Holmes. 'Release me, immediately.'

DERBYSHIRE, MAY 1887

There is a small hamlet on the haunch of the River Dove called Milldale and in it a packhorse crossing known as Viator's Bridge. It was made famous by the writer Izaak Walton in his book *The Compleat Angler* as a spot where fishermen gathered and gossiped before taking to the banks.

I knew it for a different reason. It was also where a fortune-telling hag fished for coin. Many a mill girl had crossed the old crone's palms with silver, in return for the promise of a dark handsome stranger to marry, or at least a husband who wouldn't beat her.

Lacking a better way to while away the hours of a lazy spring afternoon, I had put coin in the gypsy's hand and sat opposite her while she read my palm. Her brow furrowed and dark eyes squinted as she took an age to tell me nothing of note. Then she finished with words I would never forget. As I was about to leave, she said, 'We all have a hidden sense that can warn us of opportunities to be seized or impending dangers to be avoided. You would do well, young man, to heed yours.'

I smiled sceptically. 'I am afraid I have no such powers.'

'We *all* have them but few of us recognise them or under-stand how to use them.'

'And how should I recognise these powers?'

'You have proof of their existence every time someone tells you that they feel there is a *change* in the air, or they remark that they "just knew things would turn out exactly like they did", or they speak of a gut feeling that something bad is about to happen.'

'Those certainly are all things I have said and experienced.'

She looked pleased with herself. 'Then use such instincts. Build them like muscles. I see a restlessness in your eyes. You have the look of a hunter.'

'Some fish and game. And a rabbit or two,' I confessed.

She stared at my hands and her face grew cold. 'I think not only of fish and fowl.'

I had heard enough. 'Good day to you, ma'am.'

She rose and rushed to me. 'Here is your money back, hunter. I will not take it.' She pressed the coins into my hand. 'It has blood on it. I want none of your clink.'

I did not take it from her. Instead, it dropped to the floor and she left it there.

As I turned to leave, the gypsy shouted after me, 'Learn those senses. You will need them, for hunters are also hunted.'

I was to be reminded of this conversation one year and two days after the funeral of Michael Brannigan. Surrey had been asked by Moriarty's brother James to travel to Ireland to assist one of his men, a former colonel called Moran. In her absence, I was required to travel with Brogan Moriarty, Sirius and Lady Elizabeth to an upcoming race at Epsom, where I was told there might be business to be done, both on and off course.

The day before our planned departure, I felt all the symptoms the fortune-teller had spoken of. Something was about to change – I felt it in my gut. The hairs on my arms bristled. I was certain my life was set to take some surprising turn.

I readied myself for the task in hand. Prepared my rather unusual travel bag, comprising casual and formal clothes and an efficient 'killing kit' that suited whatever eventuality might arise. I also wanted something to read, a distraction to dull the boredom of endless hours travelling by horse and locomotive.

I visited Moriarty's library, made a rough selection of books and took them to a table to whittle down the number. Since Michael's death, I had read most voraciously. Sitting quietly and immersing myself in literature seemed to create some balance after the brutal physicality of a kill, or the hard work I put into keeping myself fit.

I was but a short way through making my choices when the door opened and Elizabeth entered. At that moment, I again experienced the very feelings that the gypsy had described. The air was charged with excitement from the first second Elizabeth's eyes caught mine.

'I hear tomorrow we are to go to Epsom together,' she remarked as she neared me.

As I looked at her, the awkwardness I had created by stealing a kiss in this very room returned.

'So I understand,' I finally replied. 'The professor informed me at breakfast.' I gestured to the books laid out on the table in front of me. 'I am looking for something suitable to pass the journey.'

She put down some books of her own and sat opposite me. 'Have you been racing before?'

'No, I haven't.'

'I adore it. At least I adore the fashions and the thrill of winning.' She added quickly, 'But not the cruelty to the horses.'

'*Is it* so cruel?'

'Don't be naive. Of course it is. All that whipping and kicking with heels. It is terribly cruel. And then there is the fixing, the deliberate ways of making them sick or injured, to ensure one wins over the other. I suspect it is even crueller than your precious boxing.'

'I had never really thought about it.'

'Then you should.' She finally looked at the book I was reading. '*Romeo and Juliet*?'

'I have read it once before and thought it worth revisiting.'

She picked it up and flicked lightly through some pages. 'Because you enjoyed it so greatly?'

'What is there not to enjoy about a young man's pursuit of his love?'

'What indeed?' She smiled coyly.

'And I prefer Shakespeare's Queen Mab to Shelley's, even though the fairy is somewhat duplicitous.'

'Do you indeed?' Her smile became flirtatious enough for me to be reminded of the fortune-teller's comments about sensing and seizing opportunity.

'You look very beautiful today. Too beautiful to be in a dusty library. Would you like to walk in the grounds with me?'

'I would not.' She laughed playfully. 'Tell me instead, how does Shakespeare's Mab differ from Shelley's?'

'I believe you know how.'

'I would like to hear *you* tell me.'

'Well, it seems to me that Shakespeare's fairy fills people's minds with hopes and dreams. Lovers with love. Soldiers with soldiering. His Mab is more *sensual*, more passionate and daring than Shelley's cynical old sprite.'

'And has this *sensual* Mab visited you in your sleep?'

'Nightly.'

'And what has she filled your sweet head with?'

'With dreams of love, of course.'

'Not slitting throats?'

'Just love. *One* pure love.'

'But, Simeon, you are a soldier now, are you not? Moriarty's newest recruit. A proud fighter in his ranks.'

'I obey him, as you do. That does not mean I dream of the life he shapes for me. I dream of you, you know I do.'

'And you know you should not.' Her gaiety faded. She rose and wandered to the shelves.

I called after her. 'Elizabeth, why do you provoke me to talk of such things only to reject me again?'

She faced the books as she answered. 'Perhaps it is because I am trying to discover your true feelings.' Then she half-turned and added, 'Perhaps it is because I cannot help myself.'

I rose and walked towards her. 'The thoughts I have for you do not come *nightly* in my dreams; they are in my mind all day and at all moments. There is not a minute within an hour when—'

She cut me off by extending both hands and pushing a book towards me. 'Take this.'

My hands involuntarily grasped the volume.

'Take it and read it. It will serve you far better than *Romeo and Juliet*.' And with that she glided past me to the door.

'Elizabeth, wait!'

She stopped and smiled. 'Read the book, Simeon. Learn the dangers that dreams and hopes can lead to. And if you need help in understanding anything, then we can discuss it on the way to Epsom. Or if you cannot wait, then you will find me in my room this evening.'

Six Days to Execution

Yesterday, I had been blinded by optimism. Dazzled by my colourful counsel and the belief he had engendered within me that I might escape the noose. But with the new dawn and the lack of further news from Mr Levine came the reversal of my moods and I found myself contemplating the worst.

There were but two more days, after which the clemency deal Holmes had offered would disappear like the pale show of light outside my postage stamp of a window. It was the only true guarantee that I would be freed and therefore able to exact the revenge that was eating me alive. Increasingly, that thought alone seemed sufficient compensation for selling the last ounce of respect I had clung onto.

My eyes roamed the walls of my cell for the millionth time. There were scratched messages on almost every brick. Lines of verse, prayers, pleas for mercy authored by the cell's previous occupants. Made no doubt with nails like the one smuggled to me in chapel. Lord knows, it was proving good for nothing more than leaving a vain mark on the masonry.

I had read most of the inscriptions within my first hour inside this godforsaken place. They were footnotes to each individual author's execution. Final efforts to leave a mark in a world that wanted rid of them.

Now as the end loomed large, I stood alongside

innumerable initials, crossed-off days and pleas for forgiveness and began my inscription.

SL 1900 . . .

It wasn't much to leave behind.

The last century had started with horses and carts and finished with trains, trams and automobiles. Machinery had begun replacing men in many jobs and electricity was replacing gas. I had been born into a world of advancement and opportunity and had become nothing more than a grave filler.

I retraced my initials and the date, hoping the motion would awaken some creative thoughts.

It didn't.

The nail had become annoyingly blunt. I tried to sharpen it on the wall next to the window. Scraped hard where bricks met the floor close to the edge of my bunk. It sank into the mortar rather than scratched over it. Clogged with dust and debris.

My heart missed a beat. This must have been the only place in the cell I had not previously scraped and poked at.

I looked to the door. Listened for the sound of gaolers. Ran the nail back and forth. The mortar was mouldy and soft. Years of damp and filth had eaten the bond between brick and floor. I scraped furiously, produced small but multiple heaps of slurry that had to be fingered away. Running the metal along the top of the brick had the same effect. Mortar slopped away like rancid butter.

I paused and listened for sounds of gaolers outside the

door. There were none. I scraped vertically this time, first on the left, then on the right of the target brick. It wobbled; with more effort it would come free. I knew that if I jammed the nail deep into the rotten mortar I could prise this single brick out of the wall.

I lay flat on the floor, working the brick up and down and side to side. It slipped back, in danger of disappearing into the blackness behind it. I couldn't let that happen. If it slipped into that space then I might not recover it and the hole would be left exposed and noticeable.

With great care, I manoeuvred the brick forward. Firstly, from the left. Then the right. Soon, I was able to get my fingers onto the edges and eased it forward. It came away completely.

I froze with shock. I had taken a brick out of the cell wall.

The rest of the wall was still intact but to me it felt like I had cracked opened a safe. The rectangular hole beyond the brick was tiny, but it was a hole.

Beyond it there was only blackness. I put my ear as close to the gap as I could get and heard a distinct sound of wind. It convinced me I had discovered a chimney, still bricked at the bottom but hopefully open at the top.

Thoughts of Jack Sheppard sprang to mind. One of his escapes had been through such a shaft.

Loud sounds on the landing caused me to stop. Hurriedly, I brushed the scrapings and filth into the small hole then replaced the brick. I grabbed a book and sat on my bunk.

Keys jangled. I realised I still had the nail in my hand, and jammed it into the back of my shoe.

The door opened. A gaoler, a vile hog of a man called Wallace, rubbed his whiskery jowls as he entered.

'Stand up, Lynch!'

My heart skipped as I rose.

He peered at my feet to check that my new leg irons were still secured to a floor ring, then glanced around the rest of the cell, before adding, 'Father Deagan is here to see you.' He stepped aside. 'Please come in, Father. Our apologies for the stink and for him over there stinkin' more than anythin'.'

The priest entered. He looked older and weaker than I remembered. 'Thank you, officer,' he managed. After pressing a handkerchief to his mouth to stifle a cough, he added, 'You may leave us now.'

The door shut. Deagan lifted his tired face and shook my hand. 'How are you, my son? I hope you are holding up as you climb your own Calvary.'

'I am fine, Father.' I made space for him on the bunk. 'Please sit down. You really do not look so well.'

'I confess to being somewhat under the weather. But I do count my blessings. God gives me the constitution to soldier on and administer his word.' He lifted a leather bag and from it produced two prayer books and two sets of red rosary beads. Without asking he passed one to me. 'I thought we might pray together. Nothing grander or more ambitious than that. A shared moment of divinity, that is all.'

'I am ashamed to say it is many years since I have prayed. So many that I cannot remember.'

'That is why I brought the book.' He closed my hand around it and then struggled to rise from the bunk. 'Please help me kneel as my old joints have grown rusty in this wet and bitter winter.'

'Of course, Father.'

I held his arm as he lowered himself to the hard floor and then knelt myself. For a second, his breath drew short and he stayed motionless until another fit of coughing was finished.

I waited patiently while he regained his composure, hoping his illness wasn't serious. Winter was a time of dying. Prison flu killed a person a week, took felons and gaolers without prejudice.

'Let me offer you some words of fortitude,' he said weakly. 'Some trusted words from Man's most trusted book.' He lifted a rosary over his head, set it in place around his neck and kissed the small black crucifix. 'The Lord is my shepherd,' he began, 'I shall not want . . .'

The words of the psalm struck chords within me and raised hopes that I feared might be false ones. Could a killer like me really pass through the valley of death into the green pastures of heaven? Was I not the embodiment of evil and was this not the time the Devil would come and claim his soul?

Father Deagan touched my arm. He pulled me out of my contemplative state and pressed me into prayers. We did the full circle of the rosary, the 'crown of roses' in all its Christocentric glory, punctuated only by the rasping of his painful cough.

When we finished, he looked to me and asked, 'Now Simeon, while you are in this state of grace, would you like me to hear your confession?'

It seemed right to say yes. Perhaps the old priest was a perfect salesman and knew that if he had me kneeling and in a state of prayer then I would finally consent. Certainly, I saw no harm in it.

I rejoined my hands and said, 'Bless me, Father, for I have sinned. I have not made a confession since I was a child and had not long since completed my first communion.'

'I understand. What is it that you wish to confess? Speak frankly and fully now, for you speak to the Lord thy God and master of your soul for all eternity.'

And I did. For the next half hour, without thought for the poor man's knees on the brutal stone floor or the strains of his obvious illness, I told him everything. That is to say, every act of theft, deceit, violence and murder I could remember. The offences were so numerous and spread over so many years that I am certain there are some I forgot to mention. I named no names. And as best I could, implicated no one else. I was certain God knew to whom I referred and I did not wish to place Father Deagan in a position where he might be tempted to break his religious oaths and make himself a target for people who would need to silence him.

The old priest listened to my sins with admirable patience, without admonishment or any sign of judgement. But with his professionalism and kindness came a determination to root out all the evil that lay in me. 'And what of the last murder you were convicted of, my son? You are in denial as to this act, yet I fear your soul is also infected by this mortal sin.'

'No Father, it is not.'

'Do you swear so in the presence of the Almighty?'

'I do, Father. It is only just and proper that the Crown hangs me for the many murders I have committed, but not the one I have not.'

'The judgement of the courts and the judgement of Christ are very different, Simeon. Lying to a court may lead to retaining your liberty; lying to the Lord leads to eternal damnation.'

'I know that, Father. I swear on my soul, I am not guilty of that abomination.'

He raised a hand to stop me going further. 'Then let us speak of remorse. Are you truly sorry and contrite for all your sins?'

'I am.'

'And do you reject Satan and all his followers and his acts?'

'I do.'

'Are you ready to meet the Lord your God, to beg for his blessed forgiveness and to throw yourself upon his mercy?'

'I am.'

He opened my prayer book again. 'Please say these words aloud, and when you speak them make sure you mean them with all of your heart.'

I looked at the text. It was the Act of Contrition. Great emotion rose within me. A thousand times or more in my life I had apologised to people and asked for their forgiveness. But this was an apology to God. My last chance to say sorry for wasting the life he had given me.

I struggled to read the words. 'Forgive me my sins, O Lord, forgive me my sins; the sins of my youth, the sins of my age, the sins of my soul, the sins of my body; my idle sins, my serious voluntary sins; the sins I know, the sins I do not know; the sins I have concealed for so long, and which are now hidden from my memory. I am truly sorry for every sin, mortal and venial, for all the sins of my childhood up to the present hour. I know my sins have wounded thy tender heart, O my Saviour; let me be freed from the bonds of evil through the bitterest Passion of my Redeemer. Amen.'

Deagan took the book from me and gave the response in full, concluding with the words of hope that all sinners long to hear: 'Through the ministry of the Church, may God give thee pardon and peace, and I absolve thee from thy sins in the name of the Father and of the Son and of the Holy Spirit. Amen.'

'Amen.'

He took my hands in his and added, 'I must leave you now, Simeon; but I will pray for your soul and so must you.

Pray for it until the last breath of life is taken from you. Do this and the glory of God and the gates of the Kingdom of Heaven will be open to you.'

'Thank you, Father.'

'Please help me to my feet.' He stretched out an arm.

As I did so, he coughed so violently his whole body shook and I felt duty bound to hold him for a good deal longer. 'Are you all right, Father?'

'No, my son, I fear I am not.' Another bout of coughing caused him to double up with stomach cramps.

'Gaoler! Gaoler, come quickly!' No sooner had the words left my mouth than the priest staggered and fell.

Keys turned in the lock and Wallace entered. 'Stand back,' he shouted. 'Get back by that window or we'll beat you back.'

'Hurry up – it's Father Deagan; he's collapsed.'

'If this is a trick, Lynch, I'll flog you so hard you'll not be able to walk to the rope.' He blew hard on a whistle.

Within the minute, half a dozen screws had rushed into the cell. The good Father was lifted up between them, carried out and my door soundly shut again.

Left behind were his bag, rosary beads and prayer books. Instinctively, I seized them.

Inside was a convict's treasure trove – a pipe, a soft leather pouch filled with tobacco, a purple-coloured silk sash, a vial of holy water, a wooden crucifix about six inches long and three inches wide and a small mirror edged in leather. It would be a strange collection for someone such as me to carry, but was, I presumed, a standard set of tools for someone in the clerical trade. There was also a set of keys, no doubt for the parish church, and a fountain pen with a broad steel nib.

Without hesitation, I took what I wanted. The sash would make a highly workable garrotte and the crucifix a useful dagger if sharpened properly. The rosaries were well strung and could help secure all manner of things, or people.

I rushed to the brick that I had loosened, removed it, stashed my hoard and replaced it. The screws would be back any moment. I knelt with my back to the door, put my hands together and prayed. Not for Father Deagan, but that I didn't get caught.

No sooner had I settled into that position than Wallace and one of his colleagues returned. They swore at me as they filled Deagan's bag with his remaining things. Swore again and left me with such a hefty boot in the middle of my back that I collapsed against the wall.

The door closed and I heard them retreat down the gallery. When they were gone, I thanked God for allowing me to steal from a priest, though I suspect the appreciation should have gone to Satan. I got up and retrieved the nail that I had hidden in my shoe.

I went to the door and checked for sounds on the landing before returning to the spot where I had made the inscription SL 1900. Father Deagan had come to save my soul. He had given me absolution and within a second of his collapse

I had reverted to my true self. I knew now what I had to write. What should be my message to the world. I scratched it deep into the grime of the wall.

> Though I walk through the valley of the shadow
> > of death,
> I fear no evil.
> For I am evil.

DERBYSHIRE, MAY 1887

The book Elizabeth had given me was Charles Maturin's *Melmoth the Wanderer*. It revealed itself to be the tale of a foolish and greedy man who sells his soul to the Devil then wanders Europe, corrupting others while trying to find someone to relieve him of his burden.

I discerned the plot of the novel in the privacy of my room, while thinking over Elizabeth's behaviour towards me. There had been a look on her face that had urged me to talk freely to her, and I had touched her heart — I was sure of it.

But she had left my thoughts and emotions spinning.

Did she really want me to take up that invitation to come to her room? She had said come with the book and she would explain it to me. But had that been more than just a literary offer?

I was filled with excitement and insecurity.

And guilt.

Guilt for in light of my newly repaired relationship with Surrey, it would be highly improper for me to pursue Elizabeth.

Darling, darling, Elizabeth.

Had she really set her sights on me?

I thought again of the old fortune-teller of Milldale and her words of opportunity. Surely, Surrey and I were destined to part. We were no more than makeweights in each other's lives. I convinced myself that it would be better for both of us to face the reality of our situation and move on with our lives.

After dinner, I took a cowardly decision that a glass or two of whisky might help resolve the matter. And I suppose it did. For that evening, slightly the worse for wear, I found myself standing outside Elizabeth's bedroom door.

I knocked. Cleared my throat and announced, 'Elizabeth, it is Simeon. I wonder if I might disturb you?'

'Come in,' she answered in a tone reminiscent of my lessons in the drawing room.

I opened the door.

The room was warm and lit by numerous candles. It smelled of soft wax and fresh roses. The curtains were drawn. Elizabeth was seated on the side of her brass bed in a white cotton nightdress. Her hair was down and she was brushing it. The light seemed to catch every strand and it looked like it had been spun from gold. She looked more beautiful than I had ever seen her.

For a time, I was unaware that I was simply standing and staring. Then I realised my clumsiness and held up my copy of *Melmoth the Wanderer*. 'Forgive my appearance at so late an hour, but you said to call if I were in need of help.'

'So I did.' She nodded at the novel I was stupidly holding aloft. 'But if your cultural *craving* is to be satisfied, Simeon, then you are by necessity going to have to come closer.'

I walked towards her, aware only of the creak of the dark floorboards beneath my feet, the rhythmical tick of a grandmother clock and the thunder of my heart. I sat beside her and looked nervously across the walls, imagining that somewhere behind the boards and bricks the professor's prying eyes were watching us. 'Forgive me, but I fear Moriarty lurks behind the walls and is spying on us.'

She took the book out of my hands, placed a cool hand to my face and kissed me lightly. 'No one is there, I promise you.' She pushed me back on the bed. 'Just as *I* am certain you were not seen coming here, be certain I have ensured *we* will not be seen while you are here. '

Elizabeth undressed me. Light and deep kisses punctuated the removal of each garment. When I was naked and breathless, she stepped into the pooling candlelight so I might see her better as she removed her nightdress. I swear the sight of her naked flesh in those flickering warm hues lit a thousand fires inside me.

'Oh my God, I want you so much,' I said, no longer caring whether Moriarty was watching or was in the room alongside us. 'I want you so very desperately.'

306

'I know you do,' she teased. 'I know it very well.'

Our love played out in a shadow dance on the wall, a wonderful waltz that was one moment frantic and the next exquisitely slow. Kiss by kiss and minute by minute I slipped away from the tense reality of the world.

I fell asleep with Elizabeth in my arms, and my pleasure doubled when I found she was still there when I awoke. Dawn light fell across us both and I studied her face while she slept. She was a good ten years older than Surrey and had wrinkles around her eyes where Surrey had none. But Elizabeth was all the more beautiful for them. The tiny flaws made her unique. Made me want her more than ever.

As the room grew lighter her eyelashes fluttered open like the wings of a tired butterfly. I saw her focus. She pieced together the events of last night then smiled sleepily, 'I am glad to see you are still here.'

'Of course I am here.' I stroked her hair. 'Why wouldn't I be? You look so beautiful when you are sleeping.'

She pushed fingers self-consciously through her hair. 'I am afraid I look my age. Which as you are aware is some-what greater than yours.'

'Everything about you is greater than me. Greater than any other person I know.'

She touched my face and smiled. 'You feel like that because you have hunted me for so long and are intoxicated by getting what you wanted. Once your mind clears, you will quickly bore of me and my aged *greatness*.'

'"Age cannot Love destroy."'

'Ha! If you are to quote Shelley then you must do so in honest fullness. "Age cannot Love destroy but *perfidy* can blast the flower, even when in most unwary hour it blooms in Fancy's bower." *Perfidy*, Simeon, *perfidy*.'

I knew she meant my betrayal of Surrey was deceitful and made me likely in time to be unfaithful to her as well. 'I only want you, Elizabeth. I will only *ever* want you.'

'Then you must tell your *other* lover that.'

'I know I must. And I will, as soon as Surrey returns. But what of you and the professor?'

She frowned. 'The professor?'

'You and he are also lovers, so—'

'We most certainly are not!' She sounded aghast. 'Is that what Miss Breed said?'

I nodded.

'Then that little dollymop has lied to you. Lied no doubt, so she could keep you for herself.'

'Don't call her that.'

'She's lower than a common toffer. She sleeps with men not to pleasure them, but to take their lives. She is a succubus.'

'Is that worse than your relationship with Moriarty? Because no matter how you protest, there is clearly a relationship of sorts.'

The remark stung her into silence.

'If he is not your lover, then what hold does he have over you?'

Her face crumpled.

I put my hands to her shoulders. 'You can confide in me. I will keep your confidence. You know that I will.'

Her eyes glistened. She blinked and a tear rolled down her cheek.

I wiped it with my hand. 'Please tell me what upsets you so much that it makes you weep to even consider speaking of it.'

'It is my father.' She spoke softly, as though the words bore a terrible weight. 'He is the reason why I am here. Why, like you and Surrey and Sirius, I am inextricably bound to the professor.' She lowered her head.

'I do not understand.' I put my hand gently under her chin and raised it so I might see her eyes. '*What* about your father?'

'I had him killed. By the professor. By Michael, to be precise.'

'I can't believe that of you.'

'He abused me, Simeon. Abused me long before my mother died and before I was even of age.'

'Dear God.'

'Eventually, he made me pregnant. Lord forgive me, but it was a blessing that the poor child was stillborn.'

I tried to comfort her, but she pushed me away. It was as if she needed the space to be able to say anything more.

'He said it was my fault. That *I made him* do those things. He said God had taken the baby from me because I had been sinful and wronged both my father on earth and Father in heaven.'

'*Father?* That evil man was no parent to you. Had I known him, I would have killed him myself.'

'Thank you.'

'Forgive me for asking, but how did you even come to be acquainted with the professor and Michael?'

'Moriarty has known me since I was a young girl. He regularly came to my father's business and our house in Scotland for dinner.'

'What kind of business did your family run?'

'Shipping. Import and export. In its prime, it had vessels and crews in both Scotland and England, trading with China, Europe and America. One day, Moriarty came to see my father but he was not at home and instead he found me . . . ' She struggled to continue.

'Found you what?'

'Close to death. I had tried to end it all, by taking laudanum and cutting my wrists.'

'Dear God.'

'Moriarty and a maid found me bleeding and unconscious on a chaise longue.'

'You poor thing.'

'The professor kept me alive while a doctor was sent for. I'd have been dead but for him. It was when he came to see me the following week that I broke down and told him what Papa had been doing to me.'

'And Moriarty offered a remedy? A permanent one?'

'He did. But not there and then. It came more than a month later, after he and my father had fallen out. The

310

professor asked if it was true that I would inherit both the house and the business if Papa died. I told him it was but that our home had been heavily mortgaged to pay debts run up by the business. He proposed to have him killed, in return for me transferring the business to him.'

'Quite a payment.'

'One I am still settling.'

'And your title?'

'My title?' she smiled ironically. 'That came after father's death. I was so low and wretched. We had just buried him and I told the professor I believed myself to be the worst of all womankind and he should have let me die. Instead, he berated me for my self-condemnation. Said I was a *lady*. Can you imagine? He insisted that I travel with him back to his home in England and stay there until I recovered, which I did. And from that moment forth, whenever he introduced me, he did so by saying, 'Meet Elizabeth, Lady Elizabeth.'

'And where did the Audsley come from?'

'My mother's maiden name. God bless her soul.'

'Now I understand. Then I shall resume the good practice of calling you *Lady Elizabeth*.'

'You will not.' She smiled gently and added, 'May I ask a favour of you, Simeon?'

'Of course.'

'Please do not take offence, but I would like to be alone now. I have said much more than I intended to. About myself. And about how I am bound, in both honour and dishonour, to the professor—'

'As are we all, ' I interjected.

'Indeed. But I am tired. Physically and emotionally tired, and I am feeling somewhat vulnerable.'

'Then let me stay and care for you.'

'We are not yet *that* close, Simeon. May never be. Now, if you please, just gather your clothes and leave. Last night was a mistake. One I would like neither of us to speak about ever again.'

She turned away from me. And though I did speak, did plead to stay and comfort her, Elizabeth said no more. She would not even look at me. Indeed, it seemed she had shut out the entire world.

SIX DAYS TO EXECUTION

NEWGATE, 12 JANUARY 1900

Theodore Levine finally materialised. He was dressed as dandily as usual, in a purple jacket, black breeches and an astonishingly tall topper, which he took off with a flourish before glaring at the gaoler loitering in the secure room we had been shown to.

'Privacy, my good man!' he shouted at the turnkey. 'Please do not have the temerity to hover like a great stink. My client has the right to confidential counsel and I am asserting it on his behalf, so be gone with you!'

Levine stared a hole in the back of the turnkey's tunic until the door had been soundly shut. He then gave me his full attention. 'A fellow named Arthur Cross has lodged an official complaint with the chief constable. An hour ago he resigned from the constabulary. He did so because he felt his letter was not going to be dealt with fairly, promptly or professionally.'

'And how is this pertinent to me?'

'I shall illuminate you. When you were arrested you were taken into custody where you were beaten, were you not?'

'I was.'

'One of those men was PC Cross.'

'I cannot recall any names. What difference does his admission make?'

'A great deal, and if you kindly afford me a little of your patience, then I shall be pleased to explain.' He reached to his side and from a case produced a document. 'As you will see from his sworn statement, he and several other officers had been instructed by their inspector to assault you.' Levine picked out their surnames with stabs of an index finger. 'Here, here and here.'

'I see.'

'I am seeking to use this assault as grounds for appeal. I will build a case that such was the level of brutality it left you traumatised and unable to properly respond to questioning.'

'Will the Crown not purport that I had such an opportunity at my trial?'

'They will, but we will assert that you were *still* in a state of trauma, that such was the brutalisation, you were in no fit state to make your case.'

'And my lawyer?'

He looked embarrassed. 'We must concede that you were inadequately represented, that counsel was incompetent. That much is true. I have dismissed the flibbertigibbet and once more you have my apologies for his failings.'

'Thank you, but sadly there is no turning back of the clock.'

'We are trying, Mr Lynch, but the clocks of Justice are rusted and stubborn.'

'Then I pray you free them soon so that I might be freed. Meanwhile, I am desperate for news of the outside world, Mr Levine – news of our mutual employers, my former colleagues and associates.'

'Yes, I imagine you are.' His countenance became more businesslike as he added, 'I am not at liberty to speak openly about our employers in these surroundings, nor is any visit possible at the moment. I hope circumstances may change but for reasons of safety, such a venture is currently out of the question. Once more, I convey to you their deepest respect and highest gratitude for your continued loyalty.'

'If only locks could be picked with your fine phrases, Mr Levine, then I should already be strolling down The Strand.'

'Sir, I mean only to honestly convey to you—'

'Save me your expensive flattery. What of Surrey Breed? Do you have any word on her?'

'I am afraid not. Despite limitless enquiries, there has been no sight or sound of her since the night of your arrest.'

The news saddened me and I couldn't help but fear the worst for her. Levine got to his feet and pushed the chair beneath the table. 'If there is nothing further then I shall go, and busy myself on your behalf.'

'That is it? Your fleeting visit is over?' My temper boiled. 'You must work harder and get me out of here, sir!' I banged a fist on the table out of frustration. 'These hands must close around the throat of my nemesis!'

'Sir, please, control yourself.' The lawyer glanced towards the door and the gaolers we both knew would be standing with their ears pressed to the other side. 'I strive relentlessly for your freedom, Mr Lynch. We have our men of straw for the case of the murdered policeman, and we have PC Cross to call into question the validity of your second murder conviction. Now, if I am to secure your liberty, I really must bid you good day. There is much to be done and very little of your time left in which to do it.'

DERBY DAY, EPSOM, MAY 1887

The journey to Epsom that day almost thirteen years ago had been awful.

Elizabeth and I found not a single moment in which to

be alone and overcome the awkwardness that arose from her confession of her debt to Moriarty and culminated in my subsequent banishment from her bedroom.

My discomfort must have been palpable, for once on the train from Derby, and again as we exited at the station, the professor questioned my peculiar quietness. I insisted that I was merely feeling under the weather and thought he had accepted this. I was wrong. As we made our way into the racecourse he pulled me to one side. 'I am no fool, Simeon, so please do not treat me like one. While I may have been inclined to ignore your relationship with Miss Breed, I am most certainly not going to approve of your obvious dalliance with Lady Elizabeth.'

'It is not—'

'Be quiet! Don't irritate me with ill-thought-out lies. It is blatantly obvious from the past few hours of avoided eye contact and leaden silences that something has occurred. And if it is what I fear it is, then it must be ended. Immediately! Do you understand me?'

'Sir, with respect, I have the most honourable of feelings towards Lady—'

'God help me, Simeon!' Moriarty pushed me backwards. He was angrier than I had ever seen. 'I did not enquire, nor do I care a jot about your feelings. I asked if you understood my demand to end your dalliance.'

'I understand your demand,' I replied firmly. 'But I am not willing to comply with it.'

'*Not willing?*' His hands balled into fists, but I knew he

would not strike me. He had not the brashness of personality to do so and this was far too public a place for him to lash out and be seen losing his temper.

'It stops! Stops right now.' He jabbed me insistently in the chest and strode away.

Ahead, I saw Elizabeth standing with Sirius. They had waited for us and had witnessed everything. Moriarty drew level with her. He said something, then snatched her by the arm and all but dragged her out of view and into the mass of racegoers.

Thackeray caught me up. 'What's wrong with the prof? He certainly seemed to 'ave 'is dander up.'

'He's just in a bad temper,' I lied. 'He was warning me that there were to be no slip-ups today. Apparently, there are many important meetings to be held.'

It was a cool and cloudy morning but the crowd had clearly not been deterred by the weather. There were tens of thousands of them and their collective noise was so deafening that it saved me from further interrogation by my northern friend. Excited people packed the paddocks and stands. Others jostled around the edge of the track for the best of positions. Above the roar of thrilled voices came lusty shouts of bookmakers, most of whom perched precariously on portable steps with giant chalkboards displaying their odds.

At Tattenham Corner there were all manner of steam rides and, not far away, a fairground with coconut shies, hoop stalls, jugglers, magicians and fortune-tellers. Sadly, we had little time for amusement. Most of the day was spent in earnest with the professor's business partners. These were men who coordinated numerous betting scams, not just at Epsom but at Chester, Aintree and Ascot as well. The Chans were not among them. The pact brokered at Primrose Hill had seen them retreat into the background and take a share of profits as 'sleeping partners'.

Our appointments included trainers who were willing to nobble not only their horses but also their opponents' animals. And we struck deals with several jockeys more than content to throw a race for not much more than a month's wages. I learned all nature of dirty tricks. Foul play included tightening a horse's shoes, running it on hard ground when the race going was soft, and simply putting a bucket of water into the animal's belly just before the off.

Circumstances continued to conspire to keep Elizabeth and me apart, until the professor peeled away to a hospitality area to meet some members of Parliament.

'Are you all right?' I asked her, tentatively.

She took my arm and walked me away from Sirius and Thackeray. 'You mean, am I still embarrassed and cross with you?'

'Yes, I suppose I do. And are you?'

'I am.' She smiled forgivingly. 'But not as much as I was last night.'

'Then for that I am grateful.'

'The professor was very angry at the way you talked to him. He said you were defiant.'

318

'He told me that he didn't want me to be with you. A dalliance, he called it.'

'I know.'

'And I told him I wouldn't obey such an order.'

'I know that as well. But you *must* obey him, Simeon. Moriarty has affection for you but it would be foolish to push him to the limits of it. As I am sure you have become aware, he likes to control everything. Everything and everyone.'

'So we are destined to be his slaves? To have no free will? No right to choose what we feel and for whom we feel it?'

'You put it a little melodramatically, but yes, that is the sum of things.' She lifted the racing card in order to change the subject. 'Did your various discussions this morning inform you of where I should place a wager?'

'Avoid the favourite – that's a horse called The Baron. And if your heart is so bold, take a flutter on an unknown called Merry Hampton.'

'You know my heart is bold; it is my mind that urges caution. What is so merry about this horse?'

'He's a sixteen-hander, strong and wiry, said to have great stamina in his legs.'

'Stamina is a quality I find most attractive,' she said flirtatiously. 'Tell me more.'

'He's a thoroughbred, owned by a man called George Baird, a fellow who also uses the alias Mr Abington.'

'Baird? I think I have heard of him.'

'You probably have. He has been in the newspapers.'

319

'Why?'

'He was banned when he was a jockey and also prosecuted for assaulting a policeman. I know of him because he's also been heavily involved in illegal prize fighting. Money is shifting to his horse, so something tells me it may be worth backing.'

Elizabeth opened her handbag. 'What are the odds?'

I looked at a board beyond her shoulder. 'Currently eleven to one.'

From her purse she produced the grand sum of ten pounds. 'Then back it for me.'

I took the money and grinned. 'I am delighted to see that your mind can be as bold as your heart.'

'Given good cause,' she answered. Then something caught her eye for she suddenly pointed, 'Look over there, Simeon! That's the Prince of Wales.'

I followed the line of her finger and saw him briefly before he disappeared in a throng of hangers-on. 'I see him.'

'Isn't it exciting? We are in the company of so many lords, ladies, barons, viscounts and knights of the realm that we may as well be at a royal garden party.'

My eyes roamed the crowd in search of the titled and privileged. New top hats and lavish bonnets bobbed on an endless sea of well-tailored gentry. It was impossible to distinguish the excessively rich from the even richer. All the ladies wore beautiful dresses, cut tight at corseted waists, carved low over generous bosoms and draped not too long in length to be caught underfoot.

Elizabeth checked her watch. 'Oh bother! I really must go. I am to stand idly at the professor's side and play the part of his doting love.'

Her impending departure irked me. 'It doesn't seem to me that you have to *play* so hard at it.'

'Don't be such a fool, Simeon. Can't you see that he has no genuine interest in me?' She caught her breath, seemed surprised by her own words. 'Please forget I said that. I have spoken quite out of turn.' She made to go.

I grabbed her arm. 'What did you mean?'

She shook me off.

I walked with her. 'Elizabeth, what did you mean?'

'Nothing.' She turned her face away from me. 'Ignore what I said.'

Suddenly, everything made sense. 'He doesn't like women, does he? The professor prefers men.'

Elizabeth did not answer. She stayed silent all the way to the tent. All the way to the side of the man she had to pretend was her lover.

A short time later, Merry Hampton won the Derby.

Won four and a half thousand pounds for its owner and more than a hundred for Elizabeth. Being less adventurous, or perhaps more sceptical, I had only placed five pounds as a wager for myself but was more than happy with the fifty-five pounds return.

I wanted to celebrate with everyone, but Moriarty insisted Elizabeth join him and Alex to host a dinner with 'family-friendly' businessmen and politicians. Afterwards, they planned to attend a private party thrown by the Prince of Wales. He said Sirius would provide protection for the evening, and I wasn't needed. I knew it was the professor's way of underlining his disapproval of my feelings towards Elizabeth.

I spent the evening alone in a local tavern with poor food and cheap ale. My mood grew melancholic and I could not help but feel that I was a puppet on strings perpetually pulled by Moriarty. Granted, this was a better rope than another that might be looped around my neck, but it was still rope.

As the ale numbed the pain, I concluded my lot was not so bad and all I really craved was the freedom to love Elizabeth and to be loved by her. If the professor granted me that, then I would kill half the world for him and the other half for her.

I woke the following morning, with a beery head and the annoyance that Moriarty, Alex and Elizabeth had already left for Derbyshire. By default, I was forced to return with Sirius, my least favourite of travelling companions.

We barely spoke en route and this gave me time to consider the deeper implications of the professor's early departure. He had travelled without security, something he seldom did. Therefore, Sirius had been left in Epsom to guard me. In my mind, this meant Moriarty was feeling vulnerable. Most probably he feared Elizabeth had confided in me, not only about his true sexuality but also his part in her father's death.

Vulnerability was something my old mentor, Bosede, had taught me to look out for. 'Every man, no matter how big or powerful, has a weakness,' he told me. 'He will seek to hide his vulnerability by taking the boldest of actions. Find that Achilles' heel and you control him and your own destiny.'

I was certain I had found Moriarty's. Elizabeth's companionship afforded him a veneer of heterosexual respectability. To be seen as half of a courting couple made him socially acceptable and allowed him to do business within conventional circles.

The journey back to Derbyshire was slow and it gave me time to reflect. Elizabeth had acted most uncharacteristically in revealing Moriarty's secret to me, and indeed her own background for that matter. It made me wonder whether she was forcing my hand. Testing me, to see whether I could use this powerful information against the professor and lessen the hold he had on her.

The day was all but over when we rolled through the gates of the Moriarty country estate. Once I had helped stable the horses my mind and body were exhausted and all I was fit for was sleep.

The following morning, I did not go to the professor, but instead sought out Alexander. I knew that in speaking to him, whatever I said would within the hour be relayed to Moriarty.

I found the lawyer alone. He was taking tea in the garden beneath the shade of some yews while perusing a copy of *The Times*.

'Hello, Alex,' I called amiably.

He looked up and seemed pleased to see me crossing the lawn. 'Simeon! How are you? Was your journey back yesterday agreeable?'

'I am very well; and we had a good journey, thank you. May I sit and seek your guidance?'

'Please do.' He regarded me with suspicion while I pulled out a chair and rightly so, for once I was seated I asked, 'Tell me, how does law and society stand in respect of buggery?'

'*Buggery*?' He abandoned his paper in shock. 'Gosh, what a question. Why do you ask?'

'Personal curiosity.'

'Well, let me see. *Hrrm*. Homosexuality is not much spoken about these days. Although it is undoubtedly common among all classes.'

'But kept secret?'

'Somewhat.'

'And the law?'

'Well, there was legislation in the sixteenth century that made buggery punishable by death. Execution was only abolished back in the sixties. Currently, there is a strong movement in Parliament and the Church to widen legislation in order to make *any* physical sexual contact between men a criminal offence.'

'And how do *you* feel about that? From your own *special* perspective?'

He looked flustered. 'You mean as a lawyer?'

'How else could I have meant it?'

'I feel such persecution to be abhorrent. As I feel all prejudice and persecution is.' He took off his hat and mopped his brow. 'It is a very beautiful day, but too hot for me to be sitting outside for any length of time. I think I must hobble back inside before I burn to a crisp.' Alex rose on his crutches and somewhat flustered added, 'My apologies, Simeon. Please do excuse me.'

I watched him swing on the sticks and cover the grass almost as quickly as I could. It was clear now. The final piece of the puzzle was solved. Alexander and Moriarty were lovers. This was why the professor trusted and valued him so much.

'Wait!' I shouted and ran after the young lawyer.

Alex halted on the pathway and half-turned to me. The expression on his face said he feared I had something uncomfortable to say.

I caught up with him. 'Tell Moriarty *I know*. I know about him and about you. Please rest assured that I would never betray either of you. Like yourselves, I simply wish to be free of opposition when it comes to matters of the heart.'

He shifted his weight in order to move again but I put a hand on his shoulder and stopped him. 'One more thing. Please also tell the professor he has my blessing to call upon Elizabeth as a companion any time he wishes. And he has my assurance that I will keep the relationship I fully intend to have with her every bit as discreet as he does his relationship with you.'

*

325

Within the hour, Moriarty called me to his study.

I knocked and waited until I heard him bellow, 'Enter!'

I opened the door and found him in a red leather captain's chair behind his desk.

He looked up from a fan of paperwork and said brusquely, 'Come in and sit down.'

As I took the seat opposite I noticed he was a little flushed. Anger, I suspected, after being appraised by Alex of our conversation.

He slid an envelope across the desk and tapped it with the fingers of his left hand. 'Here is one thousand pounds. A small fortune. You can take it, providing you walk out of here and out of all of our lives, including that of Lady Elizabeth. I promise you safe passage and that you will never see, or be troubled by any of us again. *Alternatively*,' he drummed the fingers of his right hand on the desk, 'you can stay and try to prove that your feelings towards her are as honourable as you claim. But if they are not, then you will be dealt with.'

He lifted his hands and rested both on the desk. 'Which is it to be, Simeon? Love or money? Loyalty or freedom?'

I replied without hesitation. 'You can keep your money. It cannot buy my heart or Elizabeth's.'

'Be sure, Simeon!' he snapped. 'You will *never* again have a chance to walk away from this house and this life of your own free will. Never! You do understand that, don't you?'

'I do.'

His anger dissipated. He let out a sigh and placed his

hands calmly on the desk. 'Then so be it. As I am a gentleman, I stand by my word. You are free to pursue the affections of the good Lady Elizabeth, and in return, I trust you to keep the promises you made to Alex.'

'I will. And I gladly give such undertakings directly to you.' I stood and pushed back my chair. 'But I have a condition that I must add. As a gentleman, you must not spy on us. I know about your perversions of watching from inside your secret walls.'

'*Perversions?*' His anger flared again. 'You imbecile! You think I would watch you for pleasure?'

'Why else?' I stood my ground. 'What other reason did you have for spying on Elizabeth and me when we first kissed? You even called Sirius and Surrey in to share your viewing.'

'I did it because I did *not* at that time fully trust you, Simeon. You had killed a man. You had set about Brannigan and you unquestionably acted strangely around Elizabeth. I was concerned for her safety, nothing else.'

I could see from his face that he was speaking the truth and had no option but to back down. 'I feel foolish. I apologise.'

He shook his head in frustration with me. 'Accepted. And now I expect you to be the guardian of her safety and interests.'

'I will not let you down.'

'Good. Then it seems we must rely on each other's discretion in this matter, as we do in so many other things.'

He thrust out his hand and I shook it. If Elizabeth had manipulated me into this confrontation then she had done it well.

Moriarty held my hand tightly in his and fixed me with a cold stare. 'I have a caveat for you as well.'

'Which is?'

'Make sure you speak openly to the woman you have scorned. I will be displeased if Surrey's professional performance is compromised by your personal treatment of her.'

'I will. When does she return?'

'She came back from my brother's chores in the early hours of this morning. She may still be resting.'

'Then may I leave and see her?'

'You may. Handle this well, Simeon; Surrey Breed is a dangerous young woman and you should not make her an enemy of Elizabeth or yourself.'

I left him filled with purpose and searched the house but Surrey was not there. Nor was she in the gardens. After asking the servants, I eventually found her in the grounds of the chapel, on her knees, laying fresh flowers on Michael Brannigan's grave.

Surrey turned her head on hearing my footsteps on the gravel and instantly I saw red and purple bruising down the right side of her face.

'Are you all right?' I moved more quickly towards her.

She got to her feet and I saw tears in her eyes. She wrapped her arms around me and said, 'Hold me. Hold me tight and make me feel safe.'

I embraced her. Nestled the back of her head in my hand and held her in the way I knew she liked. 'What happened to your face?'

'It's nothing. The man I killed yesterday punched me, that is all.'

I ran a hand tenderly over the purple skin.

'He looked for all the world like Michael.' Her voice was breaking with emotion. 'He was a dead ringer for him. As I watched him choke on the poison I had administered, I saw only Michael's face in pain, *Michael's* face pleading with me for help.'

For a second, I remembered the look in the old wrestler's eyes, on that awful day when I had to end his suffering. 'What had this fellow done?'

'I don't know. Neither Moriarty nor Moran, that damned former colonel of his, informed me.' She shook her head. 'In truth, I have long forgotten to ask such questions.'

'Surrey, there is something I must tell you.'

'No, there isn't.' A great sadness suffused her face. 'You don't have to tell me anything, Simeon. I already know it.'

'Sirius? Did he—'

'No, he didn't say a word. It was in your eyes. I saw it as you approached me. It was in your touch when you held me just now. What little we had, it has already gone, hasn't it?'

'I am sorry.'

'No need to be.' She sounded exhausted. 'It's not like your feelings for *her* are a surprise. This moment was always going to happen. I just wish you had been more honest with me.'

'I think I was having trouble being honest with myself.'

'The more you do this job, Simeon, the more difficulty you will have being honest with anyone, especially yourself.'

I put the palm of my hand to her injured cheek. 'Has the doctor looked at that?'

'A doctor is of no use to me.' She turned her back, faced the grave she'd been tending.

I touched her shoulder. 'Surrey, I am sorry. Truly, I—'

'Don't!' she pulled away from me. 'Please *don't* say anything more.'

'You will always be dear to me. I hope we can remain friends. Closest of friends.'

She wheeled round, laughing bitterly, 'Friends?' Her face had hardened. A steely shield had been raised. 'You are no friend. You are dead to me, Simeon. As dead and buried as poor old Michael.'

PART FOUR

And now I die, and now I was but made;
My glass is full, and now my glass is run,
And now I live, and now my life is done.

'Elegy', Chidiock Tichborne

Forty seasons in the Peak District came and went as quickly and colourfully as brushstrokes on an artist's canvas. Autumn's russets and golds washed into winter's blacks and whites; spring's lemons and limes squeezed into summer's blues and greens.

While the passage of ten full years showed only seasonal change on the landscape, the decade saw my personality altered beyond recognition. With every kill I lost a piece of my humanity. I had become two people living in one skin: an increasingly cultured, educated and kindly Simeon along with a savage and ruthless Simeon. But for my love of Elizabeth and the good fortune of her loving me in return, the base and beastly side of me would have taken control of my being. She was my certainty, my lodestar.

Unplanned and unexpected, we had a beautiful baby daughter whom we named Molly. Our princess had her mother's eyes and hair colour, though it fell in soft curls that were uniquely hers and simply refused to be straightened by comb or brush.

According to Elizabeth, Molly had both my smile and stubbornness. Certainly, the more I saw my daughter laugh, the more I smiled, and the more I smiled the more she laughed. We were symbiotically happy.

To my great surprise, the professor turned out to be more than just understanding about the birth. While he would not let us marry, as to do so would remove his cloak of heterosexuality, he did give us a detached cottage and a generous plot of land in the grounds of the family estate.

Both he and Alexander showed genuine affection for Molly and it was made abundantly clear to me that, providing I still performed my duties to the best of my ability, then my own family would never want for anything.

Conversely, my daughter's birth further separated me from Surrey. Our relationship had deteriorated from being one of intimacy to a cold state of professional acquaintance. The professor tried as much as possible to have her work with Sirius and increasingly allowed me to work alone. It was an arrangement that suited everyone.

The Moriarty empire grew across the world and so did my duties. I was called upon to kill in Austria, Switzerland, France, Holland, Spain, America and even Russia. It seemed that every time a new avenue of enterprise was opened, someone needed to be murdered in order for the others to pledge their loyalty, and to share their profits. The work proved hazardous and not without injury. I sustained numerous fractures to fingers and ribs, cuts and bruises to my face and head, even bullet and knife wounds to my body. The use of guns was dramatically on the increase and Elizabeth became desperately worried about my safety. Having a child had changed our relationship. We both ached for the day when the killing might end and I could become just a mundane but doting father.

I talked at length to Moriarty about being allowed to do something else, perhaps even manage one of his companies. He said he would be happy to consider it. But not yet. There was still work to be done – my usual kind of work.

Each murder became easier than the last. It had to. I had reached the point where I felt no more compassion than a butcher ending the existence of a chicken, cow, deer or lamb. Which of course is how Michael had trained me. 'Kill and kill again. Kill until you stop feeling.' That had been his motto. Mine, too.

Until one particular death that turned my world upside down.

Two weeks before Molly's first birthday she was vexed with teething and cried to the point of exhaustion. The poor mite was subsequently stricken with such diarrhoea, vomiting and stomach pains that Elizabeth sent for Dr Reuss. He diagnosed it as 'a stomach bug, most probably caused by an unsterile teat on a feeder bottle. A most common occurrence.' He told us not to over-worry. And having put our minds to rest left us with some soothing drops for wind.

The following day, our sweet little angel passed away.

I could not believe it and Elizabeth would not accept it. She cradled Molly in her arms and insisted she was only sleeping. I had to prise our dead child from her fingers and hold my own composure, as she wept loud enough to shake the moon while beating me with her fists.

Moriarty allowed us to lay Molly to rest in the graveyard of his family's chapel. Alexander took care of the funeral and arranged for a beautiful statue of a cherub to be commissioned in her honour.

The weeks and months that followed were the worst of my life. Blacker even than losing Philomena in that awful workhouse ward. Elizabeth blamed herself and became despondent and withdrawn. She would sit all day in the house with the curtains drawn, clutching one of Molly's tiny dresses to her breast. There seemed nothing I could do or say to shake her out of the state she had fallen into.

More than a year after the period of mourning passed, she still dressed only in black. 'I will wear something different when the hurt in my heart has diminished,' she declared. 'Until that moment, I will know we have not been forgiven.'

'For what?' I asked. 'We have done nothing wrong. The doctor said that infection was the fault of manufacture, not good practice.'

'It is not that, Simeon, and you know it. Molly was taken from us by God. Taken because of what you have done and what I have allowed to be done.'

'That is not true.'

'Is it not? I should never have taken up with you.'

'Don't say that.'

'It *is* true. You were such a lovely young man when you came to this house. Rough at the edges, but there was a sweetness in you, an innocence.'

'We are both much older, my love.'

'Older and bitterer. The sweetness went when you killed. When you murdered those men who stopped your carriage.'

I saw some truth in her remark but said nothing.

'Since then, kill by awful kill you have become hardened and our souls have blackened with every drop of blood you have shed.'

'I did what I did because I had to. Moriarty says they were all evil men deserving of evil ends. Like your father.'

Her eyes flashed with anger. 'You delude yourself. Always have done. You kill because it pleases Moriarty, because you have had no parents and you are desperate to be needed and approved of.'

'Your medicine is making you speak foolishly. You need to rest.'

'*Rest?*' She regarded me with scorn. 'There is *no* rest for me, Simeon. Nor for you. God will never let us rest, not even when we are wrapped in beggar's cloth and buried in the ground.'

Six Days to Execution

Festering in my condemned cell, Elizabeth's words returned to haunt me. She had been right; I had changed and I did kill to please Moriarty. After all, the man held my life in his hands – had done since we met in Manchester and he threatened to turn me in to the police. Parts of my kindness and my softness had disappeared with every life I had taken and as my days ebbed away in prison I wished with every atom of my body I had chosen a path less brutal. All that remained of the young Simeon, the one before he shed blood and unquestioningly buried victim after victim, was a desire to survive. To escape.

I had worked throughout the previous night on the yielding wall near my bunk. With that small, thin sliver of a nail, I hacked at bricks and mortar with all of my strength and determination. Only when my hands were cut to ribbons from holding it and my body and brain grew exhausted from lack of sleep did my endeavours cease.

Once the sky beyond the window bars shifted from black to grey I reviewed the efforts of my labours. I had dislodged almost two square feet of bricks, from the floor upwards. The section I had loosened covered an area that ran from the right-hand corner of the cell, behind my bunk and towards the door. A hefty shove and I was certain the bricks would all collapse inwards.

Because it was winter, I knew full daybreak was still at least an hour away. This gave me the courage to work a little longer. I took two rows of bricks out, one by one, and stacked them in the same order and shape so they could be replaced if necessary.

Every few minutes, I stopped and listened for sounds of screws on the gallery outside my door. Fortunately, the prison was short on manpower and not many wished to confront me on their own. Still, I was vulnerable to prying eyes or a surprise spot check. Given half a chance, I could push my bunk back to the wall and cover some of the hole but not all of it. In the dim light it might pass a cursory glance but not any real inspection.

Nervously I laboured. Within ten minutes I had removed enough bricks to discover a row of iron bars sunk into the floor beyond the wall. They were set less than a foot apart. And there were many of them.

This was the worst imaginable setback: bricks and bars – beat one and the other stops you.

I was about to replace the wall when I had an interesting thought. Screws would only put bars over a weak spot. A place they feared a prisoner might have a real possibility of escaping from. And they would only brick it up *as well* if indeed that spot were extraordinarily weak.

I lay on the floor and peered into the gap. It was too dark to see, so I stretched a hand into the hole and felt around. It was cool and damp; thick dirt and a familiar smell oozed from the gap.

Soot.

I pulled my hand out. It was black, and stank of burned coal and wood. My heart leapt. It was, as I had hoped, the foot of a chimney. I stood up, backed away and looked at the wall. There was no visible sign of a stack being there. Then I remembered that I had been put into this stinking old part of the prison because of the overcrowding and the fact that all the other condemned cells were filled to bursting. Romantically, I imagined that this was Jack Sheppard's chimney and that I was but a shimmy away from freedom.

Looking at the shape of the room, it was apparent it had once been twice the current size. That would account for why the ceiling was only half an arch – the other half must have been in the room to my right.

Judging from the decayed mortar, I guessed the division had been made fifty or more years ago. There were many tales about the history of Newgate – how it had been built in the twelfth century, ruined during the Great Fire, rebuilt in the mid-eighteenth century, set ablaze again by the Gordon rioters in 1780 and patched up ever since. In short, the gaol might well not be as secure as it seemed.

I sat and positioned myself in a way that enabled me to put my feet against two of the exposed bars. I wrapped my hands around one in the middle and pulled.

It was solid.

I pulled again. Jerked hard. Shook the bar with all my might and finally felt a little play between bar and stone. If

I put in long hours with the nail and then used more brute force, there was a chance of moving it.

But not that morning.

The patch of black at my window was now light grey. The sky steadily on its way to becoming some form of morning blue.

I replaced the wall then took pieces of torn newspaper that I used for the shitting pot, soaked them in water, rubbed them in dirt and pressed then around the bricks to fill the gaps.

At first glance it would pass as mortar but would not bear close scrutiny. If this were to be my escape route then I needed to use it in the very near future.

DERBYSHIRE, NOVEMBER 1898

Doctor Reuss diagnosed Elizabeth's condition as 'shattered nerves'. He prescribed several courses of mild opiates but she became increasingly reluctant to take them. When she did, they only left her listless and even more maudlin.

She would go days without speaking and weeks without even venturing outside the cottage. Most nights I would wake to find her crying in the room where Molly had slept. She seemed to derive no comfort from me covering her with a blanket and lying with her until morning. Each dawn brought renewal of my dim hope that this might be the day we turned a corner.

The professor often visited and tried his best to raise her from the gloom. He would sit in a chair alongside her, take her hand and reminisce about the life they had both known before I had come along.

When all the tinctures and tonics had failed, Moriarty insisted on attending her himself and using his powers of phrenology to reveal where in her brain the depressive problems persisted.

He made Elizabeth sit bolt upright on a chair and spent nigh on an hour combing his fingers through her hair. Occasionally he would break off to refer to several diagrams that showed skulls labelled with descriptions of what he called 'cerebral controls'. He interrogated her extensively on how she felt, as he prodded and probed different pressure points.

When he was done, he took me aside and urged that thrice a day I gently rubbed the top and back of her head, because beneath it lay the source of self-esteem, which he reasoned had been badly damaged by Molly's passing. He showed me vital sections close to the very centre of her skull that he called 'the Fonts of Hope' and said these should be massaged at least three to five times a day 'without fail'.

I obeyed his instructions assiduously. And even though Elizabeth seemed to derive some comfort from it, I cannot in all honesty say the practice had any lasting effect on her demeanour.

I found myself wondering if there would ever be a spark of light in our darkness, or was this awful creeping death that consumed Elizabeth God's punishment for my sins? Was not the loss of our sweet and innocent child payment enough for the squalid, sinful lives I had ended?

I bowed my head, for I knew it was not. My soul stank of the sulphurs of hell. Elizabeth was doomed and so was I. There was a pistol in the drawer of a desk in the corner of our main room. I found myself sitting with it and a glass of whisky. For a full hour, and half a bottle of the fiery liquid, I contemplated ending both our miserable lives. But I had neither the courage nor complete despair to do it. Instead, I sank to my knees and prayed to a God that certainly had no reason to listen.

FIVE DAYS TO EXECUTION

NEWGATE, 13 JANUARY 1900

Throughout this long and dreary day, my eyes never left the patch of stagnant light pooled on the floor by the window bars. For once, I was impatient for it to disappear. Night-time meant fewer turnkeys, the cover of darkness and a fresh chance to use my precious sliver of steel to try to break through the bars that stood behind that damned wall.

It was late afternoon when the sun finally sank and the insipid pool of light in my cell evaporated. A supper of stale bread, watery stew and a mug of cold tea followed. I ate quickly and waited to be 'locked down', enduring what remained of the day. Keys jangled in locks. Voices called down galleries. Screws completed their chores and settled into noisy rounds of cards and tittle-tattle.

I made my move. Feverishly, I gouged out both the real mortar and the fake that I had made with paper saturated in dust. I took away all the loosened bricks and, as I had done the previous night, stacked them along the wall so they might be slid quickly back into position if necessary.

Seated on the floor, I gripped an exposed bar with two hands and pulled with all my strength. At the same time, I planted both feet on adjacent ones and pushed with the might of a kicking mule. I felt like a human arrow pent on a crossbow.

The bars did not shift.

I rocked them as hard as I could. Sweat beaded on my brow. Sinews pulsed and strained down my arms. Still the iron would not give up its congress with the stone. I concluded that my efforts were too close to the floor to have an effect and I needed to try higher up the bars, at what might be a weaker point.

There was still no movement, and my strength was ebbing away.

I dropped to the stone floor and worked furiously with the nail, jabbing around the base where the bar met the ground, then I repeated all the pulling and straining exercises. To no avail.

I got to my feet, stepped back as far as my leg irons would

allow, ran at the bar from the side, slid and kicked it with the flat of my foot.

I felt enough 'give' to be encouraged to repeat the attack, and the bar loosened. I thumped it several more times and it began to rattle.

Keys jangled in my lock; I froze.

A screw shouted through the door, 'What's all that noise? Is it you, Lynch?'

There was no time to move the bricks back into position. If he opened up then I was done for.

'It *is* me. I am as mad as hell and letting off steam. So you just open that door you piece of prison shit and come in here, so I can vent my anger on you.'

'Fuck you, Lynch! We'll all be drinking ale when they get round to popping your head in a noose.' He banged the door and moved on.

I stayed as still as possible, listening to his feet click down the landing, and made sure he was gone before I took so much as a peek through the newly bent bars into the hole in the wall next to me.

For a moment, I wondered if he would come back, maybe with some other screws, to teach me a lesson. Or would he steer well clear, prefer a quiet life to one that could end up in serious injury?

I gambled on the latter.

One of the bars had bent. Better still, it had broken the stone where it had been set. I worked on it with the nail. Ground out all I could around the metal. Pulled hard.

Pulled left, right, backwards and forwards. Stone splintered away.

Excitedly, I grabbed the bar and heaved it towards me. Got to my knees and pulled with every ounce of effort I had left. Unable to do more, I sat back and looked at the result.

It was bent as far as it would go.

I crawled to the bars, twisted my head and angled my shoulders.

I could fit!

It was tight, but I could get through.

Quickly, I shuffled back and used the nail to pick the lock on my leg irons. Then I stuffed my pockets with the booty I had taken from Father Deagan's bag and returned to the exposed chimney.

Iron and brick had been defeated. Wind whistled down from the outside world. Somewhere up there in the darkness above my head lay freedom. Never had I so longed to be outside in the stinking, foul air of London Town.

I worked my way back inside the hole, leaned against a wall and pushed my feet against the bricks opposite me. By keeping my hands at my side and pressing hard on the wall, I was able to inch my way slowly upward.

Tired and panting, I stopped, for fear of falling. Rain fell on my face – glorious, glorious rain! One drop, two drops, then many. A delicious downpour. It renewed my muscles and I moved on.

Progress was painful and slow. At times my hand or foot

slipped on the soot-covered walls and I feared a back-breaking drop to the stone below. The climb was hard and I was not as strong as I used to be. Prison slops had sapped muscle from my frame. The higher I got the weaker I grew.

I saw moonlight, felt the cold breeze of unchained air and more of that heavenly rain. But only through a slit. I could see now that the chimney had been blocked off, except for a small rectangle. I ran my fingers around the hole. It was much less than a foot wide and not two feet in length. I could get a hand and arm through, but that was all.

After a minute or so, my fingers found some purchase and I was able to pull down on the end of the block.

Nothing gave.

I grabbed the stubborn stone with both hands, took my best grip, released my feet from the side of the chimney and dangled recklessly free.

Not even my weight would dislodge it.

I swung back into my braced position, feet planted against one wall, back firmly against the one opposite; I pulled and pushed on the block, but to no avail. My energy was spent. There was nothing more I could do for now. With heavy heart and exhausted limbs, I climbed back down.

Soaked and saddened, I replaced each and every brick as best I could. I used the last of the toilet paper to fill the wall cracks. Once my leg irons had been replaced, I endeavoured to wash my hands, face and hair but the water in the bowl almost instantly turned black as ink.

It was then that I realised I was not only covered in an unmovable amount of soot, I also stank of it. The smell was ingrained in every pore. I felt it in my eyes, tasted it in my throat. Not even the most stupid of the screws would fail to notice the smell of the chimney on me and in the room. In fact, it would only be a matter of time before they came into the cell. They would smell it down the corridor and then, like dogs, they'd track down the source.

My bowels rumbled at the thought of the kicking they would give me. And I dared not imagine the delight they would derive from discovering my attempted escape.

I worked out there was only one thing that could be done: a shocking act that would baffle them and at the same time afford me one more chance to scale that chimney.

DERBYSHIRE, AUTUMN 1899

Christmas and the winter of '98 glumly passed with no difference in Elizabeth's mood; the spring and summer of '99 followed suit. She had moved only from black to grey and at times it seemed her melancholia had become even worse than in the weeks immediately following Molly's death.

Moriarty and Alexander decided it was time for their annual escape to the home they kept in New York – a last retreat before the onset of winter. They were in the habit of travelling White Star from Liverpool and were excited that some new ship promised to land them in America in less than six full days.

As usual, Sirius travelled with them as protection, leaving Surrey and I to look after whatever 'urgent jobs' needed dealing with in Britain and Europe. Since my daughter's death and Elizabeth's depression my former lover and I had grown a little closer again. I should stress that by 'closer', I mean in the sense of friendship, rather than anything physical. Time, it seemed, had healed the wounds inflicted at the end of our relationship and Surrey had even 'looked out' for Elizabeth whenever I had to travel to perform my duties. It was with some sadness then that I learned soon after Moriarty's departure for New York that she had to leave Derbyshire for business in the northernmost part of England and would be gone for perhaps a month. The following week was the second anniversary of Molly's passing and I was anxious about the emotions it would arouse.

My fears were well-founded. When the dreadful moment came, Elizabeth cried throughout the day. The only time she spoke was while visiting Molly's graveside. The words she uttered cut me to the quick: 'I forgive you, Simeon, but the good Lord may never do so.'

That night we lay together in bed and though I held her, I knew her heart and mind were not with me. They were in the cold soil of our child's grave.

When dawn warmed the windows of the cottage, we rose from our sleepless bed and went to the kitchen so that I might brew tea and muster the resolve for a fresh day. The fire in the range had burned out and Elizabeth wrapped a blanket around her shoulders to keep off the chill. She sat in a chair by the table while I remade it with kindling, paper and coal.

By the time I had warmed the room and boiled water, she was fast asleep. I put the drink down beside her, kissed her lightly and went to walk in the garden to clear my head.

Life could not go on like this. My own mood was blackening. The dogs of depression sensed my vulnerability and were intent on hounding me into the dark hole that Elizabeth had already toppled into.

Selfishly, I tracked down Thackeray to the carriage workshop for some male companionship. I knew my mind was not capable of focusing fully on more than one thing so I was pleased to accept the distraction of helping him mend a broken chassis on a carriage.

I was even interested, for once, in his tales about horses and how they could only breathe through their noses because their mouths were too big to keep open. 'Jus' imagine wot mess that could lodge in there,' he said with amusement. 'An 'orse's gob is so big it could catch a bird in it – that's if th' animal's stupid enough to go runnin' around with its 'ead up at the right angle.'

'And a bird is misguided enough to fly into its mouth,' I pointed out.

We laughed and bantered for a good hour and a half before we took a break from the work and walked outside for a cigarette. I was lighting a rollup when the figure of a woman appeared over the distant crest of lawn. I did not recognise her at first because of the shimmering purple coat and bonnet paired with it.

Then I did.

It was Elizabeth.

My heart raced as she slowly approached us.

'My dear . . .'

'Please don't say anything.' She held a hand up to halt my exuberance. 'It is time for us to start again,' she announced determinedly. Then added in a weaker tone, 'Or at least, I am ready to *try* to do so.'

'That's wonderful.' I had to force myself not to embrace her. 'I am travelling into Matlock later; please let me know if you would feel able to come.'

'I will. But do not rush me, Simeon. Let me do this at my own pace.'

She turned swiftly so I might not see the strain on her face and, to my relief, headed towards the eastern side of the lake and not back to our cottage or the chapel grounds.

'Lady Elizabeth looks brighter,' remarked Thackeray.

'She does!' I said joyously. 'She really does.'

'Still got time to 'elp me finish up?'

'Of course. You have been my lucky mascot.'

We were about to head off when the sight of a peculiar-looking carriage entering the drive stopped us. We both put hands to our brows, to shield the sun and squint out a better view.

'What on earth is that?' I asked.

'It's 'orseless,' cried Thackeray with excitement.

I had heard of such automobiles and understood there were now many of them in London, but I had never seen one, let alone been near one.

'It's a fast bugger,' he added. 'I reckons that thing's doin' summit round ten, maybe fifteen miles 'n hour.'

We both watched dirt drift from the dusty drive as the open-topped vehicle closed in on us. A man in a black uniform and cap brought it to a halt not far away. Several other men were now visible, one at the front and two more at the rear.

'God's bollocks,' Thackeray exclaimed, amid the loud noise of the engine. 'It's the Devil 'imself.'

'*Who* is the Devil himself?'

He covered his mouth with his hand because the driver had turned off the engine and it was spluttering to a stop. 'The professor's pig of a brother, James, that's who. I'm goin'. Best keep out that bugger's way.'

I had heard much about James from Surrey and a little of the jobs that she had done for him, but we had never met.

The driver and a large, well-built fellow in his early thirties disembarked. They walked to the back, where they joined a younger, clean-shaven man who, when he stood to his full height, must have been close to seven feet tall.

A final figure appeared – James Moriarty. Quite the smallest but also the most captivating of the four. He was broad-shouldered with a thick russet beard and wiry hair. Before he moved so much as an inch away from the motorised carriage, his dark brown eyes took in everything around him.

His gaze found me for the second time and he shouted, 'You there, come over here.'

It had been a long time since someone had called to me like a servant. I strolled slowly towards him.

Moriarty unbuttoned his brown tweed jacket. A gold watch glinted in the sunlight and he lifted it for inspection. 'Hurry up now, or I'll have my men dig a hole and bury you where you stand.'

If anything, I slowed my pace in order to assess the possible dangers. The driver presented no threat, but the other three men did. The big young one would be strong but stupid. His older companion was a different proposition. He stood like a soldier and I took him to be a fellow Surrey had mentioned – Colonel Sebastian Moran, a veteran of several foreign campaigns and James's principle protector.

Then there was the master himself. While clearly past his prime, he still appeared fit and powerful. He wagged a finger at me as I neared him. '*You* – you are Simeon, are you not?'

'I am.'

'I thought so.' He smiled at his own cleverness. 'My brother said you exuded defiance, and so you do.'

'The professor is not here, sir.'

'I know. His absence is why I *am*.' His eyes darted off me. Checked left and right. Found me again. 'Walk with me. There is a matter best discussed in private.'

As we headed inside, 'the Devil' as Thackeray had called him, strode into the hall, down the west wing and directly into a study, behaving as though the house were his own.

The room smelled heavily of polish and it must not have been to his liking for he immediately slid open a window. 'Close the door.'

I did and when I turned around he was in front of the desk, leaning back against it, his hands holding the edges. The look on his face was one of great consternation. 'Brogan and that effeminate *companion* of his have been attacked in their New York home and left for dead.'

'My God! Who killed them?'

'You did not listen correctly. I said *left* for dead. Their wounds were not fatal but they are gravely ill. Both are in hospital and have lost a great deal of blood.'

I grimaced as I imagined the injuries Alex and the professor must have sustained. 'I am truly sorry to—'

'Save your words. I need action from you, not sympathy. The attacks were orchestrated by Lee Chan. It appears that his grandfather died last week and he is now completely in charge of the family's operations.'

I was bursting with questions. 'How did the Chans get to the professor and Alex? I thought Sirius was with them. And surely they had plenty of local protection as well?'

'Indeed Sirius was, and indeed they did have local men. But apparently not in sufficient numbers or excellence. Six of our guards were killed when ground security was breached in the middle of the night. Three unarmed domestic servants were also murdered and numerous other staff horribly injured.' He took a long and slow breath to calm himself, then added, 'Most disturbingly of all, it seems Mr Gunn had been corrupted by the Chans and helped facilitate the attack.'

'*Sirius*?' I was aghast. 'I cannot believe—'

'You *must* believe. I discovered his treachery when the Chinese, along with support from their British gangs, took almost overnight control of a number of our betting syndicates and racecourse operations. My men captured one of their ringleaders and under torture, *extreme torture* I might add, he gave up Gunn's involvement in return for his own miserable life.'

'And what now? Why are you here and what must be done?'

'Revenge should never be rushed.' He rounded the desk and sat in the professor's chair. 'For the moment I must take control of all affairs and act astutely on my brother's behalf. More immediately, the chateau was looted of a great many treasures and it is not inconceivable that Chan will also seek to plunder the historic and invaluable art, jewellery and sculptures that lie within these walls.'

'Which, I suppose, is how I am to help?'

'Do not suppose anything. You are not blessed with either the intelligence or experience to do it. Miss Breed has been recalled and I have something else in mind for the pair of you. Something more befitting your undeniable talents.'

Five days to Execution

The gaoler who opened my door was a man in his twenties.

When he saw me standing there, bold as brass, facing him down, he almost gagged out of fear and revulsion. I was no sight for the weak-hearted. Immediately, he shut the door and whistled for help.

I braced myself and waited, covered in my own excrement. My pot had not been emptied for about a day so I had smeared the entire contents over my clothes, hair, hands and even my face.

The screws would see this abominable act as disrespectful of them. In reality, it was designed to be the ultimate distraction from the soot and dirt of the chimney.

Feet thundered down the corridor. My door opened and gaolers flooded in. They pulled my chains until I fell, then dragged me across the floor and threw bucket after bucket of water on me. I could not catch my breath. Runny excrement filled my eyes and mouth, blinded and choked me.

They scrubbed me hard with long-handled yard brooms and beat me with them. One brush was jammed across my throat, while a young screw pulled off my clothes and threw them out onto the landing, retching while he did it. Then he kicked me like he was learning his trade, an apprenticeship in battering inmates.

Others cheered him on then scraped their brushes over my naked body, twisting my chains and flipping me over like a roasting boar. More icy water came my way. Metal buckets were flung and banged my head.

The young screw lifted my chin to see I was still alive, then let it fall, causing my face to hit the cesspit floor like a dropped egg. As I lay there, abuse piled up on me.

'Dirty bastard!'

'Filthy fucking pig.'

'You're worse than a bleedin' animal, Lynch.'

The shouting died down and faded into complete silence.

I lifted my head.

Johncock was stood over me.

I got to my knees and retched water.

He kicked me down again and spat on me.

I rose again, needing to retch more water or I would choke.

Johncock stamped on my planted hands. Ground his boots on my knuckles.

I bit through the pain until he stopped.

'I warned you, Lynch. Warned you right at the start of your stay here about what would happen if you crossed my line.' He drew back his right foot and swung it at my head.

There was no pain, just dizziness. A million bees buzzed inside my ears and swarmed my brain.

I sank into a sweet world of blackness.

The days that followed my initial encounter with James Moriarty proved tense and frustrating. He calculated that the Chans had the upper hand and would use it to brutally assert themselves.

They did.

The next week was a bloodbath. The Moriartys lost almost all their betting operations. To those caught on the ground, it must have seemed a sad surrender, for rather than sending extra men to support them, James pulled his best lieutenants out. He simply left the weakest of the lambs to be slaughtered by the most vicious of Chan's wolves.

And then came an even bigger blow. Ten days after being badly wounded in America, Alexander Rathbone died from his injuries.

Word of the kind and gentle American's demise passed around the house in Derbyshire. All our spirits fell. Surrey took charge: people were notified, curtains closed and black clothes worn out of respect and a genuine affection for him. It broke my heart to see Elizabeth forsake the brighter colours she had only just started wearing again and retreat into drab funereal cloth.

The following day, we all travelled to the professor's house in Primrose Hill, leaving the residence in Dovedale guarded by an astonishing number of men that James Moriarty had mustered.

That night, in a series of carefully orchestrated attacks,

James used the best of the lieutenants he had withdrawn from earlier battles to simultaneously destroy almost all of the Chans' London and Manchester shipping businesses.

Buildings were burned to the ground and containers looted. Key figures within the Chinese organisation were murdered and their corpses dumped in the Thames and Irwell. Before first light, police in the pay of the Moriartys swooped on houses and factories in the East End of London and arrested generations of Chinese who had illegally settled in England. Two of Lee Chan's cousins were followed to a laundry that acted as cover for their drugs trade and arrested.

The message was clear: any violence and disruption by the Chans would be met by an even more devastating response.

James chose this moment to send a personal letter to Lee Chan. It was an offer to halt hostilities, to meet on neutral territory and broker peace. 'A form of normalised business must be resumed,' he told us. 'Wise heads know when to pour brandy, not blood.'

Not unsurprisingly, his offer was met with scepticism. Chan sent word back. He would only agree to such a gathering if it was at a place of his choosing and Elizabeth were placed in the custody of his men as an insurance against foul play.

The first I heard of this demand was when Moriarty walked with me to the carriages, both horse-drawn and motorised, in the yard of the professor's London residence.

'Preposterous,' I exclaimed. 'He cannot seriously expect you to expose her to such a danger, especially without the exchange of his wife.'

'He does, and despite my protests he is unmovable on this tenet. In order to broker peace, it is imperative I comply. The time and place have been arranged.'

I grabbed his arm. 'Then you must reconsider.'

He stared at my hand. 'I *must* do *only* what I wish. And you, my dear fellow, must remember your place.'

I took my hand away. 'Then allow me to protect her.'

He let out a sigh of aggravation. 'That is not your role. Tonight, you will be with me, Moran and his assistant Frederick at the peace meeting. They are my most trusted men and you are Brogan's.'

'And Elizabeth? Who will be looking after her safety?'

He rested a hand on the brass end of the black cane he was carrying and spoke wearily. 'Miss Breed will attend to her. Thackeray will deliver them both and he will also be on hand to ensure their safe return. The Chans will believe Breed is Elizabeth's maid and that will be to our advantage. Moran will also send a contingent of his men to populate the street and intervene if necessary.'

'Forgive my impertinence, but I am not happy about these arrangements. I would much prefer it if I—'

'Goddamn you, man! Neither your happiness nor your preferences matter to me! Understand this: Chan has stip-ulated his *non-negotiable* terms for the meeting and for the moment we must be seen to acquiesce. Now let us make haste.' He pointed his cane towards the carriages. 'We will not take the Benz tonight, as we do not wish to attract attention. I will inform you of your duties en route.'

'No.'

'I beg your pardon?'

'I said no. I am not leaving until I have seen Elizabeth. Are you aware of what she has endured? What we have *both* been through?'

'I am *quite* aware of it. My concerns at the moment are for lives that may be saved, not lives already lost.'

I swallowed my anger and strode off towards our cottage.

Moriarty shouted at my back. 'She and Breed have already left.'

I stopped in my tracks. Had all this really been done and dusted behind my back? So swiftly? So slickly and irreversibly?

I turned and approached him. 'Under great duress, I presume.'

His eyes narrowed. 'Elizabeth understood that she is key to this meeting because of her perceived closeness to my brother and she very properly accepted her responsibilities. She also understood that *you* would be unduly concerned about her, even angered to the point of being impudent.'

'Can you blame me?'

'I forgive you. But only because I know such a reaction is born out of loyalty to her. Tonight you and your loyalty to my family will be needed. Simeon, my patience is wearing thin; may we *please* make progress?'

I knew I had no option but to board the carriage.

Once it was filled with Moriarty, the big young oaf Frederick and the older man Moran, the horses were whipped into life and we headed south-east across London to the meeting point. I was informed that the intended venue was a large, mid-terraced house in Harley Street, owned by a friend of Chan, a surgeon who worked at St Bartholomew's.

As we travelled, the full details of James's plan were disclosed. He told us there would be face-to-face discussions between him and Chan. The parties would then retire to separate rooms to consider their positions. At this point, Moriarty's men, armed with pistols, knives and iron bars would climb into the house through the connected attic that served the whole row of dwellings.

'They will kill all the gang leaders and Lee Chan. By removing the head of the foraging snake the vipers in the nest will perish.'

'And what if your men cannot get into the attic?' I asked.

'They are already in. Once Chan named the venue, we purchased access from a nearby resident. The Chinaman has men patrolling the street, of course, but they stand out like sore thumbs and are not much loved by the locals. We already have twenty of our people in position.'

'And throughout all this, where is Elizabeth being held?'

'She and Miss Breed will be detained in lodgings in Clerkenwell, a couple of miles from Harley Street. As there is every possibility that they may be moved from there, I have men on the street, lying in wait to follow them.'

There was not much more to be said. The three of us were there to protect Moriarty. Personal survival was his paramount concern. Tonight we were to leave the killing to others and that suited me just fine.

London jolted past the window of our carriage. I saw a black motor car up ahead, driven by a flat-capped young man. It came alongside us and passed by at twice our speed, with such noise that it scared our horses into a dance.

For some time, we were delayed by a congestion of horse-drawn omnibuses, each vying for space on a tight street corner. Our coachman cursed at the state of London's roads and grudgingly backed up the carriage to let one of them past.

The rest of the journey progressed relatively quickly and without further incident but as we approached our destination my feelings of foreboding increased.

I remembered the words of the old gypsy in Milldale about sensing danger.

Never before had I felt peril to be so close.

LONDON, NOVEMBER 1899

The house in Harley Street was a handsome white-fronted, four-storey terrace ringed by spiky, black iron railings and overlooked by gargoyles and heavily muscled men.

Inside, all was opulence. A hall of grey marble led to a

mighty oak tree of a staircase that branched east and west to galleried landings, rooms and passages on the upper floors.

The corridor we trod was adorned with a collection of classical nude sculptures that were, I imagined, worth considerably more than most surgeons could afford. Either the owner came from an enormously rich family or, more probably, the wealth had been amassed through aiding the Chans in their criminal enterprises.

The four of us were shown into a large reception room lit by a sumptuous chandelier. A giant golden mirror hung squarely over a marble fireplace. It wasn't solely for decoration. It afforded anyone seated close to the large fireplace a near-panoramic view of the room.

Fine oils of country hunts and lakeland scenes covered the other walls and created a strangely scenic backdrop for two wing chairs and large sofas covered in contrasting creams and reds.

After several minutes, the door opened. Lee Chan swept in, followed by his bodyguards. He was dressed in black out of respect for his grandfather, as were his men.

Chan bowed slightly to Moriarty, who had not dressed in black. Not for Alex. Nor for the Chans.

James reciprocated somewhat awkwardly, then, to my surprise, spoke to him in fluent Chinese.

Chan replied curtly.

Without so much as a handshake they took the chairs by the fire. Both men glanced repeatedly at the mirror above their heads, which reflected the spectacle of the rest of us, left to stand and stare at each other.

Chan continued to talk and Moriarty continued to listen. He did not blink or move. I noticed at one point he sneaked a deep breath to calm himself. I sensed his inner rage, noticed his fist, the one furthest from Chan, clench until the knuckles turned white then slowly flex and relax.

Chan finished and Moriarty responded. Neither interrupted the other. The pattern had been set and so it stayed for the following hour.

Finally, Moriarty stood. The Chinaman rose. He bowed and led his contingent out of the room.

Moriarty walked to the curtains. He twitched them open and closed – a signal to the street to set his men in action. 'Barricade that door,' he told us. 'Push the furniture against it and prepare for hell to break out.'

We acted swiftly and as quietly as possible. Once Moriarty's men descended from the attic, there would be mayhem and the Chinese would undoubtedly come for our blood.

As we waited, I wished for everything to be already over. Once I was reunited with Elizabeth we might use the cover of this current chaos to run away and start afresh somewhere. Perhaps it was not too late for us to become normal people.

Noise erupted behind the closed doors. Chinamen shouted in anger and surprise. The attack had begun. A cacophony of violence followed – raised voices, gunfire, splintering wood, crashing glass. More gunfire. Wailing. Shouting. Cries of pain.

'We need to leave.' Moran ushered Moriarty back to the window. He tried to lift the sash but it was stuck.

'We *must* get out,' cried Moriarty. 'The police will come. I cannot be discovered here.'

'Then we break the glass,' said Moran. 'Frederick, use one of the chairs.'

The big oaf picked it up like it was weightless, and hurled it through the window.

Moran kicked out the remaining shards. Moriarty took off his jacket and covered his head, presumably to hide his identity, then climbed through the broken frame. Moran was but a beat behind him.

I heard fighting on the street as well. Presumably Moriarty's men had tackled whatever guards Chan had posted there.

Frederick was staring at me as though he had forgotten what to do and needed me to instruct him. 'Go on,' I urged. '*We* need to get out as well.'

He took a pace towards the window and I wondered if he was too big to fit through. 'Out you go! You can make that.'

The big oaf grabbed me by the throat.

I was too shocked to react. His thumbs dug into my neck. It felt like his nails would pop through my skin. Years of training saved me. Instead of trying to force his huge hands from my neck, I grabbed his arms, gripped the cloth of his jacket and swung myself down and between his legs.

He lost his grip and his footing, crashed forehead first into the floor and broken glass.

I rolled to my feet, caught my breath and headed to the window. My hands were on the ledge when he grabbed and pulled me back. Again he snatched at my throat. This crazy imbecile was set on killing me. I stepped outside his reach and piled a powerful left into his belly. Air whooshed from his mouth and he doubled up.

I hit him with a hearty right-hander; his eyes glazed over and he rocked, staggered to his left, then collapsed. I was out on the street before his body had settled on the floor.

No sign of Moran, or Moriarty. They had gone, but the street was far from empty. The noise of the fight sounded like hell being emptied. Police vans were everywhere. I had no choice but to run towards them.

The Old Bill poured from their carriages. Whistles cut the night air. A copper snatched at me as I tried to pass by.

I slapped my hand in his chest and pushed him away rugby-style.

Another rozzer swung his stick at my head.

I blocked it with my left arm, cracked him with my right fist. I sprinted to the end of the road and turned into a part of town I knew well. This was a labyrinth of alleyways, a rookery that encompassed the old Knights Templar buildings to the south of the meat market. I slowed to a walk and disappeared into the shadows. The darkness stank of piss and gin.

I was not alone. I could hear others. Smell them. Sense them. Hairs bristled on the back of my neck.

Sitting in the shadows were the skeletal forms of more than a dozen homeless men and women, sheltering from the elements. I dug into my pocket, took out a handful of change and dropped it noisily. 'There's plenty of clink there. Anyone asks, I was never here.'

They clambered for the coins while I disappeared beyond them.

I still had enough money to hail a cab to take me to Clerkenwell. It was only a short distance away and I prayed this was where Moriarty and Moran were headed. Hopefully, they had already secured the safety of Elizabeth and Surrey.

Five minutes later I saw their carriage on the street corner. Alarmingly, there was no sign of the men Moriarty had promised would provide protection.

I paid my driver and made my way to the one house that was completely lit up. The curtains were drawn. Two silhouettes stood out against the cloth of a downstairs front room. From their shapes and sizes I was certain they were Moran and Moriarty.

I rushed to the front door, opened it and froze.

There was blood on the wooden boards in the hallway. Blood on the walls. Blood on the door handle in front of me.

'Elizabeth!' I rushed into the front room.

Moriarty and Moran were together in the corner, both on their knees. Hunched over something. They craned their necks my way. Looked shocked to see me.

'Simeon . . .' Moriarty's tone was disturbingly soft as he rose. 'Dear boy, I am sorry . . .'

I didn't understand what he meant. Then I saw where Moran's gaze was fixed, what their bodies had been masking In the corner, in front of them, was Elizabeth. And blood. A whole ocean of blood. Her throat had been cut. Her head was tilted back. An obscenely gaping wound showed the inside of her neck, the rawness of her throat, the root of her tongue.

I ran to her, fell to my knees.

Her eyes were white with death.

'My darling. My angel.' I lifted her head. Closed that gaping neck wound. Lunatic thoughts told me she could still be saved by my presence, my touch, my love. I pressed my cheek to hers. 'My sweetness!' She was cold as glass. 'My sweet, sweet lady.'

Moriarty tugged my shoulder. 'You have to leave her. We *must* go.'

I could not. My mind had lost all reason and my limbs would not surrender my love.

'Come on, man!' Moran tried to prise her out of my arms.

'Get the fuck away!' I struck out wildly. 'Touch her again and I *will* kill you!'

He took a step backwards and grabbed Moriarty's arm. 'It's no use. We *must* leave.' Without a further word they fled.

I sat with my back against the wall and held Elizabeth

close to me. The action made her sigh. I knew it was only air escaping dead lungs but the illusion of life was enough to break my heart. I rocked her and wept. Cried like a child while I hugged her preciously tight. Her head lay against my chest and her soft hair brushed my face as exquisitely as it had done a thousand times.

A long silhouette fell into the room, followed by another and another. The shadowy figures gathered into a dark, thin army and moved in on me.

'Jesus, Mary an' Joseph,' exclaimed a gruff old voice. 'What in God's name 'as gone on 'ere?'

'Looks like there's bin a fight, Sergeant,' replied a youthful man. 'A big fight an' 'im 'ere killed 'er there.'

I heard their voices clearly, knew who they were and what they were about to do. But I did not so much as look up from the woman I cradled in my arms. In that moment, I cared for nothing. Everything that mattered to me had just been destroyed.

It took four men to separate me from my love, to prise her beauty from my blood-soaked arms. And when they did, I broke several jaws and bones in my desperation to get back to her.

They flung me into a police wagon and beat my wailing grief into the most painful silence I had endured. Once clapped in chains, they waddled me into the station house, threw me into a cell and recruited new men to beat me again.

Throughout the night, my door opened several times and

I was aware of feet and voices gathering around me. There was at least one failed attempt to sit me up and bring me to full consciousness. It concluded with much swearing and slamming of doors. As I sank back into a fitful sleep I was aware only that Elizabeth was dead and I was presumed her murderer.

FOUR DAYS TO EXECUTION

NEWGATE, 14 JANUARY 1900

Another night in prison had come and gone by the time I reopened my eyes, felt the painful aftermath of my latest beating and pieced together what had happened following my lapse of consciousness.

Johncock had sent in the prison doctor. Fresh blankets had been brought for my bunk and clean clothes for me. Grumbling orderlies had wiped me clean with towels. The quack had put balm on my body where I had been scrubbed raw with stiff brushes. He had bandaged my head and ribs, and made me swallow something to relieve the pain — something that now left me feeling as though iron had been smelted inside me.

My fingers tentatively explored my body. The injuries could have been worse. Much worse. Through the murkiness of my aching mind, I realised that during those missing hours, those wasted hours of unconsciousness, the clemency deal offered by Sherlock Holmes had perished. My only guarantee of avoiding the noose had disappeared. My future, my life itself lay either in the hands of my lawyer and his appeal to the Home Office, or in my own as they scrabbled at the bricks that blocked the chimney in my cell. I resolved to double my efforts to remove them, but I needed to recover first. Heal a little. Gain some strength.

Soon after what passed for breakfast, I was taken into the Press Yard and left on my own in the muddy light of an icy winter morning. A chill wind buffeted me as I voluntarily made slow and painful circuits. I had to stay mobile. Work through the pain. My blistered feet had not yet properly healed from my marathon ordeal in here and unless I escaped they never would. So I walked in defiance. To give up on this right to exercise would be to give up on a possible escape route and I would not do that. Not until the hangman had choked the last breath from my body.

With every step, I carried an unseen weight, one felt heavier now than at any other time of my life.

Guilt.

As I hobbled across the yard it crushed me just as surely as stones had in the past crushed confessions from inmates who walked here. Years of guilt were piling up on me. The justifications I had given myself for the murders were disappearing on a daily scale. The weightless shadows I had seen my victims as were now dead weights in my troubled mind.

Elizabeth's death also troubled me. I blamed myself for

her demise. My role in life should solely have been that of loving and protecting her. I should not have accompanied Moriarty and Moran to Harley Street to meet Chan and his cronies. I should have gone to Clerkenwell to stand guard over my darling angel.

Because of my incarceration, I had been unable to see her laid to rest. Not dropped earth on her coffin, nor laid flowers on her grave. The only image I had was the brutal one of her lying, almost decapitated, in my arms.

James Moriarty's lawyers had seen to it that Elizabeth had been buried in the grounds of the family's chapel at Dovedale. They had acted discreetly, purchasing the undertaker's silence with threats as well as clink.

I walked more briskly in the yard, worked aching muscles and frozen bones to build strength and keep warm. Tried to use the exertion and pain to take my mind off that fateful night. But I could not. There were still too many unanswered questions.

Why had the young oaf Frederick turned on me, after Moriarty and Moran had escaped through the window?

Initially, I had simply believed the youth to have been of such low intelligence that he reacted like a startled dog, one that in the midst of being frightened inadvertently bites its master. But now I wondered if Frederick had been briefed to kill me.

As ludicrous as it seemed, James Moriarty had never hidden his dislike for Alex. He had described him bitterly as Brogan's *effeminate companion*. And very disrespectfully, he had not worn black when news had reached the house that the kindly lawyer had passed. It occurred to me that James might have planned to kill both Elizabeth and me. He would blame our deaths on the Chans and once and for all bury any witnesses to his brother's homosexuality.

Then there were questions relating to Surrey: her whereabouts after Elizabeth's murder and why she hadn't visited me or been heard of since the killing.

Had she been complicit in Elizabeth's murder, believing she would then have an open route to my heart?

I could not believe such a thing.

It was more likely that James had dismissed her from her duties and told her Elizabeth was safe with him and Moran. Given Surrey had worked for them on other occasions she would unquestionably have taken such an instruction. If all that were true, then it made sense that when Surrey learned of the awful events that ensued, she would be either too ashamed or too frightened to come out of hiding and visit me in prison.

I paused opposite the exit door in the Press Yard, blew warmth into my ice-chilled hands and tried to make sense of it all.

Probably none of what I had feared was true.

I was just driving myself mad. Most likely, a vengeful Chan had planned Elizabeth's death to hurt and humiliate the Moriarty family, and Surrey had been abducted and killed by the Chinese because she was in the way. This was what I had long believed, what fired me to escape and made me ache to kill at least one more man before I died.

The yard door opened. Huntley entered and walked my way. He wore a long coat but still slapped his upper arms to ward off the cold. 'Lynch, what happened to you wasn't right. They shouldn't have beaten you. Shouldn't have beaten you at all.'

'Is that why you're here? Come to take my written testimony against your colleagues?'

'I think you know I haven't. I have however lodged an official complaint with the keeper, but he, like everyone else, seems powerless to control Johncock. That man is a veritable force of nature inside this gaol.' He moved closer and lowered his voice. 'In truth, I need to speak to you about something else.'

'Then speak.'

'It is about Father Deagan. Considering how close you had become, I thought you might be concerned about his health, following his collapse in your cell. The Diocese has called the governor and it seems he has taken to his bed and not risen since.'

'What is his affliction?'

'I do not know. Let us hope it is not gaol flu. But for the moment he is unable to go about his duties and has sent a message that while he will try to rally and be at your side for ...' he hesitated, '... for the *final hour*, he cannot guarantee his presence.'

'The final hour? Your delicacy amuses me. Call it what

it is. *My execution*. Please let the good Father know that I wish him a speedy recovery and hope for him it is not consumption.'

'As does the Diocese. They have enquired as to whether you would like a new priest to visit.'

'No.'

'It is your right.'

'*Right?* I did not know I had *rights*,' I said sarcastically and instantly wished I hadn't. 'I am sorry; you deserve better than my bile. There is no need for another priest. I have made my peace with my maker. That is, whatever peace can be made by a man like me.'

LONDON, NOVEMBER 1899

With the new day came new policemen to rouse me, kick me and hold me accountable for the previous day's troubles. At least they let me wash in cold water and use a toilet, albeit chained, before leading me into a windowless room at the back of the station house.

Two uniformed coppers sat either side of me on a rough bench, while across a wobbly-legged table was another bobby and a plainly dressed man about five years older than me who seemed to be in charge of proceedings, for all eyes were on him.

He wore a brown lounge suite that like his stubbly cheeks and shadowy eyes had seen better days.

'I am Inspector Mather,' he announced politely. '*Felix* Mather of the Criminal Investigation Department of Scotland Yard.' He smiled, and I sensed he derived great pride from announcing himself in such a formal fashion.

'What is *your* name?'

'Terry,' I lied. 'Terry Perch.'

He opened a notebook on the table and with pen poised asked, 'Terry as in Terence and Perch as in fish?'

'Yes.'

'I like to be precise.' He made his note then looked up in earnest. 'Are you an honest man, Mr Perch? The kind to respect the police and not tell them lies?'

'I am, sir. I am exactly such a person.'

'Then describe for me the circumstances surrounding yourself and the dead young woman you were found with last night. The one whose throat had been cut and whose blood was all over you and your clothes.'

'She is my cousin, sir. A Miss Elizabeth MacIntosh.'

His pen moved to his notebook. 'How do you spell that? M small C, or Mac and capital I?'

'The latter, sir.'

'Thank you, Mr Perch. Do go on.'

'Well, I had arranged to meet her and a friend on the street corner in Clerkenwell, and when I turned up, I heard her screaming from within the nearby house. I rushed inside and well, I found her in that awful state.'

Mather made further notes. 'Where had you been beforehand?'

I struggled to answer and sensed my hesitancy aroused his suspicions. 'Forgive me sir, I have a great headache from the beating, and cannot easily remember the entire events of the evening, but I believe I visited a tavern. Yes, that is correct, I went to a tavern to see if any of my friends were there.'

'Which tavern?'

'The One Tun, on Saffron Hill.'

He raised an eyebrow. 'A known den for thieves; I wouldn't have thought an *honest* man like yourself would sup in such a place.'

'I would not have done had I known it had such a reputation.'

'It is the type of establishment where policemen and their enquiries are not welcome. A place where alibis are as cheap as ale.'

'I will steer clear of it in the future.'

'Oh, I am most certain you will never set foot inside it again.' His tone intimated that I would not have the chance to do so. He drummed the fingers of his right hand, added percussion from his left and watched the flailing digits for all of ten seconds. Finally, he looked up at me and smiled easily, as clearly was his way. 'Sir, I am a patient man. A *calm* man. I understand the emotions of those involved in death, in murder, and the conflict between the soul and the feet. The soul wishes to be clean. Pure. Such a thing can only happen with confession. The feet . . . well, the feet are different. They need to run. They ache to flee. Carry you far away from harm, from places like this station house and people like me.' He drummed his fingers again, then added, 'This is your final chance to come clean, sir, to purify yourself and save that soul of yours.' He looked away, took a deep breath and then slammed his hand down loudly on the table, making even the policemen jump. 'Damn you! You killed her, *didn't* you? You cut the poor woman's throat!'

My heart pounded. Not from fear of him but with grief. I spoke no words, only shook my head.

Mather glared at me. 'By God, man, you will swing for what you have done. Now confess your crimes and be done with it!'

'I swear on my soul, I never harmed a hair of her head.'

The inspector nodded to the beefy man at his side. The constable stood up and walked around the table. 'Hold him,' he told the men who flanked me.

They did and the constable punched me in the face. For such a big man, it was a small blow. His second effort was more impressive and by the time he sat back down I had cause to spit a tooth onto the table.

'You are a killer,' said Mather, 'a killer destined for the rope.' He turned to the back of his notebook and took from there a folded sheet of paper. He languorously straightened it out and smoothed it flat. 'You are not Terry Perch. You are Simeon Lynch, and you are wanted for the murder of PC Thomas Jackson of the Metropolitan Police Southwark Division.' He turned the paper and slid it across for me to see.

I stared at a document marked WANTED FOR MURDER and beneath it was a picture of me as a young man. I recognised it straight away. It had been taken during my time in the workhouse, when I was boxing regularly and had won a local tournament.

'I was there, Lynch,' said Mather. 'In that house, when you and Paddy Hoolihan's monsters killed my colleague. I was a young PC then and I will never forget the horror of seeing Jackson's body and that knife you put through him.'

He snatched back the paper and refolded it. 'I've looked at every murder in London since that day. Sat face to face with every cut-throat arrested in the country. I *knew* you'd turn up, eventually. Come out of the wood, like a worm. Well, now I've got you. Got you bang to bloody rights!'

PART FIVE

All you that in the condemned hold do lie,
Prepare you, for tomorrow you shall die!
Watch all, and pray, the hour is drawing near,
That you before th'Almighty must appear.
Examine well yourselves, in time repent,
That you may not t'eternal flames be sent;
And when St Sepulchre's bell tomorrow tolls,
The Lord above have mercy on your souls!

'Chant of the Execution Bellmen'

THREE DAYS TO EXECUTION

I drummed my fingers on the table to which I had been manacled. Levine was late. I had sixty hours of my life left, and he was late.

Finally, he was ushered in and to my surprise and annoyance was not alone. With him was a shabby clerk – a dreary, hunched figure swathed in a dull brown cape, the hood of which was still pulled high. Close to his chest, he clutched a tied bundle of legal books and a slim leather document case.

'Dear God, what happened to you?' Levine asked, as he saw my bandages.

'I believe I had an accident. A very unfortunate one.'

'And are you in great pain?'

'I am, and the discomfort is worsened by every second you delay telling me why you and your man are here.'

The clerk slid off his hood and I suddenly recognised him. Knew him as well as anyone in the world. A thousand thoughts flooded my mind, before I could speak.

383

'Professor.'

I was startled by the one word I uttered. Surely something more erudite or emotional should have come from my lips, but no, this was the best I could muster. 'Sweet Lord, I thought I would never see you again.'

'I came as quickly as my health and the railways and ships would allow.' His voice was strained.

I rose awkwardly.

'Sit. Please sit, my dear boy.' His right hand waved me back down. 'You look quite terrible.'

'Superficial injuries,' I lied nonchalantly. 'Michael regularly gave me more painful thrashings than the amateurs in here have managed.' As I sat, I noticed his left cheek bore a terrible burn that ran from temple to chin. 'What happened to your face?'

'This?' He touched the mark. '*This* was the work of Sirius. He shot both Alexander and myself and then set the room we were in on fire.'

'*Sirius* did that?'

'I am afraid he did.'

'I had heard of his treachery from your brother but still cannot believe it.'

'Enough of him. He is not worth us wasting our breath on. I am so terribly sorry that we are reunited under such dire and desperate circumstances. Please accept my deepest sympathies in respect of Elizabeth's passing. You know that my affections for her were akin to your own.'

'I do. And I know she had only kind thoughts of you,

which is why she did as your brother James required that night.'

His eyes avoided mine. No doubt he felt some family culpability for her fate.

I remembered my manners, and added, 'Please accept my own condolences in respect of Alex. He was a fine man and I had grown to greatly respect and admire him.'

'Thank you.'

Levine sensed our courtesies had been concluded. He cleared his throat and cut to more pressing matters. 'I understand that you wished for good news, Simeon, but I am afraid we are unable to deliver it to you. We have experienced profound difficulties in presenting your case. The home secretary has turned down the request for an appeal.'

I felt like I had been punched. 'You seemed so certain of success.'

Levine fidgeted with the hem of his jacket. 'He said there were insufficient grounds to support a review.'

Moriarty interrupted. 'Cross, the police officer we thought we had *an arrangement* with, has gone missing.'

'Missing?'

'I am afraid so. And without him,' added Levine, 'we have only his statement, which sadly is not enough.'

'Why not? Surely a signed statement is admissible?'

'Admissible, yes; but convincing, no. Without the physical presence of the witness to verify the testimony, and if necessary be cross-examined, it lacks the necessary gravitas for acquittal.'

'Then where is this damn man, Cross? He can't simply have vanished.'

'We don't know,' Levine replied. 'We accommodated him in a safe house in Marylebone. Unfortunately, our men were either lackadaisical or he outwitted them. Either way, when they checked on him last night, he had gone.'

'Dear Jesus!' I felt deflated. 'Might he just be somewhere nearby? Drunk in the filth of a tavern, or lost in the arms of a dolly?'

'I think not,' said Moriarty. 'Either Chan's men got to him, or he learned they were threatening his life. Much to my brother's chagrin, Lee Chan is still alive, Simeon and he wants all of us dead, including you.'

'And I want *him* dead. I desire it more than saving my own neck. The thought of getting out of here and killing that bastard is all that has kept me going. Now, all seems lost.' I sat back and could not hide my despair.

'Far from it!' Levine did his best to sound spirited. 'A great deal can happen in twenty-four hours and I remain confident we can find our witness and persuade him to speak on your behalf.'

'Are you?' I asked sarcastically. 'Would you wager your *own* life on it?'

'No,' answered Moriarty. 'He isn't and he wouldn't.' The professor glanced at the lawyer. 'We need to be straight and honest with him, Levine. Simeon, we have no idea where Cross is, but we will not give up, not until . . . the very last moment.'

'You mean, until my execution.'

No one contradicted me. I looked to Levine. 'I should have accepted that offer of clemency from Sherlock Holmes.'

'Holmes's offer was in return for testifying against me?' asked the professor.

'Indirectly,' confirmed Levine. 'As you know, that terrible man is obsessed with ruining your brother.'

'Always has been.' The professor leaned across the table and put his hand on my arm. 'Simeon, you must accept his inducement. You have my blessing to do so.'

'The offer has expired,' I replied. 'The deadline was yesterday.'

'Nonsense,' he snapped. 'Deadlines never expire. They are but part of a negotiation. Holmes is bluffing. Offer now to speak against me and he will have a pen in your hand quicker than a gaoler can unbolt your door.'

I did not know whether to take Moriarty seriously. 'I am surprised to hear you suggest such a thing. If I did, then the consequences for you and your family would be dire. Both you and James would be candidates for the noose.'

'You are right. That is true. But we would be able to prepare ourselves for such eventualities.' He glanced at the lawyer. 'Mr Levine is usually more reliable in coming up with loopholes and escape routes than he is proving in your case. Dear Alex, I do so miss him; he too would have had some bright thoughts in these moments of darkness.'

I was confused. Had the professor's near-death experience

in America softened him beyond all recognition? Or had the loss of Alex simply broken his spirit in the same way Elizabeth's murder had fractured mine?

'If you wish me to contact Mr Holmes for you, I can oblige.' Levine looked to Moriarty, who gave him a sad nod. Then he added, 'But first there is some information you should know. A confidence the professor wishes to convey personally.'

Moriarty scratched intensely at his beard and intertwined his fingers. His eyes caught mine and I saw something I had never seen in him before: uncertainty.

'Levine is correct, there is something I want to say.' He looked angry with himself. 'No, that is not true. There is something I *need* to say. Indeed, it is a matter I should have spoken to you about when we first met many years ago.' Hesitancy overwhelmed him. His words led nowhere. He looked down at his hands and took an inordinately long pause. Finally, he raised his head again and his eyes showed a glimpse of their old resolve.

'I am your father, Simeon. And you are my only child. My son and heir.'

'What did you say?' I had heard him clearly but needed to ensure I had not misunderstood his words.

'You are my son.'

A cold shiver ran through my veins.

Levine rose from his seat. 'I will leave you together.' He put a reassuring hand on Moriarty's shoulder before heading to the door and knocking to be let out.

The professor looked to me for a response but I could not give one. I sat in silence and stared at him, searched for words that did not come.

'It is true. I swear it.' Moriarty reached across the table but I pulled my hands away from him.

'How can this be?' I chose my words carefully. 'I mean, given your *friendship* with Alexander. The nature of how you are?'

His face grew weary. 'It was in my younger days. In that period of my life when I had not such a clear view of my true self.'

'I don't understand.'

'Then I must begin at the beginning. I came of age, reached manhood in what was an entirely different time. A different world. My own father took my lack of desire for female company as shyness. And he thought a lady of the night might bring me out of myself and teach me how to become "a proper man" as he put it.'

'And what?' I felt my anger rise. 'Are you saying that my mother was that *lady of the night*?'

'Yes, that is precisely what I am saying. Her name was Alice. Alice Armer.'

'Alice?' I repeated it, for I had never heard her name before.

'She was picked out for me.' He spoke bitterly. 'Father told me he visited the best brothels of Mayfair, to find "a new girl that hadn't yet been ruined". No expense was spared.'

'I don't believe you.' I shook my head in disbelief. 'This doesn't make sense. How would a *pure* girl end up in a brothel?'

'Her father had run off with another woman and her mother had died of the fever. That is how she ended up in the ruinous company of one of London's leading madams. Alice was elegant, lost, beguiling and taken advantage of.'

I cannot deny that his description of her intrigued me. I had killed off all fledgling curiosity about my mother and naturally such a kindly portrait touched me.

'I am not lying to you, Simeon. You are my flesh and blood.'

'And you would know that, how? Prostitutes have many clients.'

'Simeon, I—'

'Surely to God, there's a clamour of *better men than you* out there claiming to have sired me?'

He let my fury subside before he replied, 'You make a plausible point and I have a reasonable response but it is unpleasant. My father was concerned that I should not contract venereal disease. He was most terribly frightened of syphilis. A close relative had gone mad with it. Not only was Alice picked out for me, she was retained for my use.'

'What does that mean?'

'Father paid an exclusivity fee to her brothel. It was a place in London that he subsequently frequented himself and sent many important clients to. The woman running it would not have dared lie to him.' He paused to put a comforting hand to his facial injury then added, 'I did not know she was pregnant, Simeon. You must believe that. I had no idea, until after you had been born and she had died.'

'Why not? Mine was, after all, a very public birth.'

'It was. It was indeed.' He needed a moment to compose himself, then continued, 'After five, maybe six months, Father stopped taking me to see Alice. I thought nothing of it. In fact, I was relieved our mutual ordeal was over. I hoped he had concluded that I had now learned enough and didn't warrant any more expenditure.' He looked down at his hands. 'Only later, *many years later*, did I discover that my visits had been curtailed because she had been found to be pregnant and, as a consequence, thrown out onto the street.'

Although I had seldom thought about my birth mother, strong feelings now rose within me. 'They threw her out because she was pregnant? Pregnant, with no roof over her head, and they discarded her?'

'Yes.' He held his head up. 'That is so. But I did not know it. Not at the time. Believe me, Simeon, I had no idea.'

'I really do not know whether I believe a single word you have said to me.'

'It is the truth. Many, many years passed before I became aware of it.'

'How were you told?'

'I was at a party in Westminster. Alice's old madam was there. She had provided some young girls for a politician's birthday celebration. I recognised her and approached her when she was alone. We talked over canapés . . .'

'Canapés! *How nice.*'

'It was then that she told me the truth. Alice had died in childbirth and you had gone to the baker and his wife.'

'Thank God. Thank God I hadn't gone to you, or your devil of a father.'

'I tracked the Lynches down; or rather I tracked down where they had been. Their shop had become a haberdashery, Cyril was dead, you had gone to the workhouse with Philomena and she had subsequently passed.'

I felt my past unravelling. I had tightly wound all this history together like a ball of old string that I no longer needed. Tucked in its ends and stored it away in a forgotten part of my mind. Now Moriarty was painfully pulling it all apart.

'When I—'

'Stop! *Please stop.*' I let out a sigh. 'I don't think I can take any more. This is the wrong time and wrong place for me to learn of things like this.'

'Then you believe me?'

I said nothing. Painful questions entered my mind, aching to be asked. I looked at him, searching for visual clues that would confirm beyond doubt that I had sprung from him, that I was this monster's child. Our eyes were both dark. We were of similar sizes and build. Beardless, his face would not be unlike my own.

No! I told myself I would not allow it to be true. 'Why

now?' I asked him. 'Why choose to tell me all this, right at this awful moment?'

'Because you are to be hanged.' His voice shook. 'Because it is *wrong* for a man to go to his death without knowing the truth about his birth.'

His words stung me. I *was* to be hanged and I *had* lived a life of lies. Right from my birth, up to the precipice of my death. Lies and murder. That was all it had been. 'This is horse shit! You have scraped together these untruths for some reason that I cannot even begin to imagine.'

An awkward silence grew.

Finally, he spoke. 'In your heart you *know* it is true, Simeon. Why else would I have plucked you out of that den of thieves in Manchester? How else could I have traced you there?'

'Boxing. You said you saw me box—'

'*Really*, Simeon?' There was a sneer in his voice. 'Do you honestly believe that I would have opened my house and my life to a young thief who happened to be a promising boxer?'

My mind became crowded with thoughts from the past. I recalled my first days in Derbyshire. Sirius had asked me, 'Do you not have any idea *why* you are here, *who* the professor is, or why you were chosen?'

Chosen.

The word had stuck at the time. I had come to believe he had merely wished to profit from my propensity for violence. But I had always wondered about how and why I had been picked out.

Another echo from the past sounded in my mind – Sebastian, at Michael's funeral. He had told me he and other area lieutenants had been given my description and had been instructed to be on the lookout for 'a boy from London whom the professor considered special.'

Special.

One more word that now conveyed deeper implications.

Moriarty leaned across the prison table. 'Remember when we first met, when you lied to me about who you were? I said, "I know exactly who you are, young man. Know it better than you do." Do you recollect that, Simeon?'

I did but I shook my head in denial. 'I do not recall such a thing.'

'You will. You will remember many occasions that made no sense in the past but do now. They will confirm that I speak the truth.'

'And the truth is that none of this matters. As you so eloquently said, I am about to be hanged. My life, whatever is known or unknown to me, is over.'

'You may yet save yourself, Simeon.' He reached across the table again and once more I pulled my hands clear of his reach.

'I am an old man now. My time is almost done and my concern is only for you. I believed Levine would extricate you from this predicament but it seems there is some new force in this damned government that I cannot overcome.' A palpable sadness grew in his eyes. 'Should you have been freed, I would have told you the truth. Shown you your inheritance and readied you to take over when the day of my death came. Those riches can still be yours, but to claim them you need to testify against me.' He smiled resignedly. 'If I go to Holmes then there will be no deal. He will merely see to it that both of us hang, along with your uncle, of course. That would be his greatest prize.'

'Holmes is a fool.'

'No, my son, that is the one thing that he is not. Sherlock Holmes is no fool. But you are, if you don't accept his offer. Tell him your story and you will have your clemency, your life *and* if you are lucky, you may still secure your fortune.'

Moriarty and I talked for several more hours, not just about my mother and what little he knew of her, but also about Alex, whom he described as 'an uncrowned prince of a man,' and how the traitor Sirius had come into his life and his affections.

Like Surrey, Gunn had been the child of a former member of the Trinity. A paid killer; sworn in blood and oath to protect the Moriarty family and its secrets. 'His father had been a most honourable and trustworthy fellow, killed in service to the family. Sirius came to us in his late teens, when his mother took her own life.' Moriarty put his hand to his heart. 'His betrayal pains me here more than anywhere. Far more than the scars you see.' He paused reflectively then added, 'I should have anticipated it. From Judas to Brutus, betrayers have brought down emperors and empires. They are an abomination.'

'Why did he do it?'

'Sirius, it seems, had long envisaged himself as my heir apparent. He would have continued to do so had he not overheard Alexander and myself discussing my will. Until then, he had always imagined you merely as a replacement for Michael. This discovery of his came about a fortnight before we went to America. I recall it because he challenged me on the matter and admitted he had been about to knock on my study door when he had heard the discussion. In hindsight, I believe this was the genesis of his treachery.'

I looked across the table and could see the professor was close to collapsing. 'How are you feeling?'

'Not so well. The fire cooked my lungs and much of my body has also been burned. I tire easily.'

'Then you must go. Sleep and heal a little. Perhaps return tomorrow?'

He didn't fight the suggestion, just gave a sorrowful nod of his head then rose slowly, shuffled to the door and knocked for the gaoler.

We parted with emotional awkwardness. Our time together had been all too inadequate for a bastard son to even think of all the questions he wished to ask his newly declared father.

After the professor's departure, I was returned to my cell and left to contemplate the final dilemma. He wanted Levine to contact Holmes on my behalf. I had told him to wait, and said I needed to sleep on it. Not that I would manage a wink. How could I send him and his brother to the gallows, and in the process endanger every man and woman who worked for the family? No, I really could not entertain such an act.

But doubt and paranoia plagued me. Was Moriarty's tale of parentage in fact a lavish lie? A masterful manipulation to save his own skin and fortune? Over the years, the professor had perpetrated many deceptions on me. It was comfortably within his range of cunning to seek to silence me with the biggest form of emotional blackmail he could muster.

Maybe his suggestion of contacting Holmes was a clever bluff. Perhaps he knew Levine had no hope of clearing me, so to prevent me talking to Holmes he had woven this web of lies to catch and hold me in.

I dismissed the thought. Once Moriarty had said he was my father, I had seen clearly myself in him. That was why his gaze had always magnetised me. His eyes were a mirror of my own. His voice was my voice, only older and deeper. The broad, square shoulders and the way he stood – this was my form. The more I looked for similarities the more foolish I felt not to have seen them the very first moment we had met. My lord – to others, the mutual likeness must have been obvious.

I was Brogan Moriarty's son.

There was no denying it.

The name Lynch, the one so generously afforded me before I could even speak, was the biggest lie of my life. I had never been fit to carry it, or the immaculate reputation of that kindly baker and his angelic wife. Equally, I knew I should not irrevocably stain it by having a noose put around my neck and being dropped through a trap and into history as a Lynch.

I was a Moriarty.

I had lived and killed as a Moriarty. And if I had to tread those boards and stand on that trapdoor, then I should die as a Moriarty.

I curled up on my bunk and my mind was as troubled as a hornet's nest battered by sticks. Thoughts of my birth mother stung me most.

Alice.

Since childhood, I had stopped myself thinking about her. I had effectively wiped her out of my consciousness. Now I tried to imagine her as Moriarty had described. Young. Beautiful. Vulnerable. I had no face to envisage. No shape or form to picture. The only image that came to mind was the silhouette of the lady that sweet Philomena Lynch had given me as we entered the workhouse together.

I still had the shade. Faded and frayed, it had been carried from place to place and pocket to pocket for more than three decades. Never had I gone anywhere without it. It had been close to my heart when I had taken my first life. At the birth and death of my child. At the death of the woman I loved. I had held onto it during my arrest. After passing through the prison gates, the shade and the clothes that I stood in had been the only things I had been allowed to keep.

I reached beneath the bunk and slid it from its place in

between the leg joint and slats. For a moment, I held it so I could study the profile and imagine the colour of my mother's hair, strawberry-blonde like Elizabeth's, her eyes as big and blue as Molly's. I kissed the shade, put it to my heart, then most reluctantly returned it to its resting place.

I had to escape!

I would climb that damned chimney and pull out that troublesome block with my teeth if I had to. It was my only chance. I would seize it. And when I did, I would find poor Alice's bones and bury her respectfully. I would visit Elizabeth's grave and I would pray for forgiveness.

Then I would find Lee Chan.

I would find him and, so help me God, I would kill him. But I would not bury him. I would gut him like a fish and leave him by the Thames for all the lowest creatures of the earth to feast upon.

Over the next few hours, both my rage and the frigid weather changed. Rain hammered against my cell window and washed away the deposits of frost etched into the corners.

Elizabeth had loved the rain. Adored walking in it. She would sit by a lakeside bench on Moriarty's estate and be mesmerised by droplets dancing on the surface. Sometimes she would tilt her face to the sky, close her eyes and open her mouth to the downpour. Then I would kiss her, while she was still wet and cool and more alive than anyone could possibly be.

Before the great blackness came, we had sat by the fire

in our cottage and she had talked of how she'd teach Molly to dance in the rain – something her hypocritical Scottish father had chastised her for. She said she would teach our daughter a wild Celtic dance to clear the puddles from all the great lawns around us. How I longed to have seen it. I missed them both so terribly much.

After conviction, I had locked down my grief, but now it ran free inside me, its long talons trying to catch my wounded spirit and pull it down into despair and surrender.

Today and tomorrow – then I would be dead. And no just God would reunite me with my wife and daughter, for they were surely in heaven and I would go straight to the fires of hell.

It would soon be midday. They would hang me at dawn the day after tomorrow. Twelve more hours of today, twenty-four of tomorrow and perhaps six of the final day. Forty-two hours.

I had determined not to do this, to count down the hours. It only set my heart racing and my brain aching. But I couldn't help it. Try as I might, the clock in my head could not be stopped and it chimed off every hour as soundly as Big Ben.

A thump on the door and a rattle of keys was followed by a familiar command. 'Stand back by the window!'

Johncock swept in, accompanied by Huntley and two older screws. 'Getting near to the big day now, Lynch.' His face was the happiest I had ever seen it. 'Not long now. Not long at all.'

I didn't answer. His goading had long since failed to rile me.

'I 'ave to say, I really am looking forward to walking you out there.' He grinned expansively. 'I'll be as proud as a father taking 'is daughter to the marriage altar.'

There was a loud bang and one of the screws stumbled sideways. Dopily, he had leaned on the cell door believing it closed, while it had still been a little ajar. As a result, it had slammed shut.

'Imbecile!' Johncock scowled at him. 'Stand up straight, man! You should know better—'

A second noise severed his sentence – a rumble. Rows of bricks in the corner of the cell tumbled onto the floor, dislodged by the bang.

Johncock's eyes grew as large as those of a startled deer's. 'My, my, my,' he said excitedly. '*What* do we 'ave 'ere?'

I tried to look surprised.

He leaned down and sifted the rubble, picking through the debris and dust. His fingers settled on several strips of paper that I had pressed into the cracks. At first he wasn't sure what they were. Then he realised. He turned to me and smiled. 'Clever, Lynch. *Very* clever. But unfortunately for you, not clever enough.' He looked to his men. 'Get down there. Delve beneath this devil's cot and see what else 'e's been up to.'

The two screws fell to the floor. They scrabbled in the rubble and I knew it would only be seconds before they found my stash.

'I've got something, sir!' The fool that had slammed the door surfaced with Father Deagan's crucifix.

'There's more!' shouted his colleague, with the excitement of a treasure hunter. 'It's a rag or cloth of some kind.' He emerged with the silk altar sash and rosary beads.

'Anything else, Lynch?'

'Yes, sir,' I said contritely. 'There are also two nuns and a boys' choir hiding in there. They kept me awake all night.'

He punched me – a sound right-hander that hit me full in the mouth. I spat blood. Then he hit me again. My lips had already been torn, and slivers of tissue came away in my mouth. I spat again.

'Get 'im out of 'ere,' he told Huntley.

'There's a cell shortage, sir. Where shall I put him?'

Johncock glowered at Huntley. 'I don't care. Just make sure it's somewhere I can't 'ear 'im until it's time to drag 'im, weeping and wailing to the scaffold. I need to see the governor and decide what should be done with this creature.'

Johncock was back in full control. The execution was close and his time of absolute authority had come.

Huntley told the others to clear up the rubble, then he put me in walking chains and ushered me down the landing. 'You made quite a mess back there, Lynch. Almost became the new Jack Sheppard, didn't you?'

'Tried my best, Mr Huntley.' I looked directly at him. 'If you'd left me a bigger nail then I might've done a better job.'

He stopped us in our tracks. 'What do you mean? I left you no nail.'

His answer surprised me. I had been sure he had been my secret supplier.

I held up my right hand, 'I mean, had I been equipped with more than nails bitten to the quick, then I might have escaped.'

Huntley said no more. He walked me on, through a gateway and onto another landing. We left the condemned block and entered a part of the prison that housed those convicted of lesser crimes. He opened a door to his left and barked out an instruction to me. 'Step inside. You can wash your mouth out in there. I'll be back once I've sorted your cell.'

I entered and he locked the door behind me. The room was narrow and stank of shit and cheap tobacco. Gaolers' caps and coats hung from wall pegs. One side of the room was fitted with cracked and filthy sinks. Opposite was a series of toilets, some with battered green doors, some without. I guessed this was some kind of changing place for the screws.

I washed my mouth and spat in a sink. Used one of the toilets then quickly checked the windows. They were small, all barred and even higher than the one in my cell.

Huntley eventually opened up and called to me. 'Hurry up, Lynch. I've found somewhere to put you. Come on.'

We walked together in silence along the landing. He stopped, opened a cell to his right and pushed me inside.

'Here he is, boys, this is the one,' he announced before closing the door.

Four men gazed at me.

Two were slim, young and swarthy. A third was big and bald. The fourth had his back to me and was facing the window. He was of medium height and build, with jet-black hair and the start of a thinning crown.

He turned and I saw immediately that he was Chinese.

'My cousin Lee, he wishes you dead,' he said through a broken wall of teeth. 'And I also wish you dead, because you kill my friend Lin.'

'I don't think so,' I replied coolly. 'I have killed many people in my time, but never one of your kind.'

'In your cell, you kill him.'

'Ah, I remember now.' I nodded in mock respect. 'My condolences. Although I do recall that he was trying to murder me in my sleep. Perhaps you're the fellow who can tell me how he got in?'

He smiled again. 'Mr Boardman, he also wants kill you.'

'Ah, of course he does.' So I had been right. A turnkey had been in my room with the other intruder. There seemed little point telling the Chinaman the screw had killed his friend, had shanked him through the chest while I'd been merely choking him with my manacles.

The bald man cracked his knuckles and rose. He was well over six feet tall, thickly muscled. When he spoke his accent was horribly familiar. 'Yow got moy friend beaten up by young mister Chan at that owse in London, remember?'

'Yes, I remember. A Brummie bastard, if ever there was one.'

The two young convicts jumped down from the top bunk where they'd been sitting together.

The Chinaman glanced at them and then laughed. 'You relax – they the only ones don't want kill you, Mr Lynch. They just wish fuck you when you dead.'

'Oh, that *is* of great comfort,' I replied.

Baldy made his move. He grabbed for my chest with his big sausage fingers. Big mistake. I slammed my left fist into his throat. Between my knuckles was the nail I had put there while in the screws' bathroom, looking to escape through a window. He screamed and coughed blood. His eyes widened as he slowly choked.

I pulled out the nail and switched my attention to the Chinaman. *My mistake.* Baldy wobbled and fell into me. We staggered half a yard, his big arms circling my chest like twin snakes. His knees gave way but he held on, crashed me into the edge of a bunk and pulled me over. I hit the ground backwards, Baldy a dead weight across my chest and legs.

A foot stamped on my outstretched left hand, smashing down so hard that I released the nail from my fingers. The Chinaman came into my view. Dull steel moved in his right hand – a shank made from scavenged metal.

'This is for Lee.' His hand rose and fell.

I would have been dead. The shank would have sunk in my head or chest, had the cell door not banged open. It caught the Chinaman fully in the shoulder and he toppled over. Voices bellowed. Screws kicked their way into the cell.

Someone pulled Baldy's corpse off me. Blood spurted from his throat into my face.

I got to my knees. Wiped my eyes with my thumbs.

Johncock stared at me. 'By Jesus, Lynch, you just can't stay out of trouble, can you?' He dragged me to my feet. 'I think the gallows might be the safest place for you.'

'Thank you,' I said.

'Don't be thanking me. I want you dead as dearly as Huntley does. I'm just prepared to wait a little longer and see it done legally.'

Huntley? My mind could not register him as anything but a friend, let alone a secret enemy.

Johncock turned to his men. 'Get Lynch out of here and have him cleaned up and protected.'

The screws' idea of 'cleaning me up' turned out to be nothing more than issuing me with a dry set of dead man's rags, a bar of carbolic soap and a bucket of water, then turning me out into the cold of the Press Yard.

I stripped naked, washed myself clean of the Brummie's blood and changed into the tattered garments.

I had killed again.

Not the life I had wished to take, but still a life. It seemed as though I was fated to murder until God stilled my hand and man piled earth thickly upon me.

I was taken back inside the gaol and chained up in a corridor for more than an hour before they found me a new cell. It turned out to be one vacated by a convict who had died from gaol fever. Another bucket of water, more carbolic and a scrubbing brush were brought for me to clean the place.

The floors and walls were still wet when Johncock strode in. This time he ordered his men to wait outside. He looked at the dripping walls, then at me. 'Made yourself at 'ome, Lynch?'

I didn't answer. He hadn't come here to check on my comfort.

'You've done us all a favour today.' He smiled gloatingly. 'Thanks to you we were able to get a bad apple, a *very* bad apple out of our barrel.'

'You mean Huntley.'

'Aye, I do. I do indeed.'

'May I ask how I acquired such good fortune that you intervened on my behalf at *exactly* the moment you did?'

'Eyes and ears, Lynch. I have them on every landing in Newgate. Nothing 'appens in 'ere without me knowing about it sooner or later.' Water had gathered on the floor where it ran at a slope and hit the wall. Johncock placed his boot in a puddle of water then pleased himself by making a footprint on some dry stone to one side. 'From the first day you came 'ere there were contracts out on you.'

'Contracts plural?'

'Most certainly plural. There are Englishmen, Irishmen, Londoners, northerners and all manner of foreigners wanting your bones boxed and buried. Fortunately for you, only 'alf a dozen of the devils in Newgate 'ave the gumption to fulfil such a wish. I've 'ad them all watched. And when 'untley arrived I 'ad 'im watched as well.'

'Why Huntley?'

'All prim and prettified, posh and perfect, 'e was too good to be true. I can tell rotten without seeing rotten. And when he walked out of 'ere at night at the end of 'is shift, 'e changed into clothes and went places that not even the keeper could afford.'

'So you had Huntley and the most dangerous men in the prison under observation?'

'I did. The pair of pixies in the Chinaman's cell – they were two of my snitches. I 'ad them put into several cells before we identified Sun Shi as the man contracted to kill you. Indeed, 'ad you got out into the exercise yard the first time 'untley wanted you to, then you would 'ave run into 'im and 'is shank. You were only saved because those boys gave me the nod, and in doing so they confirmed my suspicions about 'untley.'

'Mr Johncock, you put the great Sherlock Holmes to shame.'

'In my opinion, there is nothing so great about 'im.' He puffed out his chest. 'Could 'e manage this gaol for a month? For a day? I think not. Twenty years I've been 'ere, and never a slip up on my watch.'

'What about Boardman?'

'Boardman?' he looked surprised.

'Your big dumb screw was the man who shanked the Chinaman you found dead in my cell. He was going for me.'

''ow do you know that?'

'Sun Shi said it. I asked him outright how his friend accessed my cell.'

'Then I will speak to 'im, and if you are correct Boardman will be dealt with.'

'And what now of Huntley?'

'The police 'ave 'im. Not that it is any concern of yours. 'e'll get 'is punishment, along with Boardman if 'e was involved as well.'

'And the bald Brummie I killed?'

'We could try you and 'ang you for it, I suppose.' He gave me a look of mischievous amusement. 'Or I could save myself a lot of paperwork and report it as self-defence. A fact that will come out if we get 'untley and Sun Shi to the Old Bailey.'

He splashed a foot in the puddled water again, stamped down his boot and lifted it to reveal a strong outline on dry stone. 'Tobias Johncock always leaves 'is mark. Every day, in one way or another, 'e always leaves 'is mark.'

Two Days to Execution

The following morning, as they cleared away the slop they called breakfast, I discovered that my new cell was something of an inconvenience to the turnkeys. Apparently, it was further from the Pinioning Room, the dreaded area in which they would bind my hands by my side so I might fall 'straighter and cleaner' through the trap. Screws liked things easy and a longer walk would give me more chance to stage a final fight for life.

When Levine and Moriarty arrived, we were afforded the privacy of a secure area near the Association Room. My lawyer was more modestly dressed than usual, in a suit of green velvet, pale ruffled shirt and green silk tie. Moriarty was still in the guise of clerk.

They had both been told of the attempt on my life and despite the fact that I was soon to hang were ironically concerned for my welfare.

'I do hope you have not suffered further injury,' remarked the lawyer. 'You have had a most terrible time since your admission.'

'Shut up, Levine,' growled Moriarty. 'Your lack of reality embarrasses me.' He looked my way. 'Simeon, I will find this Huntley fellow and I assure you he will be dealt with.'

'He is of no consequence. Chan was behind the attack, and it is he I wish to be brought to book.'

'You are certain it was Chan?'

'The cell was run by a Chinaman called Sun Shi, who said he is a cousin of Lee Chan.'

'This side of hell, they will never be reunited,' promised Moriarty.

Levine was nervous of the conversation and keen to change the subject. 'Gentlemen, let us move to legal business, as time is of the essence. Simeon, in light of our failed appeal to the home secretary we have been petitioning the monarch for clemency.' He passed me a stamped note, signed by the royal secretary. 'Unfortunately, Her Majesty is not disposed to intervene on this occasion.'

I held the letter but did not look at it. 'Yesterday, you informed me you had lost PC Cross as a witness and had an appeal denied by the home secretary. Am I correct in now assuming we are at the end of the line and I should prepare for the worst?'

'I am truly sorry,' added Moriarty. 'We have run out of options. Except for the one Holmes presented you.'

I passed the royal note back. 'Holmes's proposition is not an option.'

'Then you have decided?' Levine sounded a tad too enthusiastic for my liking.

'I have.' An involuntary sigh gave away how drained I felt. My spirit was already dead. My determination to live had been depleted. 'I am guilty of the murder of PC Jackson and, Lord knows, many more as well. So I shall not be saving my own neck only to break those of others.'

Moriarty spoke gently and slowly. 'My son, you are resolved to do a brave and honourable thing, but I beg you not to. You are young enough to start again, to find a new love and to raise a new family.'

I shook my head. '*You* of all people know that I have had but one love. One beautiful love and one beautiful child. I wish for no more. They are irreplaceable.'

'I understand your loss, and your sentiments.' His eyes misted and I am sure for a moment he thought of Alexander. 'But I would willingly give my life in return for yours.'

'But it would not be *only* yours,' I reminded him. 'Holmes seeks the neck of your brother more than yours, and it would not stop there. Everyone in your empire would be at risk.'

The ensuing silence seemed to seal the discussion. I had but one loose end, one unanswered question. 'Surrey? Do you have any further news of her?'

The professor took a deep breath. 'I do not. I asked the very same question of James and he says neither he nor Moran saw her after she went with Elizabeth.'

'So Chan killed her as well?'

'It would appear so.'

'For that error of judgement alone, I deserve to hang. Had I gone with Elizabeth then both she and Surrey would be alive today and I would not be in this wretched place.' I banged my fists on the table and struggled not to bellow out the rage that rose inside me.

Moriarty put his hands gently over my whitened knuckles. 'Do not torture yourself with regrets. The blame is solely Chan's. Not yours, nor mine, nor James's.' He could see my spirit was still fiery and added, 'You and I are not so different. I have the same rage and propensity for violence, I have just learned to hide it better. And I too lost my mother; she passed in my early teens and I missed her terribly. The business I built in America was more to honour her memory than anything. And I confess that returning to those shores always made me feel connected to her.'

He flinched and I wondered if it was the pain of remembering or the agony of his injuries, then he concluded, 'Sons who lose their mothers early are either driven to succeed or destined to die in poverty.'

From that moment forth, our moods became increasingly saturnine and I found myself longing for my own company in order to come to terms with all my feelings and the enormity of what lay ahead. 'Please do not think me rude, but I need to return to my cell and rest now.'

Moriarty looked disappointed.

'I wish to gather my thoughts,' I explained, 'come to terms with my lot and find some peace with my maker.'

'I understand. Then Levine and I will leave you for now.' He squeezed out a smile as he began to rise. 'But we will come again tomorrow and—'

'No!' I snapped. 'I am sorry, I mean, *no thank you*. I fear that from this moment onwards your presence may only

413

weaken my courage rather than fortify it. I wish to give no satisfaction to those who tie the noose around my neck.'

He looked pained by my bluntness. 'You do not wish to see me again?'

'Not this side of Newgate's unholy walls.' I rose from my seat and looked to the lawyer. 'Good day, Mr Levine. It is a great pity that your wardrobe outshone your abilities, but I thank you nonetheless.'

He afforded me a graceful bow of his head. 'I shall pray for you, sir.'

Moriarty appeared close to tears as he extended his hand. I shook it firmly and we both held tight, understanding that this would be our last contact. His flesh was my flesh. Our handshake was our bond. I looked him in the eyes. 'Will you promise to do something for me?'

'Anything within my power.'

'The life of Lee Chan. That is my dying request, father. Take his life. Kill him for me. For your son. For Elizabeth and for Molly.'

ONE DAY TO EXECUTION

NEWGATE, 17 JANUARY 1900

I saw them again last night.

Not my family, or the few I called friends. But the faces

of each and every person I had murdered. They surfaced from the black pools of my mind. Rose first as shadows, then shaped themselves into silhouettes before finally becoming the fathers and sons, brothers and lovers that I had slain. This was their moment of reckoning.

I clearly saw their faces. Mouths that had cried for help, gasped for breath or gargled blood. Eyes that had registered shock, pleaded for mercy or grown cold as glass. Now I wished I had not killed them, whatever their crimes I wished they still trod the earth.

My eyes remained shut until the physiognomy of my victims faded and they became no more than what death and I had reduced them to – mere shadows, pools of blackness.

The experience left me depressed and the mood was still on me when Johncock entered the cell and found me sitting on my bunk. 'Mr Sherlock 'olmes 'as arrived at the gate'ouse and is seeking to visit you.'

'No.' I shook my head. 'I do not have the energy for him. Turn the man around and tell him he has made a wasted journey.'

'I am not your errand boy, Lynch, and Mr 'olmes anticipated that you would respond in such a fashion.' He reached into his right-hand pocket and produced a folded note. ''e required me to give you this, and said it would alter your decision.'

'I doubt it.'

I took the note, unfolded it and read it. My heart quickened. The contents were brief but so shocking that I had to reread it before I could respond. 'Mr Holmes is correct. I have changed my mind and will see him.'

The meeting took place some ten minutes later in my cell, after one of Johncock's men had grudgingly brought two rough wooden stools and afforded us some privacy.

Holmes was wearing a brown tweed greatcoat and a generous woollen scarf in contrasting cream. He winced at the smell of the room and held the scarf to his nose to mask the stench. 'The air in here is most odorous,' he complained. 'There really should be a law against it.'

'What is the meaning of this note?' I asked, holding it up.

'I should have thought that axiomatic.' He sat on a stool and loosened his coat. 'You were foolish enough to confess to a crime that you had not committed, and I can prove your stupidity.'

'With respect, Mr Holmes, you cannot prove I was wrong. It may have escaped your brilliant powers of observation but I was actually *there* when PC Jackson died and you were not. I put a knife through his throat. I watched his legs twitch and his mouth froth. In short, I witnessed his death in its entirety.'

'With that last declaration I have no argument. The officer in question is undoubtedly dead and I fully accept that you *witnessed* his passing. But you did not kill him.'

'How can you say such a thing?'

'Do you remember when we first met inside this institution? I asked you to name the men who had been with you on that fateful night and you would not.'

'I do.'

'Well, you would have saved me a great deal of time and effort if you had been more forthcoming. No matter, I have done what I do best. I have been back to the scene of the crime. I have examined that flash house in Southwark where the murder occurred. Furthermore, I have mentally reassembled the events of your encounter, reconstructed them in my deductive mind and seen them from the true angle, one of a dispassionate and incisive observer devoid of emotion, guilt or mistaken memories.'

I was close to my wits' end. 'Then please tell me what on earth you think you have deduced, so I may at least look forward to dying in peace.'

'There is no *think* about it, sir.' He sounded offended. 'The names of the men you would not disclose are the brothers Charles and James Connor. I suppose it is to your misguided credit that despite your past differences with these fellows you chose to protect their memories – and I say memories, because both of them are dead.'

'How did you come about their names?'

'A search of public records placed you all at the same London workhouse. An unpleasant conversation with Mr Beamish, the master and a far more efficacious one with Mr Bangura, your former boxing trainer, gave me all the background information I required about you, the Connor boys and your collective exit from the institution.'

'But how did you place all of us at Hoolihan's house in Southwark?'

'That was even less taxing. The corpse of Charles Connor was found alongside that of PC Jackson. It was almost inconceivable to me that two brothers who had run away together in your company, would not have stayed together once free of the spike. Ergo, James Connor was also in that room when his brother and PC Jackson died.'

My mind turned to his earlier comment. 'You said both of the brothers are dead.'

'I did. Charles, as I believe you are aware, died from a fatal abdominal stab wound sustained in the confrontation with the police. He had other vicious but non-fatal injuries, consistent with being beaten by a truncheon.'

'And Jimmy?'

'Ah, therein lies the key to your innocence of this crime. James Connor fled the scene, presumably because he saw that his brother was dead and so too was a policeman.'

'As did I.'

'Quite. But you didn't flee together, did you?'

'No.'

'And you never saw him again?'

'No.'

'Had you done so, you might have learned that human beings are creatures of habit, especially those who kill.'

'You are baffling me, Mr Holmes.'

'To be more explicit, people who kill with knives tend to kill again with knives. Murder is habit forming and in my experience, once a habitual murderer has perfected a way to take a life, he usually sticks to it.'

418

This was uncomfortable ground for me. He was right. I also had my preferred techniques, though my preference was not for a knife but my hands. 'I still do not see your point, sir.'

'That is because I haven't yet fully made it. I pursued my theory of habitual modus operandi and I found two more murders in which the victim had been pinned to the floor with a knife through the larynx. One of those was a pawnbroker in Sheffield. The other, a jeweller in Leeds.'

'So the practice was more commonplace than you thought?'

'*No.*' He looked exasperated. 'To the contrary. It was the same man. Ten years ago, James Arthur Connor was hanged in Yorkshire. He swung from the gallows inside Armley Gaol, after being convicted of both the killings I have just described to you.'

'May the Lord have mercy on his soul. I did not know Jimmy was dead, let alone that he had been hanged. I am saddened to learn of this.'

'You shouldn't be,' said Holmes, brightly. 'When asked if he had any final words, according to several witnesses of good repute, James Connor responded, "God forgive me. I killed another. A copper in London."'

I still refused to accept the implication of what was being said. 'He didn't, though. Not unless it was a policeman other than the one I killed.'

'Dash it man, have you *no* common sense? Your friend fled London after PC Jackson's death. In fact, he spent little time anywhere, except for inside the gaols of Stafford, Stoke and Kirkdale. Furthermore, he also told three other felons in Armley, all of whom are still incarcerated there, that he had nearly been caught for killing the policeman who had murdered his brother.'

A cold shiver gripped me. I knew Jimmy would unhesitatingly have killed anyone who hurt Charlie. Holmes was right about brotherly love. My mind crackled with partial memories of that day. Flashes of facts, glowing like embers in a fire that I thought had been long extinguished.

Still I tried to deconstruct the detective's theory. 'In truth, Mr Holmes, it was *I* who fought with Jackson, not Jimmy. The knife belonged to the policeman, not one of us. He had pulled it out and stabbed Charlie. I punched him and grabbed his wrist. We fought for possession of it and struggled all around that room. Jimmy was fighting some other copper, then we all crashed into each other. We fell like idiots and when I got up and looked around, I saw the knife sunk in Jackson's throat.'

'Exactly!' Holmes wagged a finger directly in my face. 'You *saw* the knife! But do you recall *holding* it? Turning it? Positioning yourself directly above the man, then stabbing downwards with such deliberate force that it went through several layers of his flesh, tissue, muscle and organs, and pinioned him to the floor?'

'No, sir, I do not.'

'I thought not. Then how could that very thing have happened?'

'I presumed we fell. That the weight of others landing on top of us drove the knife through his neck.'

'*Presumed?*' He said the word with rich sarcasm. 'Your *presumption* is utter nonsense. At best, such a thing would be highly improbable. But given James Connor's confession that he killed his brother's murderer, it is absolutely impossible.'

Holmes stood up and backed away from the stool. 'Here is what happened. Connor saw his brother stabbed by PC Jackson while, as you said, he was engaged in fighting another officer, a man I have learned was one Benjamin Crowther. James Connor and Crowther subsequently careered into you and Jackson. All four of you fell. Crowther ended up face down over Jackson's legs. *You* were on your side, facing away from everyone and you were disorientated. You rolled out of the melee, got to your feet, saw Charles Connor was dead and then saw the knife in the policeman's throat. In that second, you made your presumption and *assumed* your guilt. Am I correct?'

'Yes, that is precisely my recollection.'

Holmes continued with more energy. 'What actually happened was that while you were still down and confused, James Connor got up. He saw the spilled knife and pounced upon it.'

Holmes put his hands together and interlocked his fingers as though holding a blade downwards. 'He was enraged. He saw his brother's murderer trapped beneath Crowther, and he struck.' Holmes fell dramatically to his knees, raised the imaginary knife and slammed his hands down. 'Connor plunged the knife into PC Jackson's throat. Double-handed, with enough force to pierce the larynx and the boards beneath it.'

The detective rose, brushed dirt from his knees, then sat back on the stool. 'In addition to the scene of that murder, I have been to the Coroner's Office and examined sketches made by the attending doctor and investigating police officers. I have consulted the best brains in Harley Street and the consensus of expert opinion is that Jackson's fatal injury is entirely consistent with the actions I just described to you, actions only attributable to James Connor. My experts also concur that *you* could not possibly have delivered that fatal wound, not from merely falling over with the deceased. Nor could it have been inflicted by another person falling onto the knife in the ridiculous way you described.' He looked at me in earnest. 'In short, Lynch, you are innocent. Of this murder at least.'

His observations left me stunned. My life might have been different – so very different. Had I known, as I left that house in Southwark, that I had not been responsible for the policeman's death, I certainly would not have given in to Moriarty's demand to leave with him that day in Manchester. Most of all, I would never have killed on his behalf.

'I am grateful for you revealing this, Mr Holmes, but I am somewhat nonplussed as to why you have done so on my behalf.'

'The answer to that is simple. Your account of how you killed Jackson made no sense, and for me there must always be sense in a confession, otherwise it is a lie or a mistake. You see, Lynch, I am quite content to see a man hang for a murder he committed, very content indeed. But I am most disturbed if one hangs for a crime he did not commit. It undermines our entire judicial system.'

'So you will present your evidence to the home secretary?'

'I have already.'

'And?'

'Dear fellow, would you still be imprisoned if I had been successful?'

'But what of your experts?'

'Dismissed as opinion. The truth is, a policeman has been killed and someone must be hanged for it. They believe it might as well be you. There is of course the second murder you were charged with. That hardly helped your case.'

'Elizabeth MacIntosh. Do you believe I killed *her*?'

'No, I do not. You had nothing to gain from it. You are an intelligent man; should you have wished to murder her you would have chosen a better time and place. But I cannot prove your innocence there, if that is what you were leading up to.'

'It was.'

'Then I must disappoint you. At first I thought there was something in the fact that the lady's throat had been cut by a right-handed man holding her from behind. I believed you to be left-handed. But on closer observation you gave away that you are ambidextrous. A rarity, and in your case unfortunate because it means you *could* have killed her.'

He produced a pipe from his pocket and inspected it but didn't light it. 'I had hoped to make a case on the direction of the blood spray found across your shirt and vest. Her killer would have been covered in it, but an area of clothing would also have been blood free, where the killer held Miss MacIntosh close to him as he made the fatal incision.'

'The police took my clothing.'

'I know they did. I made enquiries. And after conviction they disposed of it all. I was not surprised to learn that they have no records of where the garments went.'

'Then it seems all your efforts are to no avail, Mr Holmes. Being hanged for crimes I didn't commit will leave me every bit as dead as being hanged for ones I did.'

'Then testify against the Moriartys. Both James and Brogan. Begin anew.'

It was the first time he had mentioned *both* brothers and I could not keep the surprise from my eyes.

Holmes looked amused. 'Please do not tell me you thought that I did not know Brogan was the real power in the family?'

I said nothing. My loyalty was still instinctive.

'I have known it for some time. It merely suited me not to pay him the public attention I afforded his brother. Tell someone that you know their secret and they make plans accordingly. Let them believe they have fooled you and you have an advantage. I am under no illusions. James is the flame that draws the moth. Brogan is the whole candlestick. And you, Mr Lynch, you can help me burn down their empire.'

I knew I was at the point of no return. The answer I gave now would seal the fate of either myself, or my father and uncle. My heart pounded and my mouth grew dry. Was Holmes lying?

It certainly would have been easy for him to trace my connection to the Connor twins. But was the rest of it true? Had Jimmy really killed Jackson? And had the home secretary truly turned down Holmes's appeal? Might it be that Holmes never spoke to him because he wished me not to be freed unless I gave up Moriarty and his family?

My troubled mind thought up an alternative scenario – one even more worrying: had my father also known that I had not killed Jackson?

He had admitted to an almost forensic inspection of my early life. Had he discovered the same thing as Holmes but nevertheless held the threat of the noose over my head, just to control me, to manipulate me to kill for him and become what he wanted me to be – his murderous heir?

'Do something good with your life, Lynch,' implored Holmes as he watched me fight my thoughts. 'Seize this final opportunity of clemency and do not go to the grave with such terrible stains on your soul.'

I closed my eyes. My head would not clear. Blood pounded in my temples – the blood of my sworn oath. The blood of my family. I put my hand to my forehead and felt sweat beading there. I had not a clear thought in my mind. Everything was corrupted.

I opened my eyes and looked Holmes in the face. 'My answer is the same, sir. I am done with this life and the way I have lived it. I want no more deaths, of any kind, on my conscience. Good men or bad men, I do not want to send any of them prematurely to their graves. It is best that you go now; go and pay your companion the twenty pounds you owe him.'

EXECUTION DAY

NEWGATE, 18 JANUARY 1900

Through the cell bars I listened to the midnight bells toll. I tried through sheer power of will to halt those cast–iron notes in mid–chime and freeze time, but the last minutes of the last day of my life would not be held back.

The silence that followed marked the beginning of the end, brought me so close to the gates of hell that I could smell the sulphur and feel the flames. These were my final few hours.

Even the rancid air of the gaol was precious today. Closing my mouth, I breathed in fully through my nostrils and exhaled slowly, understanding for the first time what

426

a marvellous narcotic oxygen was. Greedily, I drew down breath after breath and I swear my heart beat faster and my head grew giddy.

I had lived a full life. One beyond murder, experiencing much of what all men crave. I had travelled the world. Loved and been loved. Fathered a child.

Philomena, Elizabeth and baby Molly had brought me such joy. They had touched my heart and out of the great slab of wickedness that defines me, they had sculpted the semblance of a kind man. Cyril Lynch had given me his name and taught me how to be honourable. Had Molly lived, I would have brought her up in the wholesome way that he had tried to raise me. Molly would have been a good girl. Good through and through.

And then there came Brogan Moriarty, my father. He had taken me in. Fed me. Clothed me. Educated me. Provided for me. Given me the chance to make my fortune, meet the woman I loved and have the child I adored.

And he had taught me to commit murder. To protect him and be like him, until one day I could inherit one of the biggest criminal empires in England. As unforgivable as those deeds were, he remained my father, my only living blood.

And then there was his reluctant young lover, sweet Alice, my biological mother. The woman I had maligned most of my life and had never known. Alice, the parent I would have loved to have been a son to. Perhaps if she had survived my sordid birth, then both our lives would have been different.

I laughed at my thoughts. Life, it seemed, was painfully crowded with perhapses.

The moon moved in a gentle arc across the barred window and cast silvery shadows upon the stone cell floor. I knelt, dipped my hands in them and studied the magical luminescence on my skin. I was washing my hands clean. Ridding myself of the blood I was stained with.

I stared at the silhouette beside me. A monster on his knees, clutching at nothing. This was *my* shade. The shadow of the man I had become.

I stood in the centre of the cell and it stung me to think I would never see the magnificence of the moon again. I would be hanged and cut down before the sun reached its apex and began its descent into the west. The lice that crawled in my hair would soon be overcome by corpse flies and maggots of the earth.

I was still standing when an elderly turnkey entered the cell. He was the mild-mannered fellow who had spoken kindly to me about Louise Masset's execution and said she had found peace at the end. 'Mr Johncock sent me to enquire about your final wishes.'

I laughed. 'I should like to be freed and spit in the old curmudgeon's eyes as I dance out of the gates.'

A smile tugged the corner of his lips. 'Something special perhaps from the kitchen?'

I laughed. 'Special? Their food is more likely to kill me than the knot around my neck.'

'Then a jug of ale, or cup of gin to steady the nerves?'

'I have no nerves, only regrets, and ale or gin is no solution to those.'

'As you wish. Is there a will to be lodged, or one still to be written?'

'Neither. I leave behind no more than I had when I entered this world. And before you ask; no, there is no final letter I wish to pen.' My eyes fixed again on the patch of sky beyond the bars. 'Tell me *precisely* what happens when I next leave this cell.'

He took a deep breath. 'It will be quick.'

'Tell me.'

'The Execution Detail will come. You will be taken in haste to the Pinioning Room where Mr Warbrick's assistant will secure your arms. They will walk you free of leg irons to the scaffold. You will climb the stairs and then be hooded, positioned on the trap, noosed and hanged.'

I looked at him. 'And that is it? So perfunctory?'

'It is. It will be over within minutes.'

'I pray you are right.'

'Your priest has confirmed that he will attend but asks if you would kindly allow another cleric to accompany him due to the fact his health remains poor.'

'Of course, but I prefer he does not come. His good health is more important than my bad death.'

'I am told he has already risen from his bed and is on his way.'

'He is a kind man and I am grateful.'

The turnkey looked to the window. Dawn was coming.

'I need to convey your answers to Mr Johncock. Is there anything else you wish to ask for?'

'There is nothing.'

'Then I will pray for you, Simeon Lynch. May the difficult moments in front of you pass as quickly and painlessly as possible.'

'Thank you.'

He turned and out of some kindness closed the door behind him with a respectful gentleness uncommon to the gaol.

I was alone. I put my hand in my pocket and retrieved the crumpled, faded shade that Philomena had given me. It meant so much more now than it had ever done. I kissed the worn image and held it to my heart. 'Please forgive me for all my shameful ways. For what I have done and not done. For how I have repeatedly let you and Cyril down.'

I kissed the picture again and lodged it high in a crack in the brickwork of the cell. Neither Philomena nor Alice would be enduring the gallows.

A look at the window told me dawn was at the gates.

A noise in the door lock startled me: the time had come. The door opened and Johncock stood there.

'I am ready.' I took a deep breath and proffered my wrists.

Johncock glanced to the men who followed him in. 'Take 'im to the Pinioning Room. There's a 'earty breakfast awaiting us, men – let's be done with this scum as soon as we can.'

The detail of four marched me quickly into a cell less

than twenty seconds from mine. My heart raced so fast I thought I would die before I reached the scaffold.

There were other men in the small room – Warbrick's assistants. On a shelf opposite me were coils of ropes, stacks of laundered clothes, towels and sheets.

Not sheets. Shrouds.

Then I saw it – the loose cotton hood to pull over the condemned man's head. *My* head.

I was still staring at the dreaded garment when one of Warbrick's men drew my wrists down by my side and behind my back. I didn't fight. I felt cold steel, the click of tight, fresh chains on me.

This was wrong.

I knew from what others had said that my hands needed to be by my sides.

Johncock faced me and smiled. 'We still 'ave a little time on our 'ands, Lynch. Time enough for this.' He punched me hard in the stomach.

The blow took me by surprise and was all the more painful for it. A turnkey to my side threw a right-hander that all but broke my cheekbone. Another grabbed my hair and held up my head.

Johncock hit me again. Once. Twice. Three times.

The blows dropped me to my knees and such was the pain in my stomach I was unable to breathe.

The assistant keeper bent low and held my head up as he told me, 'We're going to tell the world you screamed like a coward, Lynch. That you fought like a girl and begged not to be brought out. That you weren't man enough to face your punishment.'

I tried to get up to fight, but heavy boots thumped into my sides, and ribs. I collapsed to the floor and a heel came down onto the bottom of my spine. Steel toecaps bust bones. They straightened me out, turned me over and kicked me from shins to shoulders.

My hands were held fast behind me so I was powerless to protect myself. Boots piled into me like hammers breaking rocks.

Blackness found me. I was dying. God was being merciful. I was not going to hang ignominiously; I was going to perish here, in private, in the soft unconsciousness that now engulfed me.

I woke groggy. Blinded by blood in my eyes. Terrible pain pounded my forehead. Unable to stand, I slapped my hands on cold stone and tried to crawl.

Strong hands pulled me upright. Straightened me. Walked me.

A room swam into a hazy view.

A pew tilted left to right. I thought for a moment that I was in church. Strange faces peered at me. Looked past me and up on high.

The gallows.

The scaffold loomed large to my left. This was no church and no nightmare. I could smell the room. Hear voices. Hushes.

Panic rose in my chest.

Those holding me swung away from the pew. I glimpsed a brick wall. Warbrick's men crowded me. Forced something in my mouth.

I tasted cloth.

They tied a gag around my face. I snorted air. The instinct to survive was still there.

The hood.

The dreaded hood slipped over my head. The gaolers acted with the speed and deftness of fingersmiths. I tried to raise my hands but they were restrained. Not by rope, as I expected, nor by the manacles that previously restrained me.

I was in a straitjacket.

It had been fitted while I was unconscious. Johncock was taking me to the gallows as though I were a lunatic. A certifiable imbecile.

I tried to shout but the gag stifled my words.

Every ounce of dignity had been removed from me. They had even taken away my right to any final words. To say I was sorry.

I struggled for breath.

My feet clattered against a wooden step. Strong hands lifted me up another step, and another. My heart banged against my ribs, like it too was desperate to escape.

Wood creaked beneath my feet.

I tried to halt the movement. Pushed back. It was no use. My toes scraped across the boarding. Muffled words around me. Father Deagan's voice, weak and croaky. A prayer of some sort, low and solemn. 'Amen.'

Silence.

Johncock spoke. 'Prisoner, do you have any last words to say?'

A man behind me pulled the hood tight. The gag sank deeper into my mouth. I could not make a sound or even nod. The words I wished to utter would never be heard.

'Very well.'

Hands smoothed down the hood. Touched my throat. I felt the noose slide over the crown of my head. Over my forehead. Over my ears.

Around my neck.

It tightened.

A prayer sprang to mind: *Our Father, who art in heaven, hallowed be thy name—*

There was a bang, loud as a gunshot.

The trapdoors opened.

My feet fell into the void.

I dropped.

A sudden jerk. The rope snatched my flesh. Pain encircled my throat. My body bounced. Cries of shock spilled from those who watched.

Then nothing.

I was sure I was dead.

A whisper of voices contradicted me.

My neck hadn't broken. I was suspended. Swaying.

Swinging by my unbroken neck. Strangling slowly to death. Unable to breathe.

I snorted. Swayed left and right. Back and forth. The knot pushed my chin up and back. My spine cracked and burned with pain.

The fall had been too short. I was slowly strangling with each pendulous swing of the rope.

My feet twitched. The Morris jig. This was it. My involuntary dance of death had started. I felt irresistibly faint again.

Dear God, I was blacking out. Finally, passing away.

The swing of the rope slowed to a halt. The creak of the twine and the timbers became no more than distant murmurs and croaks.

The swaying stopped. I twirled slowly. Spun into nothingness. No breath in my body. No thought in my mind. No pain.

My life was over.

I was done.

THE DAY AFTER EXECUTION

LONDON, 19 JANUARY 1900

Mr Christopher Ellis Ackborne, a veteran reporter for the *London Evening Standard*, had been invited to witness the execution and wrote about it in the following day's edition.

In his article, he went to obsequious lengths to praise both the execution and the executioners.

> The assistant keeper of Newgate, Mr Tobias Johncock, formerly of the Queen's Guards, used his laudable professionalism to ensure that the hanging of the callous murderer Simeon Lynch was carried out, not only with military precision but also with admirable compassion and true justice. The convict, a beast of a man who had brutally murdered Elizabeth MacIntosh of Derbyshire and Police Constable Thomas J. Jackson of London, had been brought to the gallows visibly restrained after violently assaulting several gaolers and resisting their rightful duty to convey him to the scaffold. The hanging itself proved as merciful and quick as these things can be. Death was promptly certified by a doctor from the Home Office and a member of the Coroner's Office, after which the body of the murderer was duly taken away and immediately buried beneath the infamous stretch of stones within Newgate known as Dead Man's Walk.

Mr Ackborne was a journalist of good repute and undoubtedly his newspaper's well-educated readership accepted his unwholesome account as entirely truthful and accurate. Indeed, Mr Ackborne had no reason to believe that he had done anything other than report precisely and with integrity exactly what he had witnessed.

But he had made grave errors. About as grave as any journalist has ever made. He will never be told of them, nor will he ever suspect there to be any. Nor, for that matter, will any of his readers.

Only Johncock, his special detail of men and a handful of extremely discreet others will ever know the truth.

To fully understand, time must be rolled back to the minutes just before the hanging, to that tense moment when the witnesses and gaolers gathered in the execution shed.

Decorum has always dictated that the gated area beneath the gallows' trapdoors, the straw-filled pit where the body falls and is later cut down for inspection, is covered with black cloth. This 'dressing' prevents distress to the witnesses. And with good reason, for often the drop is not perfect. On several occasions, the hangman has been compelled to quickly descend the gallows, rush into the pit, and pull on the convict's legs to hasten death. Some gallowsmen have even been known to climb onto the backs and shoulders of the hanged man, to add sufficient weight to finish him off. This is not a sight mere members of the public should witness.

Like countless souls before me, I had fallen through the traps genuinely believing I was dying. And I did swing on that rope. I truly did.

But not by my neck. Unbeknown to me, the noose that had been placed over my head had also been hooked by a wire of admirable strength into the back of a corset fitted beneath my straitjacket. As a result, my weight had been distributed under my arms and across my waist, not around my neck. The choking I had experienced had been through the corseted restriction around my ribs and the panic in my head. In retrospect it is clear that the beating administered in the Pinioning Room had been devised to render me unconscious and fit the harness beneath a new set of clothes.

Dazed and confused, I had been walked out and paraded before witnesses, so those assembled could be certain of my identity and my death. I had been gagged and hooded to prevent me from shouting out and inadvertently ruining the deception.

When I fell through the trap and my body jerked and swung on that rope, I was certain that I was choking. The falling and swaying motions, coupled with the lack of oxygen caused by the gag, corset and straitjacket, conspired to convince me that I was truly being hanged by the neck until dead.

Beneath the cover of those black drapes, my legs were grabbed. But they were *lifted*, not pulled. By then, I had passed out from my heightened heart rate, limited breathing and sheer shock. I was completely unconscious when the hood and corset were removed.

A pad of chloroform was subsequently held over my nose to ensure I remained subdued and compliant. Like some piece of magical theatre, the curtains were then drawn back so witnesses could see my body, limp and lifeless.

As soon as horrified eyes had been averted, I was lifted into the rough cart that had carried away Louise Masset and trundled out of sight. My specially selected execution detail slowly moved me from the gallows to the gaol's graveyard and en route ensured many other turnkeys saw my 'corpse' and therefore, if necessary, would most willingly testify to my apparent death.

The detail took me to a freshly dug grave where they respectfully crowded around me to begin what must have looked to any accidental observer like my interment. Only instead of burial, I was given smelling salts. As I woke, startled and weak, I was strongly restrained and told to say nothing.

I can't adequately describe my shock at being woken from 'death'. The mind is a most magnificent organ, but I swear in that split second when I found myself held tightly over the edge of my burial pit I glimpsed madness. Had my mouth not been covered and my limbs not secured by strong hands I would most certainly have gone into hysterics.

Once the detail had persuaded me I was not in hell or in danger, they fixed a grey wig to my head and matched it with a full beard and glasses. Baggy prison clothes and the corset and jacket were stripped away and as the grave was slowly filled in, they dressed me in a shirt and tie and smart black suit. A matching frockcoat and a Derby hat were added and within ten minutes, I and my companions had cleared the security gates.

Outside, a vast and noisy crowd was slowly dispersing. Even though they could not watch the execution they had still felt morbidly compelled to be close to the event. Hordes swarmed us, bumped and jostled for space as they resumed the mundaneness of their lives. I found the noise and clamour terrifying as I passed unrecognised through them. My senses were horribly heightened. I could feel every contour of the cobbles beneath my feet. The smells and sounds of London assaulted me. Coal, tar, fog. Rumbles of carriages, shouting traders, the crack of a coachman's bullwhip in the frigid air.

Two men walked either side of me and they forced more than guided me towards a waiting carriage. I glanced at a woman lingering solemnly on the corner of a street we passed. Slim. Dark-haired. Almost boyish.

Surrey.

She so closely resembled my ex-lover that I could not believe it was not her.

I slowed down and started to turn to look again.

'Do not look back,' ordered one of the men. 'Get inside and say nothing. Not now, not during the journey. Afterwards, there will be time enough to speak.'

I did as instructed. Men who can save your life when your neck is secured inside the hangman's noose can end it just as easily.

The ride that followed was the most wonderful I had ever experienced. To leave Newgate alive, to watch its foul form fade in the distance with every turn of the carriage wheels was divine. I settled back and breathed a sigh of relief. Daylight seemed astonishingly bright. The winter air exhilaratingly fresh. The sky as smooth as platinum. Overhead burned a sun that seemed imbued with the warmth of God himself.

I was alive. I knew not why. But I was alive.

The journey was a long one and the stress of my ordeal and the motion of the carriage rocked me into the first throes of a troubled sleep. Perhaps the chloroform also conspired to conjure up vivid flashes of the rope, the drop and those agonising moments when I swung from the scaffold.

'Wake up!'

A hand roughly shook my shoulder. We had stopped. The carriage door was open. A man stood holding it. Back straight. Face expressionless. Eyes catching me only briefly as he studied everything all at once.

'Get out,' he ordered.

I unfolded myself, finding I could barely stand from the stiffening of my joints, straining of my spine and onset of serious bruising.

I looked around. A fine country house faced me. Tall trees stood soldier-straight on both sides of the gravelled drive. I glanced back. Iron gates were being closed and barred. Men in winter coats stamped their feet to stay warm.

'Inside.' The rough hand shoved me again.

I creaked my way to the ivy-covered entrance arch and glossy black door beneath it.

Men strode in front of and behind me. Four in all. I stumbled climbing the steps. Hands caught me and helped me up. I remembered my stuttering walk on the planks of the gallows and shuddered.

Inside, the house smelled of waxed wooden floors, silver polish and coal fires. I was taken through a cool marble entrance hall into a large oak-panelled room where a fire blazed. Three men were grouped around the hearth, warming their hands while talking. All had their backs to me.

'Simeon Lynch, sir,' announced the man with the pushing hands.

A figure turned.

I did not recognise him.

He was a large, stout fellow with a high forehead, probably in his mid to late fifties. He smiled broadly as he looked me over. 'My, my, Mr Lynch, you do look as though you have been in the wars. However, I suppose that given everything the *Crown* had planned for you, then you are in remarkably fine fettle.' He walked closer and extended his hand. 'My name is Mycroft. Mycroft Holmes.'

One of the other figures turned and I was not surprised to see it was Sherlock.

'You two are brothers?'

'I told you he wasn't very intelligent,' said the detective, who, understandably given our history, offered no hand to shake.

'Make allowances, Sherlock. Make allowances.' Mycroft looked me over, like a lord might regard the head of a stag just readied for display on his wall. 'God and government have done a remarkable job in bringing you here today, Mr Lynch, a remarkable job.'

The third man spoke and his voice was surprisingly familiar. 'More blessed are those who have sinned and repented, than those who have never sinned.'

'Father Deagan?'

'Ernest Braithwaite, at your service.' He clicked his heels and bowed his head. 'Priests and chaplains are but a small part of my vast repertoire.'

'You are looking less holy but *far* healthier,' I said, 'than when I last saw you.'

'My illness was feigned to bring another operative into the gaol to assist me with your escape. My rejuvenation is down to the removal of some rather good theatrical make-up.'

'Ernest works for me,' explained Mycroft. 'Quite a thespian before I recruited him.' He motioned to chairs spread around the blazing fire. 'Please sit, before you fall, Mr Lynch. There are precious ornaments in this room and I should hate anything to be broken.'

We all sat and a wave of warmth flowed over me as I

felt the glow of the fire and watched it crackle and spit. I extended my hands towards the flames for comfort. All eyes were on me and I felt compelled to break a lengthening silence. 'Thought I might have been in an even hotter place than this by now,' I joked, then added, directly to Mycroft, 'I am grateful to be alive, sir. But if you have saved my neck for the same reason as your brother proposed, then you may as well just call in your men and finish the job that was started at Newgate.'

'No, no, no!' He waved a dismissive hand at me. 'Sherlock has a quite blinding obsession with the Moriarties. But they are small fry to me. Whitebait in a universal sea of sharks. He believes you have killed many people but not those you were going to hang for, is that not so?'

I made no comment.

'Good God, don't be coy with us, man.' Mycroft sounded irritated. 'You confessed all to Braithwaite here, so you may as well start by being honest with me.'

'Then you know it is true,' I answered. 'There *is* blood on my hands but not a drop from the veins of those I was convicted of killing.'

'Convicted and hanged for!' retorted Mycroft, with a tone of irony. 'Once I had learned about you from Sherlock and the fact that you would not betray your employers, even when facing death, then you became of great interest to me. So I struck a deal with my brother. He could have you for his own devices, *if* he could turn you against the Moriartys. I could have you for mine, if he could not.' Mycroft beamed

444

at me again with his trophy-hunting eyes. 'So here you are. My winnings. A triumph for me, and a defeat for the country's best known and *saddest-looking* consulting detective.'

'Must I suffer this?' Sherlock slapped his hands on the arms of his chair and looked set to leave.

'Just a little longer, dear brother. Help me appraise Mr Lynch of how indebted he is to us.'

'*Really*, Mycroft?'

'Indulge me.'

Sherlock sighed. 'Oh, very well. The nail you were given was arranged by me.'

'By you?'

'Willy Watkins, the old orderly, used to be in my employ; that was before he was apprehended for handling stolen goods. I had deduced from seeing your cell, indeed *smelling* your cell, that the removal of part of the floor beneath your bunk would have given you a chance to escape.'

'I never thought about trying the floor.'

'Yes. I understand you foolishly tried to take down an entire wall rather than take up a little of what was beneath your feet.'

Mycroft chuckled.

'We had hoped you would get out of that place on your own accord,' added Braithwaite. 'Hence my collapse in your cell after your most valuable *mea culpa* and the opportunity I created for you to steal objects from my bag.'

I shook my head. 'If you had wished to truly assist me then you should have simply given me a set of keys.'

'You would only have been caught,' said Holmes. 'We discussed it with Johncock. You could never have got out of Newgate that way.'

'Johncock was one of yours?'

'Has been since his army days. A little rough around the edges, but always reliable.'

'That man damned near beat me to death. On *several* occasions.'

Mycroft's eyes lit up and a smile twitched his lips. 'Yes, our gaoler friend was shocked when we approached him about you and disclosed our belief that Huntley would facilitate your murder. He was however most pleased to have the opportunity to catch his colleague red-handed and discredit him.'

'I am sure he was.'

'The assistant keeper had cultivated quite a dislike for you,' continued Sherlock. 'Told me he had been most eager to see you swing. The murderers of innocent women and dutiful policemen are not popular in prison.'

'You know I didn't kill either.'

'I do, and since yesterday, so does Johncock,' replied Sherlock. 'I have already told you who murdered PC Jackson. Now I believe I can inform you who killed Lizzie MacIntosh, better known to you as Elizabeth Audsley.'

'And yes, we are aware that she was the mother of your deceased child,' added Mycroft.

'I already know who killed her,' I said bitterly. 'That bastard Lee Chan and his murderous Chinese cohorts.'

446

Sherlock nodded. 'Chan certainly gave the order. Just as he issued the contract to have you killed in prison. But he was not the knave who put a knife to your queen's throat.'

'Then who did?'

'One of Brogan Moriarty's employees. A person who turned against him in return for an offer of great wealth and a new life away from the Moriartys.'

I nodded. It made sense. 'I know the snake you mean: Sirius Gunn.'

'No, that is not correct. Gunn is still at large in America. The Pinkerton Agency claim he is heading to Boston. It is not he.'

'Then who?'

'Last night, I visited a place of relaxation I often frequent. I believe one time you followed me there. It is in the heart of the Chinese community and they provide me with certain medications and reliefs. I was informed by a reliable Asian contact that your lady's murder was carried out by a Miss Surrey Breed.'

'No.' My blood ran cold. 'You are wrong, sir. That can not be true.'

'I confess that I lack further substantiation for this claim, but the source that offered it to me has in the past proved unerring.'

I pictured the woman I had seen outside the gates of Newgate Gaol. The one I *thought* had been Surrey but then dismissed as merely her doppelganger.

Was she really alive?

Had my former lover, my *first* love, come to see me die? To make certain there was no chance I had escaped the noose and would ever come after her?

Anger built inside me.

Now I thought about it, I saw that it was even possible Surrey had turned traitor at the same time as Sirius, but stayed like a deadly viper within our bosom. I remembered us lying in bed together and her asking me to run away with her. I had said we could never escape Moriarty and could never dream of a better life; she had said that such an existence was not enough for her.

But why had she finally turned against him and me? Because she hated Elizabeth? Was jealous of her? Wanted to hurt me in revenge for not choosing her? I knew it could be one or all of those things. More than anyone, I understood that every murder had many reasons behind it.

I looked to Sherlock. 'Knowing what you did, could you not have stopped my execution on the basis of such knowledge?'

'Knowledge is not proof, Lynch,' he answered as though dealing with a simpleton. 'There was not sufficient time to gather any evidence of substance.'

'Nor had we the inclination to do so,' added Mycroft. 'At least not on my part. For I believed it was much better for you, and better for us, that you were seen to die on that scaffold. You understand that, don't you? Now the world thinks you are dead you can move around freely in it. You are like a ghost,' he said triumphantly, 'a deadly, murderous ghost.'

'A bogeyman,' added Braithwaite.

I could sense they had plans in mind that stretched far beyond simply saving my life. 'So what exactly do you ask of me, gentlemen? Why did you go to all this trouble?'

'Now I will leave you.' Sherlock rose and nodded to his brother. 'You know I do not want any part of this.'

'As you wish.'

The detective bade us good day.

'Don't forget to pay Doctor Watson his twenty pounds,' I shouted to his back.

He missed a stride but left without another word.

Mycroft prised his large frame out of the chair and groaned a little as he bent and removed a brass fireguard from the front of a dying coal fire. He took an iron poker from a hearth set and rattled the embers until they glowed more brightly. 'I would have thought that what we *ask* of you,' he paused, then corrected himself, 'rather, what we *demand* of you, is obvious. The British government requires you to do what you do best, Mr Lynch, which apparently is to kill discreetly, kill with regularity and kill with impunity.'

'I am to be an assassin on behalf of Queen and Country?' I couldn't help but notice the irony of once more being coerced into the worst kind of service with no option but to comply.

'Yes, you are to serve your fellow countrymen and it is a noble job that you will undertake. But let me be very clear about this: if you are caught, then Queen and Country will deny you even exist, let alone admit you are in their employ. And if you speak a word about the nature of your profession, you will discover that the men who spirited you out of Newgate will spirit you to the bottom of the Thames far quicker.'

'Of that I have no doubt.' I decided to push my luck. 'And what is to be my remuneration for this position?'

'You mean being given your life is not payment enough?' He laughed as he replaced the poker and shook coal from a bucket onto the fire. 'Let us say that you will be more than adequately housed, fed and looked after. The better you work for us, the better the life you will live. Does that suit you?'

'I suspect I do not have a say in the matter.'

'Splendid! You are mastering your position already.' He put the bucket down, stood straight and dusted off his hands. 'I have a little personal motivation for you. Something to get you into the correct frame of mind and moving along the right tracks. Braithwaite, the papers, please.'

His colleague stepped forward and handed me two sheets of paper. Neither of them bore any letter headings or names, just a very long, typed list of addresses. Next to the locations, most of which were in London or Europe, were days, dates and times. I turned the pages to see if there was any more information but there wasn't. 'What are these?' I shrugged. 'And what am I expected to do with them?'

'They are your first assignment,' answered Mycroft. 'The first of many, we hope.'

I waved the papers. 'Then you need to give me more than this. I need the names of people, their descriptions, background information—'

Mycroft cut me off with a raised palm. 'These things you already know. The addresses are places regularly frequented by Lee Chan, Sirius Gunn and Surrey Breed.'

I found myself unable to breathe.

'Chan and his Chinese cousins,' he continued, 'belong to a secret organisation called The Society of the Righteous and Harmonious Fists. We refer to them as Boxers, because they are extraordinarily violent and have peculiarly deadly ways of punching. They are rising as rebels from the rubble of a broken China and growing in strength both at home and abroad. We need to root them out, eliminate them from London, before they are impossibly large to tackle. In short, Mr Lynch, we require you to kill Mr Chan, and do it quickly.'

'Gladly,' I replied. 'It is my greatest wish to do so. I would travel to the end of the world to murder the bastard. But why have you not already done it? You have in your employ many very able men, as I witnessed today.'

'We cannot get near him. But I am certain you could inveigle your way into his company without much effort.'

'How so?'

'I'll leave that to your imagination, but for example, should you contact Gunn, perhaps send a message suggesting that you are alive and in pursuit of him, then you can be assured he will run straight to Chan, quicker than Anthony flew to Cleopatra. In which case, you would be afforded the opportunity to kill them both.' He raised an eyebrow. 'It is not impossible to imagine that along the way you might also encounter Miss Breed and have the chance to exact your fullest revenge.'

'My lord, you are no better than the Moriartys.'

'To the contrary; I am *entirely* better. After all, I now have London's best assassin working for me, not them.' He cracked a broad smile. 'Now let us see about getting you some food and rest, Mr Lynch. After all, you have work to do. A great deal of work.'

ACKNOWLEDGMENTS

Many thanks to my wise agent Luigi Bonomi, my inspirational editor Jade Chandler at Little, Brown and her wonderful colleagues, Ed Wood, Celine Kelly, Nico Taylor, Iain Hunt, Sarah Shea and Stephanie Melrose.

I'm also indebted to Sophie Hutton-Squire for her excellent copy-editing of the final draft and Dr. Mary Shannon for her generous assistance with the Victorian research – any factual deviation is entirely down to me!

As always, I'd be in a mess without Scary Jack and his team at CBW, and finally, the biggest thank you of all to Donna and Billy who give me the time, space and understanding to pursue the privilege of writing *The House of Smoke*.